THE BLACK MADONNA

First published in Great Britain in 1997 by
Nyali Press Ltd
Pinkhill Farm, Eynsham, Oxon. OX8 1JQ

A CIP catalogue record for this book is available
from the British Library.

ISBN 0 9524188 2 7

Typography and composition by
Richard Graham
Cedar Hill, Roscrea, Co. Tipperary
Set in 12pt Baskerville.

Printed and bound by
Mayfield Press (Oxford) Ltd., Ferry Hinksey Road, Oxford OX2 0DP

Dustcover painting and text illustrations by
Mick Cawston

The Black Madonna

R.W.F. Poole

Nyali Press
Eynsham

To the memory of my grandfather and the men of the Kuban Cossacks whom he led in the fight against Bolshevism.

CONTENTS

Prologue—1453

CONSTANTINOPLE was burning.

"Oh sweet Christ, that hurts."

"It's going to hurt a lot more, Excellency, but it's got to come out," said the Sergeant grimly. "Bite on this strap. Now Tomas, Stephan, hold the Excellency."

The two big Russians held the writhing man on the ground. The Sergeant took hold of the shaft of the arrow that was embedded in the Captain's shoulder and stood astride the man's chest.

"Bite hard Excellency!"

In spite of the strap in his mouth the Captain's scream echoed from the walls of the mean, narrow street; then came merciful unconsciousness. The little band of wearied, bloodied and smoke-blackened men stood in the narrow alley looking down at the limp form of their commander, whilst the Sergeant threw aside the bloody arrow, and the kneeling Tomas applied a dirty cloth to the ugly, gaping wound.

"Will he die?" said a young man.

"As God wills," said the Sergeant grimly, "but if we don't get off this fucking street, we are all going to die. It won't be long before the Turks find us again."

The men listened to the distant cries and screams, and the cackling of burning buildings. It was the smoke from the burning buildings that had allowed the little band of Russian mercenaries to break off their fight against the overwhelming force of Turkish Janissaries who had pushed them back, street by street—the smoke and the fact that the Janissaries had discovered a convent. The Russians could still hear the screams of the nuns beyond the smoke. The Sergeant crossed himself.

The Captain moaned.

1

"The Excellency is coming to," said Tomas.

"Poor sod," said the Sergeant. "Well?" this to the man who had been scouting up the street behind them.

"It's a dead end, Serg. We're stuffed."

"Deep shit."

"What's up the end, then?"

"Just a little church."

"Well, for fuck's sake let's get in there. Pick him up you two."

The little church filled the end of the alley. The large studded door was closed. Stephan tried the handle.

"Locked."

"Well break the bloody thing down, then! If the Turks catch us here, we're dead."

Two men with axes started to batter the door.

The door suddenly swung open. The little priest looked up at the bloody band with a gentle smile:

"A knock would have sufficed."

"We need shelter, Father."

"Enter in God's name and God's peace, my son."

"Not much of that out here, Father," said the Sergeant as the men piled into the little church. "Lock that door fast, sharp."

"The young man is wounded," said the old priest as the men laid the moaning Captain on the floor.

"We're all knocked about a bit Father, but the Excellency is bad hurt."

"I have some spirits here and I will dress his wound, otherwise it will get bad and he might die. Take him up by the shrine and let the Lady look on him. She has great healing powers."

"Jesus Christ, Father, you've got a woman here?"

The little priest smiled:

"My son, this is the shrine of the Black Madonna. There is her icon above the altar." He pointed and the men gaped at the little icon. The gold shone dully in the dim light; the Madonna and Child in the icon were both jet black. "She has wonderful powers."

"Well, she'll need them all, when those bloody Turks get here."

"Have faith my son. I think that it would be better if none of us was here when the heathen come. In fact the Lady and I were both about to leave when you came."

"Leave? How?"

"The Black Madonna has many secrets," said the little priest. He reached up and lifted the little icon out of the alcove above the altar. "She has been here in this church for hundreds of years. Now, I think that her time here is over. You must take her with you and swear to look after her, then she will look after you."

"I'll swear black is white if she gets us home."

"Then swear loyalty to her, all of you."

He handed the icon to the Sergeant, who then, after a moment's hesitation, held it to his lips. One by one the Russians passed it from hand to hand and kissed the icon and crossed themselves.

"Good," said the priest. He handed the icon back to the Sergeant. "Now." The priest reached into the alcove and touched something. Very slowly the altar of the little shrine moved outwards to reveal the dark opening of a passage. "I told you that the Black Madonna has many secrets. Now off you go and may God and the Lady bring you safe to your home."

"What about you Father?"

"This church is my home. I think that now the Lady is in safe hands I will stay and give the heathen my blessing when they come."

"They'll nail you to the bloody door, Father."

"Just as they nailed Christ to the bloody cross, my son. Now go, and the Lady go with you."

1 Two Captains of Horse

THE Duckwing cock had the Grey by the back of the head, his beak gripping the bloodstained comb viciously. Both cocks were well bloodied. The vicious steel spurs bound onto their legs had done their work. Blood was sprayed around the pit. It was London in 1803. The Duckwing released his hold and pecked his opponent several times then seized the back of his head again and shook him. The Grey was crouched, his wings spread and his eyes half closed. He was finished. `

The yelling around the pit rose to a new crescendo. Charles was on his feet:

"Get up, you gutless bastard, get up and fight! I've got fifty guineas on you!"

"You're about to be fifty guineas the poorer, my boy. The Grey's finished."

"Nonsense, nonsense I tell you! The bastard's got plenty of fight left in him. Fight damn you, fight!"

The Duckwing continued to worry the limp body of its opponent with its cruel beak, until the owner, scowling with disappointment, stepped into the ring and stopped the fight by deftly wringing the Grey's neck.

"He'll make good soup," said Major Barnardo, "and that's where your fifty clinkers have gone, Charles, into the soup with the cock. Good fight though."

"Gutless bastard!" growled Captain Lord Charles Fitz-Hugh of The Royal Horse Guards. "You'll take a note of hand?"

The Major got out his leather-bound betting book with satisfied deliberation:

"From a fellow officer and an undoubted gentleman, that goes without saying."

"What! What! Fight over? Who won, what?"

5

The long figure of Captain Sparke had been slumped, snoring gently and belching occasionally, on the bench throughout the fight, his chin resting on the knob of his cane and his beaver hat tipped over his eyes.

"The Duckwing cock won it," said Major Barnardo cheerfully.

"Oh jolly good, what! Which did I back, Charles?"

Charles growled: "You backed the Duckwing, Hugo."

"Jolly good! Do I owe you, or do you owe me?"

For a moment, Charles's eyes flickered.

"Charles owes you a pony," said Major Barnardo.

"Not your day, Charles, my boy. Time your luck changed. Fancy another punt?"

"Hell and damnation!" Charles growled. "I've had enough of this bloody place. Let's go to Ma Huggetts."

Major Barnardo chuckled:

"Fancy yourself lucky in love, eh? Mind you the only luck you need at Ma Huggetts is not catching the pox. But yes, I fancy a bit of doxy myself."

They had to help Captain Sparke through the yelling, stinking crowd. Iky Solomon, the owner of the pit, was standing by the door:

"Leaving already, gents? There's a prime pair of Ginger cocks in the next fight. One from Squire Huddle of Cheshire—such good birds the Cheshire Fancy run." He leaned across to Charles in a confidential manner. "Try a flutter on the Cheshire cock, Captain. On my life, he's a good one."

"You won't have a life if you don't fuck off out the way," growled Charles.

"His Lordship is in poor fettle, my jolly old Solly," said Major Barnardo. "He has a different kind of cocking in mind."

Captain Sparke began to sing.

"Hell's teeth," said Charles, "let's get out of here."

"I'm damned if I'm carrying Hugo all the way to Ma Huggetts through all this shit."

The dark street was ankle deep in filth.

"We'll never find a growler this side of the Strand."

"There's a carriage there," said Major Barnardo. It was a smart, closed carriage, with a liveried coachman on the box and a liveried groom holding the horses' heads. "Hey cully! Whose yoke is this?"

"My Lord Bruton's," came the reply.

"Old Jimmy! Well, he won't mind. Take us to Jermyn Street, cully."

"My orders are to wait for his Lordship."

"The hell with this!"

Charles moved like a whip-lash. In a bound he was on the box of the carriage. He seized the portly little coachman by the collar of his coat, and pitched him into the filth of the street.

"Quick, man! Push Hugo in!"

Charles seized the reins from the dash-board and the whip from its holder. He laid the lash across the rumps of the startled horses. The horses plunged forward.

With a frightened yell the groom leaped wildly to one side and the carriage was swaying and bucketing down the street, whilst Major Barnardo, inside the coach and shaking with laughter the while, was still trying to drag the limp form of Captain Sparke through the door.

The bedclothes were rancid, and the stained pillows stank of sweat—but Charles was past caring. He took another pull from the brandy bottle and lay back on the pillows. He could feel the slut's hot mouth on him, her fingers gently stroking his balls. He did not think that her ministrations would be successful, but she was skilful and he felt himself stirring.

"What's your name girl?" he muttered, his eyes closed.

"Millie, Milord. My, my! What a big boy His Lordship is! Prime meat makes a girl quite hungry!"

"Help yourself, Millie."

He felt the girl straddle him—felt her wet warmth enve-lope him, smelt the earthy feral scent of her. He gave a bellow of pleasure as her frantically heaving loins brought him to a climax. Then he passed out.

The shaft of sunlight that found its way through the dirty window of the room woke Charles. His head was falling apart. He sat up slowly on the filthy bed and groped for his tumbled clothes. He began to curse. Millie had taken his invitation to help herself rather too literally. The girl was gone and so was the leather pouch with his few remaining guineas.

* * *

Mischa was screaming. He knew that he was screaming, but he also knew that no sound was coming out because the water was filling his head and his lungs: filling him, bursting him as he struggled towards the dim light of the surface. But, however hard he struggled, the girl held him down. He was trapped in the long golden tresses of her hair. The hair encircled and held him like strands of kelp. All the time her face stared at him: a face once beautiful, but now bloated and whitened by long immersion: a face battered and bruised by the rocks of the rapids: a face that he had once kissed and loved, now swollen and hideous.

The face was trying to reach his as the hair enmeshed him and dragged him down—down, down into the darkness, where something foul and hideous waited to seize him. He tried to scream again. Then a shaft of light came to him and he managed to break free and struggle up towards the surface and emerge gasping.

The beam of early morning sunlight playing on his face brought him awake, and the scream died in his head as he lay gasping and sweating in the sodden bed. The dream faded in the light as he took in the solid and reassuring things about him: the old oak cupboard, the wooden chair on which his clothes were tumbled, the pictures on the wall that he had known since childhood: familiar things with happy memories, all bathed in the bright light of a new day which drove away the things of nightmare—drove them back deep into his subconscious. But he knew that they lurked there and that their horror would return to haunt his dreams. The girl would never go away. He shuddered.

There was a knock on the door and old Johannes came shambling in with a can of hot water and a mug of steaming coffee.

"Good morning, Herr Mischa. The day is fine. Your father is awake. God is in his Heaven and the world is no worse than it was yesterday."

The old man looked at the sweating face of the young man and at the tumbled bed. 'The boy has had a bad night,' he thought to himself, 'the night hags have ridden him hard,' and Johannes knew which hag it would have been—all the village knew. He shrugged mentally. The boy had too tender a conscience. It was a shitty world in which shitty things happened, and that was all there was to it. Johannes did not dream.

"Fat bacon again!"

Graf Friedrich Czerny prodded the waxy coloured slice of fat, with small pink islands of meat in it, that covered his wooden platter.

"Have we nothing else in the larder?"

Father and son sat at the table in the great hall of Schloss Lippitz and gloomily surveyed their breakfast.

"Fat is good for you, Herr Graf," said the imperturbable Johannes, "especially for some one as skinny as you. You need the fat this cold weather..."

"It's summer, dammit!"

"And some schnapps in your coffee," Johannes continued imperturbably. He banged a bottle of the colourless spirit on the table and limped towards the door that led to the kitchen regions before firing his Parthian shot. "You better eat and drink whilst you can; if the cursed French come again, you'll have neither pigs nor schnapps."

Johannes exited and banged the door behind him triumphantly. He always liked the last word.

With some reluctance father and son began to eat their breakfast. The Graf poured some schnapps into his empty coffee cup and swirled it around so that the warmth of the cup brought out the full power of the liquor.

"The old bastard has a point there, my boy. I am pleased that you are going to be away out of it."

"I really feel that I ought to be staying with my regiment, Father."

"I know how you feel about it, boy, but this posting to St Petersburg is very important, and it is your duty to go. Soldiers do as they're told. You must do your duty by the Emperor, but I'm all for you doing it where you ain't so likely to get skewered by the French. Just remember that you have a duty to the family as well."

Mischa pushed a piece of bacon round his platter and sighed inwardly. He knew that this subject would rear its head before his departure. As the only son and heir to Lippitz, the question of procreation and inheritance was never far from his father's mind: 'If only,' the father thought, 'the boy would find some nice suitable girl and do his duty by the family, if only...'

If only—Mischa crumbled some bread abstractly. For a moment a vision of golden hair and pouting lips flickered across his mind, and he felt an answering stirring in his loins; then his mind filled with the images of the nightmare. The crust of the bread cracked and crumbled as his huge hand clenched and pulverised it.

The old Graf looked across at the great brooding, bear-like, figure of the younger man, and felt a twinge of his son's anguish.

Father and son were so alike in so many ways. They were both men of large stature and great physical strength; both were capable of immense rages, which broke and thundered like summer storms, and passed as quickly and were just as likely to end in gales of laughter. But, where the father was an intensely physical man and an outgoing person, the son was much more shy, introverted and gentle. 'Too gentle,' the old man thought, 'far too like his late mother, God rest her soul, for his own good.'

Mischa's mother had been sweet, gentle and beautiful, and the old Graf had loved her as he never loved anyone else. He had met and wooed her in Vienna, when he was a dashing young subaltern. She had been so gentle and fragile-looking that Friedrich had been frightened of breaking her, like some beautiful china doll.

In the end, it could be said that he did break his gentle wife. Their life together had been a golden magical period for the Graf. He had been amazed by the passion and physical intensity of their lovemaking. There had been great joy and happiness when the Gräfin finally became pregnant. How they looked forward to their first born!

The birth was long and hard. The Gräfin was delivered of a fine healthy boy, but the birth broke her. She took a fever and died within a week.

The grief of Mischa's father was terrible. He really felt that he had killed his wife, and he mourned her. Indeed he never really recovered from the death. He never considered marrying again.

It is true that various village girls warmed his bed from time to time, but that was a matter of need and had nothing to do with love. All his love was now centred on his son. It amazed people to see how gentle the great, gruff, roaring Graf was with the boy. It was because he saw so much of the mother in the child that he loved him the more and feared for him. It was a harsh, uncertain world that Mischa grew up in, and his father, who had feared neither God nor man, was frightened for his only son and heir.

He was frightened for him now, as he looked at Mischa's troubled face across the table. He wished that he could help the boy, but he did not know how. Perhaps it was a good thing that he was going away.

"Damn and blast this bloody bacon," said the Graf, seeking refuge from thought in expletive. "Tell you what, boy, why don't you go and find the Hunter. Get us a deer! A bit of venison would be just the job—I'm sick of bloody pig. Bit of fresh air would do you good, what?"

Mischa rode up the steep track through the beech woods behind the castle. The morning sunlight dappled through the leaves of the great trees. The two great rough-coated deer hounds played and tumbled around his horse, with the joy of freedom from the kennel and the knowledge of work ahead.

The track led out of the woods into a great upland pasture, from which the whole valley and the lazy meanderings of the River Lipp could be seen. At one end of the pasture, and at the top of the escarpment, there was a rock crag. Sitting on the top of the crag, with smoke from his pipe curling up into to the still warm air, was a figure in the familiar battered broad-brimmed hat, and the rather tattered cloak that he seemed to wear whatever the weather. Mischa had known that the Hunter would be there. What he did not know was how he knew.

The Hunter had been part of Mischa's life from time out of his memory. It had never occurred to Mischa to ask who he was, or where he came from, and no one had ever offered any explanation. The Hunter was just there—in the same way that the sun shone and streams flowed and the wind blew. The Hunter was like an element, and Mischa had never known him as anything else except— 'The Hunter'.

The Hunter had made daisy chains with him. The Hunter had showed him how to tickle trout in the streams; how to sniggle a rabbit and, with the Hunter, Mischa had shot his first deer. He always seemed to be there when Mischa needed him, always in the broad-brimmed hat and the tattered cloak, always with the lined, handsome face—handsome in spite of the scarred socket where one eye had been torn out. He looked the same age now as he did when Mischa first remembered him. It did not seem to matter.

As Mischa cantered across the firm turf of the pasture, the two dogs spied the hunched figure of the Hunter and raced to greet him. The Hunter ruffled their great rough heads as the dogs whined and wriggled in their pleasure at seeing him. All dogs loved the Hunter, and the great deerhounds loved him, especially as they knew that his presence meant work—work they were bred for and loved. The Hunter tapped his pipe out on the rock and rose to his feet, his weathered face crinkled in a smile of greeting.

Mischa remembered how as a child he had been fascinated by the cicatrices of the withered eye socket. He remembered how, with the directness of youth, he had asked the Hunter about the missing eye. The man had laughed and just said that everybody had to lose something to gain wisdom.

"Good morning, Mischa."

"Good morning, Hunter."

Mischa raised his cap to the ragged man as he had always done.

"You need a deer for the larder." It was a statement, not a question. "Your father is tiring of pig meat, perhaps?"

Both men laughed with the ease of long friendship.

"I know of a good buck. Let us go."

The two men set off across the pasture, the Hunter's long effortless stride easily matching the pace of Mischa's horse. They came to a small valley in the open upland, with outcrops of rock on either side and a small hill-stream racing and tumbling over its boulder-strewn bed in the bottom. The Hunter pointed to a pile of large boulders, from which a clump of stunted birches sprang. This vantage point commanded a view of the valley at a narrow point.

"Tie the horse back in those trees, then get yourself and the dogs tucked in there. The buck is feeding further up the valley,"—the Hunter wet a finger and held it up to test the wind—"I will work myself round upwind of the buck, and when he touches my taint on the wind, he will move down towards you. Be ready."

He set off at an angle across the open country, his long loose-kneed stride eating up the ground so that he soon disappeared into a distant screen of pine trees.

Mischa found a spot which gave a good view of the valley. The dogs, grim and silent now, although quivering with excitement, lay down obediently behind him. He poured powder from his horn into the barrel of the musket, rammed a wad into place to hold the powder, then the smooth round lead ball and, finally, another wad. With great care he primed the pan of the musket and checked the flint, which, hitting back the striker, would produce a spark that would ignite the powder and then the charge in the breech of the barrel.

The musket had one of the fairly new rifled barrels, that gave far more accuracy and range than the old smooth-bore weapons.

Then he settled down to wait.

Silence and stillness settled over the little valley. From some distance a cow bellowed for her calf, otherwise there was only birdsong in the morning calm. A wren appeared on a birch twig beside him and sat looking at this curious addition to its territory. Mischa stayed motionless, and the little drab bird hopped from twig to twig, twisting its head from side to side as it examined these strange creatures. Mischa smiled to himself. It was then that a flicker of movement caught his eye—in the scrub down by the stream. He was alert immediately.

The buck was a big one, with a good six-point head. He was moving without haste, but every now and then he would pause and look behind him, his nose twitching, to catch another snatch of the man-scent that was worrying him. His mobile ears twitched to catch the slightest sound. He was alert but not unduly alarmed. His present course would bring him within a hundred yards of Mischa's hiding place.

Mischa laid a warning hand on the heads of the dogs, who were quivering with eagerness.

The buck moved closer. With great care, Mischa eased back the hammer on the musket from the safe half-cock position to full-cock. In spite of his care, he could not totally avoid the click of the hammer. The buck's super sensitive hearing picked up the sound and it paused. Damn!

The buck was in range—just—but was partially screened by a birch sapling. Damn!

The buck was alert now and, looking directly at Mischa's hiding place, he sensed danger. Mischa would have to take the shot. *Now!*

Boom!

Damn! damn! damn!

The lead ball, propelled at low velocity by black powder,

glanced on a twig of the birch sapling. The buck was hit, but not vitally. The adrenaline sent him bounding forward towards the cover of the trees further down the valley.

"Go!"

Like twin bolts from a crossbow, the two great deerhounds were gone. The buck was nearing the shelter of the trees, but the wound was slowing him. Then the two hounds were on him, pulling him down, and Mischa was running, reaching for the long hunting knife on his belt.

The Hunter appeared, seemingly from nowhere, as Mischa and the two hounds, still heaving and panting from the chase, stood around the carcass of the dead buck whilst Mischa, hat in hand, delivered the age-old eulogy to the spirit of the dead animal.

The Hunter sat himself on a sun-warmed rock and watched whilst Mischa bent over the carcass and performed the gralloch, removing the buck's pluck end guts.

"So you're off to Russia." It was a statement.

Mischa straightened up from his task and absent-mindedly wiped his forehead with a gory hand, leaving a streak of blood on his brow.

"Yes, but I told Father that I would much rather be with the regiment. I think that there is bound to be action against the French soon."

"As sure as flies on a carcass."

"I think that Father is rather pleased that I am going to be out of the way and safe."

"Ah, the son and heir!"

"Yes."

It seemed as though a cloud passed over the Hunter's face.

"Mischa, I've known you since you were born and I've known your family since... well, it does not matter when, and I have always had a special care for them. But you should not think that there is no danger in Russia. There is a darkness there,"—the Hunter's face had taken on a strange look, as though he were looking at something far away and did not like what he saw—"You must remember that Russia is on the edge between east and west, and there is a special darkness in the east—a darkness that you might disappear in."

"What do you mean?"

"I don't know what I mean yet. It is too far for me to see. It is beyond, beyond... beyond my power, but it is dark, dark, dark!"

Mischa stared at the Hunter. He seemed to be in some sort of trance—a troubled dream. Mischa had never seen him like this before. The Hunter had always been a thing of certainty. Suddenly the Hunter seemed to shake himself, rather as a dog does when it emerges from water, and was his old self again.

"Right, my boy, let's get that deer back to the castle and cheer your father up a bit," his face clouded again for a moment. "Just remember what I said: take care in Russia."

* * *

The Khan threw another dipper-full of water on the hot stones. A fresh burst of steam added to the already stifling heat in the felt yurt. The Khan settled back, cross-legged, on his mat, great rivers of sweat running down his hard-muscled, naked body.

He shifted the wad of khat from his cheek and resumed his rhythmic chewing. The drug was already taking effect, lifting his mind from his body, so that he seemed to be hovering over his physical husk, looking down on his huge squat crouching body. He felt the euphoria lift his floating other self, raising it to a higher plain of consciousness and moving into the grey mists that swirled around it. He felt himself moving faster and faster, and, as his spirit moved through the mists, they became darker, blacker and more menacing.

Then the mist cleared. He could see the far away plateau with the little stone hut. The scene shifted to the smoke-filled interior of the hut, and the little wizened figure with its stiff leg hunched over the miserable fire.

"You have come then," said the voice.

It was a dry, creaking voice, quiet and yet full of menace—

the menace of something from a bottomless pit that crawled and seethed with unimaginable evil. The Khan was frightened. He was always frightened of the Shaman, but then a slave is always frightened of his master and his power. It was a portion of that power that he craved; evil is a heady drug.

"Yes, Master, I have come."

Silence—a silence that was even more menacing than the voice.

"What is it that you want, my son?"

"To serve my Master, as always."

"You must beware, my son. There are troubles coming to you. They will come from the west. Even I cannot see them clearly yet. They are shrouded in the mists of another power—a power in the west. But this I tell you, you must beware of a dark woman and a golden woman: they represent power and death. You must possess them both, or they will destroy you and harm my purpose. This much I understand at the moment. Power and death, my son, think on that. Now go."

The last words slithered away into the darkness, and the Khan felt himself whirling backwards through the mists until once more he saw his body below him, slumped and sweating in the steam.

The Khan emerged from his dream. The steam and the heat were dissipating, the sweat was cooling on his body. He arose and stretched his cramped limbs. Emerging from the steam lodge, he plunged immediately into the ice cold water of the mountain stream that tumbled past the camp.

He came out of the water, dripping and ravenous as always after meeting the Shaman, but before he ate there was another appetite to be appeased. As he towelled himself and felt the sun's warmth seeping into his body, he sensed another heat rising in him. As he wrapped a robe round him, his hardness pressed against the cloth. He must eat, but first...

He took up the knout—the twisted leather whip—that lay with his other clothing beside the steam lodge, and made his way to his own yurt.

The captured Russian woman was tied, naked, to the pole of the yurt. As soon as she saw the Khan, she began to scream.

* * *

"No, Sir! Dammit, Sir! Not another bloody penny, Sir! D'yer hear me? What a damned young hound you are! A disgrace, Sir!—a damned disgrace, d'yer hear me, Sir?"

The Marquis of Fowey was in full spate. Charles sighed inwardly and sat there silent and expressionless, biting the metaphorical bullet. It was a scene that had been played many times before, and Charles knew that the only thing to do was to stay silent until the storm was past. That was the great thing about the Marquis: his rage was like a lightning storm, thunderous but soon past.

Charles had known that there would be lightning when he returned to Bardwick House, the family seat in Gloucestershire, with a view to extracting more money from his father.

At last the old man sat back in his chair, his rage spent. Charles and his father were sitting on opposite sides of a table in the great library at Bardwick, where the Marquis was wont to deal with 'matters of state'. His younger son's profligate ways with the family money definitely merited a full state occasion.

The Marquis looked at his son under his heavy-hooded eyelids, which, together with the great beak of the FitzHugh nose, made him look like an old hawk. The Marquis had a soft spot for his younger son, an affection that he was unable to feel for his elder son and heir, the Earl of Tamar.

Tamar was everything that he should be, frugal—'tight as a duck's buttocks' was the unfortunate phrase that his doting father had once used—dutiful and fully aware of his responsibilities to family, King and country. He was a pillar of the Government and was obviously destined for high office.

He was also—and again his father's description may be used—'a thorough-going little prig'.

The Marquis found little sympathy with his virtuous eldest

son, whilst in Charles he could see so much of himself when young. It has always been said of the FitzHughs that 'one generation had to recoup, what the previous one had squandered.' The Marquis was a squanderer by nature and habit, and the younger son a definite sapling off the same tree. Nevertheless, the father knew that the time had come to call a halt. Hoggett, the lawyer, had informed him that Lord Charles's debts were of a ruinous nature.

The old man rang the bell that stood before him on the table. The footman, who had been standing outside the door of the library, made a smooth and immediate entry.

"Wine," said the Marquis.

Whilst they waited for the servant's return, the father sat with his chin sunk in his stock tie, his eyes brooding and the bony fingers of his right hand stroking his cheek. Charles recognised the signs of deep consideration and knew better than to interrupt. Father and son sat in silence until the wine had been brought and poured and the footman had left the room.

The Marquis raised his glass, sniffed the wine, took a mouthful, put the glass down and turned his hooded eyes on Charles.

"Now, boy, what am I going to do with you?"

* * *

"Fucking Roosia, that's where, wherever fucking Roosia is," said Trooper Bone, sprawled in an armchair in the butler's sitting room at Bardwick House.

"Good Heavens, Mr Bone."

Sidgwick the butler leaned across the table between the two chairs, where they were sitting in front of the fire, and poured some more wine into Bone's glass.

"Roosia sounds a long way off. His Lordship's finally cut up rough with Lord Charles, eh?"

"Not a penny more, that's what his Lordship told the Captain. Very nice glass of Madeira, this, Mr Sidgwick. Not a penny more, unless the Captain gets out the country, toot bloody sweet. He come to me, the Captain, and he says,

'Bone,' he says, 'we're off to Roosia. No? do you mind, Bone? How would you fancy going to Roosia, Bone? Just pack our traps, Bone, we're off to Roosia.'"

"But why Roosia?"

"Well, it seems that there's this General Barclay de Tolley, a Scots geezer. Now he's some sort of cousin of his Lordship's, and he's a high up in the army of the king out there— a Czar they call it. So his Lordship says, 'Right. my boy, off you go to Cousin Barclay de Tolley and make your own bleeding fortune, instead of trying to spend all mine.'"

"I suppose you aren't forced to go, Mr Bone?"

"No, I ain't forced to go, but I been the little bugger's orderly now for ten years and as officers go he ain't a bad one. If I go back to the regiment, Gawd knows what might happen, not with the Regimental Corporal Major hating my guts. No, I reckon I better stay with the Captain. Besides, the silly bugger gets in enough trouble when I am looking after him, Gawd only knows what would happen without me to keep an eye on him."

"Another glass of wine, Mr Bone, to drink good fortune to your journey?"

"I reckon we'll bleeding well need it," said Bone gloomily.

* * *

The old priest was troubled. He was troubled because the young man who sat on the other side of the table from him was troubled, and the old priest knew exactly why.

He sighed to himself. It was an old, old story—a story as old as men and women. The old priest had heard Mischa's first confession, and had known him all his life. When he looked at the fine upstanding young man, who now sat opposite him fingering a barely touched glass of wine and staring at the table with down cast eyes, he still saw the child: the child that he had blessed as a still-squalling swaddled bundle, the child who had given his first faltering confession of a window broken with a stone, a cake stolen from the kitchen.

He also saw the golden-haired peasant girl, little more than a child herself, who had found herself carrying a child:

a child fathered in a summer of fragrant hay meadows and soft shade beside the gently flowing river: a child fathered in love and gentleness by the young man before him, who had given and taken love freely and happily offered.

All this he had known from the girl's whispered shame in the confessional.

He had tried to temper that shame with words of God's love. But the man who might have eased the shame was no longer there. He was away with his regiment. and, if he gave thought to the little peasant girl and her love, he sent no word of it. In this silence the girl's shame and loneliness grew with the child inside her. She could not tell her father who was a hard flinty man, as hard as the land he worked. She could not tell her mother who was worn down with work and care, and ten other children. She could only tell the old priest and, gentle as he was, he could not shield her from the cruelty of the world—a world from which she knew her condition could not much longer be hidden.

The knowledge of Mischa's imminent homecoming had pushed the girl beyond the edge of her moral precipice. She drowned herself and her unborn child in the river Lipp. All the village knew this, but the old priest gave her the last comfort that he could, by declaring firmly that it had been an accident whilst the river was in spate, and allowing her sad little body to be laid to rest in consecrated ground. It was a matter that he was quite prepared to stand up for when he finally met his Maker.

Mischa had arrived home on the day of the girl's disappearance. He had joined the search. He had been there, two days later, when they had lifted the pathetic little corpse from the eddying pool below the mill race. He had seen the face that he had once kissed, bloated by the immersion and already nibbled by the eels. He had seen the long golden hair that was now tangled with weed. It was the face and hair that now came to him in his dreams. He was a tortured man.

The old priest sighed again and took a sip of his wine. There was so much of the mother in the boy. Perhaps he was too gentle—God forgive him for the thought—but it was a hard world. The girl was dead and the young man had a life to live.

"My son," said the old man, "I think that. it is a good thing that you are going away. What happened was a great tragedy and a sin; I know you know that. You will never be able to escape that, but it may be good that you are leaving here. Life is full of tragedy and you cannot escape that either. You have a long journey before you, in every sense, and I hope and pray that during your journey you may come to a better understanding of life and love."

Mischa looked up at the kindly lined face that he had known so long.

"Father, how can I ever love again, when it just seems to bring suffering and death?"

"'Ever' is a long time, Mischa. Leave 'ever' to God. Now, let us go into the church and pray together that through your journey you will find peace and love."

2 St Petersburg

"**W**AKEY, wakey, Sir!" Bone firmly shook the shoulder of the shrouded figure huddled in the narrow bunk.

"Fuck off, Bone, I'm dying!" came the muffled response and the rough blankets were pulled even tighter round the head of the corpse.

Bone grinned maliciously.

"Come on, Sir, show a leg, as the matelots say. The Captain sent me down to rouse you. We're in the river now and it's like a millpond—and St Petersburg's in sight."

"Sod it, sod you and sod off!"

Bone sighed. He knew the moods of his officer only too well, and this was going to be a trying one.

"I've got a nice cup of tea for you, Sir, and the Captain sent you down a nice tot of rum—to settle your stomach like."

A pale, tousled and horrified face appeared from under the blankets.

"Jesus Christ, Bone! I'm dying and you start waving that stinking, poxy, sailors' rum under my nose. Oh, sweet Jesus, where's that bucket?"

Bone put the odoriferous bucket close to the bunk. The smell of old vomit, combined with a waft from the glass of treacly rum, caused an instant spasm in Charles's insides, and he hung gasping and retching over the edge of the bunk. In truth he had little left to offer. The short steep waves of the Baltic had already exacted maximum tribute from the man; Charles had not enjoyed his voyage.

Bone watched in grim amusement. The motion of the barque had not inconvenienced him in the least. He had feasted on salt pork and plum duff, and had taken a tidy sum off the Bo'sun at cards. He had enjoyed the trip so far, especially with his officer being confined to his bunk—

23

'whores dee combat,' as Bone so delicately put it.

"Give us a shout when you're ready, Sir, and I bring some hot water and shave you. The way your hand's shaking you'll cut your throat if you try it yourself. Must have you looking your best for Roosia and the General."

Charles groaned and retched again.

"A bonny enough sight, eh Milord? Right! Get the tops'ls off her, if it please you, Mr Murdie. The tenders are on their way to us."

"Aye, Aye, Sir!"

The First Mate bellowed his orders, and the shrilling of the Bo'sun's pipe sent the crew scuttling into the rigging.

Charles, still looking pale and haggard, but smartly dressed now, stood by the rail of the poop deck and watched the elegant baroque waterfront of St Petersburg gradually draw nearer.

"As you say, Captain Maitland, a bonny enough sight, and I shall not be sorry to get me feet on land again."

Captain Maitland's weather-roughened face cracked into a dour smile:

"Aye, my Lord, I doubt but ye've taken little pleasure from the voyage. The North Sea and the Baltic have hardly smiled on you."

Charles shuddered at the heaving, creaking, pitching, wind-howling memories.

"What's this like in winter?"

Even on the wide river the late summer heat was starting to seep through Charles's coat.

"Frozen," said the laconic Scot.

The two large oar-propelled tenders approached the barque; she would be towed to her berth on the waterfront.

As the tenders swept by a waft of foulness almost caused Charles to vomit again:

"Christ, Captain! What's that stench?"

The Captain frowned at Charles's outburst, but just replied:

"Convicts. The tenders are rowed by convicts—it is the

stench of unrighteousness, and no doubt a swift path to repentance."

"Religious chappie, are you?"

"An Elder of the Kirk, my Lord."

"Oh well, you're probably the wrong chap to ask, then."

"Ask what?"

"Well, you know how it is—two weeks bobbing up and down and spewing me guts out—there's three things I want through my teeth: a glass of wine, a decent meal, and a tart's tongue."

The Captain regarded Charles sternly:

"My Lord if you will take my advice and heed the words of Holy Scripture, when you go ashore you will keep your hand on your wallet and your cock in your trousers; otherwise you're likely to be robbed, poxed, and damned in very short order."

Bone had just come on deck from packing Charles's traps in the cabin. He muttered to himself: 'That's right, you tell him Cap'n, and it won't do a monkey's fuck's worth of good.'

"God's teeth, but that feels better, Bone! Good old terra firma, eh?"

"Yessir."

The two men stood on the quayside along their pile of luggage, waiting whilst a sailor came nimbly down the gangplank with the last of Charles's chests balanced on his shoulder.

Charles was in expansive mode now that the horrors of the sea crossing were behind him. He was back on dry land, about to start a new adventure, and cheerfully conscious of the bag of golden guineas in his portmanteau. This, and a draft on a Russian bank, had been his father's parting gift, together with the promise of a small monthly remittance for as long as he stayed out of England—'I ain't going to say never darken the doorstep again, my boy, but just don't come back with empty pockets.'

Charles felt in his waistcoat pocket and flipped the sailor a crown, which the man deftly caught:

"There, cully, piss that against the wall."

The sailor gave a black-toothed grin and knuckled his forehead.

"Now, Bone, see if you can jack up a carriage, and we'll go and find Cousin General Barclay de Tolley—if we don't find something better first. It looks quite a promising place."

Whether Czar Peter the Great would have been pleased with such a dismissive description of his attempt to build a 'Venice of the North' is doubtful; after all, its fine classical buildings had been designed and built by the best architects and builders that money could attract from all over Europe.

Charles did not have a very advanced aesthetic sense. Classical façades meant little to him; he was far more interested in the pleasurable possibilities that might lurk behind and within. His first impression of the wide avenues and fine stone buildings was favourable—the better the buildings the more chance of mischief. He settled himself on one of his chests, and let the bawling and bustle of the quayside flow round him. He was hungry, thirsty and randy—more or less in that order.

Charles could see the line of carriages drawn up along the quayside and he idly watched Bone surrounded by a group of hirsute, gesticulating, drivers. He hoped the fellow would get it sorted quickly. He pushed his cap over his eyes and almost dozed in the growing heat of the day.

"Excuse me, Sir."

"All set, Bone?"

"Well no Sir, begging your pardon, Sir, but none of them blighters speak English and I don't reckon that any of them reads much either. I tried showing the bit of paper with the General's address on, but they just shrugged and gabbled at me in foreign."

Charles sighed:

"Well I suppose they *are* foreign, Bone. Or I suppose, to be fair, it is us who are the foreigners."

"I'm no bloody foreigner, Sir! I'm English.!"

Charles sighed again:

"Yes, Bone, I do believe that you are. Unfortunately, it

ain't getting us very far at the moment."

"Shall I pop back to the ship and get the Captain to sort something out for us? He must speak a bit of the lingo."

"I think that Captain Maitland was pleased to see us go. I sensed a heavy pall of disapproval hanging over him. But, yes, that may have to be the answer. I ain't sitting on this poxy quay for the rest of the day."

"Excuse me, Excellency."

Charles turned. The small neat man had a small neat moustache and small neat side-whiskers. He was twisting a beaver hat in his small neat hands.

"Excuse me Excellency, I am Polikoff, I am agent for shipping here. I am agent for Captain Maitland. Perhaps I can be of service to you."

The voice was oleaginous and servile. Charles screwed the eye-glass into his right eye and had a proper look at the little man. 'Thoroughly nasty little shit' was his first thought; 'needs must' was his second.

"Speak English do you cully?"

The little man bobbed and simpered and bowed.

"Oh yes, Excellency, thank you Excellency. I am much working with English like Captain Maitland."

"He's not English—just a haggis shagger," growled Bone.

"Please?"

"Pay no attention, my dear old Polikoff, my man is just being English. We shall be delighted to avail ourselves of your services for which I shall, of course, feel obliged to re-imburse you. Now, we need a carriage."

In fact they needed two carriages: one for Bone and all the luggage, one for Charles and Polikoff.

As they drove, Polikoff pointed out the buildings. In spite of himself, Charles was impressed. Even if the thought that Czar Peter had attempted to encapsulate the whole of western culture in stone, and had then attempted to dump it on a northern swamp, did not occur to him, he did think the buildings 'damned fine'. He also thought the great wide streets, seething with traffic, 'damned fine' and that, by comparison, St James's was a mean street.

As an ex-soldier he was interested in the mass of uniforms and their colourful display he saw in the streets. However, the sights soon palled and more urgent needs reasserted themselves.

"Tell me, dear old Polikoff, rather than go to the merry general, is there anywhere where a little sport might be had, where a chap might be diverted for a while?"

"Excellency?"

"My dear old boy, I've been at sea for two weeks. A chap has needs you know—appetites, d'yersee."

Light dawned over Polikoff and he smiled a broad smile.

"Ah Excellency, of course, you want fuck."

"That's it then Bone. Polikoff and I are just going to pop in here for a little light refreshment of body and soul. You push off to the General with the baggage. My compliments to the General and tell him that I just wanted to rearrange my clothing, so that I can present myself clean, dry and lightly oiled—good that, what, Polikoff?"

"The Milor is a most witty person."

"You sure that this is a good idea, Sir? I mean I don't like the look of this place. Think I ought to stay with you?"

Under Polikoff's direction, the carriages had turned off the broad expanse of the Nevsky Prospekt, and had twisted and turned through a succession of increasingly mean streets, before pulling up in front of a large dilapidated house from which came the sound of music; there were several dubious-looking characters lounging on the steps of the place. To Bone's practised—if pugillistically battered—nose, the place smelt of 'Trouble'.

"Shove off, Bone, I'll be all right. Polikoff will look after me, won't you cully?"

"Yes, yes, yes, Bone! I look after Milor real good."

"That's what worries me," thought Bone.

"Yes, yes, yes, shove off Bone!"

"I'll shove that fucking nose right up his arse in a minute, the slimy little git," thought Bone.

"I show the Milor a real good time."

The little Russian's face broke into a very wide grin of anticipatory pleasure.

'Like a fucking shite hawk watching a chicken run,' thought the street-wise Trooper Bone.

And out loud:

"Very good, Sir. And you," he turned to Polikoff. "You look after his Lordship real good or, by the Lord Harry, I'll look after *you* real good."

"Oh, I look after the Milor very good. Now *departez*, Bone."

Still smiling, the little man gave the carriage drivers some rapid orders in Russian. As the carriages jolted off down the street, Bone looked behind and saw Polikoff bowing and scraping Charles into the building. He also saw the ripple of interest run through the bystanders, who jostled through the door in their wake. Bone's driver turned and said something to him in Russian. Bone shrugged his incomprehension. The man laughed and drew his finger across his throat.

She was a handsome well-fleshed slut.

Her expert fingers quickly brought Charles up to the 'Present', as he fumbled with the ample breasts that flowed out of her bodice. She said something enquiring in Russian.

"No speeko the lingo, old dear," said Charles as he pushed her off his lap onto the bed, "but who needs words, what?"

The girl giggled and, turning onto all fours, flipped her skirt up over her back with a practised gesture, and presented Charles with the large white globes of her naked bottom.

"You're a right mare, and no mistake. Well, I'm just the stallion you need for a rousting—prepare to receive cavalry!"

General Barclay de Tolley was not pleased. He glowered at ex-Trooper Bone, who was standing stiffly to attention before his desk.

"The damned young fool! Not an hour in the city and he's into the stew pot," he said, in his harsh Aberdeen accent.

"Why did ye no stop him, man? Ye must have seen what sort of a place yon was?"

Bone stared straight ahead.

"Begging your pardon, Sir, but it's not my place to stop his Lordship. I did try to persuade him, like, but he's very headstrong, is his Lordship."

"From what I hear, his head is the least of his troubles. Ah well, just so, no doubt you did your best for the young fool. Now what did you say this place was called?"

"It sounded something like Strogov's, Sir."

The ADC standing beside the desk, who, like all educated Russians of the time spoke excellent English, made a wry face.

"Heard of it have ye?" asked the General, looking up under his beetling brows.

"Not a good place, Excellency, I fear."

"Who's commanding the duty troop?"

"Major Lubin, Excellency."

"Right! Get him here on the double and stand the troop to. We better get your lord back before the bastards eat him."

"Permission to speak, Sir."

The General nodded.

"Permission to accompany rescue party, Sir!"

"Aye, weel, we may need the corpse identified," said the General with grim jocosity. Bone thought of Polikoff and cracked his mighty knuckles with anticipation.

"A right little snorter, cully, you did me a good steer there. She could really gallop, what? I must say, this is a jolly place."

Charles looked round the shouting, smoke-filled room. Polikoff smiled his smile.

"The Milor is enjoying himself? Now we have a little more to drink, yes?"

"Well, why not? But I must go soon—meet the General, d'yersee."

"You try this special wodka. Make you fit to meet a hundred generals. Make you fit to meet the Apostle Peter himself."

Polikoff filled the glasses and handed one to Charles.

"Now, Milor, you must drink it down in one—old Russian custom."

The choking fit bent Charles almost double.

"Jesus Christ! What on earth was that stuff?"

"I tell you werry special wodka."

Polikoff refilled Charles's glass, but he was suddenly aware that the room was beginning to blur, and that his head felt funny. He was dimly aware of figures gathering around his table.

"I think I had better be going, cully, got to see the General." He was aware that his words had started to slur.

He started to rise from his chair, but strong hands from behind him pushed him back into the seat. Polikoff smiled at him from across the table.

"Oh no, Milor, do not go yet! Stay with Polikoff and all your new friends. Don't you worry—we are going to take care of you, just like I told that scum, Bone."

Charles was aware of a new tone in Polikoff's voice, but his head was swimming and the room had started to revolve around him; he was slipping away, and was only dimly aware of the crash of the door being burst open.

The Cossack troop was drawn up in the yard of the headquarters building when Bone and Major Lubin emerged from their interview with the General.

Lubin was a tall, languid young man with extravagant moustachios and an air of relaxed ferocity about him. He spoke excellent English and was licking his lips at the thought of 'a little sport', as he put it.

"I fear that your officer is not in a good place," he said to Bone. "We may have to crack a head or two today," obviously relishing the prospect.

Bone studied the troop with a professional eye. They were Lifeguard Kuban Cossacks in long red tunics and tall red hats. They sat their wiry little horses with the relaxed air of men who were part of the horses they rode. They were mostly of powerful physique with flowing hair and beards,

and Bone thought that they were as hard a bunch of ruffians
as he had seen. 'I don't know what the Regimental Corporal
Major would make of this lot,' he thought, 'but I'm bloody
glad they're on my side.'

Two orderlies came forward with two horses. Lubin
swung into the saddle, set his red forage cap at a rakish angle,
and addressed the troop in Russian. The troop growled with
pleasure, one or two of them laughing. Lubin turned to
Bone, who was now mounted.

"I tell them they can have any whores that your lord has
left over. They are very keen, my little band of angels!"

At a shouted command from the Sergeant, the troop
wheeled into column. They burst out of the gate at a canter
and headed west down the broad street. Bone, riding next to
Lubin, noted how the crowd scrambled to part in front of the
cantering troop. Lubin, looking straight ahead, deviated neither to left nor right. Pedestrians and horsemen scattered to
let them through. A cart driver, who struggled to move his
clumsy vehicle out of the way in time, received a casual back-
handed slash from Lubin's leather-thonged knout, sending
him tumbling to the ground with blood streaming from his
face.

'Strewth,' thought Bone, 'these are some rough bastards.'

The troop sliced through the crowded street like wire
through cheese, their lances slung over their shoulders. They
arrived at the doorway where Bone had last seen Charles
with Polikoff; the steps were empty and the door closed.

Lubin swung a leg over the pommel of his saddle and slid
easily to the ground. He barked an order, and two huge Cossacks immediately smashed the door in.

For a moment the inmates of the crowded room froze,
then the Cossacks were amongst them, roaring and swinging
their knouts with uninhibited relish. There was instant panic
with men and women scrambling, scratching and screaming
to escape. They tried to get four deep through the doors at
the back with the Cossacks harrying them like wolves in a
sheep fold, roaring with laughter and bloodlust.

There was a crash of glass as one man dived head first

through a window, only to find himself lying in the filth with a lance at his throat.

Bone was one of the first through the door. He immediately took in the figure of Charles slumped over a table. Bone was quickly beside him. He felt Charles's pulse: strong enough.

"You silly little bugger," he said out loud. "You never bloody learn, do you."

With that he hefted Charles's slim form over his shoulder and carried him out easily into the street where he plonked him down on the pavement and sat him against the wall.

"English Milord! You savvy?" he said to the Cossacks on guard there.

The Cossacks roared with laughter: "English Milord," they said to each other.

Bone shook the slumped figure.

"Now, Sir, you just sit there quiet like until I get back, you understand."—Charles gave a feeble moan—"Well, I don't think that you're going anywhere, but I've just got a little business to attend to."

Bone went back into the house.

The Cossacks were having a wonderful time; they were comprehensively wrecking the place and the people therein. From the rooms at the back came loud screaming—for the Cossacks had got amongst the whores. Lubin was sitting at an unwrecked table with a bottle of vodka in front of him, watching the mayhem with benevolent interest.

Bone saluted: "Excuse me, Sir, beg leave to report that I've got his Lordship outside, but I reckon he's drugged."

"Only death is more certain," said Lubin languidly. "My little wolves are really enjoying themselves, so I will let them play a little longer."

"Excuse me, Sir, but I don't suppose you've seen anything of a greasy-looking little beggar with side-whiskers and a little moustache?"

"Ah ha!" said Lubin with a flicker of interest, "I do believe I saw such a creature go through the door over there."

"Thank you, Sir."

The room behind the door was empty, but there was a huge cupboard in the corner. Bone marched up to the cupboard and wrenched the door open. Polikoff was curled up inside in a foetal position. He looked up in horror, and then relief.

"Ah, Bone," he said, with an attempt at a smile, "thank the saints that you have come. I was trying to protect the Milor with my life."

Bone's evil grin wiped the smile off Polikoff's face. Bone said nothing. He just reached out a huge hand, and, seizing Polikoff by his shirt front, dragged him out of the cupboard and into the main room where Lubin was still sitting placidly amongst the wreckage.

"This is him, Sir! This is the one that trapped his Lordship."

Lubin took out his eyeglass and surveyed the gibbering, shivering Polikoff.

"A nasty bit of human carrion. I wonder how long he will last in the mines."

At this Polikoff fell to his knees in front of Lubin and clutched his ankles.

"No! No! Have mercy, Excellency!"

Lubin kicked him languidly.

"Do you want him?" he asked Bone.

"I was going to break his bloody neck, but just look at the snivelling wretch. It ain't worth it."

"I agree that he's worthless, but... Sergeant!"

"Excellency?"

The huge bearded Sergeant came across the room, his knout swinging from his wrist. Lubin gave an order.

"This animal has put snot on my boots," said Lubin to Bone.

Polikoff's screams rang in Bone's head for some time afterwards.

"Ye're a bluidy wee waster!" said General Barclay de Tolley.

"Sir!" said Charles, who was standing rigidly to attention staring at the wall above the General's head.

On the wall was an icon of the Madonna and Child. It was unusual in that both the figures were black. Charles tried to look the Madonna in the eye as the tirade rumbled and grumbled from the table below. He was to describe it afterwards as the biggest bollocking he had had in ages, and Charles was something of a connoisseur.

General Barclay de Tolley was a formidable figure, as befitted a man who a few years later would lead thousands of Cossacks into Paris—the furthest west that any Russian army has ever advanced before or since—yet Charles found the Madonna's gaze arresting, as though the picture was trying to draw him towards it. He found that his concentration was becoming more and more committed to the picture, and the General was becoming like the vague rumble of distant gunfire; he found the sad and gentle stare almost worse than the tirade below. A thunderous bang on the table jerked his attention back to the General who was glowering up at him from under his huge bushy eyebrows.

"Man! FitzHugh, are ye listening to a bluidy word I'm saying?"

"Sir!"

The General looked at him reflectively, and then turned his head for a moment to look at the icon.

"Ah!" he said, "the Lady gave you the eye, did she?"

"Well, yes Sir. I did find her somewhat compelling."

The General gave a 'hrrmph' that might almost have been a laugh.

"More compelling that some old general blethering on and telling ye what ye have no heard afore, eh?"

"Well, Sir..."

"Yes, Sir! Well FitzHugh, ye would do well to heed yon Lady because she's worth more than any poor general."

"Why, Sir? Who is she?"

"That, man, is the Black Madonna. Mind, yon is only a copy. The original hangs safe and sound at the church of St Lazar in Pyatigorsk. For the Cossacks that icon represents the personal blessing and safe keeping of Our Lady on each and every one of them. They believe that if the Black Madonna is carried with them when they go into battle then they can't be beat. Ye may think that that is a lot of auld wives' nonsense, but the point is that they believe it, and they'll fight for it in a way that they would fight for no human leader. So ye do well to heed her. But now, just for a moment, heed me."

"Sir!" said Charles, looking down at the grizzled veteran.

"If it were not for the regard and kinship of your father, I would be minded to put ye on the first ship out of here. There is no doubt but you're nothing but trouble, young man. But, I suppose I must find you something to do—preferably as far away from me as possible. In the meantime, find Major Dorlov, give him my compliments, and tell him to keep you busy and out of my sight. I hear that you are a swordsman of sorts?"

"Tolerable, Sir."

"Right. Well, training recruits in sword-drill might sweat some of the muck out of ye. Now get out of here."

"Sir!"

Charles saluted smartly, about-turned and marched out of the General's presence. Somehow he felt a pair of eyes boring into his back, and he did not think they were those of General Barclay de Tolley.

"Rittmeister Graf Czerny has arrived and is waiting in the ante room, Herr General," said the ADC as he placed the last document on the table for the General's signature.

"Ah ha! Splendid!"—General von Hohenfels's generous muttontop whiskers shook with pleasure—"Send him in! Send him in! But I almost forgot—any word from the Ministry yet about that meeting?"

"No, Herr General. I have made further representations but they say Prince Malikoff is still out on manoeuvres and is not available."

"Manoeuvres? Manoeuvres? The only manoeuvres that bastard's on are horizontal and debilitating. I saw him myself at the opera two nights ago. How does anything get done in this blighted country?"

"On the whole it doesn't, Herr General," said the ADC

smoothly, whipping the document away swiftly.

The head of the Imperial Austrian Military Mission in St Petersburg was not unaccustomed to mangling documents ready to hand when frustrated by the somewhat relaxed attitudes to life and duty of his Russian counterparts.

"Barrgh!" said the General, taking a generous handful of whisker and twisting it—a sure sign of frustration. "Damn these wretched bastards! Well, anything else?"

"Just Czerny, Herr General."

"Of course! Of course!" The General's face lightened. "Well, what are you waiting for? Send him in."

"Very good, Sir," said the ADC, before making one of the seamless exits that ADCs have to learn.

Mischa was sitting bolt upright on one of the small and uncomfortable chairs in the ante room. He was tired and worn with travel, but on arrival at St Petersburg he had not hesitated to change into full dress uniform and report to the Military Mission. He had been watching the door, and straightened up as it opened and the ADC appeared.

"The General will see you now, Czerny."

Mischa got to his feet rather nervously, adjusted the pelisse on his left shoulder, straightened his shako and, carrying his sabre with his left hand, marched through the door that the ADC was holding open. He crashed to a halt in front of the bewhiskered figure at the table and saluted.

"Rittmeister Mischa Czerny reporting…"

"Yes, yes, my boy, I know who you are, dammit! I've known you since you were a baby, dammit boy! At ease and all that sort of thing. Now sit down and tell me all about your father. Why, dammit, I remember your father and I…"

Major Prince Dorlov was sitting at ease on his charger. Behind him, on the wide expanse of the parade ground outside the barracks, a troop of recruits sat on their wiry horses.

Cossacks are brought up to ride and have little need of instruction in horsemanship; but on acceptance into one of the

Guard Regiments, they needed training in basic drills and
military manoeuvres. Each man would bring his own mount
with him—the hardy little horses of the steppe that looked no
more than ponies, but which would carry a man and his
equipment and eat up the miles, day after day.

They were all watching the Englishman.

A line of wooden pegs had been driven into the clay of the
area, now made muddy by the autumn rain. In the near distance Dorlov could see Charles mounted on his charger,
lance at the rest, waiting for the signal. Dorlov waved a languid arm. Charles's lance point came down and his horse
jumped from the stand into a mud-spurting gallop. Bending
easily in the saddle, Charles drove the razor-sharp point at
the first peg, splitting it cleanly. The speed of the horse never
slackened as the thud of its hooves grew more distinct. With
unerring ease Charles split peg after peg.

A murmur of approbation rose from the troop and, as
Charles spitted the last peg and raised it triumphantly on his
lance point, a spontaneous 'Hurrah!' rose from the Cossacks,
only to be silenced by a growl from Dorlov.

The bloody Englishman could ride, he concluded grudg-
ingly, but he was not going to have the man cheered by his
own Cossacks. Damn the man! He was cocky enough as it
was, and too damned clever by half with the cards—Charles
had trounced the Prince in last night's game *and* had remained upright whilst the Prince had finally slid beneath the
table. Poor Dorlov did not like being beaten. After all, he was
a prince.

Charles came trotting back, foam dripping from his
horse's bit, the last peg still impaled on his point. He reigned
in opposite Dorlov and lowered the lance so that the point
and peg hovered in front of Dorlov's chest.

"There you are, old boy, a present for you."

Dorlov's face remained expressionless, but he seethed inwardly—damn the man showing off in front of *his* men! He
would dearly have loved to wipe the insolent grin off the

fellow's face. He snapped a command and a dismounted orderly came running forward to take Charles's lance. Charles swung his horse in beside Dorlov and grinned at him.

"How was that, old thing? Cheered your lads up, what?"

Dorlov snapped an order for the Sergeant to take his troop back to barracks, whilst he and Charles followed at an easy pace.

"You ride well on the parade ground," said Dorlov. "I imagine that you also go well across country?"

"The living best,"—Charles had never been burdened with false modesty.

"That is good. The Grand Duke Alexei's boar hounds meet at Gorodny tomorrow. Perhaps you would care to accompany me?"

"Absolutely splendid!"

Charles's eyes lit up at the thought of hunting. The volcano of the prince's temper glowed deep in its crater.

"Good," said the prince out loud, and to himself, 'I will ride you into the ground you smug English bastard.'

Said Charles to himself, 'Catch me if you can, my merry old Ivan.'

"Come in, my boy, and sit down," said General von Hohenfels. "Oh, but pour yourself a glass of wine,"—he waved towards the decanter on a tray beside the door—"and pour one for me while you're at it."

Mischa did as he was told and put the glass in front of the old man. He had become very fond of the old General since he had arrived at St Petersburg; all the members of the Mission were fond of their avuncular commander, but they also had a great respect for his ability and his temper, which was all the more feared for being rarely seen.

"Well, my boy," said the General, putting down his glass and licking the wine from his bushy moustache with a satisfied expression, "you seem to have settled in very well since you have joined us. You work well and conscientiously—

perhaps too conscientiously. Getting out a bit, are you? I know that I've seen you at some of the official receptions, but I hope you're getting around—balls and that sort of thing. This is the time of year when all the families start coming in from their summering on their estates. You should be attending some of these occasions—part of the job you know. Dashing young chap like you—bet you're a hand with the ladies, eh?"

"Well, Sir, I..."

"Mitzendorff tells me that you spend far too much time with your head stuck in reports and things. Part of our job here is to keep the Russians sweet—won't do that with your head in a report. You must get out, meet people, get a bit of fresh air too. I tell you what! Old Grand Duke Alexei has a capital pack of boar hounds on his estate. He's invited me for a day; why don't you come along? Bit of sport will do us both good, eh?"

3 Noblesse Oblige

THE Gorodny Estate had been laid out for hunting on the French pattern. Old Grand Duke Alexei had served in the Paris Embassy in the days of the King. He had much admired the way that the royal forests had been planned, with a web of broad straight rides spreading out and intersecting from a series of interconnecting hubs. Many serfs had laboured for years to establish a similar system in the tangled Russian forests around Gorodny.

Charles and Dorlov had sent their horses on with grooms, and went bowling on to the meet in Dorlov's carriage. The day was fine after several days of continuous heavy rain. An early frost was helping to bring the leaves to their autumn colours.

Charles sniffed the air as he huddled into the fur collar of his driving coat. He smelled all the familiar smells of autumn —of damp earth and rotting leaves—it smelled like a typical hunting morning. He closed his eyes, and for a moment he could hear the hounds singing in their kennels at Bardwick House; he could hear their cry in the well-kept woodlands of the park, and see the lithe red form of a fox slipping across one of the broad rides. For a moment Charles felt very homesick for England.

He was aroused from his reverie by a grunt from his companion. Dorlov had not spoken a word since he had picked Charles up at his quarters. Dorlov had been in poor fettle, but then Charles had never known Dorlov to be anything else.

Charles was hardly a sensitive soul, but he suspected that Dorlov did not like him—couldn't think why—it was hardly his fault, Charles felt, that the man was such an infernal muff at cards, at drinking and with women. Not that Charles knew

41

much of Dorlov's ineptitude with women, it was only what he had heard from the Grand Duchess Olga—and he had a feeling that, when the fellow found out where the Grand Duchess was currently reposing her favours, there might well be trouble. The thought sent a tremor of excitement through him; trouble was exciting.

The meet was at one of the circular clearings in the forest: a hub from which long straight rides stretched out to connect with other clearings.

The clearing was a milling mass of carriages and horses. From the carriages fur-wrapped ladies wove webs with their eyes, whilst male admirers buzzed them like wasps around a honey trap. Some horses were being led about by grooms; some already had their riders in the saddle.

There were a few ladies riding side-saddle; one of these was the Grand Duchess Olga. It was the first time that Charles had seen her on a horse and he did think she looked a damned handsome woman; but then he *knew* that she was a damned handsome woman. He also noticed that Dorlov was stroking his beard into place as he watched her.

"Damned fine woman, ain't she?" said Charles with all the innocence that he could muster.

Dorlov gave him a sideways look.

"The Grand Duchess is a great lady," he said chillingly.

"She looks as though she goes well," said Charles in the same innocent tone.

But, as he said it, he pictured the magnificent naked body above him, and felt the steel-muscled thighs gripping him as they had the other night. 'The Grand Duchess goes extremely well, if you did but know it, my fine Russian bucko,' he thought to himself.

Dorlov gave one of his sullen grunts. The carriage ground to a halt.

"Ah, my merry English friend," said a languid voice, and Charles looked up to see Major Lubin, sitting easily on his horse.

Since Lubin had extracted Charles from the brothel, they had become regular companions. Through his monocle,

Lubin regarded the world with the same amused, cynical detachment as Charles did. They enjoyed each other's company, and Lubin had introduced Charles into some of the best houses in St Petersburg.

He had also arranged lodgings for him in a house kept by a comely widow of his acquaintance: "She will help you with your Russian," Lubin had told him.

"Sounds pretty much the same as it does in English," Bone had grumbled as the sounds floated down the stairs from the bedroom. However, Bone's own Russian lessons were progressing most satisfactorily on the pillow of the widow's plump but attractive housekeeper. All in all, both master and man seemed to be adapting extremely well to their strange environment.

"Ah, here are your horses, I think," said Lubin. "Come on, Dorlov, buck up a bit, you look like a bear with piles this morning."

Dorlov grunted, threw off his rug and began shouting at his orderly for no good reason. His gaze was fixed on the Grand Duchess Olga.

"Right," said Lubin, when Charles was mounted. "Since friend Dorlov seems somewhat out of sorts this morning, I will introduce you to the Grand Duke Alexei and the Grand Duchess, although I believe you are already acquainted."

Indeed, the Grand Duchess most graciously offered him a slim, kid-gloved, hand to be kissed.

"You must," she said, "come and meet my husband."

The Grand Duke Alexei was at least twice as old as his wife. He was fat and jolly. His passions had long been limited to the chase and the table. For years he had been content for his wife's passions to be taken care of elsewhere, but he required her to give a blow by blow account of her adventures, during the telling of which the old rogue would sip and slurp and roar with laughter, slapping his plump thighs at the more entertaining morsels.

At the edge of the clearing stood a little dacha, and at a well-laden table in front of the dacha sat a hugely fat old man, wrapped in a cloak. His moustache and beard were

already well stained with food. Also seated at the table was
another hirsute elderly man in the uniform of a General of
the Imperial Austrian Army. Charles recognised him as the
head of the Austrian Military Mission, whom he had seen at
receptions. Beside him sat a large, quiet-looking man in the
uniform of a Rittmeister of Kaiser Cuirassiers.

Unbeknownst to him, Charles had already occasioned His
Imperial Highness much mirth to the extent that he had almost choked on a quail during the account of one of
Charles's more athletic moments, and he had had to have his
imperial back vigorously pummelled by a hastily summoned
major domo. He therefore greeted the Englishman with
great cordiality, introduced him to General von Hohenfels—
the General bowed in a genial manner—and Rittmeister
Czerny who was serving with the Austrian mission.

The Grand Duke hoped that they would both enjoy their
first day with his hounds. The foresters had a fine old boar
harboured. The day looked fine.

"Ah, my English friend, I have fine English hounds and
an English huntsman."

The hounds were grouped in an orderly fashion at the edge
of the clearing. In their midst, dressed in the long-skirted red
coat and the velvet cap, such as would be seen on any huntsman in England, sat a little ferret-faced man, whose sad
weeping eyes and swollen purple nose suggested the regular
consumption of beverages other than milk.

Charles recognised him at once:

"Good heavens, Jolly! Is that you?"

"Aye, it's me Milord," said the little man in lugubrious
tones, executing an extravagant sweep of his cap. "Aye, it's
me and a pretty place you find me in."

Charles remembered Jolly when, clear of eye and hard of
visage, he had hunted Lord Borrowdale's hounds, and gone
the living best across the new thorn ox fences that were then
just starting to criss-cross the open ground of Leicestershire
after the Enclosures Act had removed the rights on the open
Common land. He also remembered that Jolly had suc-

cumbed to that all too common complaint of hunt servants—
the sipping of readily offered gin.

"How came you here, man?"

"Oh, bad luck, Milord, bad luck. I lost my position
through no fault of my own, you understand, and jobs such
as a man of my talents deserve were hard to find, or didn't
suit a man what had been an Earl's huntsman. But things
were agin me, Milord, things were agin me."

'A–gin you, more like,' thought Charles.

"Anyway, I was with this Colonel Wimperis and suddenly
he ups and says, 'Jolly,' he says, 'Jolly, I shot me bolt and the
Jews are after me. So I've sold the hounds to some Roosian
Duke,' he says. 'You can go with 'em or you can go to blazes,'
he says, 'I'm off to Boulogne.' So here I am, Milord, stuck in
this howling, bloody wilderness, and..."

"Yes, well done Jolly," said Charles quickly, realising that
this was a tale of misery that was likely to have no ending except in the vodka bottle, which was obviously going to be the
end of Jolly's story. "I hope we have a good day. Good to see
you again, Jolly."

And he moved rapidly away, leaving the sad piece of human flotsam still muttering amongst his hounds.

Hounds moved off, followed by the mounted cavalcade. This
was in turn followed by a line of carriages, led by that of the
Grand Duke who was accompanied by the Austrian General.

Charles found himself riding beside the young Austrian
Rittmeister, whom he had noticed at the meet. He seemed a
serious, quiet man. Charles eyed him speculatively, wondering how lucky this large young bear was with the cards and
dice. Charles's funds were running a little low, and the pigeons that he had already plucked were tending to take flight
at his approach. He needed a new mark.

"Charles FitzHugh, Royal Horse Guards, at your service,
Sir," sweeping his hat off with a bow from the saddle. The
man saluted gravely and formally:

"Mischa Czerny, Kaiser Cuirassiers," he said. "I have seen
you in the distance at receptions and balls and, of course,

your reputation is well known in the capital."

Charles looked up sharply but, apart from a twitch of the heavy moustache, the big man's face remained gravely expressionless—unless there was a twinkle of irony at the back of the eyes.

"Humph! Yes, well, your servant Sir," said Charles, extending a hand which was taken in Mischa's huge grasp.

'The man's a bloody bear,' thought Charles.

"At your service, Lord FitzHugh."

The two men smiled.

"I fear that Prince Dorlov is not having a happy time," said a languid voice.

Lubin had swung his horse in beside them.

The three men turned their attention to Dorlov, who, some way ahead of them, was riding alongside the Grand Duchess. The Grand Duchess was lavishing her entire attention on the elderly man who rode on her other side. Dorlov was being markedly ignored. It was obvious that this was doing nothing to improve his state of mind.

"Poor Dorlov! He had a brief moment of glory when the Grand Duchess dispensed some of her famous sweetmeats to him. However, it is rumoured that his greed is hardly matched by his ability. It is also rumoured that the Grand Duke found the account of Dorlov's efforts so boring that he fell asleep in the middle of the telling. Moreover, one hears that Her Imperial Highness is now receiving much better service. Only gossip, of course, but Dorlov is not pleased, and would dearly like to know who has jocked him off—so to speak."

Lubin inserted his monocle and smiled benignly at Charles, who kept his eyes firmly to the front.

"She is certainly a most beautiful and gracious-looking lady," said Mischa.

Lubin adjusted his eye glass again, and gave the young Austrian a cool appraising stare.

"Just so," he drawled. "Well, perhaps I should introduce you. What think you, Charles?"

"Don't matter to me."

The Grand Duchess seemed much taken with the young Czerny. She had always had a weakness for large men. She insisted that he ride beside her and tell her all about himself.

"Oh dear!" said Lubin to Charles. "I sense the smell of unhappiness from Dorlov. I do hope that his somewhat limited mind will not fix on Czerny as his rival. That could lead to unpleasantness."

"You, Lubin," said Charles, "are a shit-stirring bastard."

Both men burst out laughing.

The boar was old and solitary. The size of a small pony, he would have turned the scales at well over five hundred pounds. After a night rootling for acorns, he was crouched contentedly in a stand of young oaks. Occasionally he would move his jaws, so that the massive tusks ground against each other, being thus continually stropped into razor sharpness.

At dawn that morning old Boris, the head forester, had found the boar's footprints leading into the compartment of trees, and had given a little murmur of excitement at their size; this was a big boar. He had circled the section of trees to make sure that the pig had not come out, and was laid up for the day. Then he had hastened back to the meet where, twisting his cap in his hands, he had made his report to His Imperial Highness.

As he trotted down the ride with his hounds, Ben Jolly was not a happy man. "A great, huge boar," old Boris had said. Jolly did not like great, huge boars; there would be some hounds hurt, maybe some killed.

He adjusted the short broad-bladed sword that hung at his waist. Custom dictated that, when the boar stood at bay, it had to be dispatched with a thrust to the heart with a sword by the first man up. 'Serving the boar,' they called it. 'Bloody outlandish custom,' Jolly called it. He would ride cautious, like, and let one of them crazy foreigners get there first. Ben was no bloody fool—not him! God, what he would not give for a drink of decent gin right now!

Old Boris was waiting for him at the oak thicket, whilst

Jolly cheered his hounds into the covert, dreaming of gin.

With skilled ease, the Grand Duchess Olga had extracted all
the personal details of the shy young man riding beside her.
She found Rittmeister Czerny most interesting. His large
frame, manly bearing and obvious lack of guile attracted her;
he was most charming in a quiet and unassuming way. She
suspected that he was not experienced with women—and she
liked to bring on a young horse from time to time. She began
to exert her own considerable charm. It would serve that
sulking misery Dorlov right.

From the depths of a thicket a hound spoke; then came a
crash of hound music.

"Listen!" said the Grand Duchess, laying a tiny gloved
hand on Mischa's arm in full sight and glare of Prince Dorlov.
"The boar is roused."

She glanced slyly at the prince as she said it.

The old boar had been hunted before. He grunted as he first
heard the sound of Jolly's voice. He stretched and listened.
The human sounds and scent came down the wind to his
delicate nostrils. He did not wait, but set off through the cop-
pice at that strange awkward-looking trot of a running pig, in
a gait that looks so deceptively slow but eats up the miles. He
heard the first triumphant hound challenge as his couching
place was found and his scent picked up.

The boar went.

"Listen!" said the Grand Duchess, laying her hand on Mischa's arm again.

They could hear the sound of something large crashing
through the young oak trees. The mounted field waited in
expectant silence as the sound got nearer. There was a gasp
of excitement as the boar broke out onto the broad ride.

"My God!" gasped Charles. "What a bloody corker!"

The massive pig paused for a moment and cocked a fierce
and wicked eye at the horses; then he was across the ride and
away into the forest. The curled hunting horns sounded the

call *The Boar*. Jolly's little English hunting horn twanged to urge the hounds on as they came swinging and roaring across the ride on the rank scent of the running pig.

The hunt was on.

The Grand Duke's forest covered many thousands of *desyatinas* and the going for the horses was good on the well-kept rides.

It was easy to keep in touch with the hounds by their cry, and to watch both hounds and pig as they crossed the open spaces. The Grand Duchess rode with an effortless grace. The Grand Duke was also very much in contention. He knew his forest, and his carriage racketed along the rides, the coachman urged on by ducal blasphemy and the occasional welt of the ducal stick across his shoulders. Age and greed may have relegated the old man to a carriage, but he had lost none of his passion for the chase.

"I do not think this pig will stand up too long," said Lubin as he cantered beside Charles and Mischa. "He is too big, and the day is too warm; he will blow up fairly quickly."

"You may be right, old boy," said Charles. "I don't know much about pig hunting, but I'll be damned if that old feller doesn't look like going a bit."

"It is the young pigs that usually run the best," suggested Mischa.

The Grand Duchess gave him the full benefit of her smile.

"That is my experience too, Herr Rittmeister. They have more stamina than the ageing boar.

Dorlov intercepted the sly glance in his direction. The powder train of his temper was now well and truly ignited.

For an hour or more the forest echoed to the sound of hound and horn. Hunted pigs often circle, but the big old boar had been running fairly straight. The heat of the autumn day was increasing and the horses were rank with sweat, but still the pace showed no sign of faltering. The hunt was approaching the edge of the forest.

"D'yer think the pig will ever leave the forest?" Charles

asked Lubin.

"It would be unusual, but if he does go out onto the open steppe, then we are in for a real hunt. I may have done this boar an injustice."

In front of them the cry of the hounds took on a different tone—they were running in the open. The twanging of Jolly's horn announced the *Gone Away*.

At the end of the broad ride the forest finished abruptly, and before them lay the rolling open plain of the steppe. As the riders debouched into the open, they could see hounds running in a tight bunch half a *verst* away, and in the distance the black dot of the boar.

"Damn! Didn't I say he was a corker?" cried Charles.

The open rolling grassland that stretched away to the horizon was rougher going than the manicured rides of the forest, but the going was sound enough. Many of the mounted followers had been thrown out by the pig taking to the open. They were waiting for the hunt to swing back into the trees; for them the day's sport was over.

It was a small select band that got away with hounds—the Grand Duchess, Mischa, Charles, Lubin, Dorlov and a handful of others following the hunched little red-coated figure of Jolly.

The rolling steppe was split by wooded, swampy gullies. On the edge of one of these the party halted their sweating, panting horses, as they listened to hounds running in the birch and willow scrub below them. Mischa mopped his brow and took out his pocket watch.

"Two and a half hours."

"Won't stand up long, eh Lubin?"

"Mea culpa! Mea culpa! A Cossack by definition is never wrong. What I meant, of course, is that he won't stand up much longer. Perhaps the Grand Duchess has an opinion?"

The Grand Duchess had lifted her veil slightly to get the benefit of the cooling breeze.

"My opinion is that matters of love and hunting are almost impossible to predict. Is that not so Herr Rittmeister?"

Again the dazzling smile, and Mischa felt himself blushing.

But, before he could reply, there was a sudden change in the cry of the hounds; it took on a deeper, more continuous baying note.

"If that was a fox, I'd say they were marking to ground," said Charles, "but it would have to be a bloody great hole to get that beggar in."

"Look!" Lubin was pointing with his whip to an open space in the valley.

The boar was shambling across this clearing with the hounds flanking him and crowding behind him. The boar suddenly turned and took a swipe with his tusks. The experienced hounds whipped back, but one young bitch was not quick enough, and the razor-like tusks laid her shoulder open to the bone.

"Oh my Gawd!" cried Jolly. "Poor little Seamstress!"

The boar continued down the valley with the wary hounds baying behind him. They disappeared into a thicket of scrub and sedge. The baying reached a new crescendo and became static.

"He's at bay!" shouted Lubin, suddenly losing his customary languidness. "Come on—we must be quick!"

The riders bucketed their horses down the steep slope of the slack to where a stream ran in the bottom and disappeared into the thicket. Somewhere in the middle of this the boar was at bay.

"Be quick! Be quick!" cried the Grand Duchess. The men leapt from their panting and exhausted horses.

The thicket turned out to be a swamp in which the men were soon struggling up to their knees in stinking mud as they forced their way through the reeds.

"Go on, gentlemen! Go on! Don't wait for me!" cried Jolly who was making haste slowly through the swamp.

To himself he muttered, 'Aye! You go on you mad bastards—better you be carved up than Ben Jolly!'

The baying got closer as the men panted and forced their way through the swamp and into a small clearing. The huge boar was standing on a small tussock island in the muddy stream. Hounds were all around him in a trampled circle of

mud and broken reeds. There was already blood in the mud
and a screaming hound lay with its guts protruding from a
slashed belly. Every now and then another hound would be
emboldened enough to dart in at the boar, but the slashing
tusks kept the circle.

Amazingly there was already a peasant on the scene; a
very big bearded man in a slouch hat who was leaning on an
oaken staff. Charles reflected how extraordinary it was that
local people always seemed to sprout out of the ground on
these occasions—he imagined the chap might be a shepherd
or something.

Mischa pulled out his short sword and started to make a
wary approach. He had done this before in the forests at
home and knew that timing was all important. You got one
chance with a boar—especially a 'wicked' one like this—muff
the chance and it was the boar's turn.

Something snagged his foot and he found himself
sprawling face down in the mud, his knife spinning away into
the reeds. Then he realised that Dorlov was standing over
him—by God, the bastard had tripped him!

"Stay there, my pretty boy," said the sneering voice, "this
is man's work."

He began to circle the boar.

"You may need this," said a gruff familiar voice.

Mischa raised his mud-caked face in surprise. The slouch-
hatted peasant was holding out a broad-bladed short sword to
him.

"Holy Jesus! Hunter! How came you..."

"No time now, boy, take it!"

Mischa took the sword and several things happened at
once.

Dorlov lunged at the boar.

Some hounds surged forward, unbalancing him, and his
thrust hit the boar's shoulder a glancing blow.

The pig squealed and swung on him.

Dorlov fell flat on his back.

Mischa moved with lightning speed.

He thrust the razor-sharp sword behind the boar's shoulder and into the vital organs.

The pig screamed again and swung.

Mischa felt sudden searing pain in his thigh, but he threw all his weight onto the knife hilt to force the pig down.

The hounds—emboldened by the man's presence—also piled in and added their weight to drag down the boar. Two of them were tossed bleeding into the air by the boar's death throws.

Mischa continued to push down on the knife with all his might. The boar might be clinically dead, but the adrenaline was still pumping in the system and the animal was still dangerous. The pain in Mischa's ripped thigh was now excruciating, and he could feel the warm blood pouring down his leg.

The pig's struggles weakened, but Mischa still held on grimly although his wound was making him dizzy. Dimly he could hear the shouts of the other men struggling through the mire towards him. Then he could hold out no longer, and a blackness swept over him. He collapsed in the blood-stained mud, and the eager hounds trampled over him as they worried the carcass of the great boar.

"Well, my boy, how are you feeling?"

Mischa swam up from the depths of the laudanum-induced sleep and blinked in the bright sunshine that poured through the windows of the room. He had no idea where he was. The recent past was a series of agonising dreams interspersed with blackness. He could remember being carried out of the swamp. He could remember the jolting, pain-filled journey in the carriage with the Grand Duke swearing and belabouring the coachman. He could remember a gentle hand cradling his head and wiping his brow with a fine lace handkerchief—he could even see the pattern of the lace.

Then the pictures became more and more distorted, and his last coherent memory was a draught of strange tasting liquid being poured down his throat: then oblivion.

As consciousness returned he became aware of the group of people around the bed: there was his General who had just spoken, there were Charles and Lubin, and there was a fussy little man in a dark suit with a snuff-sprinkled shirt front who was burrowing into a large black bag on the table and muttering continuously.

"Really gentlemen, I do most heartily recommend that the patient be left in the utmost peace if I am to effect a full recovery."

No one paid him the slightest heed.

Mischa moved, and swore as the pain in his leg began to reassert itself.

"Now that's better, cully," said Charles cheerfully. "If he can swear like that, then he ain't going to die just yet."

"Where am I?"

"You, cully, are in a Grand Ducal bed in a Grand Ducal palace on Grand Ducal orders. Their Imperial Highnesses were most gruntled by your tussle with the boar. You're quite a little hero, saving Dorlov's skin and all—not that I'm totally sure that *that* should be counted unto you for righteousness."

Mischa tried to sit up and swore again at the pain.

"Dorlov! He…"

"Yes, yes, my boy,"—the old general was twisting his whiskers in perturbation—"Prince Dorlov is quite unharmed and owes you a debt of gratitude. You behaved quite splendidly as behoves an Austrian officer. But you have lost a lot of blood and you must rest. Is that not right, doctor?"

"That is exactly what I have been trying to tell you, gentlemen,"—the little man took a massive pinch of snuff and sneezed violently into a large handkerchief—"if we are to avoid the fatal fevers that so often attend upon wounds of this sort, then rest, quiet and proper medical attention are essential. I have been particularly charged by His Imperial Highness…"

"Who will send you to doctor the convicts in Siberia if this young man dies," said a silvery voice.

The Grand Duchess swept across the room, followed by a man servant carrying a silver salver upon which was a decanter and some glasses. The men around the bed all bowed. Mischa tried to sit up.

"Lie back Herr Rittmeister, and try not to be a fool as well as a hero." The Grand Duchess let her imperious gaze sweep round the room and settle on the little doctor, who was now sweating profusely. "Well, doctor, and what pray is your professional opinion of the patient?"

The little doctor coughed, shuffled his feet and mopped his brow.

"As I was telling these gentlemen, Your Imperial Highness, the young man has suffered a grievous wound..."

"We all know *that*, man!"

"Yes, yes—quite so—forgive me Your Imperial Highness. A grievous wound, as I said, and there has been much loss of blood resulting in a considerable weakening of the system. However, I have been unable to detect any sign of the evil humours that might well be expected to result from such a wound in the conditions in which it was received, and..."

"Fiddle-faddle, man! If you are as good a doctor as you are a windbag, then there is hope."

"The patient is young and fit, and has so far shown no sign of the fevers concomitant with such a condition..."

"Enough! Show me the wound!"

"But Your Imperial Highness! The Rittmeister is quite unclothed in his nether regions."

"Holy Mother, doctor! He is only a man. Is there anything down there that God did not make?"

The little doctor went cerise with embarrassment. Charles lifted a kerchief to his face and managed to turn a laugh into a cough.

The doctor leaned forward and pulled back the sheet, revealing Mischa naked except for his shirt and the heavily bandaged thigh. With a serene expression, the Grand Duchess leaned over the bed and gave close attention to what was revealed. To Mischa's dismay and intense embarrassment he felt his body acting in a wholly involuntary manner, and he could see the movement under his shirt.

The little doctor, now totally unnerved, was babbling on about the patient's need for rest.

"And precious little rest he will get with all you old women

fussing about him,"—the Grand Duchess straightened up—
"Now go! All of you! Out! This minute! I prescribe wine for
this young man, and I intend to make sure he takes his
draught!"

The silent footman poured two glasses of wine and placed
the salver on the table beside the bed.

"Shoo! Shoo! The lot of you!"

The imperious woman made gestures as though she was
chasing chickens off a vegetable patch. The men retreated in
rout and disorder. The little doctor, bringing up the rear,
stepped out backwards bowing continuously and causing him
to become totally entangled with the footman so that both fell
in a heap in the doorway to peals of imperial laughter.

"Men are such fools! Are you a fool, Herr Rittmeister?"

"It seems highly probable, Your Imperial Highness."

"A brave fool, at any rate,"—she sat on the gilded chair
beside the bed—"I'll wish to inspect your wound again."

With no more ado, she pulled the sheet down again. Mischa closed his eyes. He was well aware that his
embarrassment must now be plainly visible.

"Quite the hero it seems."

Mischa kept his eyes closed as a cool hand stroked his
cheek. Mischa opened his eyes. The Grand Duchess's face was
bent over him, the eyes heavily lidded, the lips parted and
swollen.

"The doctor says that you need rest and ease, Herr
Rittmeister. It is my duty to see that your ease is as pleasant
as possible."

* * *

The Khan had chewed the leaf the night before. In his
dreams he had soared over steppe and mountain. He had
spun through dark caverns where faceless things of unspeak-
able vileness had tried to seize him. He had galloped through
fire and blood and infernal violence. These were the dreams
that the Shaman gave him: to excite him, to urge him to violence.

Now he was coming back from the swirling mists, back

from the splendid and terrifying deeps to the meanness of a
mountain hut. He grunted and stirred on the verminous furs
that served him as a bed. As he returned to consciousness he
was aware of the Russian woman crouching beside him; she
would not dare to touch him unbidden.

For a time he studied her through half-open eyes. He had
kept her for far longer than was his wont. After the initial excitement of taking and breaking captive women, he quickly
tired of them and passed them on to his men—they did not
usually last long. This one was different. She was good looking and came from high-bred stock; this had added to the
Khan's pleasure in breaking her. There was nothing haughty
about her now; she was his slut.

All these infidel women were sluts underneath, but this
one was different. Although she screamed and writhed under
the whip, she took the subsequent rape with pleasure. When
he took her, the Khan found her wet and suppliant with desire. She would wrap her long legs around him, score his
back with her nails, and writhe with ecstasy under his
thrusting body.

The slut actually enjoyed the whip. This intrigued the
Khan, even if it did not altogether please him; pleasure was
something that he took, not something he gave. The Khan
felt that a little pain—someone else's pain—was an essential
condiment for pleasure. However, he would keep this woman
for a time; she was very inventive. He would keep her until
the Golden One came.

The Khan closed his eyes for a moment and the picture of
the Golden One floated across his mind: now, *she* would be
one to break—the very thought aroused him.

He opened his eyes and crooked a finger at the Russian
woman. Without a word she took off her robe and knelt beside him. The Khan reached up a rough hand and began to
fondle one of the large, dark-nippled breasts. The woman
gave a moan and the nipple stiffened under his fingers. He
squeezed the nipple hard and the woman threw back her
head with a small scream. The Khan smiled. He ran his fingers down over her stomach and entwined them in her pubic

hair. The woman moaned again and spread her thighs, allowing the Khan's rough finger to penetrate the hot wetness: 'the bitch is begging for it,' he thought.

The Russian woman leaned quickly forward, pulling a fur aside to reveal the Khan's swollen sex. She dropped her head and took him in her mouth with frantic urgency. For a moment the Khan let her have her way. Then, seizing her by the hair, he dragged her head back until she was wincing with pain.

"Who said that you could suck me, bitch?"

"No one, Master, I just..."

"What do you want?"

"Please fuck me, Master, please!"

"You'd like that, wouldn't you?"

"Yes, Master!"

The Khan came to his feet in one movement. A blow from his open hand sent the woman sprawling across the hut.

"Bitch!" he bellowed, the spittle of rage flying from his mouth. "The only pleasure here is mine!"

He dragged the woman to her feet by the hair and, seizing her wrists, he secured them with a leather thong, then tied the thong to a hook in one of the beams. With a rough hand he parted her thighs, and rubbed her swollen flesh until she was again screaming and begging in ecstasy.

Then he went to the hut door and shouted an order.

A girl had been captured in a raid two days before. She was sobbing as she was dragged to the Khan's door. The Khan grunted and seized the girl's hair, forcing her head back further until he could see the fear in her eyes. That was good. Fear was good. The Khan enjoyed the fear of others. It was better than the chewing leaf, and better than the fermented mare's milk; better than the wine and vodka that he took from the Russian villages and towns that he raided and burned. Fear was the great gift that he had been given by the Shaman; it was the ultimate drug of pleasure.

"Now," said the Khan to the Russian woman, "you can watch *my* pleasure."

And throwing the still sobbing girl on the rugs, he raped

her with enormous satisfaction.

* * *

Anna liked the early mornings: the crisp coolness before the
heat of day, the time to get the chores done.

She hooked the two wooden buckets on, picked up the little three-legged milking stool and slipped the carved wooden
yoke across her shoulders. Anna opened the gate of the little
yard and stepped out into the wide village street. It was a
long straggly village, with a wide dirt road running through
the middle and set with wide grass verges on either side.
Ducks and geese swam in the open ditches that separated the
verges from the houses. Old Heidi, the house cow, who was
tethered on a verge, tossed her head and gave Anna a re-
sentful look as she approached.

"Ah! Liebe Heidi, do you think that I am late?"

Heidi lowered her head and let Anna scratch her between
her horns.

"There, old lady, you like that don't you? Now will you let
your milk down for Anna, like a good girl?"

Anna put down her stool and sat beside the cow. She set a
bucket under the cow's bulging udder and pulled her scarf
over her head. Pressing her head into the cow's side, she felt
underneath for the first two teats and began the gentle
stroking that soon dropped into a rhythm. The first spurts of
warm, fresh milk squirted into the bucket.

Anna liked milking. With her head pressed into Heidi's
sweet-smelling flank, she could dream a bit. Anna was a
dreamer. Mutti often scolded her for it.

"That girl walks around with her head in the clouds," she
would say.

Papa would give his deep gravelly laugh in his beard.

"Let the girl dream a bit," he would say. "God knows that
life is hard enough. Let her have her dreams whilst she can."

Mutti would snort.

"Dreaming would not fill any meal buckets, and dreaming
won't keep the bandits away."

"The Cossacks do that."

"Cossacks! They're as bad as bandits."

The village was entirely populated by German Lutherans. They had come there from Württemberg a century before. The Great Czar Peter had been vastly impressed by German thrift and efficiency. Many German peasants had been actively and financially encouraged to leave their stony acres for settlements on better land in Russia. The Czar hoped that their example would be good for his own shiftless peasants. The hard work and sober ways of the Germans had enabled them to make a good living from the fertile land along the river valley, and to exist in reasonable harmony with the Cossack inhabitants of neighbouring villages scattered over the steppe.

Anna finished her milking and divided the milk equally between the two buckets for balance. She scratched Heidi between the horns again and gave her a kiss. Heidi was a good cow.

The sun was already warm on the girl's back and she felt the first prickling of sweat. She pushed the scarf back from her head and let her long golden hair hang free.

As she set off back down the street, she noticed a huddle of men that had formed in the middle of the road. The pastor was there, her father and several other of the senior men in the village. They were listening to a man she knew vaguely by sight. He came from another village further over the steppe, closer to the mountains. You could not see the mountains from the valley, but Anna knew that if you climbed to the top of the hill behind the village, you could see the jagged line of peaks in the distance, with the mighty snow-clad peak of Elbrus soaring above them.

The sight of the great mountain chain always awed Anna and frightened her a little. Her father had once taken her to the teeming horse fair by the Malka river, at the foot of the mountains and in the country of the Kabardines, who were famous for their horses. To this fair came all the wild tribes out of the hills: 'all bandits,' her father had said.

"Bandits," said Anna's father, detaching himself from the group to join Anna.

Anna's father was a big jovial man, but Anna noted that today he looked grim as he walked along beside her.

"Bandits. They raided Maxan village two nights ago—drove off the cattle, burned several houses, killed three men."

Anna stopped and looked at her father.

"But Maxan is only forty *versts* from here."

"They are getting bolder."

"What about the soldiers?"

"They are running about like headless chickens as usual. And there's more."

Anna stared at her father's serious face.

"The bandits took three women with them."

Anna gave a gasp and put a hand to her mouth in horror.

"Oh, God help them!"

"God help them, indeed," said her father grimly. "I don't think anyone else will."

Kurt had hobbled his horse and let it graze. He sat at ease in the warm sun, his battered slouch hat shading his eyes. Below his hilltop vantage point on the rolling range, the communal village cattle herd grazed peacefully, sleek and shiny in their summer coats. A *verst* away, on the other side of the herd, Joachim, the other herdsman, sat slouched in his saddle. Kurt could see the curl of smoke from Joachim's pipe in the still air. A movement below caught Kurt's eye—a glimpse of white. Then the grey horse emerged from the scrubby wood above the village and there was a flash of gold in the sun.

'Love and lunch,' said Kurt to himself as the grey horse drew nearer at a steady canter, with Anna's golden hair streaming behind her.

She would, Kurt knew, be riding bareback, with her skirts rucked showing her long slim legs. As Kurt thought of the long slim legs and the lovely face, he found himself imagining the wondrous mystery of all that lay between. He felt a growing heat in his groin and firmly thrust the thoughts away from him. What was it that St Paul had said: 'Better to marry than burn with lust.'

Well, he and Anna would soon be wed, and then what was

now lust would be a most proper procreational procedure—a duty to be performed with the Church's blessing. Kurt allowed his hunger pangs to cool his ardour, and fixed his mind on the food the laughing girl was bringing him. Her laughter and delight at seeing him made him smile too, although he felt that after they were married Anna would have to adopt a more serious approach to life. He often found her levity unsettling: lots of children—that was the answer.

The telescope focused on the laughing face of the girl, and then the slim white thighs as she rode the horse with a natural grace.

Two *versts* away across the valley, the Khan with three men sat their horses in the cover of a grove of scrub oaks. The Khan found the telescope very useful; he had taken it from a captured Russian officer, who had found no further use for it in view of his rather prolonged demise.

He had studied the village and the very splendid-looking herd of cattle before, during his scouting operations. It would certainly make a good plump prize—he could almost smell the burning houses but it was further from the safety of the mountains than he had so far ventured. But then, in the course of the reconnaissance trip, he had seen the girl, the Golden One. He had seen her first at the horse fair by the Malka, and had felt instantaneous desire. Now that he knew where she lived, it was only a matter of time and opportunity.

He watched her laughing face magnified by the lenses. He thought that she would not be laughing by the time that he had done with her. The pleasure of this thought made him laugh out loud as he returned the telescope to its case.

4 A Sirius Affair

CHARLES FitzHugh was slumped on the chaise longue in the sitting room of his quarters. He was comfortably undressed in a silk dressing gown, shirt, trousers and a tasselled smoking cap. A bottle of rather moderate Russian wine lay to hand. He was smoking a rather moderate cigar, and was leafing through a pile of old *Bystander* magazines that a friend at the Embassy had passed on to him. All in all he was moderately comfortable and massively bored. He pricked his ears at the knock on the door.

"Excuse me, Sir," Trooper Bone put his massive shaven head round the door, "the Rittmeister Czerny's called. I said I didn't know if you was in, Sir."

"Ah ha!" cried Charles rising to his feet and scattering magazines. "The estimable Czerny's afoot again! Show him in, Bone, show him in! Have we got any decent Champagne left?"

"Only a couple of bottles, Sir."

"Well, pop round to the grog shop and get some more."

Bone scratched his bristly head:

"Thing is, Sir, the old Armenian is getting a bit tight with the credit."

"Tell him I'll get the Cossacks to pay him out in full, if he don't cough up."

"Very good, Sir."

Bone withdrew in short order. The door opened again:

"The Rittmeister Czerny, Sir."

Mischa hobbled into the room, leaning heavily on a stick.

"My dear fellow! How absolutely splendid to see you! Come sit down! Still going a bit short, I see."

Mischa dropped gratefully into a chair.

"Yes, thank you, the pain is greatly eased and the doctor has declared that I shall make a full recovery."

"And the Grand Duchess—what does she say?"

"Her Imperial Highness has been most gracious and kind."

"I'm sure of it, dear boy. You've been to ground there for so long we all thought that she must have gobbled you up."

Mischa stiffened in his chair:

"What, please, does it mean, this gobbling up?"

'Christ,' thought Charles, 'he's about as touchy as a maiden aunt. He'll start blathering on about a woman's honour next.'

"I must inform you that Her Imperial Highness is a most gracious and honourable lady."

"Never thought anything else, dear boy," said Charles smoothly. "Her grace and honour are legendary in St Petersburg."—and, to himself, 'but not as legendary as certain other graceful and honourable attributes, of which I have had the undoubted honour of availing myself; and if you ain't done the same, then more fool you, my little pickled cabbage eater.' And, out loud, "Now allow me to offer you something to drink, a little Champagne perhaps?"

"I had not intended to take up your time. I only wished to thank you for your help."

"My dear chap, think nothing of it. Now, a little wine: take a little wine for your stomach's sake, for your constant infirmity."

Mischa's stiff back relented somewhat.

"I did not realise that you read the Holy Bible."

"Read it? I had it thrust down my throat when I was a child. M'tutor was a real Holy Joe."

"Ah, well, a little wine would be most agreeable."

"*Bone!* Wine!"

At Charles's insistence, the two young men dined together in a tavern. The truth was that, in spite of the great difference in their temperaments, they had come, rather warily, to enjoy each other's company.

Charles took rather mischievous pleasure in probing Mischa's rather prim exterior. Mischa found himself fascinated, in spite of himself, by Charles's rake-hell attitude to life. It was an attraction of opposites.

"You must realise," said Charles, as he wrestled with a piece of gristly meat—"Christ, I hope I don't come across poor Fido's collar buckle in minute; can they produce no decent meat in this God-forsaken country?—You must realise that your sojourn in the Imperial bosom..."

Mischa put his knife down with a bang.

"I really must protest. I can assure you that Her Imperial..."

"Yes! Yes! I know. Pure as driven snow—Caesar's wife, Caesar's wife absolutely. I know that and so does everybody else. It's just that you must understand that your writhing in agony on the Imperial bed ain't gone unnoticed, d'yersee, and whilst I know that everything was quite proper and above board, there are those crude fellows of the baser sort. Well, you know how people talk, and there are those whose nebs have been well and truly unjointed."

"Who could harbour such unworthy thoughts?"

Charles took a hefty draught of wine:

"Major Dorlov, perhaps? He definitely has a crude and base thought process—if he has one at all."

"Dorlov? What is the matter to him?"

"Well, let us say that Dorlov has long been an admirer of the Grand Duchess and all her absolutely splendid virtues: spanieled her at heel, all that sort of thing. Then suddenly you save his life, end up between the Imperial sheets and unexpectedly Dorlov don't get no more sweetmeats, d'yersee?"

"You surely are not saying that Dorlov thinks...?"

"Who knows what Dorlov thinks, or even if he is capable of any intellectual exercise. What I am trying to tell you is that, somewhere out there, there is a very unhappy Major the Prince, who regards you as the source of his unhappiness and that you should be like Agag, and tread delicately."

"Agag?"

"Some chappie in the Old Testament. He trod delicately, but it availed him nothing: untimely demise, I remember."

"You really think that Dorlov might seek to harm me? I

did save him."

"For which," said Charles cheerfully, "the poor chap finds it hard to forgive you. You undoubtedly saved his life and lost him his face. All I am saying is to watch your back and stay out of dark alleys."

"I can hardly believe that such a thing might be contemplated by a gentleman."

"This is Russia, cully. Nothing is what it seems and almost anything is possible. Come on, I'll walk you back to your quarters."

In the crisp autumn evening the two young men strolled arm in arm down the wide street, turning into the tree-shaded square where Mischa had his lodgings.

"Stop!" said Charles. "That's your door ain't it?"

The square was ill-lit and they stood staring into the gloom.

"Yes," said Mischa, "what...?"

"There's a feller lurking by the door,"—Charles's long experience of debt collectors and bum bailiffs had sharpened his senses—"let's bolt the beggar!"

He switched into his amorously-won colloquial Russian:

"Hola fellow! Who are you? Show yourself!"

The man who emerged from the shadows was wearing a uniform that Charles recognised as that worn by the Forest Guards of the Grand Duke Alexei. By his side was a huge dog:

"A thousand pardons, Excellency, but I have a message from Her Imperial Highness for the Rittmeister Czerny."

"Have you, by Jove? Well, let's see it then."

The man handed Mischa an envelope. The letter inside was on a sheet of paper unheaded and unsigned. It said simply: 'His name is Sirius. You need someone to look after you.'

"Great Heaven! The dog? It is for me?"

"That's right Excellency," said the man stolidly. "My orders were to bring him to you and make sure that I handed him over personal. I waited here for you." Then, warming to his theme, "He's only a young dog, Excellency, but he comes of the finest stock in His Imperial Highness's kennel and I have myself seen him bring down a wolf on his own, he..."

But Mischa was no longer listening. He approached the great Borzoi and offered him the back of his hand. Sirius sniffed the proffered hand and gave a small wag of his bushy tail. Very gently, Mischa reached out and stroked the shaggy head. This time the tail moved more definitely.

"He likes you, Excellency."

The man handed Mischa the leash. Mischa fumbled in his pocket and produced a gold coin.

"God's blessing on you and the dog, Excellency."

With that the man saluted and faded into the darkness.

Sirius sniffed Mischa's trousers and then sat down beside him.

"Is he not magnificent, Charles?" exclaimed Mischa.

"You must have been a damned good patient. I happen to know that old Alexei's Borzois are some of the most sought after in the realm. Dorlov's been angling for one for years. He told me so, in an unguarded moment."

"Dorlov again?"

"Exactly, Dorlov again." Charles bent and ruffled Sirius's head. "Well, cully, you had better look after your lord and master; I fear that there may be tears before bed time."

'Wine is a mocker and strong drink is raging.'

Prince Dorlov was raging, indeed his raging was the talk of the city and he was using much strong drink to fuel his anger. His rage was directed at the two foreign officers.

He suspected that separately and severally they had been responsible for his removal from the favour of the Grand Duchess—there could be no other reason. He could not know and certainly could not comprehend that his own inadequacy as a lover might have had something to do with his loss. Such a possibility would never have occurred to the Prince. A prince, by definition, could never be inadequate. His suspicions had turned to certainty when the damned Austrian had not only basely foiled his attempt to serve the boar and perhaps re-establish his place with the Grand Duchess, but had also finished up in her bed as a hero. What was worse, a hero for supposedly saving his, Dorlov's, life! What nonsense! And people believed it!

He bellowed for the servants and more wine.

And now the bloody Austrian was strutting the streets with one of the Grand Duke's famous Borzois following him at heel. Damned kraut eater! Dorlov had tried for years to get one of those dogs. It was almost unheard of for any to go outside the family.

The servant was justly terrified of his master's mood and his hand trembled as he refilled the glass. A few drops spilt on the table. With a roar of fury, Dorlov seized the man by the throat and shook him into unconsciousness. But, in his mind and his fury, it was Mischa whose throat he gripped. Pushing the unconscious man aside with his foot, Dorlov returned to his chair and his brooding. He would have to deal with the damned Austrian. The servant began to whimper. Dorlov kicked him.

It had all been very simple really—just a case of Dorlov biding his time—then a crowded room, a deliberate jostling of Mischa and the spilling of Mischa's wine down the front of Dorlov's snow-white uniform, succeeded by Dorlov's accusation that Mischa was a 'clumsy peasant' and the sudden hush that fell on the room as the two men faced each other. Mischa, who had gone suddenly pale and drawn, suggested that Dorlov withdraw his remark. Dorlov refused with maximum insolence. The die was then cast. It was now a matter of honour.

"Pistols," said Charles. "Our noble prince wants pistols."

As Mischa was the challenger in the 'Affair of Honour', Prince Dorlov had the choice of weapons.

Charles, who had immediately offered his services as Second to Mischa, had been to meet Dorlov's Second and make the proper gentlemanly arrangements. The two young men were sitting in Charles's rooms discussing the matter:

"Well, of course, the beggar would want pistols. The word is that he is a crack shot. How are you with the pistol, eh?"

Mischa, who was slumped in a battered armchair with Sirius's great rough head resting on his thigh, sipped his brandy before answering.

"Tolerable."

Charles leaned across the table that stood between their chairs and refilled his friend's glass:

"Don't mind my asking, cully, but have you done this before?"

"Never."

"Ah! Ever killed anybody?"

"Never," said Mischa firmly.

But as he said it, a vision of floating blond hair flowed through his mind and he winced involuntarily.

Sirius felt the electricity of discomfort course through his master and raised his head to look at Mischa's face. Mischa ran a finger down the rough hair of the dog's muzzle. Charles failed to notice his friend's spasm of guilt.

"Ah!" he said.

"Have you?"

Charles took a sip from his glass before replying:

"Well yes, I have, as a matter of fact twice—fought that is. Never killed anybody though. Seldom happens, you know."

"May I hear your experiences?"

Mischa was frowning slightly and staring at his toe caps.

"Well, the first time was pistols. Some damned sutler from a line regiment that no one had ever heard of called me out, said I had insulted a lady friend of his. He had found out that I had been giving his doxy a damned good rousting—which was more than he seemed able to do—and got jealous, d'yersee? So pistols at dawn and all that: twenty five paces, turn and fire. So the muff fires first and misses clean and there am I still loaded, so I bring my pistol down and aim at him and d'yer know what? The muff shits his breeches! So I raises my pistol and fires in the air and says, 'You will perceive, Sir, that I am able both to be continent and to hold my weapon in the erect position.' Damned good that I thought, what?"

Charles gave a bark of laughter at the recollection.

"And the other occasion?"

"Oh some damned young coxcomb; I took a lot of money off him at cards and he took exception to my mode of play. It was swords that time."

"And?"

"Oh, I just pinked the little shit in the shoulder and he bled a lot and they stopped the fight—honour satisfied and all that. I remember we had some cold duck for breakfast. That's the thing about duelling, you feel damned hungry afterwards."

"If you survive."

Charles turned to his friend:

"Worried?"

Mischa did not reply, but sat with his chin sunk on his chest. Charles leaned across and put a hand on his arm. This time he spoke quietly:

"Look, cully, the waiting is the worst time. Don't worry about being frightened. The man who ain't frightened is a fool, and you ain't a fool, but take it from me that once you're out there and the blood starts pumping, you'll be cool as a cucumber. Now what have you got in the way of pistols?"

At this moment there was a knock on the door and Bone came in.

"'Scuse me, Sir, but I've just had this queer-looking cove come to the door. Big bearded bloke in a bugger of a hat, but spoke English like a toff, begging your pardon, Sir. Brought a parcel for the Rittmeister. Wouldn't stop. Said...—and Bone furrowed his brow with the effort of recollection—"Said he'd see you on the day, meaning the Rittmeister, Sir."

Puzzled, Mischa took the carefully wrapped package and opened it.

Inside was a polished wooden case, and in the case a pair of pistols on their velvet beds. The metal was beautifully engraved and had a deep, deadly, sheen. Charles whistled.

"My God! A pair of Mantons! The very best! You could shoot the eye out of a gnat with those."

Mischa stared at the beautifully worked pistols for some time, then said softly: "Hunter!"

Mischa shivered in the dawn chill, in spite of the heavy cloak that he wore over his shirt. Sirius sat beside him, motionless except for the nostrils that constantly whiffed, monitoring all the scents of the morning. Mischa could feel the dog's body pressed against his leg.

There was a mist lying over the marsh to his right, and the mist enabled him to look at the red ball of the sun that was already rising over the surrounding birch woods. A fallen tree presented a tangle of twigs and branches. A wren was hopping from twig to twig, turning its head and watching him with the curiosity of its kind. From a branch of a nearby beech tree a squirrel scolded him. Mischa drank in the sights, sounds and smells of the dawn woodland—so reminiscent of autumn dawns at Lippitz.

He no longer felt any fear, just a stark emptiness that these might be his last sights on earth and that he would never see Lippitz again. Some time in the next hour, he too might disappear into the dark void where the girl with the golden hair, and his child, had gone before. Mischa had tried very hard to pray in the dark wakeful hours of the night, but the emptiness would not go away.

He stood alone by the carriage in which he and Charles had driven to the woodland meadow, huddled in his cloak. Some way off there were more carriages and a knot of people, where Mischa knew that Charles was in conversation with the surgeon. There was the usual group of onlookers for whom the duel would be a bit of sport; from this group came a sudden bark of laughter. Mischa did not feel much like laughing.

"I think that a drop of this would not harm you," said a deep voice at his elbow.

Mischa turned with a start; he had not heard anyone approach, nor had Sirius emitted the low grumble that usually greeted the approach of any stranger. Indeed the dog had got to his feet and was wagging his tail as though in pleased recognition. The big bearded man with the scarred eye socket and the ragged cloak was leaning on his staff and holding out a large silver flask on which the figure of an eight legged horse was engraved.

"Hunter!" said Mischa in astonishment. "What are you doing here?"

"Oh, I just happened to be passing."

"And the pistols? I..."

"This is no time for questions, my boy. Now take a drink of this—remind you of home."

Mischa took a swig from the flask and spluttered. Obstler! The fiery pear eau de vie of Austria.

"Take another."

And Mischa felt the fiery liquid coursing down his gullet and had a fit of coughing.

"If there's any left for a thirsty Second," came Charles's voice. "Good morning, Mr Hunter."

"Good morning, Charles."

"You know each other?" spluttered Mischa in great surprise.

"I am an old friend of the family," said the Hunter gravely.

There came the sound of horses and wheels, and a closed carriage loomed out of the mist across the meadow.

"Here comes the wicked prince," said Charles.

Prince Dorlov and his Second got out of their carriage. For a moment, Mischa and Dorlov looked at each other. They bowed formally. The Prince smiled a small cold smile and turned to his Second. Charles went over to speak to them. He came back with a furrowed brow:

"He wants to turn and fire at twelve paces. As you know that normal distance is twenty-five paces and you ain't forced to accept his idea, but..."

"Honour demands that I should," said Mischa dryly.

Charles nodded gloomily:

"It does make it more dangerous," he said simply.

Lubin strolled over from the group of onlookers; the early sun made his monocle glint.

"A word," he said, taking Mischa by the arm. "Now, I have

seen Dorlov fight before. He relies on speed. The moment he turns he will fire. My advice is not to try to match his speed, just make sure that you hit him, eh Charles?"

Charles nodded. He was busy charging, loading and priming the Manton pistols, a job over which he took the greatest care. Then, holding the two pistols by the barrel, he laid them across his left forearm, approached Prince Dorlov and bowed. Dorlov returned his bow and studied the two pistols:

"Mantons!" he said. "At least your friend has the pistols of a gentleman."

"I assure you, Sir," said Charles in icy tones, "that you will never be more opposite to a gentleman than you are at this moment."

The Prince smiled his sour smile and said nothing. He reached out and touched a pistol butt. His Second took the chosen pistol from Charles.

Charles coughed:

"Gentlemen!" he said. "We are here to settle an affair of honour. I am duty bound to ask both parties whether they are still intent on this matter, or whether there is a hope of settling the matter peaceably."

Mischa and Dorlov remained silent.

"Very well, then, the duel must take its course. You both know the rules of an honourable engagement. You will stand back to back. When I give the word you will both march forward for twelve paces which I will count. On the twelfth pace you may turn and fire at will. May Almighty God have mercy on you both. Gentlemen! Prepare yourselves!"

Mischa slipped the heavy cloak off his shoulders, and felt the morning chill strike through his thin shirt. It was not the only chill, he felt. He hefted the pistol in his hand and, in spite of the tension, he could not but admire the wonderful balance of the weapon. He just hoped...

"Hrrmph!" Mischa turned and the Hunter was standing behind him, stroking his flowing beard. "Now—these particular pistols have a slight idiosyncrasy. They tend to fire a trifle high, just something that I pointed out to Joe Manton.

From what I hear of Prince Dorlov he takes great pride in putting the ball through his opponent's head. Remember what I have told you when hunting deer, and go for the body, for the vitals."

Mischa's eyes widened: "But, Hunter..."

"Gentlemen, come forward."

The two men approached.

"Now stand back to back."

Mischa could feel the warmth from Dorlov's back as they took up position.

"Gentlemen! Cock your pistols."

The double click of the two hammers sounded loud in the silence that had fallen on the meadow. Then Mischa heard the thin cheep of the wren. The little bird was still flitting round its fallen tree.

"Gentlemen, are you ready?"

Both men nodded silently.

"Then, march! One... Two..."

Mischa felt a coldness in his gut, and could feel it spread upwards to his brain. Everything was clear as crystal and he felt coiled like a spring.

"Seven... Eight..."

'Holy Mother! Look a upon a humble sinner,' he murmured to himself. 'Hail Mary...'

"Eleven! Twelve!"

To Mischa, it all seemed to happen incredibly slowly. As he spun on his heel, he saw the flash from the other pistol then the puff of black smoke. Then there was a burning pain as something hot and angry scored his cheek.

His reaction was instinctive. He pointed the pistol as though he was pointing a finger at Dorlov and squeezed the trigger.

For a moment the cloud of black powder smoke blocked his vision. As it cleared, he saw that Dorlov was still standing, the gun still clutched in his hand. Mischa felt an instant of relief—'we both missed' was his thought.

Then—still it seemed very slowly—the pistol fell from Dorlov's grip and, with both hands, he clutched his solar plexus, from which a spreading tide of crimson was staining his white shirt. Dorlov seemed to fold in two and crumple to the ground.

There was an instant of stillness as the powder smoke still hung in the quiet air. Then Dorlov's Second was on his knees lifting his principal's head. A thin trickle of blood ran from the corner of the fallen man's mouth. He tried to say something, then his head fell back.

The surgeon was also kneeling beside Dorlov now, his bag open beside him, his ear to Dorlov's face.

The surgeon straightened up, crossed himself and, reaching forward, he pulled down the eyelids. The silence was broken by Charles's drawl:

"Well, doctor, there ain't much you can do for the dead. Lavish a bit of your care on the living, what? Hey! Steady on, old boy!"

For Mischa, the blood streaming from his torn cheek, had slowly sunk to his knees. Charles went to catch him, but Mischa was kneeling with clasped hands:

"Hail Mary, full of grace..."

"Give him a sniff of your flask, Mr Hunter," said Charles. "Do him more good than all that God bothering."

"Sometimes, my dear Charles," said the Hunter mildly, as he unscrewed his flask, "a little God bothering does not come amiss."

Sirius sniffed the fresh blood on his master's face and reached out a long pink tongue.

General Barclay de Tolley and General von Hohenfels sat in silence either side of Barclay's desk. A bottle of whisky stood between them on the desk, and a glass of the brown liquid in front of each of them. The silence of thought was only broken by General Barclay de Tolley tapping the desk with a pencil. At last the Scotsman took a swig from his glass, wiped his moustache on the back of his hand and sighed:

"Aye, it's a bad business right enough Gustav."

Von Hohenfels twisted his luxuriant whiskers, as he always did in moments of stress:

"But dammit Charley, it was a fair fight. I mean I don't approve of duelling, but young cocks will fight."

"Aye, aye, just so, just so, but the trouble is your young stag killed a prince and a prince that the Czar was very fond of, the dear knows why—*de mortuis nil nisi bonum*—but yon Dorlov was a poisonous young cur. It's my opinion that your young man did the world a favour, but my palace contacts tell me that His Imperial Majesty ain't going to see it quite like that."

"But an affair of honour between gentlemen, Charley..."

General Barclay de Tolley gave a wry smile:

"This is Russia, Gustav, and you have na known it as long as I have. Nothing in Russia is what it seems. The Russians may strut about and act the gentleman, but take it from me, they're no but heathen savages under the skin. Scratch the skin and the wolf pops out. I'm afraid that young Czerny has done a damn sight more than scratch the skin. Man, do ye not realise how easy it is for a man to disappear in this damned country?"

Barclay de Tolley scratched his chin and poured some more whisky into each glass:

"You must get Czerny out and far away from here."

"But if I send him home, that will count against him."

"Aye, just so—let's now drink and think. This damned highland fire water rots the guts. but it's grand for the brain."

Once again, silence fell on the room. General Barclay de Tolley pulled out his snuff box, tapped some of the powder into the hollow of a thumb joint, sniffed noisily and then sneezed explosively into a huge red spotted handkerchief. Barclay de Tolley wiped his moustache, and a slow smile spread over his craggy face:

"Eureka, as yon wee Greek loon said, I may have an answer. There's one of my laddies called Lubin. He's a Major of the Kuban Cossacks. Now, he and his squadron, who've been on Lifeguard duties here, are due to rejoin their regiment at Pyatigorsk. Lubin is a canny enough lad and will keep his mouth shut. Now suppose we sent young Czerny down with him?"

"Pyatigorsk? Where in the world is that?"

"Just about on the edge. A thousand miles and a world south of here, on the edge of the Caucasus—a right whoor of a place, with bandits behind every boulder. Your man will have all the fighting he's got the stomach for down there and, if he lives, it will be with honour."

Von Hohenfels took a draught of whisky, and coughed and spluttered as it burned his gullet. Barclay de Tolley watched with wry amusement:

"Did I not tell you that it was a damned heathen drink? But what about my idea? What do yea say?"

Still puce in the face with coughing, the old Austrian nodded vigorously:

"Good! Good!"

"Right! I will make the necessary arrangements, and"—he gave a wolfish grin—"this will be a grand chance to get rid of one of my own little problems. We'll pull the necks of two young cocks at once."

He reached out and rang the little hand bell to summon his ADC.

"A damned awful time of year to be setting out for the south," said Lubin, languidly surveying his orders. "Bound to get snowed up somewhere. A bit of company won't come amiss."

"Pack up, Bone, we've been posted."

"Sir! Permission to ask where we're going, Sir!"

"Pottergorse—or some such bloody awful place. All I know is that it's south and the genial General Barclay de Tolley gave me that child-eating smile of his and said, 'It's about as far up the world's fundament as I can stuff you, laddie.'"

"Well if it's south, it might be a bit warmer than here, Sir. From what I hear, you freeze your bollocks off in the winters here."

"If all that I hear about the natives where we're going is true, Bone, I wouldn't be too sanguine about retaining your stones anyway."

"Bit hairy arssed are they, Sir?"

"Absolutely ghastly from what I'm told."

"Just as well we're moving, Sir. That old Armenian is getting very iffy about his bill."

"Be sure to remember not to pay him, Bone."

"Sir!"

"So, Sirius, it seems that we are being deported from St Petersburg. What do you think of that?"

The big dog stood with his head resting on Mischa's knee as he sat in his chair. Sirius's big dark eyes were fixed on his master's face and his feathery tail waved gently at the sound of the man's voice.

"Pyatigorsk! What do you think we shall find there Sirius? Honour? Adventure? Romance? We have not been too successful with any of them so far, have we?"

Mischa reached forward, and with a finger scratched the nerve under the dog's lower jaw. Sirius closed his eyes with pleasure.

"Well, dog, I hope that you and Our Lady will look after me—someone's got to."

5 German Gold

THE wind was rising from the east. Although the fire had been made in a sheltered spot amongst the rocks, the wind still found its way through the boulders and made the flames scatter. The Hunter was crouched by the fire with his thick cloak wrapped around him and his hat pulled down.

He was above the normal human feelings of heat and cold, but he did have a feeling of unease. This had nothing to do with the chill of the wind that soughed over the miles of rolling steppe where the snow wreaths still lay in the sheltered hollows, it was a malaise of the soul—if an elemental force can be said to have such a thing.

The fact was that the Hunter was far from home and, if he was not breaking the rules, he was extending the existential parameters beyond anything that he had done before. The Hunter's realm lay in the forests and mountains of Europe and, although the boundaries of his influence were ill-defined, if they were defined at all, he felt that he was at the limit. The further east he had travelled, the more he had felt as though his powers were draining, bleeding away. And the further east he went the more he had become aware of an opposing field of force that got stronger as he felt the diminution of his own—hence his malaise.

The Hunter hunched over the fire. He shivered slightly and pulled his cloak tighter around him.

The wind was still rising and the frosty stars that had twinkled when he made his camp had disappeared behind a thickening wrack of cloud. There was a wolf-like howl to the wind now, and a shower of sleet rattled the stunted trees that surrounded the camp. The darkness was deepening as the wind rose. As the Hunter watched and waited, he felt that it was a darkness beyond the deepest night. It was a darkness that seemed to writhe and swirl around the camp like a mist of blackness that was blowing in from the depths of the endless eastern steppe.

The wind was shrieking round the rocks now and the Hunter threw some more branches on the fire, making it crackle and flare up in a shower of sparks. He watched the flames intently, keeping his mind blank and waiting for the message that he knew would come. It was as though the mist that had swirled around the camp, swirled into his mind.

Then it began to clear and a picture began to form. The picture was of an upland meadow, rough with sour grasses and bents, and powdered with snow. At the end of the meadow was a small stone hut, with smoke coming from a hole in the roof. The Hunter felt his mind being drawn, sucked into the hut, with its interior wreathed in swirls of smoke.

He could see the figure sitting on the ground beside the miserable fire. The man was small; one leg stuck out stiffly, as though it had been injured and could not bend properly. His face was wizened and seamed like an old apple. He had the cold unblinking eye of a reptile.

"What do you want?"

The voice was dry and flat—the words seemed to slither:

"What do you want?"

"You know who I am," said the Hunter.

"I know who you are and what you are. What are you doing here?"

"I wanted to look at you."

The laugh was like the grinding of ice on a glacier.

"No man looks at me willingly!"

"I am not a man," said the Hunter simply.

The little figure was silent for a moment:

"Do you know who I am?"

"I know who you are, but you use many different names."

"Here, I am known as the Shaman. It is a form that fools of human nature can adjust to."

"The Shaman was a human?"

"Oh yes—he was a holy man, whom the Russians caught

and used cruelly,"—there was a dry cackle of a laugh—
"hence this twisted leg. The twisted leg perverted the man's
mind so that it became easy to possess it and bend it to my
purpose."

"And what is that purpose?"

The Hunter shivered in spite of himself and threw another branch on the fire.

"You know my purpose. You have seen it many times
when tides of people from the east have swept into the west."

"And have been pushed back by my people."

The dry laugh came again.

"Your people? You have no people. Who worships at your
shrines now? Who has taken your holy places? The followers
of a Jewish carpenter! You have become a tale told by old
women to frighten children—bah!" The Shaman spat into his
smoky fire.

The Hunter raised his face and gave a small smile:

"What about the Lady, the Madonna?"

"Bah! Madonnas!"

"That is your weakness—you do not understand Madonnas properly. You don't understand that in all the holy places
you talk about there is a figure of a Lady, and that Lady was
there even before I was. She is the eternal truth. You will
know that all through my journeys in the heart of Europe, I
pass statues of the Lady facing east and standing on a ser-
pent, standing on you, my friend. You fear the Lady. She saw
you off the last time and you are frightened that She will defeat you again. Now here She is in what you think of as your
realm in the form of the Black Madonna. You know that the
icon of the Black Madonna is a powerful spiritual force
amongst the people here. As long as it exists, or is thought to
exist, your power will be weakened."

For a moment the Shaman was silent, rubbing his game
leg as though it pained him:

"Don't worry, my friend. I have the matter in hand. The
Black Madonna has a price on her head: a price to be paid in
German gold—a nice touch, don't you think? And for that
price the icon of the Black Madonna will be smashed and the

power of the Lady with it. Then the west will open for me."

There was a shower of sparks as the pile of burning branches collapsed in on themselves and the picture in the flames was gone. The mist was also gone. In the clear frosty sky above the stars twinkled in their courses.

The Hunter shook his head and sighed. There looked to be testing times ahead. With another sigh, he took the flask from his cloak.

* * *

"Grüss Gott," said the deep voice.

Anna started. She had been dreaming with her head tucked into Heidi's flank as her small hands worked gently bringing the warm milk down from the cow's udder. In her startlement she nearly kicked over the bucket.

"Goodness! You frightened me! You should not creep up on people like that."

"My humble apologies," said the man and, removing his hat, he made a deep and graceful bow.

Not many people had bowed to Anna and she felt the warmth of the blood rising to her cheeks.

"Hmm!" she said with an attempt at severity; then her humour bubbled through. "Heidi would have been very cross if all that milk had gone to waste."

"She is a fine cow," said the man gravely, and reaching out, he scratched Heidi in the exact place between the horns that she enjoyed so much.

The cow stretched out her head in pleasure.

"She likes you and she is a good judge of character."

Anna looked at the man with interest and curiosity. He was a huge, rough-bearded man, wrapped in a much patched cloak, and with a disgraceful broad-brimmed hat rammed down on his grizzled locks. He had a stout oaken staff in one hand, and on his back he carried a large pack. He looked dusty and stained with travel. But the thing that really caught the girl's attention was the dreadful scar of the empty eye socket. She stared at it with horrified fascination, then, realising what she was doing, blushed and raised her hand to her mouth with a gasp of dismay. The man's weathered face broke into the most wonderful smile:

"Is it the eye?"

"Yes! No! Look, I'm sorry. It was very rude of me. I did not mean to stare."

"Child! Child! Do not concern yourself. It is an old and, if I say so myself, honourable scar. It does not worry me, so don't let it worry you."

Anna found herself smiling too. Her milking was finished, so she rose to her feet and put her buckets carefully to one side. Then she held out her hand:

"My name is Anna."

Her small brown hand disappeared in the stranger's huge hairy paw.

"They call me Hunter," he said.

"You are German?"

"Well, sort of."

"Here we are all Germans; although our families have lived here for a hundred years, we still speak German and keep up the old ways."

"So I have heard."

"Have you walked all the way from Germany?"

"I travel in different ways," said the Hunter vaguely.

"What do you do?"

Anna still had the simple directness of a child. The Hunter jerked a thumb at his pack:

"I am an itinerant blacksmith—if you've broken it, I'll mend it."

"Anyway, I expect you're hungry. Are you hungry as a hunter perhaps?"

They both laughed.

The girl yoked up her buckets and said, "Come—I will ask Mutti to give you breakfast."

"You are a kind girl Anna. I hope your mother won't mind."

Mutti had fussed like an old hen when Anna led the huge stranger through the door of the little house. How could

Anna be so stupid, bringing a guest at this hour and Mutti
hardly proper, and the house all upside down? And what
would the stranger think? And who was he anyway? And
what did Anna mean bringing in men off the street? Really
the child was becoming quite impossible, and the sooner she
was married and out from under Mutti's feet the better. She
really did not know…

While Mutti fussed and banged pots and pans about, Papa
got to his feet and shook the stranger's hand and gravely
bade him welcome in God's name. Hospitality, said Papa, was
a sacred duty.

So the Hunter sat and ate his plate of rather thin gruel
and sipped his mug of rather sour ale, for which they had all
duly thanked God. All the time he watched and listened as
Papa grumbled gently in the way that farmers do, always
have and always will; as Mutti fussed and scolded and bustled
and put an extra ladle full onto Hunter's plate; as Anna and
Matthias, her young brother, squabbled and giggled, until
gravely rebuked by Papa.

It was a happy family scene, but the Hunter's thoughts
were not happy. There was a cloud hanging over the happiness of these people and it was getting thicker and darker.
These people were, after all, his people. He must try to warn
them, but would they listen? His thoughts were interrupted
by Papa saying that Anna had told him that the Hunter was a
blacksmith.

"That's right; if you have a forge, I have the skill."

"Well there's plenty of things that need doing in the village, but we are not rich people. There is not much gold."

But the Hunter was looking at Anna, at lovely, laughing,
golden Anna and his thought was grim: 'German Gold' he
thought.

* * *

Lubin had been right: it had been a damned awful time of
year to be setting out from St Petersburg. It had been a
bad winter and they had, in Charles's words, been
'snowed-up, ballsed-up, fucked-up and fed-up'. His com-

ments on Voronezh, a dreary town on the steppe where they had been weather-bound, were that if anyone even mentioned Voronezh to him again he would ram it right up that person's fundament, because that was where Voronezh richly deserved to be.

It would have been amazing if the months spent in close and enforced proximity with each other had not affected the relationship of the three men.

Lubin, with his totally relaxed and sleepy approach to life, had been the emollient that prevented the rough surfaces of Mischa and Charles grinding on each other, especially during periods of immobility.

Charles's quicksilver temperament was ill-suited to inactivity. He used to alleviate his boredom by teasing Mischa, whose grave and apparently placid acceptance of the delays and tribulations of the journey Charles found inexplicable and annoying.

Only once did he manage to pierce Mischa's calm, and that was in their miserable lodgings in the miserable town of Voronezh in the middle of a raging blizzard. It was some trifling matter, but Mischa's patience finally snapped and with a roar he had seized Charles by the throat and pinned him against the wall. Lubin had saved the day by pointing out that, 'Charles would make such a nasty stain on the wall, my dear.' When Charles had stopped choking and was able to gasp out something about 'seeking satisfaction as a gentleman,' Lubin shook his head and said that 'no one could possibly be a gentleman in Voronezh.' The poison drained away.

All in all the three young men came out of the journey very well and, as the spring bloomed, so did their friendship.

"Excellency! Excellency! I have the honour to report that it is time to wake up."

Mischa opened an eye and peered out from the cocoon of blankets in which he had huddled through the night. There was a white rime of frost on the blankets and his moustache was stiff with frozen condensation from his breath.

Mischa liked the early mornings and, throwing the blankets aside, he rose lithely to his feet.

"Come on, dog! You're a star! Rise!"

Sirius, who shared his master's blankets, poked his head out, sniffed the frost and withdrew his head again.

"Idle devil!"

The sharpness of the frosty air bit Mischa and he was glad to slip into the heavy cloak that Vladislav held open for him.

"I have hot water for your shaving, Excellency."

Mischa looked with approval at his Cossack orderly.

Back in St Petersburg Lubin had drawled, pointing to the man who stood rigidly at attention:

"I will give you Vladislav Ivanov to look after you. He is an excellent horseman, has slightly more than marginal intelligence and, most importance of all, he is an expert thief. You will never go without whilst Vladislav Ivanov looks after you, will he Ivanov? He is also impertinent and laughs too much—for this he should be whipped."

"It will be an honour to serve his Excellency," Vladislav had replied stolidly.

In fact there was nothing stolid about Vladislav. He was a small man, smart and sharp as a whip and as quick as a small hawk that he so much resembled.

Vladislav held the little looking glass, whilst Mischa, crouched by the growing warmth of the newly crackling fire, shaved. This was their morning ritual. From the other side of the fire came the other morning ritual:

"Wakey! Wakey! Sir," with Bone shaking the large huddle of blankets.

"Fuck off, Bone! Just fuck off!"

By the time the red ball of the sun had risen over the horizon into a clear cloudless sky, the troop was in line of march, the men huddled in their cloaks and the breath of men and horses pluming in the chill air. Before them the steppe stretched to the horizon, brown, dead and almost flat with the remains of snow still lying in the small gullies. The steppe had been the horizon for months:

"Ain't there no end to this bloody steppe, Vlad?"

Bone and Vladislav were riding knee to knee.

"Is the bloody end of the bloody world, Bone," said Vlad, grinning from ear to ear.

"Knowing our luck, we'll fall off the fucking edge then," said Bone gloomily.

The flat plain started to rise and gradually became more undulating, with scrubby woodlands in the gullies and boggy bottoms thick with reeds. It reminded Charles of English downland, but on a huge scale. He said so to Mischa. Mischa nodded:

"It is good to see something like a hill again. I must say I miss the mountains."

"You'll have your belly full of mountains, where we're going," said Lubin. "Sirius in form today? There ain't much for supper."

"Well, dog?" said Mischa, turning his head.

Sirius had quickly learned to ride on a pad of blanket behind his master's saddle. He put his great shaggy head over Mischa's shoulder and licked his nose.

"We'll take that as a yes," said Lubin and shouted an order.

Laughing and joking at the thought of sport and a break in the routine of the march, the Cossacks formed line abreast in skirmishing order across the steppe. The clear morning air rang with their shouts and slap of their knouts on their boots.

The shouts and the whistles roused the buck from the clump of scrub where he had been couched. The sight of him produced a volley of holloas from the line of horsemen which immediately broke into a gallop.

The buck covered the open ground with great fluid bounds, heading for the cover of the tall reed bed at the bottom of the slope.

Mischa could feel Sirius's quivering tension against his back, as the dog leaned on him to help keep his balance on the galloping horse.

"Go!" shouted Mischa.

The dog shot from the back of the horse and landed galloping, without missing a beat. He went away from the line of
horsemen as though he had been shot from a gun, his back
arching with power he covered the ground in huge strides,
urged on by the cries behind him.

He closed on the buck.

The buck was nearing the safety of the reeds.

"Ten roubles says the buck gets away," said Bone to Vlad
as they galloped.

"Sirius will catch the buck and your money, Bone."

The buck, seeing the dog getting closer, put in a desperate jink.

Sirius matched his turn and even gained ground.

Another few strides and the buck would be in the reeds.

Sirius seemed to surge forward and, seizing the buck's
flank, brought him crashing down.

"Hurrah! Hurrah! Hurrah!" came the Russian cheer as
the Cossacks spurred their horses to get to the kill.

"Well done, old man," said Mischa as he stroked the
panting Sirius's blood-stained head.

"Damned good, what!" said Charles.

"Ah ha! Fresh meat!" Lubin was furiously polishing his
monocle.

"That's ten roubles you owe me," said Vlad to Bone, as he
slid from his horse and pulled out his knife.

It was Lubin who saw it first—a distant cone-shaped peak that
came into view on the horizon of the rolling steppe. He
pointed to it with his knout:

"Mashook," he said. "That is one of the mountains around
Pyatigorsk."

A happy chattering arose from the column. Most of the
Cossacks came from the villages around Pyatigorsk.

"How far?" asked Charles.

Lubin shrugged:

"God willing, we only have one more night on the steppe.
Tomorrow we should dine at the fort."

"What is the town like?" asked Mischa.

"A pleasant enough place for the wilderness. It was just a Cossack village twenty years ago, then they discovered that the waters from the springs were of some particular virtue, especially for those whose livers are being corroded by alcohol."

Charles grumbled, "That must be just about everybody in this desert. Ain't much else to do with your liver here."

Lubin ignored him:

"It has developed into quite a spa. It is a long time since I have been here, but there was a lot of building going on. In her letters, Mama tells me that it has become quite a social centre and of course the fort guarantees protection from the bandits."

"The bandits come as far as this from the mountains?" asked Mischa.

Lubin gave another of his languid shrugs:

"If you lived in those stinking mountains with nothing to eat but snow and rocks, you would probably go a-raiding too. Hunger is a great spur. Besides, to those mountain scum, raiding is a sport as well as a means of filling the cupboard, ain't that right Sergeant Major?"

The huge, massively bearded, Sergeant Major gave a grim chuckle:

"A lance in the belly is a fine cure for hunger, Excellency. We've helped quite a few of the scum to Paradise, or Gehenna, over the years."

"What religion are these chappies, then?"

"Anything you like, Charles. There's about fifty different tribes up in the mountains. Some are Christians, of sorts, some are Moslem and some worship the devil for all I know— they certainly behave like it anyway."

As they rode, the cone-shaped hill rose on the horizon and other cones came into view, until it was clear that what they were looking at was the shattered rim of a long extinct volcano.

"See," said Vlad to Bone. "See the five mountains? The Karbadine people say they are the remains of Mashook who was a mighty warrior in ancient times. He was in love with a girl called Pishtar, but he was betrayed and his enemies caught him and cut him into five pieces. Those five mountains are the pieces. Outside the town there is a lake where the girl drowned herself in her grief. She cried such tears that the lake became salt, and now you can float in it."

"*You* can, if you want to," said Bone doggedly. "I ain't going near any bloody lake, even if it does have a bleeding maiden at the bottom of it."

The hills grew in size and, as the column breasted another slope, a jagged white line appeared on the distant southern horizon: the snow-capped peaks of the Caucasus mountains, shining coldly against the cloudless blue of the sky. They looked beautiful but cruel, and Mischa felt a chill run down his spine as though a cold draught from the snow fields had run across his back.

He felt that somewhere in those distant mountains, fate was going to play a hand with him.

* * *

"Give the bellows another pump, Matthias" said the Hunter. "I want some heat in that fire."

The boy reached up both hands to the long handle of the bellows and pulled down with all his might. The air hissed through the charcoal in the fire bed and made it glow with heat. The Hunter thrust the piece of metal deep into the heart of the fire and watched critically until it glowed, red and white. Then seizing it with the tongs, he laid it swiftly on the anvil and beat it into shape with quick deft strokes.

The noise of the hammering covered the sound of the footsteps of the men, who were now standing in the doorway of the forge. The Hunter, who was well aware of their coming although he had his back to them, affected to be ignorant of their presence. It was only after he had shaped the glowing metal around the horn of the anvil and dropped it into the pail of water—with the accompanying hiss and cloud of steam—that he pretended to notice their presence for the first time.

He had sensed that there was trouble coming and here it
was: trouble in the forms of the pastor, several of the village
elders, Anna's father, looking very ill at ease, and Kurt. The
Hunter had known that Kurt would stick his righteous nose
into the business.

Kurt had disapproved of his presence in the village from
the very beginning. He thoroughly disapproved of itinerants
of any sort, however skilled they might be. He also thoroughly disapproved of his, Kurt's, fiancée picking a ragged
traveller up off the street and taking him home with her. His
disapproval had increased as he watched the easy rapport
that the Hunter had established with Anna—how he teased
her, joked with her and made her laugh. The Good Lord and
Kurt knew that Anna was far too frivolous by nature. Kurt
took a serious view of frivolity and he was quite certain that
the Good Lord did too. Kurt had no doubts but that the
Good Lord shared his views on most things. He felt that he
had established this position in his long solemn discussions
with the pastor.

Both men shared a sense of their own rectitude and their
unfailing interpretation of the wishes of the Good Lord. Both
Kurt and the pastor—and, by definition, their God—heartily
disapproved of Anna's behaviour and of the Hunter, whom
both men instinctively felt to be a subversive influence. Who
was this man, this unknown man, to come into a god-fearing
village, alternately making people laugh and then frightening
them with his tales of lurking danger? The whole even tenor
of village life was being upset by this stranger, fine blacksmith
though he undoubtedly was. The pastor felt that this usurpa-
tion of his authority could not be allowed to continue. It was
not as though the man even came to church, where he might
well have profited from the pastor's lengthy sermons. No, the
vagabond blacksmith would have to go.

The pastor, backed up by Kurt, had put his message to
the village council. The council had been reluctant at first;
after all, the man was a good smith and there were many jobs
that needed doing. But when the pastor pointed out that a
broken plough share was as nothing to the damage that

might be done to the immortal souls of the villagers, especially to the souls of some of the women, who, frail vessels
that they were, might be led away from the strait path—Kurt
agreed heartily with this—then the duty of the council was
plain. The council agreed, only Anna's father dissenting. He
liked having the Hunter about. The Hunter made him laugh
with his tales and there was not a lot of laughter in the village. But, in the end, Papa could not ignore the will of the
majority.

The Hunter listened to the stern words of the pastor in
silence, and without expression on his face. The pastor got
flustered by the man's unflinching gaze and his carefully
prepared diatribe crumbled at the end. When the pastor
staggered to a stop, the Hunter turned to Matthias:

"No more pumping—let the flame die."

Then, without another word, he took off his leather
apron, packed his tools and strode out of the forge. The dis-
comforted council parted hastily to let him through with
Matthias trotting after him.

Mutti and Matthias both cried as he loaded his pack.

Papa stood shamefaced and downcast until the Hunter
took his hand and gripped his arm and wished God's Blessing on them all. Then he was gone.

He was gone when Anna returned from seeking a hen
that was laying astray. Her anger was as hot and scalding as
her tears. Leaving her family shocked into silent immobility,
she seized a fresh baked loaf and a lump of cheese from the
table and ran out of the house.

She ran and ran, out of the village and down the road.
The road stretched down the valley and beside the river. It
was empty.

"Anna," a voice said.

She looked about wildly, and there, leaning against an ash
tree, was the Hunter; she would have sworn he had not been
there a minute ago. Still sobbing in fury she handed him the
bread and cheese. Very gently he put an arm round her and
let her sob on his chest.

"It's so unfair!" she said in a muffled voice.

"There is no fairness in life, child. Now listen: there are difficult times ahead and you must be brave and strong to cope with them. I will do all in my power to help you, but"— and here the Hunter seemed to hear a snake-like hissing— "power does not always run as it should."

"I don't understand."

"It is better that you don't, but one day you will. Now go with God."

* * *

"Well, I must say it looks quite a jolly place," said Charles.

The town of Pyatigorsk lay on the slopes of Mashook, one of the cone-shaped hills that the travellers had seen from afar. Behind this hill lay a rough circle of other pointed hills marking the remains of the ancient volcano. It is from the volcanic depths that the springs bubble up the sulphurous waters that are so beneficial to both the inner and the outer man. The taste of the water is so revolting that its healing properties cannot be doubted.

It was these cleansing effects that caused people to come there and found a spa. The town was still expanding on the hillside. Broad avenues had been laid out, and rows of trees planted along them that would one day give agreeable shade to the streets. The new houses were set back from the streets, with access through gateways that opened onto pleasant courtyards, at the back of which sat the houses.

Above the town, amongst the trees of the hillside, could be seen the onion-shaped domes of St Lazar's church. Beside the church was the wooden palisaded rampart that enclosed the fort, to which the column of Cossacks was making its way.

Below the town and around the swift flowing river, was the old Cossack village, with its crooked twisting earth roads, and still surrounded by the dry stone walls that had served as protection against intruders of all sorts. This was home to many of the men in the column; others came from the out-lying villages in the area.

Word of the column's arrival spread quickly and, by the time it arrived at the gate of the fort, it carried a long tail of townspeople. Relatives rushed in to touch and greet the troopers. Children were hoisted up in front of saddles. Larger youths seized hold of stirrup leathers and ran alongside the column. There were cries of greeting and tears of joy.

"Dammit!" said Charles to Lubin. "There are some damned pretty fillies around."

Lubin screwed in his eye glass and looked at Charles sardonically:

"And if you value your prime asset, you will keep it in your trousers as far as the Cossack women are concerned. You will find that there are many bored ladies, come here to take the waters, who might be persuaded to regard your favours as part of the restorative process."

"You're a cynical sod, Lubin."

"Deep calleth unto deep, Charles."

After the column had been dismissed on the parade ground of the fort, the three young men reported to the Commanding Officer.

Colonel Viktor Ryshkov was a grizzled veteran of the frontier, and a Cossack of the Kuban. Although a tall man of well over six foot, he was so broad that he still managed to look squat. His face was almost entirely hidden behind an enormous steel-grey beard, through which two hard eyes still managed to twinkle, and from the depths of which there was an occasional wolfish flash of teeth.

He rose from behind his desk like a bear plunging out of a thicket and, with a bass roar of delight, enfolded Lubin in his massive arms and kissed him on both cheeks:

"Welcome, my boy! Welcome! You've had a long hard journey of it."

'My God!' thought Charles. 'I hope the old bear ain't going to cuddle me!'

"And whom has God and the army sent with you?"

The Colonel turned to Charles and Mischa, who were both standing stiffly to attention. Lubin introduced them and handed the Colonel the dispatches he had brought with him.

Ryshkov read through them growling basely to himself in his beard, and glancing at the two men from time to time. At last he folded up the dispatch and threw it onto his desk:

"So, two young men of troublesome temperament, it seems—a whoring, gambling, English and an Austrian bear who goes round slaughtering princes, eh?"

Mischa stiffened:

"Sir! I assure you that it was a fair and honourable encounter, that I very much regret the fatal outcome, and.."

"Bah! Rubbish! You think I care how many stinking useless princes you shoot? What I care is that I have two extra officers, whom I can use and, believe me my fine young bear, there won't be any fair and honourable encounters here. With the bandit scum in the mountains, it is 'kill or be killed'. You stop to think of honour and you'll get a lance through your vitals. Now my boy"—the Colonel turned to Lubin—"your aunt is longing to see you. You and your friends will dine with us tonight. I expect that you are sick of borsch and horse-meat porridge. Then you can have a few days' leave and go and visit your mother, eh?"

Lubin's aunt Sara was a handsome woman with a quiet manner and a dry sense of humour. She was delighted to see her nephew and made the two foreigners most welcome. In spite of the Colonel's great roaring manner, Mischa felt certain that Sara's character matched his in a quiet strength.

The dinner was a splendid meal of fish and meat and game—fine fare after months of poor and monotonous food on the journey.

Whilst Charles had always maintained that he had not yet found a drinkable wine in Russia, he did not seem to be stinting himself that night.

All the officers of the garrison were at the dinner, and several notables from the town. As the wine—and then the vodka—flowed, tongues became loosened.

A young officer who sat opposite Mischa became voluble about a patrol, from which he had just returned, chasing bandits. These particular bandits were becoming ever more daring and venturing further and further from the mountains, and yet, he said, they were as slippery as eels and seemed to wriggle out of any trap set for them:

"They have the devil's own luck," he said, "and devils they are; the man who leads them is the biggest devil of them all, he is some sort of Khan, and is a legend amongst the mountain people. Do you know what they call him?"

Mischa waited.

"Well, in the local language, it translates, 'Pain in the Arse', and d'yer know why?"—a shadow passed over the young man's face, and he tossed his glass of vodka down in one gulp—"Because he impales his prisoners."

6   A Night of Evil

*T*HE Cossacks stood in silent ranks on the parade ground. The air was still, and the only sound was the distant chanting from the church of St Lazar. By degrees the sound got louder and closer. There was a faint stirring in the ranks as though some mild electric charge was running through them.

Charles, Mischa and Sirius stood apart as onlookers. Ryshkov, with his customary bluntness, had said: "Come if you want to, but this is Cossack business; better that you stand aside and watch."

The chanting got louder, and the head of the procession appeared at the gate of the fort—young girls in white dresses spreading petals of spring flowers, priests heavy with beards and brocades, smooth-faced acolytes swinging incense thuribles, a bishop of immense hairiness, senior officers and prominent people from the town. In the middle of the procession four officers carried an ornately gilded baldaquin. Beneath the baldaquin the priest of St Lazar carried a small dark-coloured icon.

"So that's the famous Black Madonna, in the flesh so to speak."

"You have seen her before?" said Mischa with interest.

"Not in person, old dear, but I do remember a copy of her hanging on the wall of old de Tolley's office when he was giving me the first of many bullings. I sort of fixed my eyes on her and I could swear that she was staring back."

"No doubt with a certain amount of disapproval," said Mischa dryly.

"Well, d'yer know, I thought that the lady had a certain twinkle in her eye."

"Our Lord Jesus Christ came on earth to save sinners."

"Well, that's all right then, because if they were all smug

97

self-righteous bastards like you, he'd be bored stiff. What's
that about there being, 'more joy in heaven over one sinner
that repenteth'?"

"But *you* don't repent."

"Saving it all up, dear boy. I'll have a bloody good blub at
the end and repent like anything. That'll have the heavenly
choir singing. Anyway I reckon that this Lady has a soft spot
for sinners, if she likes the Cossacks. Unless you had a sin
nailed to the floor, these bastards would steal it. Now look at
them—butter wouldn't melt in their stinking mouths."

Mischa looked at the ranks of wild-bearded, hawk-faced
men. They stood hatless with heads bowed. As the chanting,
incense-heavy procession approached, each rank fell to its
knees, rather as a swathe of grass falls before the scythe. Each
man had his eyes fixed on the icon.

As it processed through the ranks, the heavily hirsute
bishop mechanically dipped his wisp-tailed aspergillum in the
bowl of holy water carried by a young priest and sprinkled
the kneeling men. As the water touched him, each man
crossed himself. The devotion in the hard-bitten faces was
obvious and touching. A feeling of faith rose from the crowd
like some kind of miasma. The two watchers were silenced
and Sirius began a low whining.

The chanting procession wound its way through the ranks
and then through the gate of the fort and down into the
town. Many of the Cossacks remained on their knees, and
only gradually got to their feet and started to drift away.
They were like men in a trance.

"Look at them," said Charles, "they really believe. The
poor bastards really believe."

"But what do you believe in, Charles?"

"Nothing! There is nothing to believe in. I'll leave all that
to you. But if I had to believe in something then I might start
with Her Ladyship there: The Black Madonna."

Spring had come to Pyatigorsk. The sun shone, and the
slopes above the town were loud with birdsong and heavy
with the scent of lilac. Lubin's squadron had fallen in on the

parade ground of the fort. Charles and Mischa were sitting apart and at ease on their horses, whilst Lubin and the Squadron Sergeant Major did their inspection.

The two foreigners were to accompany the patrol as supernumeraries—'to gain experience'—Colonel Ryshkov had said:

"I'm not letting two pretty virgins like you loose in the whorehouse that this area has become, until you've dipped your wicks."

The Colonel had roared with laughter at this witticism.

Charles enjoyed the joke.

Mischa still felt faintly shocked by Ryshkov's manner. He did not consider it seemly for colonels to be so coarse, but, as he reminded himself with a sigh, 'this is Russia.'

Lubin's inspection was thorough:

"Dirty pistol, Sarn't Major!"

"*Excellency!* You're a filthy pig's turd! Fall out for punishment."

The guilty Cossack promptly dismounted and marched round to the front of the parade, where a large Sergeant stood holding a stout stick. The Cossack stood rigidly to attention as he received a summary twenty lashes across his back.

"No messing about, eh?" said Charles. "Might as well be back at Knightsbridge. Old Lubin ain't as soft as he looks."

"This is a fighting patrol," said Mischa.

"If you can call chasing a few hairy-arssed bandits *fighting*."

"I hope that we get the chance to find out."

Charles gave his crooked smile:

"You're quite a fire-eater on the quiet, ain't you my little pickled cabbage?"

"Charles! You know I object to..."

"All right! All right! Herr Rittmeister, I apologise. It's just that you can be so damned prickly."

"I only wish to do my duty."

"I bet that's what you said to the Grand Duchess, what?"

"Captain FitzHugh! May I remind you..."

"Stop it the pair of you!" came Lubin's lazy drawl. "Really, you two are just like a couple of old maids quarrelling over a piece of ribbon. One more squeak out of either of you and I'll leave you behind—understand?"

* * *

"You must realise, Anna, that the man was a bad influence. He was upsetting people in the village. It was an unfortunate decision of your father to take the man in. I am so pleased that we, that is the pastor and the elders, were able to convince your father of the bad situation..."

Kurt's voice droned on. Anna had heard it all before, many times. Kurt was like that when he picked up a subject; he was like a dog picking up a bone and chewing it over and over again, or, Anna thought with an inner giggle, like some great bullock chewing its cud.

Kurt was on the hill with the cattle again—how sleek and well they looked on the fresh spring grass. Anna had brought out his food, as was proper for a loving betrothed, and was being treated to Kurt's lecture on the subject of the expulsion of the Hunter. Anna lay on her front on the sun-warmed grass with her head propped in her hands and her legs over her back.

Kurt may have interpreted this as proper and dutiful subservience, but, in fact, Anna was not listening at all. She was watching an ant carrying a huge and unwieldy piece of leaf and struggling with it through the rough grass: 'Poor ant,' she thought, 'life is such a struggle for you, and I could end your struggle with one stamp of my foot. But I won't. We are all ants in this world and we just have to keep struggling and doing the best we can. I am struggling, little ant, because I am sitting here, listening to my great bullock of a man chewing over the contents of the rumen that he calls a brain, over and over and over again.'

She cast a sly glance under her cascade of hair at Kurt sitting on the rock above her. He was like a bullock she thought. Then she thought, 'Well, if he is, marriage won't be much fun.' Then she shifted her gaze to the bulge between

Kurt's thighs, accentuated by his tight leather breeches. 'I wonder what he's like *there*,' she thought.

Anna, virgin that she was, was in no doubt about what happened between men and women and, as she thought of it, she felt a glow. Anna wanted it to happen to her. She thought—she knew—that she would enjoy it. Sometimes, in the small dark hours, she dreamed her dream of the White Knight, who would sweep her onto his saddle and gallop off with her to his castle where he would do the most wonderful things to her, the very thought of which...

"...so you see it was all for the good of the village."

'My God! He was still droning on.'

Anna lifted her head and saw them: a long line of tiny ants crawling across the steppe to the north of the village. Riders!

"Look!"

Kurt paused in his flow: "What?"

"Horsemen!"

"Where?"

"There! There!"

Kurt followed the direction of Anna's pointing finger. At last he made out the distant column:

"Soldiers from the fort, I expect, coming from the north."

Anna sprang to her feet:

"I'll go and tell the village."

"There's no need. The look-outs on the picquet hill will have seen them. Stay here with me for a bit longer, Anna. Anna, you know that I like you to stay..."

But Anna was already taking the hobbles off her grey horse and, seizing the reins, she vaulted onto its back. Kurt had a quick vision of flashing smile, flowing golden hair and a glimpse of long milk-white thighs. Then the girl was gone in a flat-out gallop, leaving him still sitting open mouthed on the rock. The glimpse of the white thighs stayed with him. 'Soon,' he thought, 'soon...'—and his breeches became quite uncomfortably tight.

* * *

The column halted on top of the ridge. Ever since the squadron had headed south from Pyatigorsk, on the main road, the country had become more and more rolling. Lubin had explained that this was the country of the Kabardins, a Moslem people famous as breeders of horses and as cattle thieves. The Kabardins had accepted Russian suzerainty some years before.

Always, as they rode, the jagged white wall of the Caucasus mountains filled the horizon. The dusty road was busy with carts and wagons for this was the main trade route to the south.

The column moved at a steady jog which came naturally to the tough little Cossack horses and ate up the miles.

It was late in the day when the Cossacks halted on a wide ridge, overlooking a broad valley. A river, white with snow melt from the mountains, tumbled through a rocky bed in the bottom. On the other side of the valley, the ground became steeper—great rolling grassy hills with cascades of woodland. The hills spread and climbed into the distance, the foot-hills of the great mountains.

Below the Cossacks, in the valley bottom, a long village straggled along the banks of the river. The brightly coloured wooden houses lay either side of a wide street with grassy verges. Around the village were neatly fenced fields and garden plots. Smoke rose from the chimneys and spread in the still afternoon air. The smell of burning wood reached the men on the ridge. It all looked neat, prosperous, and peaceful.

Mischa said as much to Lubin. Lubin grunted:

"Then they should pray very hard to God and Our Lady that it stays that way. Not that they have much to do with Our Lady."

"Musselman chappies, are they?" asked Charles.

"German Lutherans," said Lubin. "We call that 'the German Village'. There are German settlements scattered over Russia. The great Czar Peter brought them in to teach us Russians the virtues of hard work and thrift. Not many of them got this far south and east."

"Can't say I've seen much sign of hard work and thrift amongst you chaps."

"My dear Charles, those are matters for serfs, not for gentlemen. It is Protestants who believe in the work ethic."

"Dammit! I'm Church of England!"

"And a shining example for us all, if I may say so. What does the Holy Roman Church say on this matter, Mischa?"

Mischa did not reply. He had taken his telescope from its case and had been glassing the opposite slope. Sirius, sitting behind his master's saddle, rested his head on Mischa's shoulder, as though he too wanted a turn with the glass.

Mischa caught a flash of something white moving rapidly towards the village. He focused his glass on it. For an awful moment, he thought that he was going to choke—the slender figure bent over the neck of the galloping grey horse, the long golden hair streaming behind it—the vision flashing through his mind of long golden hair floating amongst the weeds of the river at Lippitz, a vision that still haunted his dreams and brought him awake, panting and bathed in sweat.

For a moment longer, he watched the flying figure. Then he closed his glass with a snap. It could not be. All that lay a thousand miles to the west and rotting in a grave. It was only in his mind that it still lived and festered.

"What? Sorry?"

"It is no matter. I was only asking what the Catholic Church's view on hard work and thrift might be?"

"I'm sure that the Holy Father would be in favour," said Mischa absently.

"Well, there's damned little sign of it amongst our verminous priests," said Lubin sourly. "What did you spy across the valley?"

"Nothing—just a girl on a horse—nothing," but the slim lithe figure persisted in his mind.

Charles scratched his nose with his whip:

"You hear that Lubin? Our bear has noticed a gel, and on a horse. Which d'yer think excited him most, eh? Good looking is she, Mischa? I'll tell you what, I'll have the girl and you can have the horse."

"Damn you, Charles!"

"Ah ha! I smell a raw nerve! Fancy a nice little peasant girl do you? I bet I can lay her before you."

Mischa stiffened in his saddle, but Lubin gently pushed him back with the butt of his knout:

"Listen well. This is a respectable village and we treat it as such. Both of you, keep your breeches buttoned unless you want a piss. Sarn't Major!"

"Excellency!"

"Tell the men."

"Excellency!"

The Sergeant Major turned and addressed the column:

"Listen, my lambs: this is a German village and the Germans are much respected. You do not steal. You do not hit. You do not try to touch up any of the women. Any of you scum cause trouble and I will personally open his back from arse to neck. Understood?"

There was a rumble of wolfish laughter from the squadron.

Lubin turned to his senior troop leader:

"We'll camp tonight by the river. You sort it. We will ride into the village and make our number with the elders."

* * *

It was all Heidi's fault. After the excitement of her gallop from the hill, Anna was slightly deflated to hear that the village already knew about the approaching column.

"A Cossack patrol from Pyatigorsk," said Papa. "One of the picquets rode in earlier and told the pastor. They are camping down by the river tonight."

"They'll have every chicken in the village stolen," said Mutti, "and that's if we're lucky. No woman will be safe—you mark my words."

"The soldiers are for our protection, Mutti," said Papa, mildly.

"And who protects us from the soldiers, tell me that."

Mutti was bustling about the kitchen, banging things around and obviously getting in one of her states.

"And where are you going, girl?"

"Just to take Heidi down to the river, Mutti."

"Yes, well, keep away from those Cossacks, understand?"

"Yes, Mutti."

Anna undid Heidi's rope from its peg and set off for the river. She knew that she should do what Mutti told her and go the other way, but strangers were a rare thing in the village, and she thought that a peek at the patrol would be all right—after all she need not go near them, and it was easier to get to the river from that side of the village.

Walking down the street with Heidi trailing placidly behind her—Heidi was such a docile cow—Anna slipped into her dream world, the world where her Knight Errant waited for her.

It was the sound of horses' hooves and the jingling of bits that woke her from her reverie and made her look up to see the three men riding towards her. The one with the small moustache and the monocle was obviously Russian; she recognised the uniform. The other two men looked foreign. One was huge, 'like a bear,' Anna thought, but it was the eyes she noticed—such sad, kind eyes in a face that looked rough hewn from stone. The other one was tall and slim with extravagant whiskers. All three men were looking at her.

All of this she had time to see before Heidi decided to have a temperament. It was that dog's fault. Heidi was accustomed to dogs, but when something the size of a wolf suddenly leaped off the big man's horse, Heidi, that most placid of cows, kicked up her heels and bolted with the devil dog bounding, grinning, alongside her.

Anna tried hard to hang on to the rope, but was pulled off her feet and through the dust as she clung on desperately and screamed at Heidi and the devil dog to stop. She had to let go and lay in the dust, sobbing with rage.

The reactions of the three men to this interesting sight were instinctive. Lubin screwed his monocle into his eye and settled down to watch the show with amused detachment. Mischa set spurs to his horse and set out in pursuit of Heidi, roaring abuse at Sirius.

Charles slid from his saddle and approaching the supine and furious Anna, picked her up and began to dust her down with a silk handkerchief, with particular attention to wiping the tears of fury that coursed down her face. This only succeeded in smearing the filth over the girl's cheeks, but it did allow Charles to take her in a firm and commanding hold, which confirmed his first visual impression that under that simple peasant's dress lay something extremely vital and desirable.

In spite of all of this, Anna's gaze was fixed on the big bear, as, leaning from his saddle with practised ease, he came alongside the galloping Heidi—who was still bucking and kicking in an idiot sense of freedom—and seized the rope that trailed from her headcollar. As soon as Heidi felt herself caught, she settled once more into her more accustomed, docile self. Her small rebellion over, she trotted back quietly alongside Mischa's horse, followed by a chastened Sirius.

Anna broke away from Charles's ministrations, which had been momentarily pleasing but were now becoming somewhat intrusive. Mischa looked down at her with a slight smile and handed her Heidi's rope. In spite of her smeared face, her torn dress and her tangled hair, he did think that she looked extremely beautiful. His pleasure was increased by the fact that now he had time to look at the girl close up; he could see that in fact, apart from the golden hair, she looked nothing like the peasant girl of Lippitz, whose memory still haunted his sleeping hours.

This was a quite different sort of girl: a slim, warm blood of a girl, with an almost classical beauty. In spite of himself he could not stop his eyes straying to where the torn dress revealed a firm, pink-nippled breast. He felt something stir in him.

Anna, feeling his gaze and realising for the first time what was on show, clutched her dress together and, with a fine burst of fury, turned on the three men and berated them for incompetent clowns. What right had they to come riding into the village as though they owned it, frightening innocent cows and causing maidens to be dragged through the dust? They were bandits! They were worse than bandits! They were... and as for their dogs, as big as bulls! The three men looked in amazement at this golden, screaming, streak of fury.

At this moment a large and gentle hand took Anna's shoulder and Papa was there, wrapping his coat round her to cover her embarrassment. With a last wail of anger, Anna turned and buried her head in his chest.

By this time an interested crowd had gathered. Mutti came from the house waving a duster and clucking like an old hen. Matthias quietly took Heidi's rope from Anna. The pastor came pushing importantly through the crowd.

Lubin, who had barely managed to contain his laughter, composed his features and leaning from his horse offered the pastor a languid hand. He apologised for the disturbance and explained the presence of the patrol. They had, he said, only entered the village to pay their respects to the elders. The other two, he explained, were foreign officers attached to his command and no harm had been intended to any of the villagers. He particularly wished to apologise to the Fräulein for any hurt and inconvenience suffered.

As he said this, Lubin doffed his forage cap and executed a graceful bow from his saddle. He did not think that his ambassadorial duties went so far as to cause him the great personal inconvenience of actually dismounting.

The pastor gravely, and rather pompously, accepted the apology on behalf of the villagers, said that they were very pleased to have a patrol in the area in light of the bandit problems, and had the Major heard any more of bandit activity?

Lubin stroked his moustache and said that he thought it most unlikely that the bandits would venture this far from their mountain strongholds, but that the villagers could be sure that the army was always vigilant. He gravely accepted the offer of a sheep to feed his officers.

Anna, who was now much recovered and safely wrapped
in Papa's coat, felt able to offer her thanks to the big foreigner for catching Heidi. She was amazed when he accepted
her thanks in German, and also apologised for her distress
and for the behaviour of his dog.

The bear swung from his saddle and sternly summoned
Sirius. Sirius came creeping—he knew that he had sinned.
Mischa seized him below the jaw and raised the dog's head so
that he could gaze into the dog's eyes.

"Sirius!" he said, still in German, "you have shamed me
and upset this most beautiful young lady."—Anna felt herself
going rather pink—"Now, Sir, you must be punished! Lubin,
your whip, if you please!"

Leaning over, Lubin offered his whip.

"No!"

The cry was muffled, then Anna broke away from Papa
and, running to Sirius, knelt and threw her arms round his
great rough neck.

"No! You shan't whip him!"

Still kneeling she looked up straight into Mischa's eyes.
For a long moment, the two stared at each other, then Mischa's rather stern face crinkled with a smile:

"Perhaps the Fräulein wishes to whip the devil dog herself?"

The devil dog licked Anna's nose.

Anna shook him gently by the scruff of his neck:

"You are indeed a wicked and sinful dog! but then you
consort with wicked and sinful men..."—she looked up at
Mischa again, and became aware that her breasts were starting to show through the torn blouse once more and that
Mischa's gaze was drawn to them—"who think sinful
thoughts. Therefore, devil dog, you shall not be whipped."

She bent and kissed the end of Sirius's nose:

"There! Now one day you might turn into a prince!"

Her irrepressible humour welled up in a chuckle of delight at her own absurdity, and looking up at Mischa again,
Anna suddenly flashed her brilliant smile. Then, ducking
through the crowd, she ran to catch up Matthias who was

leading Heidi home.

Mischa watched her long graceful strides as she ran up the street and once again felt the stirring of desire. He was never to forget the deep, warm, chuckle, or that sudden, brilliant smile.

"Damned neat little filly, that," came Charles's voice at his elbow. "Look at her move! And as neat a pair of titties as I've seen in a long time—had me hand on them too, dammit! But I wouldn't mind giving her a good gallop! What say you Mischa!"

"For goodness sake, Charles"—Mischa felt a surge of anger—"do you have to look at every woman, as though she is a whore?"

Charles shrugged:

"They mostly are, old boy, when it comes down to it."

* * *

The Khan listened to the report of his scout in silence. The Cossack patrol was a nuisance; it upset his plans. But, a few days and they would be gone clear of the area. This was good because they would not be back in the near future. He could wait. There was plenty of time for the raid and plenty of time to make the Golden One his whore. He rolled some leaf between his hands and stuffing it into his mouth, sat back contentedly to wait and savour the pleasures to come.

* * *

With a jingle of bits and a clatter of hooves, the Cossack patrol rode through the village on the following morning. The villagers turned out to wave.

"By Jove!" said Charles, "there's our sporting cow!"

And there was Heidi firmly held by Matthias at the back of the crowd. "General salute, I think," and Charles went through the formal movements with his whip. Sirius, beside Mischa's horse, totally ignored Heidi and went past with ears and tail erect. "No sign of your slut, though, Mischa. Pity—I thought at least she might have come out to wave to *me*, after I'd dandled her poonts so delicately. I expect that you scared her off with that great boot face of yours."

Mischa had been out of sorts all morning and had hardly spoken, except to snap at Vlad over the temperature of his shaving water. He sat stolidly on his horse, facing straight to his front, but his eyes had been roaming and, in spite of himself, he had been hoping to catch just a hint of gold amongst the crowd. There were several golden heads but not the one he had been looking for.

The last of the houses was left behind and the patrol was on the broad road between the neatly fenced fields of the village. There had been no sign of the girl. Mischa's feelings were a mixture of relief and disappointment; that bubbling laugh still rang in his head.

There came the sound of a galloping horse behind them. The Sergeant Major turned in his saddle, his hand dropping automatically to the hilt of his sabre.

The grey horse came flying past the column, gathering a rising tide of cheers from the Cossacks as it came, the cheers increasing as the lissom form of the girl—riding astride with natural ease and with her golden hair blowing behind her—became apparent. As she came abreast of Mischa, whose mouth had fallen open in astonishment, she pulled up in a shower of stones and dust and sat her fretting horse. For a moment they just looked at each other. Then came that brilliant smile:

"Shut your mouth, Herr Rittmeister or it will fill with flies. Here! I brought this for the devil dog"—she held out a perfect yellow rose, still wet with the morning dew—"he has better manners than his owner."

With that she thrust the rose into Mischa's hand and, reining her horse hard round, she was away up a side lane in a shower of dust, followed by the cheers and holloas of the delighted troopers.

"My God! That's some girl!" said Charles. "I wouldn't mind the chance of larning *her* a few manners."

Strange to tell, these was were almost the self-same words that the Khan was using to himself as he watched the little scene from a far hill through his looted telescope.

* * *

Anna's behaviour was the matter of some comment in the village during the next few days, as it fell back into its old peaceful routine after the excitement of the patrol's visit. Most of the comment was not favourable and of the 'that girl will come to no good' variety.

"The sooner Kurt gets that girl married and settled down, the better it will certainly be for both of them."

This was the position that the pastor put very forcefully to Mutti and Papa on one of his visits. Poor Mutti was frightened of the pastor, and damnation, in about equal quantities, and the pastor's stern admonitions about the dangers to Anna's immortal soul and the particular horrors that hell held in store for flighty young women, reduced her to floods of tears.

There were more tears when Kurt also took his turn. Kurt had been mortified by what he referred to as 'the goings on with the Cossacks'. His evening visits to Anna's house were made tedious by his sermons—almost as tedious as the pastor's—about the duties and attitudes required for marriage and motherhood. He was also extremely jealous.

Matters came to a head one evening with Mutti in tears, Papa smoking his pipe with unusual vigour—as might indicate strong emotion—and Kurt laying down the law of children, church and kitchen. Anna snapped, and leaping to her feet in a blaze of tearful anger, told Kurt that she never wished to speak to him again.

That night her wish was very nearly granted.

They came in the dead dark hours before the dawn. The village dogs had been uneasy all night, as though scenting that something bad was about. A dark sullen wind from the east had sprung up at the darkening, and its sour sighing over the roofs was like a howling of wolves.

It was the pastor who was first aware of trouble. A light sleeper, he was aroused from slumber by the sound of crackling. Rushing to his window, he saw the flickering light in the altar window of the wooden church and even as he watched there was a rush of fire up the little steeple, which imploded and fell inwards with a final crash from the bell. Seizing a bible the pastor rushed out into the street. He felt a crashing blow to the back of his head, then darkness.

By this time the village was wakening, and people were running out into the street in their night clothes or hastily gathered coats and cloaks. It was here that the horsemen fell upon them like wolves in a sheep fold.

More houses were burning and the flames lit up a hellish scene of milling, running, panic-stricken villagers and everywhere amongst them the dark shapes of the wheeling, trampling riders, their sabres rising and falling and the blood spilling into the dust of the road.

The first screams woke Anna. She had finally sunk into an uneasy sleep after lying awake unhappy and listening to the howl of the wind. She leaped from her bed and bumped into Matthias.

"What in the name of Christ is happening?"

"I don't know, Anna; I just heard these awful noises. I'm frightened."

Anna put her arm round the boy's thin shoulders:

"Hush now! We must find Mutti and Papa."

They crept into the kitchen.

The kitchen was lit through the window from the ghastly glow of the fires. By this light she could see that Papa had the old musket and his two pistols on the table. He was loading them with his customary quiet thoroughness. Mutti, all her fussing to one side now, was handing him powder horn and balls.

"Papa! Papa! What is it?"

"Bandits," said Papa priming the pan of one of the pistols. "Now listen, there is no time for anything else. Anna! Take

Matthias and these two pistols—you know how to use them. Get out through the back window and be careful. Go to the place behind the pigsty, where you used to hide when you were children. Stay there and do not move until well into daylight."

"But, Papa..."

"There is no time, child. Just for once, do as I tell you! And those pistols..."

"Yes, Papa?"

"They are for you and Matthias. Do not let the bandits get either of you alive, or you'll find there's hell in this world as well as the next."

"But you and Mutti...?"

"We are old. Now for God's sake and our sake, *go!*"

The four embraced, and could feel tears on the cheeks of one another. Then Anna pulled herself together. Hastily putting on a coat, she picked up her father's belt from the back of the chair and, buckling it round her, stuck the two pistols through it. Then, taking Matthias by the arm, she pushed the small shocked boy through the door to the back room.

She turned for one last look at her parents.

Mutti was praying and Papa was lighting his pipe.

Hell had come to the village. It was a hell, acrid with the smoke of burning houses, the flames of which showed the flitting shapes of the demons about their business: that business being the systematic plundering of the village.

There were the crashes of splintering doors being forced in. Any man who offered resistance was slaughtered. The women were dragged out screaming, and casually raped in any place available—including the street. Some of the younger ones were put aside for future sport. The very old and the very young were often thrown back into the flames of their houses.

Through all these ghastly scenes moved the dreadful figure of the Khan, hunched and brooding on his horse as he

rode up and down the street. He made no move to take part
in the mayhem; he just watched with a savage satisfaction as
the work continued.

By the time of the first grey light, most of the work was
done. The shivering, sobbing, terrified, survivors had been
driven like cattle, with knout and lance point, to the centre of
the village, where they huddled in terror. It was to these horrified people that the devil himself appeared, riding slowly
out of the acrid smoke on his great black horse, his black
cloak wrapped around him—he was indeed a creature from
the depths of the pit.

The Khan sat his horse and surveyed the shivering crowd
of women, children and men in front of him. He smiled. This
was always a good moment for him. This was *Power* and the
thought caused his loins to stir. Unhurried he sat and surveyed the crowd carefully and with interest. No, she was not
there.

She would not have been killed. The Khan's orders had
been specific and, even in the fury and lust of rape and de-
struction, the Khan's orders were always remembered and
obeyed. She, the Golden One, must be hidden.

At this moment there was a distraction. Two bandits came
dragging the stumbling figure of the pastor, still semi-
conscious after the blow to his head. They let him sink to his
knees in front of the Khan's horse.

"Their priest, Master," said one simply.

"Stand him up!"

The men lifted the pastor to his feet where he stood
swaying for a moment, before rallying and lifting his blood-
stained head to look at the Khan.

"Why?" he implored.

The Khan considered this question with interest; it had
never been asked of him before:

"For pleasure and profit." His voice came as a hoarse
growl.

The pastor seemed to gather some strength from deep

inside himself, and slowly and painfully straightened up. His voice that had been thin and cracked, now seemed to regain some of the strength of the pulpit:

"You are the devil incarnate! In the name of God and of Christ crucified, I curse you and yours and..."

The Khan gave a slight nod, and a musket butt in the stomach sent the pastor sagging and retching to the ground.

"In the name of your God and Christ crucified, eh?" said the Khan. "Let it be so—on that tree."

He pointed to the great oak that stood at the centre of the village.

The pastor was a brave man. He made no sound, except a mumble of prayer when they hammered the first nails into his hands, but when they came to the knees and feet, the pain overcame him, and the prayers turned into a long thin scream of agony, mercifully cut short when he fainted.

A great wailing and crying went up from the terrified villagers. The bandits set about them with their knouts until the noise was reduced to a whimpering.

"Now!" The Khan did not need to raise his voice, his harsh raven-like croak could be clearly heard: "I might butcher you all, but that takes time and I want to be away. There is just one more thing that I need. Give me that and I might spare the rest of you. In this village there is a girl with long golden hair. She is called Anna. I want her."

"No!"

A figure, ghastly with matted blood, rose from the bushes in a nearby garden.

Kurt's first thought when he had realised that there was a raid, had been to get to Anna and protect her. Seeing the confusion and mayhem in the street, he had been trying to make his way through the gardens to her house, when a pistol ball smashed his shoulder. He had tried to continue, clutching his useless arm, but he had fallen trying to climb a fence. The pain overcame him and drove him into blackness, and he had lain amongst the shrubs unnoticed.

His return to consciousness had been slow and painful. He had heard the screams and shouts and had realised that his only hope of survival was in lying as still and as quiet as he could. Kurt was no coward, but he was in no condition to help anybody.

Through the stems of the shrubs he had heard and witnessed the crucifixion of the pastor, and had bitten his lip until it bled. He longed to leap to his feet and lay about the pastor's tormentors, like Christ amongst the money lenders. He knew that it would have availed him nothing. So he lay and listened and prayed for the deliverance of his people, but then came the Khan's demand for Anna. He could stand no more.

"No!"

Two of the bandits leaped over the low fence and threw Kurt bodily into the road. He landed on his broken shoulder and screamed.

The Khan gave a croak of laughter:

"Now that's more like it. I know you," he said to the writhing Kurt. "I've seen you through my little glass: you and the Golden One. You will know where she is and *you* will tell me."

"No!" said Kurt again, through gritted teeth.

"Show him!" snapped the Khan.

Grinning hugely, a muscular bandit stepped forward, pulled the wooden fence away from a gate post and, with a few deft strokes of an axe, put a long sharp point to the top of the post.

"That one," said the Khan, pointing to a grey-bearded man leaning on a stick. "It's time he died anyway."

The bandits thought this immensely funny. Two of them seized the old man, stripped off his torn clothing and, lifting his shrivelled body with ease by shoulders and knees so that he was bent double, they raised him till the point of the stake touched his rectum, then pushed down.

The scream seemed to go on for ever, then stopped suddenly in a ghastly silence as the old man's body still twitched and shuddered in an appalling dance of death.

"Now! Tell me where the girl is."

Kurt, wracked with pain and choked with horror, shook his head.

"Another stake!"

"No!"

This time it was a woman's voice; a woman who broke from the crowd and came to Kurt, sobbing and throwing her arms around him.

"No! Please! He is my only son."

"Very touching."

"If I tell you where the girl is, will you spare my son?"

"If you tell me, woman, I will not impale your son, on my word of honour."

"Mother, no!"

"I must, son, I must. Never mind that slut. All of this is her fault."

"No! In God's name, no!"

Kurt's mother pointed past the smouldering ruin which had been Anna's house:

"At the bottom of the garden at the back. Behind the pig-sty. There is a hiding place there. She and my Kurt used to hide there when they were children. But I knew. A mother always knows. Just save my boy as you promised."

"I will keep my promise."

The Khan shouted an order and men went leaping away past the ruins of the house.

Anna and Matthias had been lying clasped in each other's arms. The little lean-to behind the pigsty was where the brushwood faggots were kept. Years ago, Anna had hollowed out a space at the back. By pulling the faggots back over the entrance there was a dark little womb-like space with just room for two.

Brother and sister had listened with horror to the sound

of the raid. They had heard the smashing of the door and the blast of Papa's musket. Later they heard the crackle of the flames. They heard the screams. Then the sounds had become more distant. Grey light filtered through the screen of faggots. Dawn was coming. Surely the bandits would not stay long in the daylight.

Perhaps the Cossacks would come back with the devil dog and his owner. Perhaps...

Anna stiffened. She heard the voices and the approach of running feet. The men came straight to the pigsty and paused outside the lean-to. They were panting and laughing and she could smell their rank odour. They knew.

"Oh A-n-n-a! Come out!" Then more coarse laughter.

Anna paused no more; she cocked the pistols.

"Close your eyes, darling boy," she said. "We will soon be with Mutti and Papa. Oh God, forgive me!"

And putting the pistol to the child's head she pulled the trigger.

The explosion had the men tearing at the brush wood.

Anna felt very cold and calm now. As the first leering bearded face appeared through the opening in the brushwood, she put the other pistol to her own temple and pulled the trigger.

The pistol misfired.

Anna felt nothing. She felt nothing as the callused hands pulled her still wet with her brother's blood from her hiding place. She felt nothing as the hands slid over her body, squeezing her breasts and exploring with rough fingers between her thighs. She felt nothing when the large bandit pulled her against him and stared rubbing himself against her buttocks.

She could hear the rough laughter. She could hear the coarse words that hissed in her ear about all the things that they would do to her after 'the Master' had finished with her, and thrown her out like a bone to be worried over by the pack. She would be ready for anything then, they told her, a willing and well-broken whore, ready for their sport. But now she must be kept for the Master; she would be a well-ridden mare by the time he had had his way.

All these things she heard. She smelled the rancid breath as they were hissed in her ear, and the foul stink of the unwashed bodies. But she felt nothing. It was as though she was two persons. One was the ragged and bloodstained girl who was being manhandled and dragged towards the street. The other person was a tall and beautiful girl who walked proud and free and who could not be touched, whatever happened to the husk of her body.

This girl left the shattered corpse of her small brother, walked past the smoking ruins of what had been her home and had become the tomb of her parents. This was the girl who cold, erect and silent was bundled into the street, in front of the cowering villagers and the encircling bandits. Two of her captors pulled her into the centre of the circle.

"Loose her!" croaked a voice.

It was a voice full of death and pain and burning villages. Anna looked straight ahead, erect and expressionless. A great black horse was pushed in front of her. She could see a booted leg. Still she did not look up.

"Look at me, bitch!" said the voice.

Anna did not move.

A hand from behind seized her hair and forced her head back. For the first time she looked on the Khan and felt evil ooze over her like slime. In spite of herself she shuddered, then her inner self took charge. She must hold herself together. Whatever terrible things this man might do to her body, she must make sure that he never touched her soul.

"Do you know who I am, girl?"

Anna gathered her silence round her like a protective cloak. The Khan's beard twitched in a smile:

"Dumb eh? Well, bitch, you will learn who I am soon enough, and I will make you sing like a nightingale."

"Anna!"

The voice came feebly from the edge of the crowd and pierced Anna's shell. She looked round. Kurt lay on the ground cradled in his mother's arms.

"Oh, Kurt!" cried Anna in spite of herself and, tearing herself away, knelt beside him.

"Jezebel!" Kurt's mother hissed. "This is all because of you."

Anna paid no attention, but reached out a hand to the young man.

"Oh Kurt!"

"Very touching!" came the snarl. "The bitch speaks after all. Take her! We must go."

Once again Anna was seized and bundled onto the back of a horse, her feet tied to the stirrup leathers and her wrists to the pommel of the saddle. A noose was put round her neck and the loose end tied to her wrists, in such a way that she was obliged to bend to avoid tightening the noose.

"Now him!" the Khan pointed his whip at Kurt.

"No!" screamed his mother. She ran forward and seized the Khan's booted foot. "No! You promised if I told you where the girl was..."

The Khan's voice was like silk:

"I promised not to impale your pup and I always keep my word. I am merciful. He may stay with his betrothed—whilst he can."

He snapped an order. Kurt was hustled roughly to his feet. Anna could see the pain on his face, but he made no sound. His wrists were tied together, then attached to a long cord, the other end of which was knotted to where Anna's wrists were tied.

In spite of the agony of his shattered shoulder, Kurt raised his bound wrists and placed his hands on Anna's. They did not speak, just looked at each other. Kurt was crying. In spite of her forced inner detachment, Anna could not resist Kurt's pain. She could feel the hot tears running down her face.

"Good," came the Khan's croak. "The ice is melting. Enjoy your time together. Now we march."

All the cattle and horses of the village had been gathered and the road was loud with lowing and whinnying as, with whistles and shouts, the bandits got them moving. The little band of surviving villagers stood shocked, silent and shaking in the smoke-stained morning air as they saw the wealth of their village being driven past them, their treasured personal possessions packed onto the backs of horses.

The Khan reined his horse in front of the terrified people.

"You are lucky that I am in a good mood," he said. "You may live to tell the soldiers of the Khan's mercy."

With a shout of laughter he swung his horse away.

A bandit reached over from his saddle and took the reins of Anna's horse, jerking it into movement. For a moment, Kurt's hands stayed on Anna's, then dropped away. He clung to Anna's stirrup leather. Their eyes still held each other as he walked beside her.

The riders broke into a jog trot.

Kurt had to run.

Then, with one last pain-ridden glance, Kurt was forced to let go of the stirrup leather and he disappeared from Anna's sight.

Anna could not turn her head and could only watch in silent horror as the rope that attached Kurt's wrists to her saddle lengthened, then became taut as Kurt staggered and eventually fell.

The stones in the road flayed the skin from his body inch by inch, but he never made a sound.

At last a bandit brought his horse alongside Anna's mount and, leaning over, he cut the taut rope. He gave Anna a wolfish grin:

"There's no point in pulling dead meat about."

* * *

"What's the matter with Sirius?" asked Charles.

The Cossacks were camped by a stream two days' march from the village. The three officers were sprawled at ease around a fire. Sirius had been behaving oddly all evening, restless and whining.

"I don't know," said Mischa, ruffling the big dog's head. "What is it, my son?"

"Perhaps there's a bitch in that German village, he's got a lech for," said Charles slyly.

Mischa refused to rise. His hand was on the prayer book in his pocket, in which a yellow rose was pressed. He just grunted and, rolling himself in his blankets, prepared for sleep under the stars.

"Come on Sirius! Come to bed."

But Sirius continued his restless prowling all through the night, and in the grey light of the pre-dawn he began to howl.

7 In the Valley of Death

"**B**ONE!"

"Sir!"

"My compliments to Rittmeister Czerny and tell him for Christ's sake to shut that bloody dog up. I've hardly had a wink of sleep."

Thus saying, Captain Lord Charles FitzHugh pulled his blankets over his head to shut out the cold grey dawn of the steppe and the fine grey drizzle that had come with it.

"Come on, Sir, it's revally and here's a nice cup of Rosie."

"Sod you, Bone. Sod your fucking tea and sod that sodding dog," said the pile of blankets.

"Very good, Sir," said ex-Trooper Bone, totally unmoved by his officer's tantrum, "but it's still revally."

"Sirius! Come here!"

The big dog crept to Mischa, whining and miserable, his ears back and his hairy tail between his legs. Mischa gently ruffled the hair on the great head and stroked the ears between his fingers.

"What on earth's the matter, old man? You've been in a fuss and a state all night."

"What's the trouble with Sirius, Mischa?"—Major Lubin approached the fire where Mischa was sitting—"Perhaps it's this damned miserable morning. Spring time in the Caucasus, eh?"

Sirius suddenly came to attention, standing rigid, ears and tail cocked. Then with a couple of little barks, he bounded towards a figure looming out of the drizzle and leaped around him ecstatically. The figure resolved itself into a huge bearded man with a wide-brimmed hat and a ragged cloak wrapped round him.

"Good heavens!" said Mischa getting to his feet. "Hunter!

123

What on earth are you doing here?"

Lubin wiped his monocle with a handkerchief:

"Damn this rain! I heard no challenge from the picquets! My God! I'll have the skin off somebody's back for this— Sarn't Major!"

"No! No!" said the Hunter, shaking the moisture from his hat so that the little fire sizzled. "Your picquets are not to blame. They cannot see what isn't there."

"Dammit! You're here and we can see you."

Even as they watched the Hunter disappeared.

"Dammit! What an extraordinary feller! Where's the beggar gone now?"

"Here!" said a voice over Lubin's left shoulder, causing Lubin's monocle to pop out of his eye.

"Dammit!" he said again, furiously screwing the glass back into his eye.

"Noise! Noise! Noise! If it's not that bloody dog, it's you old women wittering on."

Charles came stumbling up to the fire, hugging himself against the chill. Bone appeared silently behind him, draped his cloak over his shoulders and, still without a word, reached round to fasten the clasp.

"Oh bugger off, Bone!" then, "Good Heavens, Mr Hunter! What are you doing here?"

"Ah! So you can see him too," said Lubin.

"Of course, I can see him. He's standing right behind you."

"Is he, indeed, well I wouldn't care to bet on it." Lubin looked gloomy.

"Enough!" said the Hunter, "I am not here to play games. There's trouble."

"Where?" Lubin dropped his normal languid attitude.

"The German village."

"But we were there. What? Two days ago. What the devil's happened?"

"The Devil has happened. The bandits came."

"My God! When?"

"In the night."

Lubin opened his mouth to ask how the Hunter knew all this, then shut his mouth again. There are some questions best left unasked. Instead he strode off shouting for his troop commanders and the Sergeant Major.

Vlad was hurriedly packing Mischa's valise and, in doing so, dropped Mischa's prayer book. The yellow rose that had been pressed between the pages, spilled out onto the ground. Sirius sniffed it and whined. Mischa picked it up carefully and put it back between the pages before handing the book to Vlad.

Then he turned to ask the Hunter a question, but the Hunter had disappeared. 'Anyway,' Mischa thought, 'there are some questions best left unasked; then there was hope.'

All that day the Cossacks rode at a steady distance-devouring trot, a screen of scouts moving ahead of the patrol; there was nothing languid about Lubin's approach to action.

By evening the forced pace brought them to the brow of the hill above the German village. The drizzle had cleared away, leaving a clear, watery-skied evening.

"Jesus!" Charles stood up in his stirrups.

"Suffering Christ!" Mischa was aghast.

"Trot march!" commanded Lubin.

The blackened remains of the once neat houses were still smouldering as the patrol rode along the ruined street. As they did so the bloodied and begrimed survivors crept out of whatever shelter in which they had managed to huddle. They had been too shocked and frightened to do anything else. The bodies still lay in the streets. The body of the old man was still hideously impaled on the post. The pastor was also mercifully dead on his tree.

After the bandits had gone, some of the villagers had tried to get him down, but his agony had been such that they had become frightened and backed away. His screams and prayers for death became so terrible that one of his church wardens picked up the musket that he had been too frightened to use during the bandit raid and, putting it to the pastor's head, he had closed his eyes and pulled the trigger.

The survivors clamoured round Lubin, telling him of the horror of the previous night, when their peaceful village had been cast into hell.

"I say," Charles pointed. "Ain't that our cow? You remember, Mischa."

Mischa, looking at the bloated and swollen corpse of poor Heidi lying in the road, did indeed remember. He turned to an old man, one side of whose face was encrusted with blood from a sabre cut:

"What happened to the girl—the girl with the cow?"

The old man spat.

"They took her. The bandits took her. She was the reason they came here—the whore!"

"Whore? What do you mean, whore?" Mischa turned on the man ferociously.

"Well if she wasn't before, she will be by now."

The old man shrugged and spat again.

Anna ached. The leather thongs that bound her wrists to the pommel of the saddle cut into her skin. The rough leather of the saddle chafed her naked thighs. The running noose round her neck kept her crouched forward in an unnatural position so that her back ached.

Her whole body was pain. She could feel this pain and in a way she welcomed it, because inside she felt nothing; she felt no fear, no hurt, no sorrow. Inside, it was as though her soul had died. It was as though there were two Annas. There was a detached Anna who hovered over the wretched, grimy, stained, husk of a girl jolting along on a jogging horse. It was only the physical pain that reminded her that she was still alive.

It was the physical pain that made her groan occasionally. This greatly amused the bandit who was leading her horse. It greatly amused him, also, to tell Anna of the great delights that lay in store for her, and the esoteric methods that his lord, the Khan, used to 'pleasure' his women. He also told her in graphic detail of the Khan's legendary physical attributes:

"He will make you scream, slut, how you will scream! Then, when he has finished with you, you will scream for us."—he reached across and ran a filthy hand through Anna's golden hair—"My name is Aslan, and when the time comes, I will give you cause to remember it."

The Khan was impatient and wracked with lust. He wished now that he had taken Anna, there and then in the village, in front of all the people. He had done this with the Russian woman when he had captured her. It was a fine way of starting the breaking-in process and a fine display of power.

But he wanted to savour this one. He had waited a long time for her. He could wait a little longer, but not much. He was impatient with the pace. It had been a rich village and the Khan was pleased with the great herd of cattle: good cattle and fine horses that would fetch a high price when taken over the border amongst the Chechens and Ossetians. But cattle travelled slowly.

He made a decision. He called for his nephew, his principal lieutenant—the Khan liked to keep his business in the family, in the clan. He told the nephew to keep enough men with him to bring the cattle and horses on to Tearnause. He would go ahead with the others and the loot; he had some urgent business to attend to. The nephew grinned a wolf-like grin; his uncle would take the 'urgent business' with him. The Khan grunted and ran his tongue round his thin lips.

"What about the Cossacks, Uncle?"

The Khan snorted:

"Cossacks! All they're thinking about is getting back to Pyatigorsk. It'll be a week before they even hear of our little jaunt. We'll be safely tucked up in the mountains before they've even had time for a decent shit."

The Khan's territory was based on a steep valley that ran up from the foothills, getting deeper and steeper the while, to the very foot of the mighty Mount Elbrus. The jagged mountains on either side of this large valley were both a protection from attack and a place of refuge for agile mountain men in time of trouble. The only entrance to this valley was a rocky road that ran along the valley floor, beside the snow-fed, rushing river, and at last climbed over a steep, narrow—and easily defended—pass to the lands and tribes on the other side of Elbrus.

The Khan's main base was a village at the head of the valley; but there were a series of villages below this, each one of which provided a line of defence against intruders.

Tearnause was the lowest of these villages and was almost a small town, with a market, where those from the steppes and foothills traded with the wild mountainy men and tribes from beyond Elbrus. The market supplied the Khan with a healthy income. He was a keen business man and it occurred to him that Anna would fetch a good price in the market, once he had finished with her. It then occurred to him that in the meantime he might well sell the Russian woman on. Too many women were a nuisance, and there were the four wives safe at home at the top of the valley to be considered. Their needs had been somewhat neglected of late.

The Khan sighed at the burden of his duties; the fat sows only produced daughters anyway—more women. The Khan wanted a son; more than anything he wanted a son. A man was nothing without a male heir. What use were daughters to him? No, family duties could wait whilst he dealt with his 'urgent business'.

He felt a hot surge of lust and, reining his horse round, he cantered back down the column to where Anna sat bound and bowed on her horse. The Khan pulled his horse up alongside Anna, and reaching across with a black-haired hand, casually ripped down the front of her torn nightdress revealing the well rounded pink-nippled breasts. With the butt of his whip the Khan rubbed each nipple in turn. Anna moaned.

Still saying nothing, the Khan reached across and, with a finger and thumb still stained with the night's blood, he squeezed a nipple until Anna, in spite of herself, screamed with the pain and tried to throw her head back in an instinctive reaction. The noose tightened and the scream died in a choking gurgle.

The surrounding bandits roared with laughter.

The Russian woman prepared herself with care, rubbing her body with scented oils and carefully brushing out her long hair—the long hair that the Khan liked to seize and force her to her knees in front of him.

She gave a little shiver of pleasurable fear at the thought of it. She knew from experience what her master was like when he returned from a raid: how he would stride through the door, stinking of blood, sweat and lust. She knew that he would use her roughly, grunting and roaring on top of her as he loosed all his pent-up tensions; but first she would have to tease him with her lips and her tongue, tasting the rank male scent of his massive body.

She thought of the burning heat of him thrusting inside her and shivered again—his pleasure had become her pleasure—he was her master.

The Russian woman was kept at Tearnause in the Khan's house there. She had long realised that there was no escape for her from the village and she had a certain freedom now, and was allowed to wander round the wretched market place, always accompanied by the silent slave girl who acted as her maid. The girl was silent because she had screamed too much when first brought there as a captive. The Khan had had her tongue cut out—a lesson that had not been lost on the Russian woman.

The girl was rubbing the oils into the Russian woman's back and her fingers lingered over the woman's rounded buttocks. The woman arched her back with pleasure and the fingers delved a little deeper.

Anna was drifting in and out of consciousness. Her whole body was wracked with pain and exhaustion. What was worse was that the numbness of the shock that had anaesthetised her mind was beginning to wear off. The full horror of the recent past and the present was beginning to seep in.

As to the future, she fought desperately to keep that out of her mind; if the night and the ride had been hell, then the future would plumb its deepest caverns. She tried to pray, but where was God that He should let such horror happen? The Khan was never far from her side and, in spite of the increased pace, he would still reach over from time to time and run a filthy hand over her body. Her flesh crawled at his touch. She knew that this was as nothing to what was to come.

Anna was jolted back into consciousness by the sudden realisation that they had stopped. She was dimly aware of a jagged stone wall and a barrier across the road. The barrier was dragged aside by armed men and Anna saw that they were riding into a village. It was a mean place, with rough stone houses clinging to the steep rocky hillside amidst a scattering of scrawny trees. Below the rocky track that passed as a street, the houses spread down the hillside to the roaring torrent of a river that tumbled over its boulder-strewn bed. On either side of the valley, barren rock hillsides, with a scattering of woods in the gullies, soared up to become ragged mountain peaks.

Anna searched desperately in her mind for some crumb of comfort. There came to her the deep voice of her father reading the words of the 23rd Psalm: *'The Lord is my shepherd...'* She felt that this was indeed *'the valley of the shadow of death.'*

The inhabitants of the mean houses came rushing to the sides of the road to greet the returning bandits, laughing and screeching with delight as the men boasted of their great deeds, and of the huge herd of plump cattle and fine horses that were following on behind—a fine dividend for a valley whose main industry was robbery.

The ragged, black-teethed women screeched with mirth at the sight of Anna.

"Another fine mare for the lord to ride."

Handfuls of filth, scooped from the road, splattered over Anna.

The Khan roared with laughter:

"Don't worry, I'll have you cleaned up before I take my pleasure with you."

It was too much, and Anna felt the hot tears, that she had

kept back so long, course over her downcast cheeks.

They turned through a gate in a dry-stone wall and Anna could see that they were in the courtyard of a house that was less mean than the others. Her bonds were cut and rough hands pulled her out of the saddle. She would have crumpled to the ground with fatigue but was held upright.

The Khan sat on his horse, bellowing. Through her mist of pain and tears, Anna saw a tall, handsome, dark-haired woman appear in the doorway of the house, a smile fixed on her face.

The Russian woman had heard the clatter of hooves and the cries of the crowd. As the gates of the courtyard were opened, she had put on her best smile and went to the door to greet her master but, at the sight of Anna, her smile vanished and a cold fear gripped her head. She could see that this poor, filthy, blood-stained creature, sagging between two bandits, was young and extremely beautiful. She could also see the way the Khan was looking at the girl. She knew that look. It was the way that the Khan had been accustomed to look at her. She had a rival.

At this moment a man came running through the gate and, approaching the Khan, tugged at his boot. The Khan, who had been licking Anna with his eyes, growled at this interruption:

"Well! What in Satan's name do you want?"

The man beckoned for the Khan to bend down and whispered something to him.

"*What!*"—the Khan straightened up as though he had been shot in the back—"*What! All of them?*"

The man nodded, backing nervously away.

"*All four of them?*"

The man still nodded.

"Hell and damnation! Where are they?"

"At the hetman's house," stammered the thoroughly discomfited man, who knew what tended to happen to carriers of bad news.

"*Damn! Damn! Damn!* You," he shouted, pointing his whip

at the Russian woman, "take this bitch, and get her cleaned up and ready for me when I return, or I'll take the skin off your back."

"What has happened, Lord?" asked one of the bandits. "Are the Cossacks coming?"

"Cossacks? You think I would make a fuss over a few verminous Cossacks?" Then his voice dropped, and he suddenly had a hunted look. "My wives have come down the valley—all four of them. I wish the bloody Cossacks *would* come."

With a visible effort the Khan pulled himself together:

"And you,"—pointing his whip at the Russian woman again—"make sure that the slut's a virgin."

The Russian woman's smile remained fixed.

They were sitting in a line on some hastily arranged cushions in what passed as the best room in the hetman's house:

'Like four bundles of dirty washing,' the Khan thought as he paused in the doorway and arranged his face into what he fondly imagined to be an ingratiating smile.

The four women were ranged in order of seniority. The youngest at the end of the line was obviously and heavily pregnant. The Khan's face softened a bit as he regarded her—this time it had to be a son. He could not bear the thought of more daughters. His house at the head of the valley had become a bear garden and all the bears were female.

The Khan spent as little time there as politeness and duty allowed. His marriages were all political, the ladies all representing important clan factions whose goodwill the Khan required to maintain his position. He had never heard the phrase 'uneasy lies the head that wears a crown,' but in the snake pit of tribal and local politics, the Khan knew the importance of protecting his back. His marriages were vital for this; domestic harmony must be maintained at all costs.

"And how are the jewels in my crown?" he cried with an expansive gesture that sought to embrace them all.

The four women regarded him in stony silence, all except the youngest who simpered a little.

"This is indeed a wonderful welcome for a returning

warrior, I come laden with gifts for you."

The silence continued, until the Senior Wife hawked and spat a gob of phlegm onto the already filthy floor.

"We have come to speak to you, husband."

"Yes! Yes! And so you shall, but first look at the gifts that I have brought you,"—he shouted an order and two men came in laden with things looted from the German village—"See, fine cloth! And look, see these splendid copper cooking pots. My wives will have the finest kitchen in the Caucasus. Quickly, fools! Lay them out!"

The two men unpacked the bundles hurriedly, and laid the items out in a row in front of the silent women.

"And for the one who bears my son, I bring this fine gold necklace."

He ran the gold chain through his fingers with some reluctance, for he loved the feel of gold and hated to part with it. Then he held it out to the pregnant one who, simpering again, reached out for it eagerly. The collective growl from the other three women stopped them both. The Khan felt a trickle of cold sweat run down his back. This was rebellion, a palace revolt. He ought to whip the lot of them—except the one carrying his son, of course—but he dare not and the women knew it.

The Senior Wife stuck out a horny foot and kicked a pot, sending it clattering across the room.

Number Two Wife picked up a fine silk scarf and ostentatiously wiped her nose on it.

Number Three Wife, who was never terribly quick on the uptake, was still pondering on an appropriate method of protest, when the Senior Wife spoke again:

"Baubles! Trinkets! That is all you ever want to think about husband! Are we whores to be bought with such tomfoolery?"

"Lights of my life! You are my wives and..."

"Exactly husband! We are your wives and when did you last do your duty by us?"

The Khan plucked at his beard, a sure sign of disquietude —for the life of him he just could not remember, but he rallied gamely:

"Not done my duty! How, pray then, is she carrying my son?"

He gestured towards Number Four Wife, who could not help simpering again: after all, she was the youngest and best favoured of the four, not that she would ever have dared say so. She was properly frightened of the Senior Wife, who was very handy with a mule stick.

"How do you know that it is a son?" the Senior Wife was remorseless.

"Well, after all those daughters..."

"And whose fault was that, husband?"

"It's the man's seed that sows the corn," said Number Two Wife in sepulchral tones.

All this time, Number Three Wife had been rocking to and fro as though generating the energy to speak. At last she gathered sufficient momentum:

"We want sons, too."

"What?"

"We want sons, too."

The Khan actually pulled a small tuft out of his beard. The pain made his eyes water momentarily.

"Well, I am sure that in the fullness of time..."

The Senior Wife gave a dry cackle of a laugh:

"You seem to forget husband that without a sowing, there can be no harvest. The time has come to its fullness."

The Khan rocked visibly back on his heels.

"What, now?"

The three women nodded in unison.

"All of you?"

"All of us."

The Khan began to chew a hank of his moustache:

"Ladies! Supreme objects of my desire! It will of course be my pleasure and honour to visit you, as soon as certain matters of business have been taken care of. A leader's work is never done..."

"Now!" said Number Three Wife.

"Here!" said Number Two Wife.

"And you don't leave until we have all agreed that you have done your duty satisfactorily."

"But I have urgent matters to attend to!"

The Senior Wife dropped another gob of phlegm accurately between his boots:

"Your new whore will just have to wait her turn."

The Khan sighed. He was beaten and he knew it. He looked at the Senior Wife without great enthusiasm. His personal and private feeling was that one beard in a marriage was quite enough, but...

Anna had been dragged into the Russian woman's hut by two bandits. She stood there, shivering, shocked and exhausted—only vaguely aware of her surroundings—it was all just part of the nightmare in which she was now living. She wondered through the mist of suffering whether she did want to go on living. Life seemed to hold only the prospect of new horror.

"She's all yours," said one of the bandits, fondling Anna's naked breasts.

Taking one of her nipples between finger and thumb, he squeezed until the pain made Anna throw her head back.

"Don't bruise the merchandise," said his companion. "His Excellency don't like spoiled goods."

"She'll be bruised enough by the time he's finished with her; then I'll bruise the bitch properly."

The other man licked his lips, his eyes on the Russian woman:

"A well-broken mare is a better ride. They all know how to give pleasure by the time that the Khan has finished with them. It will be great pleasure."

They both looked at the Russian woman and laughed. The Russian woman kept her smile fixed on her face, but felt the fear that she always lived with grip her more tightly.

"She does look a tight-arsed bitch, that Russian."

"Well, you're an expert on that little problem," said his companion, and they left the hut slapping each other on the back and laughing happily.

The Russian woman shut the door of the hut and leaned

back against it, taking deep breaths to calm her incipient panic. She was under no illusions as to what would happen to her if the Khan tired of her. She did not see Anna as an object of pity. She saw her as a threat to her position and survival. The girl must be frightened and humiliated to such an extent that she would prove to be a great disappointment for her master. He would then realise the Russian woman's skill and expertise was such that he would discard this other slut and throw her husk to his wolves.

Anna was still standing, her head bowed in misery. The Russian woman walked across to her, lifted her chin roughly and slapped her face with the other hand:

"Listen to me, girl, I am the mistress here and you will do exactly as I say."

She thrust her face close to Anna's so that the girl smelled her scented body:

"I am to prepare you for my master and his pleasure, although I think he will find little pleasure in a streak of skinny misery like you. Then he will find out that it needs a real woman to give him the pleasure that he wants. I shall watch whilst he breaks you. He likes me to watch. *He* also likes to watch. Perhaps he will want you to give *me* a little pleasure— and you will do exactly what you are told—then perhaps you will survive a little longer, do you understand?"

As she was talking, she began to fondle Anna's breasts.

"No! Please!" Anna shuddered with horror.

"Oh yes! Now strip!"

"No!"

The Russian woman slapped her again. She crooked her finger and the mute slave came from the corner where she had been waiting.

"Strip her!"

Anna stood in dull fear and misery, but the girl's hands were gentle on her and she looked into the eyes of the ravaged face. There she saw a sparkle of sympathy. That brief flash of silent comfort gave Anna a small surge of inner strength. She straightened up and stared straight ahead as the now filthy rags were stripped from her body.

"Skin and bone!" said the Russian woman. "The master won't like that. We'd have to fatten you up a bit if you were going to survive, but you'll be being ridden round the village before that. Now wash her."

From a cauldron hanging over the fire in the corner, the mute ladled some warm water into a basin.

Once again, the girl's hands were gentle as she washed the accumulated filth and blood from Anna's body and combed the mats from the long blond hair. The very fact of being clean again revived Anna still further, but she remained still and silent.

"Now the scented oil. Yes, but I think that I will do this myself."

The feel of the Russian woman's hands made Anna want to cringe, but she still stood straight and stared at the wall, even when the woman's hands lingered between her buttocks.

"Hmm! Perhaps we might make something of you after all. Now lie down."

The woman pointed to the pile of furs. Anna did not move.

"I warned you!" The woman's voice was thick.

She seized Anna by the hair and dragged her to the furs. Anna screamed with the pain.

"Bring the collar! We'll tether the bitch."

The mute came carrying a large leather collar with a long rope attached to it. The Russian woman buckled the collar round Anna's neck.

"Now! Let us see if this rose bud is indeed intact."

Spreading Anna's legs, the Russian woman stroked her finger down through the golden triangle of curls and began to probe between them.

Something snapped in Anna's mind—like a great flash of lightning, as though her whole mind was suffused with blood. She smashed a fist into the Russian woman's face and, as the woman reeled back in shock and pain, Anna seized the loose length of the trailing rope and, wrapping it round the woman's neck, she began to pull with an almost superhuman strength. Then blackness overcame her.

The mute squatted on her haunches and watched closely as the Russian woman's eyes bulged, her tongue protruded and her face engorged. Only when the body finally stopped twitching, did she loosen Anna's hands from the rope and gently push her back.

Anna's eyes were wide and her body rigid with shock. The mute gently pushed her back onto the furs, where she sat motionless and unstirring whilst the mute removed the collar from her neck and methodically coiled up the rope. Ignoring the twisted body of her erstwhile mistress, the mute returned to squat in her corner. For the first time in many, many, months she was smiling.

* * *

"How are the horses, Sarn't Major?"

The giant Squadron Sergeant Major ran his fingers through a massive beard.

"All sound, Excellency, but they have just done a sixty *verst* forced march."

"Sound for action?"

"They are Cossack horses, Excellency."

"Right then—loosen girths, a light feed, and see the men get some food."

"It is an honour to obey your order, Excellency."

The Sergeant Major gave the traditional response of the Russian army and marched away down the dismounted column, bellowing orders.

Lubin, Charles, Mischa and the troop commanders were in conference by the still-smouldering ruins of the church. Lubin took out his monocle and polished it.

"We must follow these bastards."

"Do we know where they have gone?" asked one of the troop commanders.

"They should be easy to track with all those horses and cattle," said Mischa rubbing his bristly chin—he needed a shave, and he hated being unshaven.

"And they ain't going to be travelling too fast, not with all those cattle."

"We have another advantage," said Lubin. "The bandits will not expect their nastiness to have been discovered so soon. They think that they will have their loot safely back in the mountains before the hounds hit off their scent."

Mischa thought of the girl with the golden hair and felt his stomach churn. He clenched his hands and murmured to himself: *"Hail Mary, full of grace, have mercy on that poor child."*

"Ha! Ha!" said Charles. "A bit of sport, eh? A bit of the old cut and thrust, what!"

He drew his sword and ran his thumb along the edge:

"Bone!"

"Sir!"

"You must have been opening your granny's letters with this. Find a grindstone and get an edge on it."

"Sir!"

"I must say," said Charles, "this Khan chap does sound a bit of a swine. The sooner we get him filleted the better."

"You must catch your fish before you cook it," came a deep voice.

They all turned. No one had seen the Hunter since his appearance at the camp. Sirius bounded around him in delight.

"...and the Khan is a slippery fish indeed."

"Do you know where he is?" asked Lubin.

"It is my opinion that he will be too fly to stay with the cattle. He will have left most of the band with them and ridden on to his valley. Do you want my advice?"

"I have learned to value it," said Lubin, dryly.

"Very well then, you must make the most of your surprise. The Khan will not expect pursuit so quickly. If you stop to take the cattle, word will get to him and the valley will be a hornet's nest. My feeling is that he will have stopped at the first village in the valley for a little celebration of his triumph and will be off his guard. Give the cattle a wide berth—you can get them on the way back—ride straight for the rat's nest."

"And cut off the king rat's tail with a carving knife, what?"

"And the girl?" asked Mischa.

The Hunter gave him a long steady stare:

"You must hurry."

* * *

The Khan was weary and was slumped in the saddle as he rode down the village street. Whenever he had been in the past, a bull amongst a herd of cows, he had vaguely thought that that might be no bad form of reincarnation; now he was by no means so certain. He had spent two days penned up in the hetman's house about his pleasurable duty—he shuddered at the word.

The Senior Wife had been particularly demanding. He had fondly imagined that at her age she would be past all that, or, at least, thankful for small mercies, instead of which... And he shuddered again.

What he really needed now was a good sleep, but first he wanted to see how the Russian woman had got on with her task, and to feast his eyes on his prize, his golden prize. Perhaps the sight of it would reinvigorate him—and the Russian woman was an inventive slut... Anyway, there was no hurry: the waiting would make the defloration all the more exciting for him when it came.

The guard at the yard gate hurried to take the Khan's horse. All was well, he told the Khan, no one had been in or out of the house, except for the slave girl going to fetch food. There had been no sign of the Russian woman, but no doubt she was making all ready for the Excellency's return. The guard had the good sense to say all of this with a straight face.

With increasingly keen anticipation, the Khan strode across the yard and threw open the door of the house.

The stench hit him.

"Hell's blood!"

The Khan was no stranger to horror, but the blackened, bloated face with the protruding tongue and staring eyes, that looked up at him from the floor, made him recoil with a yell that brought the guards running.

The Khan forced himself back through the door and took

in the scene within.

The Russian woman lay in the middle of the floor in a haze of flies. In the far corner Anna, naked, was sitting with her arms clasped around her knees and her head bent. She never moved nor raised her head at all the noise and shouting. The little mute was crouched beside Anna with her arms round her, as though trying to protect her from horrors present and future. She stared up at the towering figure of the Khan with terror in her eyes. This revived the Khan mightily.

"Get that sack of offal out of here," he bellowed at the men. "And get this floor swabbed down. You"—he pointed at the guards—"spawn of Satan, I will talk to later. Just now, I have other shashlik to roast."

And, turning, he gave the little mute the full horror of his smile.

Once the room was clear, the Khan drove the other men out and shut the door.

The little slave girl pulled Anna to her more tightly. The Khan seized Anna by a wrist and pulled her roughly to her feet, leaving the other girl sprawling.

Anna stood swaying weakly her head still bowed.

The Khan spent a long moment, his eyes licking over Anna's naked body, then he seized her hair and roughly jerked her head back. Pain spasmed her face but she made no sound.

"Still nothing to say for yourself, eh? I've got two damned mutes it seems. Well, let's see what the other will do."

He pulled the other girl to her feet, wide-eyed and gurgling with fear.

"Now you tell me what happened."

The wretched girl could only make animal sounds.

The Khan ripped away the rag of the girl's dress so that her small breasts were exposed. The little mute was paralysed with terror as the Khan unsheathed his knife, and very carefully with the point drew a line down one breast, marking it with a line of blood spots.

"Now," said the Khan in a silky voice, "if you do not want to lose more than your tongue, show me what happened."

The girl pointed frantically to the corner where the rope and collar lay neatly coiled. Then she gripped her own throat and mimed a choking.

"Ah ha!" said the Khan. "I think that I see this. We have a wildcat here. She had better be tethered. Fetch the rope."

The terrified girl scuttled to the corner.

Anna made no resistance as the collar was placed round her neck, nor when the rope was thrown over the beam and pulled tight, forcing her head up. Once more she had retreated to an inner place, deep inside herself, where she huddled in the comforting darkness. It was as though she had detached her real self from her body and had become an observer of what was happening to it. Her body made no sound nor sign as the Khan ran his hands over her, feeling, probing and squeezing. She could smell his foul breath and see the cruelty in his eyes and on his wet lips, but she was determined that whilst he might touch her, he should not reach her.

The Khan was disappointed. He liked his women to struggle and scream a bit in order to arouse him. This one might as well be a side of beef, he thought, and after his marital exertions he wanted something special to rekindle his lust. His eye fell on the whip that he had used on the Russian woman and which he kept hanging on the wall as a reminder of the need for domestic harmony.

He licked his lips.

"You, girl,"—he turned to the mute crouched in her corner—"bring me the whip! Quickly now, or I'll open your back to the bone!"

The terrified girl sprang to her feet, fetched the whip and, dropping to her knees in front of the Khan, held it up to him. The Khan smiled his chilling smile:

"Now, whip her."

His voice was silky soft.

With a gasp of horror the girl shook her head.

"If you disobey me, I will cut off both your breasts and then your nose."

Very slowly, the girl got to her feet. She walked across to

Anna and standing in front of her for a moment, reached up a hand to touch her face. She stared briefly into Anna's eyes, beseeching her forgiveness. Then she moved behind her and shook out the whip.

The searing pain of the first blow across her buttocks brought Anna out of her inner hiding-place. She screamed.

The Khan, sitting at ease on a stool, clapped his hands softly:

"Very good! Now she is waking up a bit. Again! And harder this time!"

Anna screamed again.

The Khan smiled. He could feel himself hardening.

* * *

"Very good," said Lubin, closing his spy-glass. "Very good; just that miserable wooden barrier across the entrance to the village and a couple of half-asleep sentries. I do not think that they are expecting guests."

"What a pity! I don't suppose they'll even have the kettle on," quipped Charles.

The three men were lying on a low ridge overlooking Tearnause. In the hidden hollow behind them the Cossack squadron was drawn up. They had ridden fast through high and remote hill passes, avoiding the slow-moving herd of cattle proceeding up the valley, although they had once seen its dust cloud in the distance below them.

The men slid cautiously back from the sky-line and then scrambled down the slope to rejoin the squadron.

Lubin swung into his saddle and turned to his men:

"Now my wolves, I have a tasty meal of flesh for you. Eat well!"

There was a growl of pleasure from the Cossacks.

Anna had fainted.

The collar threatened to choke her.

"Which," said the Khan, "would be a pity after all our hard work. Let her down, slut, and fetch a bucket of water. I want her awake to experience properly the delights that I shall bring her."

He chuckled at his own humour.

Swiftly the little mute undid the rope and Anna slumped to the floor, limp and unconscious. Getting to his feet, the Khan turned Anna over roughly and examined the bloody weals across her white buttocks.

"Oh now, that I find very interesting," and his voice was thick. "Fetch that water and be quick about it."

The Khan reached out to explore, his fingers sliding...

The musket shot brought him to his feet.

Then another, and distant shouting.

"What...?"

The door burst open:

"Cossacks!" yelled the guard. "Hundreds of the bastards. They're through the barricade and killing everyone."

The Khan's reaction was instantaneous. He was on his feet, out of the door and into the saddle of his charger all in one movement, leaving Anna naked and unconscious on the floor. The big black horse plunged in the excitement of the moment.

"What shall we do?" shouted the guard.

"Fight! Fight to the last man! I will bring reinforcements!"

The Khan wheeled his horse and was away up a side street in a clatter of hooves, leaving the screams and shots on the main street above him far behind.

With lance, sabre and pistol, the Cossacks spread through the town like a flow of molten lava. With the main party of the bandits still back with the stolen cattle, the resistance was ragged and disorganised—but real enough in places, as Mischa and Charles found out. With a section of Cossacks they were advancing cautiously up a narrow street, when a shot rang out from a house.

Charles's horse collapsed on its knees and rolled to the ground. Charles was fortunate to be thrown clear. He did not feel quite so fortunate to be on his feet to meet the screaming charge of horsemen that poured out of a side alley. Then a horse shouldered him aside and a huge hand gripped his collar:

"Ups-a-daisy, Sir!" said Trooper Bone. "Get up behind me, like. Can't have a hofficer afoot. No you don't, you bearded bastard!"

This last to a bandit who made a desperate attempt to slash at Charles as he vaulted up behind Bone. The bandit fell screaming from Bone's back-handed slash across the face and fell to the ground under the trampling hooves.

To Mischa it was all sound and fury: bearded, yelling faces, plunging horses. His training took over, and he cut, thrust and parried with machine-like precision, until suddenly it was over and the bloodied sabre was dangling from his wrist. The street was empty in front of them. There were only the screams behind as the Cossacks finished off the wounded with their lances. He shook his head and his eyes met the grinning face of Vlad who, he realised, must have been at his side through the skirmish:

"Well done, Excellency! You sliced up three pieces of offal."

Mischa shook his head again. He could remember no details, just confusion.

'Perhaps it is always like that,' he thought.

The Khan flung himself from his horse in the hetman's yard:

"Alarm! Alarm!" he yelled. "Attack! Attack!"

The four wives were sitting in their row and, in spite of the emergency, the Khan shuddered slightly as he saw them. The memories of the last two days were still fresh in his mind.

"What is the alarm, husband?" asked the Senior Wife.

"Bloody Cossacks!" He seized the arm of the youngest wife to pull her to her feet. "Quick we must go. I must save my son."

As the heavily pregnant girl tried to struggle to her feet, Number Three Wife reached out a plump hand to grab her other arm. The wretched girl caught in this tug-of-war began to wail.

"No husband," the Senior Wife spoke again, "we are all as likely to be carrying your sons as she is—after your, er, ministrations."

"Ministrations!" giggled Number Three. "What a funny name for it. I thought that it was ever so nice, any way. In fact, I wouldn't mind..."

"Silence!" said the Senior Wife. "We all go, or none goes."

"If we stay, we'll all be killed!"

"If you go roaming about the streets now, husband, you will certainly be killed. We will find a way to hide you."

"Ministrations," said Number Three Wife, with a glance that she might have thought of as being coy.

The Khan shuddered again.

Charles and Bone rode up to where Mischa was sitting his horse, seemingly in a daze.

"You all right, old boy? Nothing damaged, I hope?"

Mischa shook himself like a wet dog and came out of his reverie.

"No! No! I'm fine—just a bit..."

"Here have a drink."

Charles pulled his flask out of his coat pocket and handed it across to Mischa. Bone licked his lips.

"Yes, all right, Bone, you can have a drink in a minute. The Rittmeister's need is greater than yours, as is mine."

"Sir!"

"I must say, they're damned good sport these bandits. How many did you bag?"

Mischa remained silent and thoughtful.

"His Excellency killed three of the pigs," said Vlad with pride.

"I say! Jolly good for you cully! How many did we bag, Bone?"

"1 reckon you got two, Sir, and we shared the bastard that was trying to skewer you."

"Splendid!"

Mischa took a deep swig from the flask and choked as the fiery liquid burned his throat. This brought him back to full consciousness and for the first time he took in the fact that Charles and Bone were mounted tandem:

"You've lost your horse?"

"Yes, bit hairy that. Bone pulled me out. Yes all right, Bone, you can have a drink now. Anyway, Bone and I are off to find a horse—should be plenty going spare, what. By the way, where's your dog?"

Mischa started. He knew that Sirius had been loping alongside him when they charged the barricade. Now he realised that the dog was nowhere to be seen.

The Cossacks spread through the town, mopping up the small pockets of resistance that remained and doing the things that they enjoyed most: lifting anything of possible value and raping any woman who looked remotely presentable. Their passage was marked by smoke as they set fire to the miserable hovels that made up most of the village.

Lubin and his escort rode along the main street. A wounded bandit, with a rope round his neck and a lance point in the small of his back, shambled along in front of the party. He had been persuaded to tell his captors that he thought the Khan might well be at the hetman's house, to where he was leading them.

The great black stallion was still tethered outside the house. Lubin adjusted his monocle:

"Ah! A Khanish looking sort of horse! Ask him."

He nodded towards the prisoner. The man squealed as the lance point dug into his back.

"Yes! Yes! Excellency!"

"Right, Sarn't Major! Round the back! The rest of you come with me!"

The door crashed inwards and Lubin, sabre in hand, lead the rush into the house.

"There's some women in here, Excellency!"

Lubin pushed through the grinning troopers. There were four women sitting in a row on a stained carpet. He noted that one was heavy in pregnancy and hysteria. The plump woman next to her had her hands over her face, but a bright eye peeped out through her fingers. The two older women watched passively as the men crowded into the room.

Lubin regarded the women with some distaste:

'If this is what their women look like,' he thought, 'it is small wonder the bandits are keen to steal other people's.'

"Do they speak Russian?" he said.

"Only a little, Excellency." It was the senior woman who answered his questions.

No they had not seen the Khan, they were relatives of the hetman and had just come for a visit; and now all the men had deserted them and left them there at the mercy of the Cossacks who would undoubtedly ravish them—here her voice broke into a wail and hiding her face in her hands she rocked to and fro. The wailing and rocking was taken up with enthusiasm by the others, and the Cossacks roared with merriment.

"What rape *them*? Why that one has a bigger beard than you, Igor!"

At this moment, the Sergeant Major appeared from the back of the house.

"Nothing , Excellency—there's nothing out there but the back yard and the well. I think our bird has flown."

"Damn!" said Lubin. "I would have liked to pull his neck. Right, we'll waste no more time here."

"Do you still want this piece of dog shit, Excellency?"

The Sergeant Major gave the prisoner a casual kick.

"No, throw him down the well,"—Lubin turned away—"and bring that horse. We'll not let it go to waste here."

Sirius felt much better. A dog has certain priorities, and Sirius had been hungry. Let all those humans shout and gallop about if they wanted to, but he had not eaten properly for twenty-four hours.

He had smelled cooking. He let the tide of battle flow away from him and followed his nose. The nose led him into a tumble-down hovel. In the far corner of the single room a woman and some children were cowering. Sirius ignored them. On the floor was a dish and some bowls. The family had obviously been about to eat when the alarm was raised. The dish contained a congealing mess of fatty mutton. Sirius sniffed it fastidiously. A piece of wood flew past his head:

"Shoo!" said the woman in a loud whisper.

Hackles raised and teeth bared, Sirius took a leap towards the hapless family.

They cowered back into their corner away from this huge snarling monster, this devil dog.

Satisfied that he would no longer be disturbed, Sirius returned to the dish and took his time picking out the more edible bits. One of the children began to cry. Sirius cast an eye in its direction and curled a lip; the cry was instantly stifled.

Once he was satisfied that all the choice bits were eaten, the devil dog had a last sniff, cocked his leg on the pot and trotted out into the street to see what else the place might bring forth. Behind him the wails rose without any more interruption.

The mean, narrow street was empty and silent, the sounds of continuing battle now far off, but to a dog the street was full of smells. Sirius's nose whiffled as he revelled in the scents of blood, sweat and human fear. Still following his nose he trotted easily along the street. He stopped suddenly, his head raised and his nose working. He moved further down the street and stopped again. The scent came to him again, but stronger this time. He broke into a lope and came to the open gate of a yard. There was no doubt about the scent now. Sirius raced across the yard to the door of the house and began to scratch and whine at it.

Anna slowly swam back up through the dark mists of consciousness and into a reality of pain—pain that ran like a red tide through all her body—but there was some relief.

Someone was very gently bathing her face with cool water. She opened her eyes. The little mute was bent over her, making soft murmuring noises. As Anna's eyes opened the little girl gave a gurgle of happiness.

Anna tried to say something, but nothing would come.

The mute sat looking at her, as the girl struggled to speak, then she put her hand over Anna's mouth and gently shook her head.

Anna let her head fall back as she realised that she too was mute.

At this moment something started scratching at the door.

There came a whine.

With a small wail, the little mute buried her face in Anna's bosom.

The two girls clung to each other.

Anna closed her eyes and listened to the scratching and whining. She was not a bit frightened. Indeed for the first time in what seemed an age she felt a small warming of hope.

The Khan was extremely uncomfortable. He was standing in a large wooden bucket and clinging to the rope that suspended it. The slightest movement made the bucket sway perilously. The cold from the slimy walls was eating into him. Below him the cold circle of black water made him shiver all the more. He tried to keep his gaze upwards at the opposing circle of blue sky to which he longed to return. The Khan was down the well and his mind—which alternated between fear and anger—was firm on only one thing: when he got out of this stinking well, someone was going to pay for his indignity. For the moment he could do nothing but grind his teeth.

He could hear the shouting and the stamping in the yard above. It all sounded far away. The Khan gripped the rope; surely they would not bother to look down the well. The noise receded and he relaxed, as much as that was possible; his arms were starting to ache.

There was a sudden resurgence of the noise: footsteps and shouting and, above it all, someone yelling in terror—a noise that the Khan knew well and usually relished. This time he felt terror of his own as the noise got nearer. They were coming to the well!

He clung even tighter to the rope. In the name of whatever gods he could think of, why was this happening to him? Why was the world against him? All he ever did was try to earn a bit of a living in a hard world.

The Khan felt self pity surge over him; those damned Cossacks and their damned Black Madonna, that was his problem. The Shaman was right: the Black Madonna must be destroyed and with Her the power of the Cossacks. He would...

The light from the top of the well was suddenly blacked out.

Someone was leaning over the rim of the well.

Someone was falling into the well.

The Khan closed his eyes and huddled as far against the wall as he could.

The scream filled the well.

The falling body cannoned into the Khan's shoulder, nearly knocking him out of his bucket. Gritting his teeth and screwing his eyes shut, he clung to the rope as the bucket rocked in the splash.

The Khan slowly opened his eyes and, as he did, a streaming head arose coughing and spluttering from the black waters, and a desperate hand clutched at the bucket, threatening to tip it over. The Khan snarled:

"Aargh!"

"Lord! Help me!" wailed a voice.

The man was surging in the water and the bucket was rocking perilously.

"Aslan! Is that you?"

"Yes, Lord, and I am wounded. Help me or I'm afraid I will drown."

"Yes,"—the Khan smiled—"I'm very much afraid that you will."

He ground his boot heel into the fingers of the clutching hand, forcing it to let go of the rocking bucket. With a last despairing wail, the head and hand of Aslan disappeared beneath the surface.

Then there were only bubbles.

The Khan restored equilibrium to the bucket.

He felt mightily cheered.

"Christ, Bone! This bloody street's like a knacker's yard,"— Bone's horse snorted at the smell of blood as it picked its way amongst the scattered bodies—"Let's get back to what passes for the main street in this poxy place. There's no sign of any sort of horse down here."

"There's a dog barking in there, Sir."

"Jesus wept, Bone, the whole fucking place is full of barking dogs!"

Bone turned his horse into a yard:

"There you are, Sir! I thought that I recognised the bark; it's Sirius, Sir."

"By Jove! So it is," said Charles, sliding off the horse. "And what's he got behind that door that he's so excited about, eh? Now Sirius, my lad, what's all this fuss about?"

Sirius responded to Charles's voice with a brief wag of his tail, but continued the furious assault with his paws on the door.

"Must be something tasty, what, Bone! Take post here and Sirius and I will investigate."

Charles drew his sword and kicked the door open.

Sirius went bounding inside, with Charles hard behind him.

"Well! Well! Well! And what have we here?"

The mute girl gave her strangled scream as the huge dog came bounding in. Her shattered nerves broke and she rolled away from the great fangs that she imagined to be about to fasten on her throat.

Sirius ignored her and performed a little dance of delight around Anna before commencing to lick her face vigorously. Anna moaned and, throwing her arms round the great dog's neck, buried her face in his shaggy mane. Now she let the tears come: hot scalding tears of relief.

The mute felt no sense of relief as she stood flattened against the wall. She looked past the dog to the man with the sword, and the look on his face as he looked at the two women—-one naked and the other nearly so. The girl knew all about men with swords and the heavy-eyed, thick-lipped expressions of lust that followed killing. She had been to this place many times and perhaps she could save Anna from it. Summoning all her courage she stood in front of Charles and pulled her torn dress apart to display her breasts. She stood stock still and held her breath.

Breathing quickly Charles took in the scene. The mute was a skinny little thing, whereas the naked blond girl was undoubtedly desirable in every possible way—if a trifle shop soiled. As though reading his thoughts, Sirius turned his head and bared his teeth at him with a low rumbling growl. For a moment Charles turned his sword towards the dog and the two faced each other. Then Charles shrugged: a woman was a woman, and if the little girl was skinny, well, the meat was sweeter close to the bone. With the point of the sword he lifted up the ragged skirt of her dress.

As the sword was sheathed she breathed again.

"Well, well," said Charles, slowly and deliberately licking his lips, "it looks as though I had drawn the wrong weapon."

"Well Mischa, did you have good killing?"

Mischa found that he was unable to match Lubin's jaunty mood:

"Well enough, I suppose, but I've lost both Charles and my dog. Charles's horse was killed and he went off with Bone to look for one."

"That sounds exceeding careless of you. I have just the horse for Charles, here. We have liberated him."

He pointed to the great black stallion that was being led by one of the Cossacks.

"Excellency! I have the honour to report that we saw the Captain's servant in a yard just down this street. We asked him if he was all right and he said that his master was inside the house trying out a mare."

A growl of laughter ran through the Cossacks.

Lubin raised his eyes as though seeking divine guidance.

"Really, Mischa, I do wish Charles would sometimes give his intellect a rest. We had better go and restore him to the more physical world."

"I don't think you should be going in there, Sir, begging your pardon, Sir."

"I have no intention of doing so, Bone, but you may give Captain FitzHugh my compliments and, when he can spare a moment, we have a *horse* for him to ride."

"Yes, Sir, very good, Sir."

With some reluctance, Bone turned toward the door. At that moment it opened and Charles came swaggering out, buttoning up his breeches.

"Well, I'm blessed. A welcoming committee! Deuced kind of you fellows."

"We have brought a horse for you," said Lubin with his lazy smile.

"Hmm! Yes." Charles studied the Khan's horse "Not a bad sort, not bad at all. By the way," he half turned to Mischa, "your dog and your cow girl are both in there. Amongst others," he added in a self-satisfied manner.

"My dog and my *what?*"

"Yes, yes, your little cow girl, the one that stuck a rose in your teeth."

"My God!" Mischa's face coloured. "You haven't..."

"My dear old boy, would I do a thing like that? Never touched her, although I would say somebody's had a damned good try. Anyway, your dog's slobbering all over her. No, never touched her. Gave the other a bloody good tupping though."

So saying, he vaulted neatly onto the back of the black stallion.

Just as neatly, the black stallion bucked him off.

8 The Silence of Tambukan

THE dining room of the Officers' Mess at the fort was thick with smoke and the smell of heavily scented, but unwashed bodies. Collars were loosened as the men sweated from an excess of food and the heat of the ill-ventilated room. Voices also loosened and loudend as the glasses of vodka were thrown down ready throats, as toast after toast was proposed and answered.

Spirits were high after the success of Lubin's patrol. Many bandits had been killed. The horses and cattle—with a few judicious deductions in the line of duty—had been restored to the survivors of the German village. It was true that the Khan had escaped, but he was licking his wounds in his mountain lair. The officers felt that they had much to celebrate.

Colonel Ryshkov roared and shouted, banging the table with a huge fist.

Amongst the noise, Mischa sat silent and preoccupied. He drank the toasts absently. The truth was that alcohol had little effect on him and his mind was elsewhere. Ever since he had burst into that stinking hut in Tearnause and seen Anna's nakedness, he could not get the sight of her body out of his mind. He could not forget the silky warmth of her skin as he had lifted her to wrap a cloak around her, and his hand had brushed one of her breasts. He could not forget her slim thighs or the triangle of golden hair between them, the feel of her limp body as he lifted her. Nor could he forget the shame as he realised that he wanted to possess that body: to feel the slim arms and the long legs wrapped round him and to feel her lips whispering urgently in his ear, just as another golden girl had done in what now seemed like another world. He

155

realised that he wanted Anna more than anything else in the world and burned with both shame and lust. He had prayed earnestly to the Lady to be rid of this burden and to make him pure, as he had promised Her before. But, even as he prayed, Anna's form would slip into his mind. Mischa was in turmoil.

Charles's voice broke into his reverie. To mounting cheers and laughter, Charles was regaling the company with the tale of his exploits in Tearnause:

"...so there was old Sirius scratting at this door. So I says to myself, 'Ho-ho, my lad, where there's hounds there's bound to be sport.' So I kicks the door in and has a look inside. Blow me down what do I see but two women, one of them stark naked. 'Charles me boy,' says I, 'this just might be your lucky day.' 'Officers only here,' I says to Bone, 'you just stand guard.' 'I'll do the standing in here,' thinks I, and in I went. There's this blond wench on the floor. Yum-yum—to the victor the spoils. Then this little slut comes out to me and damme if she don't open her dress and shove her poonts at me. Well she ain't a looker like the other one, but she's lively and full of gratitude for her saviour, so I bent her over a stool and gave her a bloody good gallop.

"Then I had a look at the other—what a body! If my shot locker hadn't been empty... But you ask Mischa. He gave the wench a good fumble when he was wrapping her up in a cloak. Have you ridden her yet, Mischa? Perhaps she wants a real horseman in the saddle, what? Never mind old boy, I reckon there's plenty there for both of us."

To a roar of vodka-hoarse approval, Charles rose unsteadily to his feet, his face flushed:

"I give you a toast, an English toast; 'Here's to the hen that never refuses and lets the cock tread whenever he chooses.' Well, as the doxy don't speak, she can't say no!"

There was a roar of laughter that gradually subsided as Mischa got to his feet, his face set:

"You will not speak about the girl like that again."

Charles's mouth dropped open with surprise:

"Oh come on Mischa, she's only a peasant slut. They're at

it like rabbits all the time. I expect that girl fucked half the village..."

With a roar of rage Mischa exploded, all his pent-up guilt and frustration bursting forth. The glass full of vodka took Charles full in the face.

There was a sudden silence.

For a long moment Charles stood there, the vodka dripping from his face, his expression tight and hard:

"For that, Sir, I demand satisfaction."

"My God, Sir, you shall have it!"

Mischa leaned on the table with his two massive fists. The temper that he feared so much was now well and truly out. A vein throbbed in his forehead.

The knout hit the table with a crash.

All eyes turned to Colonel Ryshkov.

"Enough! I would remind you two puppies that you are here as guests and that this regiment is on active service. There can and will be no duelling. Try it and I'll hang the pair of you. I will also remind you that the girl is here under the protection of my wife. Try anything on and I'll give you to *her*—you would prefer a hanging! Now you two young cocks will shake hands and keep your differences to yourselves; otherwise, by Christ and all the Saints, I'll have you both shipped back to St Petersburg and to hell for all I care."

The savage old man was towering over the now silent table. Neither Mischa nor Charles, looking at the jutting beard and the hard, hawk eyes could doubt that Ryshkov meant what he said.

Slowly and reluctantly, Charles offered his hand across the table. After a slight pause Mischa grasped it but their eyes as they looked at each other told a different story.

"Until later," said Charles.

"Amen," said Mischa.

As Mischa, with Sirius at heel, rounded the corner of the main administration building in the fort at Pyatigorsk he heard the sound of shouting. He saw a group of Cossacks who were roaring and bellowing with laughter. Mischa sighed

as he saw the object of the merriment. In the middle of the
barrack square stood a great black horse. It stood quietly with
the reins loose on its neck and an empty saddle on its back.
The horse's ears where pricked and it was watching with obvious interest something that lay on the ground in front of it.
The horse even reached out its muzzle to give the object a
gentle nudge. The object raised a hand and slapped at the
horse's nose. The big black snorted and leaped backwards.
Trooper Bone stepped forward and caught the reins. The
horse snorted again and rubbed its muzzle up and down the
front of Bone's tunic:

"Easy, lad, easy now—whoa'se a man, now!"

Bone quietened the horse, talking the soothing, mean-
ingless words that generations of horsemen have used,
stroking the neck and gentling the ears. The horse nuzzled
him again.

The object on the ground, got slowly to its feet and dusted
itself down.

"Hell's bloody teeth!"

Charles slapped the dirt from his breeches.

"Good morning, FitzHugh: a little early morning equita-
tion practice?"—Mischa's politeness had an icy edge to it—
"Perhaps the Riding Master would recommend a blanket
ride?"

Trooper Bone made a noise that might, or might not have
been a cough and made himself very busy with some minute
adjustment to the horse's bridle. The watching Cossacks had
no such inhibitions and slapped their thighs with mirth.

"Damn you, Czerny! And you can wipe that greasy, German, grin off your face and your bloody dog."

"I am Austrian and I'm not grinning and..."

Mischa felt his temper rising and turned away. The bad
blood from the other night still simmered between the two
young men.

Charles slapped the dust off his cap and rammed it onto
his head:

"Damned horse! I will gaffer the bastard!"

The struggle between Charles and the captured black

stallion had been providing entertainment for the garrison ever since Lubin's squadron had returned from its bloody patrol. Lubin concealed a considerable gift for language and poetry behind his languid exterior. He had named the horse 'Bahram'—an obscure reference to the work of the Persian poet, Omar Khayyam: *"and Bahram, that great hunter, the wild ass stamps o'er his head, as he lies fast asleep."*

"After all, Charles," he had drawled, "the horse does seem to spend an awful lot of time stampin' over your head."

"I'll make a wild ass out of the bastard before I've finished with him."

"That's good; you'll have some company."

Lubin's monocle gleamed with something that might have been laughter.

Charles snarled. He felt that the honour of The Royal Horse Guards, not to mention his own, was at stake, especially with Mischa present.

His back rigid with fury, he marched across to where Bone was standing holding Bahram:

"Don't you think it might be better to give it a rest, Sir?"

"Bugger you, Bone! Give me a leg up!"

"Sir!"

Charles fisted the reins and bent his left leg up behind him. Bone took the ankle of the boot and hefted Charles easily into the saddle. Bahram stood like a rock.

Charles gathered the reins and touched the horse with his heels:

"Walk on!"

Bahram walked sedately down the parade ground. The watching Cossacks were silent now.

Charles clicked his teeth and the horse broke into a smooth, floating trot.

"He's a bloody lovely mover, Sir," said Bone to Mischa.

"He is, indeed, a very fine horse. The Captain seems to have the measure of him, now."

"Well, Sir, give him his due, he can ride most things on four legs. I seen him ride a bloody great old sow at Knightsbridge once, for a bet like..."

Bahram turned neatly and came trotting back. Charles touched him with his heels again and the horse broke into a canter.

"...I mean he is a lovely horseman, the Captain."

Sirius began to whine.

The explosion was brief and absolute.

The Lovely Horseman made a perfect parabola in the air, before rolling through the dust with a cry of:

"Oh shit!"

"Shit's about it," said Bone moving to pick his officer up.

Bahram obviously felt that he had contributed enough to the morning's entertainment and was galloping down the parade ground, reins and stirrups flying, pursued by a trail of laughing Cossacks and an ecstatic Sirius.

Mischa felt that a tactical withdrawal was in order and, sticking his riding whip under his arm, he whistled up his panting dog and set off for the Commanding Officer's house.

Sarah Ryshkova was sitting in a chair in the little garden of the house, under the shade of an ancient oak tree. She had a glass of tea on the table beside her and was smoking a small cigar. Sarah Ryshkova was a tall elegant woman with rather bony good looks and a directness of manner that many found disconcerting. She was reputed to be the only thing in the world that Colonel Ryshkov, her husband, was afraid of.

"My aunt Sarah," Lubin had once said to Mischa, "is a formidable woman. She has accompanied uncle Viktor on most of his campaigns."

As a result of this she habitually wore the baggy breeches and soft boots that male Cossacks wore—she still spent a lot of time on a horse.

"As a young bride, or so legend has it," Lubin had continued, "and when my uncle was absent from home, a Chechen climbed through her window one night with a view to working his wicked way—I wonder what the Chechen for 'Charles' is? Aunt Sarah was a considerable beauty, but not your fragile sort. She laid him out with a musket butt."

At this point Lubin paused and his eyes took on a dreamy look.

"What happened then?" Mischa prompted him.

"According to the legend, she had the man tied to a horse and sent back whence he came with a testicle in each pocket. It is said that aunt Sarah removed them herself. The Cossacks have an enormous respect for her."

Mischa had also formed an enormous respect for the lady, but not through fear. Ever since their arrival, she had made Charles and Mischa most welcome, treating them as members of the family. As soon as the patrol had returned from Tearnause, bringing with it the two badly traumatised young women, roughly bundled up in men's clothing and cloaks for their journey, Sarah had had them brought immediately to her house and had taken personal charge of their treatment.

"Herr Rittmeister! Your report if you please!"

"Madame Ryshkova! I have the honour to report that Captain Lord FitzHugh is experiencing certain difficulties with his new charger."

"The Captain has been dismounting without permission again?"

"I beg leave to report, Madame: several times."

"And Sirius, what have you to report?"

Sirius pushed a cold wet nose into the woman's hand.

They both laughed the easy laughter of friends. Aunt Sarah got to her feet and looped her arm through Mischa's:

"On my oath, Mischa, I fear that that horse will break Charles before he breaks it."

"The horse does appear to have a certain sense of humour."

"And Charles—how is his sense of humour?"

"Taking something of a battering, along with the rest of him, I should say."

Aunt Sarah sighed and shook her head. Then she looked at Mischa with a mischievous smile:

"And you Mischa, what brings you here? Have you brought your sense of humour or, perhaps, you have just come to take a glass of tea with an old woman?"

"That would indeed be an honour—and no one could possibly think of you as old."

"La, Sir! I do believe that you might be trying to flirt with me. Perhaps you should save your amorous skills for a more worthy target, eh?"

"I have no amorous skills, Madame."

Sarah looked up at the serious face of the large young man and thought to herself: 'No I truly believe that you believe that, my young friend—as if I had not got enough wounded birds round here.'

"How is she, Madame?"

"I fear that there is little change. She is a healthy girl and the physical damage has healed quickly, but the mind..."

"She still hasn't spoken?"

"Not a word, or even a sound. She just sits staring straight in front of her. If I speak to her, it's as though she does not hear me. So if I want her to do something I speak to the little mute girl and she goes to Anna and takes her by the hand, then Anna follows her. The little girl shows her what to do and she does it. Then she goes back to the silent stare."

"Has there been any news from the German village?"

"Bad, I'm afraid. The girl's relations are all dead and the other survivors want nothing to do with her. They won't have her back—think she is bewitched or some damned nonsense and think that the village was destroyed because of her. The only change we got from them was the child's name.

"Have you managed to find out the mute girl's name yet?"

"No. I have tried all the names that I can think of, but she just shakes her head. God knows what heathen tribe the poor child came from and she can't tell us. I have just taken to calling her 'Waif'. She seems quite happy with that. Now, Sir, what can I do for you?"

Mischa looked down at his toe caps, then met Sarah's penetrating gaze.

"I wonder if it would be possible for me to see Anna?"

It came out in a rush. Sarah paused for a moment, still staring into his eyes:

"No, I don't think so. Both girls are terrified at the sight of a man, except, for some reason, my husband, although he terrifies everybody else—including you two young men by all accounts. You would do well to heed him."

Mischa stiffened:

"I assure you, Madame, my intentions are entirely honourable."

"A young man with entirely honourable intentions to a beautiful young woman is something that I have yet to meet," said Sarah dryly. "No, you may not see her, but I will take your dog to see her. That seems to be one male that she is pleased to see."

Mischa felt a sharp stab of disappointment, but he managed a stiff smile:

"Of course, I will be honoured to offer my dog, if he will go with you, that is. I am not sure..." But Sirius had already bounded away and was whining and scratching at the door of the house.

Anna was sitting in a chair by the window, through which she stared with a fixed gaze, as though she was watching and waiting for something or somebody.

Apart from the rough baggy breeches, she wore a loose peasant shirt, that was open at the throat and showed the first swell of her breasts and the long graceful line of her neck. The suffering-induced leanness of her face only served to accentuate its perfect high cheek-boned structure, framed by the long straight golden hair. The Waif was standing behind Anna. On hearing the scratching at the door, she gave a startled cry, leaped backwards and huddled against the wall. As Sarah opened the door she spoke soothingly to her:

"It's all right, Waif, it's only Sirius who has called to see you both. You remember him?"

Sirius gave a small 'woof' and bounding across the room, did a little dance in front of Waif. The girl's taught face relaxed. She dropped to her knees and kissed Sirius on the nose. Sirius rolled an eye and nuzzled the girl's face.

Through all of this, Anna had remained motionless, her gaze fixed on the horizon beyond the window.

Sirius decided that he had done his duty by Waif and, breaking from her embrace, he trotted across the room and stuck his wet, cold nose into Anna's hands as they lay folded

in her lap. Anna remained motionless. Sirius began to whine,
rather as a puppy whines to its mother. When there was still
no reaction, Sirius reared up and, placing his feet in Anna's
lap, he began to lick her face. Anna shifted her head as
though aware of Sirius for the first time. The pink tongue
flicked out again and wet the girl's face. For the first time, her
features began to move and contort. Her hands reached up
to tighten in the rough hair of the big dog's neck, as he stood
laughing in her face. A smile flicked across Anna's face. Then
it was as though a dam had burst and the tears came coursing
down. She threw her arms around the dog's neck and buried
her streaming face in his shaggy mane.

Sarah crossed herself:

"Thanks be to Christ! I believe the gate is breaking
down."

* * *

"Come, sisters! More effort!" commanded the Senior Wife

"He's very heavy," panted Wife Number Two.

"Yes! He is heavy," Wife Number Three giggled. "I
thought that, when he…"

"Sister! Save your breath for the work!"

The three women were cranking away at the windlass on
the well.

The youngest, prettiest and most pregnant wife was bent
over the edge of the well, monitoring the Khan's upward
progress and alternately uttering squeals of encouragement
to him and to the other wives:

"It's all right, husband…, keep winding, sisters… I can see
your head now, husband… I can see his head now, sisters…
Don't worry, husband, we'll get you out."

"We? I like the 'we'," puffed Wife Number Two.

"She's pregnant."

"I thought we were all pregnant?" Wife Number Three
paused in puzzlement.

"Heave, you stupid girl! Of course we are all pregnant; it's
just that we need to make certain."

The Senior Wife tugged on the handle.

"Make certain? Does that mean..."

"Yes, girl, yes!"

"Oh good!" squeaked Wife Number Three and threw herself into winding with renewed vigour.

Very slowly the bearded, dripping face of the Khan appeared over the edge of the well.

"He's here! He's here!" cried the youngest.

"Oh Good!" squealed Number Three, letting go of the handle.

The Khan's head suddenly disappeared again and the well echoed with threats and curses.

"You stupid girl!" the two senior wives shouted together.

Snivelling quietly, Number Three Wife threw her not inconsiderable bulk back onto the windlass.

The Khan's head reappeared, followed by his shoulders and torso. Seizing the edge of the wall he hauled himself out of the well and onto dry ground, where he stood dripping gently.

He spread his arms:

"My flowers! My jewels!"

The youngest and most pregnant slobbered kisses and tears on his hand. Number Three Wife flung herself weeping at his feet, clutching his ankles—the Khan thought that rather good. The two older women, still panting from their exertions, watched him dry-eyed.

"Enough of this," said the Senior Wife. "We must be away —the Cossacks!"

"Cossacks?" the Khan started. "Are they still here?"

"We would hardly have bothered to haul you up if they were still here to make your balls into shashlik. The pigs have gone. They've burned most of the village, raped and plundered, but they've gone. But you never know, if they think that you are still here, they might come back and roast you yet."

The Senior Wife's acid tones always annoyed the Khan: the fat old sow—he would like to roast *her* on a spit like shashlik. That would be better than having to... almost anything would be better than that. He pulled himself together.

"Quite! Quite! Well done, my flowers, now someone get my horse and we will be away to the hills. I have the safety of you, the precious stones of my life, to think about."

"Your horse is gone."

"Gone? My beautiful black stallion. Gone? Stolen by the Cossacks?"

The Senior Wife spat:

"Well, you stole it in the first place. But don't worry, husband, we have a mount for you to lead us all to safety on."

"Donkeys! That it should come to this! I, the Khan, the scourge of the Russians, the Great Impaler, the man whom half the Caucasus use to frighten their children to sleep. To think that I, the Great Destroyer, should be mounted"—the Khan spat—"should be mounted on a donkey."

"You can always walk, if you wish to, husband," said the Senior Wife.

"Perhaps we should have left him down the well." Wife Number Two allowed her handsome moustache to twitch in what might have been a smile.

"Oh no!" Wife Number Three protested. "We want our lord rested and fully fit to perform his duties."

She giggled coyly at her sally. The Khan shuddered.

The youngest and most pregnant wife took no part in this. She had her eyes shut and was practising lullabies in a voice that the Khan mentally compared to a cinder caught under a door. He fell silent and let his mind wander back to the splendid sport that he had enjoyed at the German village.

From there his mind filled with the Golden One and her wonderful body, a body that he had actually had in his hands—he could still feel the warm silkiness of her. He could still see the girl twisting as the thong of the whip bit into her white skin. He could still hear her screams. By the sacred wood and stone, he would have given her something to scream about if only he had had the time. He could imagine her writhing under him, imagine the pain and fear in her face as he used her again and again and...

At this moment his donkey stumbled and pitched the

Khan ignominiously onto the ground. The four wives sat staring at him. Number Three Wife found it quite hard to control her feelings; the Lord did look so funny sitting there snarling and twisting his beard.

"You should keep your mind on the business in hand, husband."

"What in the name of the gates of hell, do you think I'm doing." The Khan got to his feet, dusted himself off and kicked his donkey in the ribs—"and why are we going up this god-forsaken goat track?"

The track they were on was a steep and rocky one that wound through a precipitous pine forest with the dirty ice of a glacier grinding through a steep valley to their right.

"And if we had gone up the valley road and the Cossacks had come back, what then? Think of the sport they would have had with you on a donkey."

The Khan grunted and twisted his beard. The Senior Wife was quite right, of course, but he was damned if he was going to say so.

As the path climbed higher the trees thinned out and the great snow clad bulk of Elbrus filled the horizon. They came out onto some stony plateau: land that rose to the forbidding rocky slopes in front of them.

"Why are we going this way?"

The Khan recognised the track that they had just joined as the one that led to the Shaman's hut high out in the white mountains.

"To keep you safe, husband, and also the Shaman wants to see you."

"How do you know that?"

The woman shrugged and said nothing. The Khan thought of his coming interview with the Shaman and was silent.

"Tonight," said Wife Number Two, "we will stop at my village. There you can gather your strength, husband."

"Oh good!" Wife Number Three was full of eagerness. "Does that mean 'ministrations'?"

The Khan shuddered again.

The Khan hated walking, but not for much fine gold would he have arrived at his meeting with the Shaman on a donkey. His request for one of the wretched horses that hobbled about the clan village of Wife Number Two had been firmly refused. The story of the debacle at Tearnause had galloped ahead of him with all the speed that bad news always manages.

The Khan had been left under no illusion by the village elders that his conduct of the raid and his personal conduct thereafter was felt to have been wanting. This was especially so as the news of the recapture of the horses and cattle by the Cossacks, with considerable losses amongst the bandits, was seeping through to the mountain fastness. The Khan had lost face amongst the loose confederation of tribes that he ruled. He knew full well that his Khanate would be a matter of debate and that he stood to lose his power, and maybe other things as well. This was why his meeting with the Shaman was so vital. He needed all the backing of that strange figure's shadowy authority. He was not looking forward to the meeting.

Few people met the Shaman. One reason for this was that the isolation of his dwelling place in a shadowy cleft high on the slopes of Elbrus did not encourage casual visitors. The other was that the Shaman's equally shadowy powers were well known—if not well defined. People were not sure what the full extent of his spiritual powers were. Few had ever tried to find out. Even fewer returned.

The Khan's mood, as he followed the rough path that twisted ever upwards beside a rushing torrent, white with snow-melt, was hardly sunny. As though to match his mood, the early sunshine was disappearing and a ragged wrack of black cloud appeared over the great snow-covered shoulder of the mountain. The Khan wrapped his cloak more tightly round him and cursed the weather.

At last the path levelled out into a small boulder-strewn alpine meadow. Some stunted trees struggled to survive on the steep rocky slopes that enclosed the space. At the far end of the meadow stood the small stone hut, with a wisp of smoke from the smokehole in the roof. It was a desolate place, and the Khan shivered in spite of his cloak. It was a place that he was always more pleased to leave then to arrive at.

The little wizened man was sitting as he always seemed to be, staring into the small fire, the smoke from which filled the wretched hut before seeping out through the hole in the roof. The Khan sometimes wondered about the Shaman's age; in all the years that he had known him and been his disciple, the old man looked just the same. He sat, as always, with one leg tucked under him. His right leg stuck out awkwardly. The leg, skewered and broken by a Cossack lance many years before, could not be bent.

The old man neither spoke nor looked up as the Khan's shape darkened the open door way, he just pointed to a spot on the other side of the fire. The Khan sat awkwardly, trying not to cough at the smoke. The Shaman picked up a dish that lay beside him on the floor. Leaning forward he thrust it through the smoke to where the Khan sat. He saw the familiar leaves. The old man spoke for the first time:

"Chew and listen to my thoughts."

The Khan said nothing. He took a leaf, rubbed it lightly between his hands and putting it into his mouth, he began to chew. He felt the first bitter taste of the juice run down his throat. Then came the feeling of light-headedness, as though he were floating and seeing everything with a brilliant clarity. The smoke seemed to disappear and the drab misery of his surroundings became transformed with brilliant colours. Opposite him the figure of the Shaman seemed to grow and float towards him. It was as though the old man's face was close to his and enlarged with amazing clarity so that he could see every tiny wrinkle on his skin.

When the Shaman spoke, his voice came not just from the moving lips, but from all around him, so that the words seemed to envelope the Khan:

"My son, you have not done well. I put my trust in you and you have failed me; I put the golden prize that you wanted into your hands and you lost it through your own stupidity. Not only that, but through your stupidity and lust you lost many good men. You know that there is much muttering amongst the clans about your leadership.

"Your authority hangs by a thread and I can snap that thread. You know that our people are not kind to leaders who fail them. The Cossack sewage is stronger than ever. The only way to break their power is to take the icon of the Black Madonna from them. They believe that She protects them and guides them, and that as long as She is with them they cannot fail.

"War is coming. I can feel it in my bones. The Cossacks will go to the war and will want to take the Black Madonna with them as a certain shield. Your task is to take that shield from them—to send them to fight without it. Then they will be destroyed and my curse on them will be fulfilled. You must destroy their power for me and for all the spirits of the mountains. If you fail, then you must be destroyed."

The Khan tried very hard to speak, but although he moved his lips, the power of the drug seemed to paralyse his tongue. The Shaman's words rang in his head as though they were the reverberations of a gong. Then the clarity began to fade and the colours with them. The Khan found himself drifting into unconsciousness and the dreams that came with it. The dreams were always full of fantastic images, usually pleasurable and exciting. Often they included golden women who twined themselves around him and roused him to great heights of pleasure. This time the dream was full of evil twisting shapes and women whose teeth were made of knives. They wanted to destroy him.

When the Khan woke, he was soaked in a cold sweat. He was alone in the fetid mountain hut, where the smoke swirled. He got carefully to his feet and looked outside the hut. There was no sign of the Shaman. The Khan began his long walk back down the mountain, with the old man's words ringing in his brain. He found that he had a filthy headache.

* * *

As the summer wore on, rumours of war in the west filtered through to Pyatigorsk. Not that the garrison paid much attention to them. The Cossacks were much too busy with their own work of containing the wild tribes of the Caucasus and impressing them forcefully of the benefits of being ruled by His Imperial Majesty, The Czar of All The Russias.

This meant constant raids and patrols. Charles and Mischa saw many burning villages and much bloody work. It was true that the Khan's wings seemed to have been clipped, but intelligence reports suggested that he was regrouping and licking his wounds in his mountain fastness.

Anna's recovery continued, to the extent that she was occasionally seen walking in Sarah's garden. She still did not speak and, mindful of the Colonel's instructions, no man dare go near her. Colonel Ryshkov shrugged and said that if he had to have three women in his house, he found it a mercy that only one of them could talk. Anna still insisted on wearing her breeches and boots and acknowledged no one except Sarah and Waif. The only other exception was Sirius. If ever Sirius was absent without his master's leave, Mischa always knew where to find the dog.

He did not mind—it gave him an excuse to call and ask after Anna.

Charles was not amused. His problems with Bahram continued.

On patrol Bahram behaved in exemplary fashion. His speed and agility had extracted Charles from sticky situations on more than one occasion: situations that Charles's impetuosity were often responsible for.

Back at the fort, Bahram obviously felt that he was off duty and honour-bound to drop his rider on any and every occasion. This ongoing tussle gave pleasure to everybody except Charles. It even gave pleasure to Anna, who eventually ventured out of the Ryshkov's garden to watch the show. She would stand with Sirius at the edge of the parade ground, waiting for the moment when Bahram's mighty back would bunch and Charles would hit the ground.

The day came when Charles's patience snapped and his

horsemanship deserted him. This may have been because he had a slight fever and a stinking hangover from trying to drown it. Once more Bahram, after performing with utter docility for some time, dropped his shoulder whilst Charles was leaning out of the saddle at full gallop, trying to lift a tent peg with the tip of his lance. Charles landed badly, the shaft of the lance underneath him. He was hurt and angry. Bone brought Bahram back and this time Charles lost his temper. He seized Bahram by the bridle and raised his whip. Bahram, eyes rolling and nostrils distended backed away from the up-raised arm:

"You bastard! I will teach you bloody manners!"

At this moment, Charles felt his raised arm caught. The whip was torn from his hand. He turned round in a rage and found Anna clutching his arm, her normally expressionless face taut with fury.

"Damn you, woman! Let me go."

Still the girl clung on, staring silently at him.

Charles's rages subsided as quickly as they rose. He saw a chance for fun, and he made an elaborate bow:

"Very well, Madame, if you think that you can do better, please delight us all."

Anna stared at him for another moment, then loosing his arm, she walked up to Bahram, his eyes still showing white and frightened. The girl raised her hand to his nose and fondled it gently. Then, inch by inch, she worked her hand up his head, stroked an ear and soothed his neck.

The horse stopped snorting and pulling away, and stood rock still, as Anna gathered up the reins and, without touching a stirrup iron, vaulted lightly into the saddle. She trotted up and down the parade ground once with Sirius bounding happily alongside. Then, without a backwards glance, she trotted out of the gate of the fort and onto the open slopes of the mountain. She put the horse into a canter and the three disappeared amongst the lilac trees.

"My dears," said Lubin, screwing his monocle into his eye and addressing the open-mouthed Charles and Mischa, "I would say that between you, you have lost a horse and a dog."

The two men were silent.

"You'll probably have to marry the girl to get either of them back," Lubin added and walked away, whistling happily.

It was an unhappy time for Mischa. His mind was full of confusing thoughts about Anna and every distant sight of her made things worse. To add to his unhappiness he had to admit to himself that he missed the friendship of Charles. The two men continued to treat each other with frosty politeness.

Mischa took to taking long rides out on the steppe with Sirius loping along, hoping that a deer or a hare would pop up.

"At least I've got you, old man," Mischa would say, ruffling the big dog's head.

But some days he did not even have the dog. Sirius always seemed to know when Anna was riding and would desert his master. Mischa's loneliness increased.

It was a summer's day of great loveliness. Mischa rode down through the tree-lined streets of the town and out onto the great rolling grasslands of the steppe that stretched away to the far horizon. In spite of the beauty of the day, his mood was bleak. The heat of the day increased and he could feel the sweat trickling down his back. Breasting a hill he came upon a small valley with a stunted grove of trees and a small stream. There was shade and water for man, horse and dog— if his bloody dog had not gone off yet again. He trotted down the slope, slid out of the saddle and, whilst his horse drank, he knelt and scooped the water up to his own parched mouth.

"Good morning, Mischa," said a deep voice.

Mischa started. With a soldier's caution, he had checked the surrounding area before dismounting. He would have sworn that it was deserted.

The Hunter was sitting at ease under an ash tree. Mischa could not believe that he had missed seeing him.

"Hunter!" he cried with surprise and pleasure. "My goodness, but it's good to see you."

Mischa hobbled his horse and turned it loose to graze by the stream. He sat himself down beside the Hunter with his back against the tree and, whilst the strange old man's pipe smoke curled up amongst the shafts of sunlight that filtered through the leafy cover, Mischa talked.

He talked as he had never talked to anyone except the old priest at Lippitz. He talked of the Slovenian peasant girl and the tragedy of his love for her and his guilt. He talked of Anna and the turmoil of his feelings for her. He talked of Charles and the sadness of their quarrel. The Hunter sat still and silent, puffing his pipe and listening. When Mischa had finished and sat with drooping head as though totally exhausted, the Hunter sighed a deep sigh and leaned forward to tap out his pipe on a protruding tree root.

"What a heavy burden, even for a broad young back like yours to carry. I have watched you bending under the weight of it and have grieved for you. The shedding of it is something that you have to arrange for yourself, otherwise you will never truly be rid of it, but perhaps there are some things that you should know that might help you on the cold, dark and dangerous road that undoubtedly lies ahead of you. You are truly fascinated by this girl are you not?"

Mischa nodded silently.

"Then there are some things that you should know about this girl and the awful burden that *she* has to carry. Then you might be able to help her and by doing so, ease the weight of your own pack of troubles."

The Hunter paused, his brow furrowed as he packed and re-lit his malodorous old pipe. Then he explained about the weight of horror, terror and guilt under the blackness of which Anna's mind was buried—the dreadful night of the raid, the shooting of her own brother, the strangling of the Russian woman and the girl's torture by the Khan; how she could no longer bring herself to wear a woman's clothing that enhanced the beauty that the girl felt was at the root of all the suffering. At the end of the tale, Mischa was aghast:

"My God! It's a wonder that the girl is not raving mad."

"She's on the brink," The Hunter was sombre, "and she can only be brought back gently and by degrees. Move too quickly and she might go over the edge."

"What can I do?"

To the south of Pyatigorsk there is the circular volcanic lake of Tambukan fringed with trees and reeds. The lake is devoid of fish and fowl for the simple reason that it is so saline that a man may float in it. That is one reason. The other is that this is the lake where the Princess Pishtar drowned herself. As a mark of respect for her sacrifice, no birds will go there.

Anna was well aware of the old legend and her lonely rides with Bahram and Sirius often took her to this wild spot. There she would dismount and sit with her arms clasped round her knees, staring at the lake, whilst Bahram grazed quietly nearby and Sirius lay beside her panting. The still-shining circle of the lake soothed her and kept the blackness at bay and, if the blackness finally threatened to overwhelm her, then perhaps the Princess would welcome her into the lake. The lake looked so peaceful, so still—a place where there might be an end to all foul thoughts.

On her rides out to the lake she seldom saw anyone save the occasional distant herdsman on the steppe, which rolled away on all sides, with the jagged peaks of Pyatigorsk behind her. Always in front of her on the skyline was the serrated white wall of the Caucasus mountains. She could not avoid looking at them and could not avoid a shudder when she did; even the heat of the summer sun could not touch the bitter mountain cold in her mind.

The sun was warm on Anna's back and the stridulation of the grasshoppers all around soothed her. She watched a hawk soaring high above her and wished that she too could soar away, leaving the dark festering of her mind in a stinking heap on the ground. To soar away—or to enter the dark peaceful depths of the lake...

Sirius suddenly came alert; his ears sticking up, he began to whine.

Bahram raised his head, ears cocked, watching something.

Anna was instantly alert. Then she saw the distant figure of a lone horseman, moving at a steady trot across the rolling sea of grass.

The horseman was heading towards her.

Anna had time to mount Bahram and run, but she felt a great weariness come over her: there would be no more running. Anyway, perhaps the horseman was just a passer-by. If not..., her hand felt the hilt of the Cossack dagger she carried in her belt. No one would take her again.

Sirius got to his feet and began to bark, wagging his tail at the same time.

Bahram whinnied and got an answering whinny from the distant horse.

Anna was aghast. It was as though her companions were deliberately trying to attract the rider's attention.

Sure enough, the rider paused and, hearing the distant barking, swung his horse towards it.

Anna got to her feet, tense and poised. She eased the dagger in its sheath.

The rider came nearer and took on shape and feature.

Anna felt herself slowly relaxing.

Mischa had been cursing himself for a fool. He had diverted a long way from his direct route to the fort to get to the lake. He knew that the girl sometimes went there, but there was no reason that she should be there today. He had sat his horse for some time in indecision where a rough track lead off the main road in the direction of the lake—should he try it? He was tired and hot and thirsty. He dropped the reins on his horse's neck. Instead of setting off for the fort and its stable, the horse turned onto the track. Mischa shrugged.

It was as he neared the lake that he began cursing himself for a fool and his horse for a bigger one. Then came the shrill whinny, which his horse answered.

Then Mischa heard the distant barking. He knew that voice.

Mischa could see the great black horse standing with its head up and ears pricked watching his approach. He could see the slim erect figure standing stiffly, and he could see Sirius who came bounding across the rough grass to meet him, and danced round and round Mischa's horse woofing with delight.

"Treacherous mongrel!"—Mischa feigned disinterest at the gambolling dog—"Ungrateful cur! All right, let us see if you have forgotten everything in your absence. *UP!*"

With a sinuous bound Sirius leaped to the place behind Mischa's saddle where he had travelled so many miles. He stuck a wet nose in the back of the man's neck and began to lick an ear.

"Damn you, you bloody ingrate!"

Mischa was laughing in spite of himself. He was still laughing as he reined in his horse in front of Anna. At the sight of her set, drawn face, the laughter died in him.

Anna stood very stiffly, as though at attention. Even as he sat on his horse, Mischa could feel the coiled spring of the tension inside her. He looked at her in her ridiculous baggy breeches, with her long hair drawn severely back and tied with a band of silk. This served to accentuate the leanness of her face and its wonderful bone structure 'My God! But she's beautiful,' he said to himself, and found himself wondering how that wonderful body would feel close to his, how... with an effort he pulled his mind back.

Still sitting his horse, Mischa swept his cap off and bowed from the saddle. When he spoke, he spoke in German.

"Good morning, Fräulein, I have been on an errand and have news for you. Will you allow me to dismount?"

The girl did not move and her face remained totally immobile. Mischa sensed that any moment she might leap onto Bahram and be gone. He sat very still, his reins loose, whilst his horse snatched mouthfuls of the rough grass. 'We might as well be in a wax museum,' he thought dryly to himself.

"I have been to your village," he said gently.

The girl started, almost as though someone had slapped her. 'Oh God!' prayed Mischa, 'I've gone too far—she's going to bolt!'

At this moment, Sirius leaped from his seat and, going up to the girl, stuck his wet nose in her hand. Anna visibly relaxed and ran her fingers through the rough mane of hair on the dog's neck, making a small crooning noise.

"May I dismount, Fräulein?"

The girl gave Mischa a long searching stare, then gave a small nod. Mischa swung out of the saddle and stood in front of the girl twisting his hat in his hands; in truth, he felt very nervous. The girl was looking directly into his face and he could not but be aware of the huge green eyes.

"F-Fräulein…"

Damn! That childhood stammer, that sometimes returned in moments of stress. He started again:

"Fräulein, I took it upon myself to visit your village. I am sure you will be glad to hear that recovery and rebuilding are under way."

Damn! That sounded pompous! The green eyes were still staring straight at him and there was no flicker of emotion. Mischa shuffled his feet, wet his dry lips and started again:

"I also went to see the graves of your family. Your father, mother and brother were all laid together in the same grave. You will be glad to know that they have been properly and respectfully buried. The new pastor assures me that they were buried with the full rites of your church, and that the whole village turned out to honour them. They have raised a simple wooden cross over the grave. I… I… I…"—oh! that wretched stutter—"I… the pastor says that it would not be a good idea for you to think of returning to the village at present. I, I'm truly sorry."

The green eyes closed, tightly screwed up, and as Mischa

watched, rigid in his discomfort, he could see the glistening of a tear.

"So I brought you this," he blurted out—he had got it all wrong.

He cursed himself for a clumsy, interfering fool. He opened the saddle bag and took out the little wooden cross, roughly and simply made with twine, the two pieces of wood blackened and charred. Very slowly the green eyes opened again, wet and brimming with tears. Mischa held out the little cross:

"I went to your house and I took two pieces of wood from the house and I tied this cross for you. If I did wrong, I am truly sorry. I..."

Very slowly, Anna reached out a hand and took the cross that Mischa was offering.

For a long moment, she looked at it, the tears coursing down her cheeks now. She knelt down and raised the cross to her lips, then she bent her head as though in prayer. Mischa stood stiff and silent, not knowing what to do. He longed to take the girl in his arms and comfort her, but he did not dare.

It seemed an age before the girl got to her feet. The bout of crying was finished but she was sniffing. Without a word, Mischa took the large silk handkerchief from his pocket and presented it. The girl paused for a moment, then wiped her eyes and blew her nose. She stood looking into Mischa's eyes and for a fraction of a second the eyes lit up and there was a fleeting flash of a smile. The she tucked the cross into the front of her shirt and in one easy movement swung into Bahram's saddle. She turned the horse as though to gallop away. Then she paused, swung back and raising the fingers of her right hand to her lips, she leaned from the saddle and briefly brushed Mischa's lips with finger tips. Then she was gone—Bahram at full stretch across the steppe and Sirius, barking and galloping alongside.

Mischa was left alone and open-mouthed, twisting the

handkerchief in his hands.

The handkerchief was still wet with Anna's tears. Mischa raised it to his lips and stowed it away in the inside pocket of his coat, before swinging slowly into the saddle and setting off in the track of the flying dot on the horizon. Mischa had a lot to think about.

The old priest of St Lazar belched appreciatively, wiped his beard on the back of his hand and patted the bulge of his belly under the stained soutane. The meal of greasy mutton had been much to his satisfaction. He looked forward to a quiet hour or two of meditation in a comfortable chair before the time for evening prayers, but prior to that it was his custom to take a brief stroll round his onion-domed church that looked down on Pyatigorsk. He belched again as he entered the church through the vestry and engaged on one of his internal arguments that he liked to hold with himself—this time as to whether Saints broke wind during their earthly lives.

This so engrossed him that at first he thought the church was entirely empty. It surprised him vaguely—in as much as he had any capacity for surprise left—because there was usually at least one of the old babuschkas who haunted the church hard at prayer. It was then that he saw the lone figure standing still and erect just inside the main door. The figure stood black against the sunlight that beat in through the doorway and the distant view of the steppe, and beyond it the jagged white fangs of the far off Caucasus mountains.

In spite of his somewhat faded eyesight, the old man recognised the figure instantly: it was the German girl. Like everybody else in the town, the priest knew the story and had felt a passing twinge of pity.

'Passing' because the great compassion for suffering that had brought the old man to the priesthood had all but worn down. He had heard and seen so much suffering and the world did not seem one wit the better for it. He could still offer the words and face of comfort, but his heart had dried, the fire burned down. He was looking forward to his rest. Still, something about the motionless figure stirred him. Somewhere in the ashes of his faith and compassion an ember glowed slightly.

He saw the girl stiffen as he approached. She looked like a deer poised for flight. The old man spoke gently:

"Can I help you child?"

For a long time the girl stared at him—he knew that she did not speak. Then she put a hand inside her shirt and brought out a little wooden cross made of two pieces of charred wood tied together with twine. She held it towards him. The priest reached out a tentative hand and took it. He was bewildered, but he realised that this rough little cross was of immense importance to the girl, and even as he watched two large tears ran down her face.

"What is it, child? Can you not tell me?"

The girl shook her head vehemently and then made a sign as of someone writing. The priest was thoroughly engaged now and, making a sign for Anna to wait, he went to the vestry and returned with pencil and paper.

"Sit there child and write."

The girl sat and very carefully wrote three words in Russian. She handed the paper to the old man. He read:

'Mama, Papa, Matthias.'

The priest felt overwhelmed by a grief such as he thought that the years had long burned out of him. He raised the little cross.

"You wish me to take this as an offering for your loved ones?"

Her head bent and weeping, the girl nodded.

"You wish me to chose a saint for you?"

Anna raised her head and shook it vigorously. She pointed. The priest followed her finger. In the middle of the church stood an elaborate shrine, bright with silver and gilt decoration. In the centre of the shrine was the icon of the Black Madonna. The girl was pointing directly at it. The priest hesitated. This would not be according to custom. Then, in spite of the warmth of the day, he felt a shudder run down his back, not of cold, nor fear, but of power. It was a long time since he had felt a charge like that.

He beckoned the girl and they set off up the aisle to the shrine. At the altar rail, he signed to the girl to stop. She did not, but followed him into the innermost area in front of the altar—a place where only a priest may tread.

He started to protest, but the charge again rippled down his spine and he remained silent. With Anna by his side, the priest crossed himself, genuflected, then reaching up he put the little cross below the icon. Then girl and priest knelt in the holy place. The old man looked at the girl, her head bent, her lips moving. She was praying.

The priest prayed too and, for the first time in many years, spoke to God.

9 Riding the Storm

'**W**E'RE going west!' A buzz of excitement ran through the group of assembled officers as Colonel Ryshkov regarded them from under his bushy eyebrows:

"It's war, my children. The little corporal from Corsica has apparently given up his idea of invading England and is marching his armies into Germany. The Little Father, our Czar, has decided that the French poodle should be put back in its kennel. The Imperial Army under Marshal Kutusov is already in Austria. We are to be mobilised and march west to join them"—the Colonel turned his gaze on Mischa—"and together we will whip the cur. I am awaiting orders for us to march and join the main army. We will leave a holding garrison here at the fort. In the meantime the General has ordered that the Black Madonna must be taken to Divisional Headquarters. Her presence there will hearten all the Cossack troops. They will not want to go into battle without the presence of Our Lady." The Colonel crossed himself. "Major Lubin will organise an escort for the icon to ensure Her safety. Now, my lambs, go and prepare your men for war."

The building shook as the officers stamped their feet and roared out the Russian 'Hoorah!' As the other officers tumbled out of the building, talking excitedly, Mischa and Charles remained standing in front of the Colonel. Ryshkov sank back in his chair and steepled his fingers:

"And what do you young game cocks want?"

Mischa came stiffly to attention:

"I request your permission to accompany Major Lubin, Colonel."

"Hmm! And you, Captain FitzHugh?"

Charles also came to attention:

"I also request permission to join the escort, Colonel."

The two young men stared stiffly to their fronts, neither looking at the other.

"Hmm," said the Colonel again, "both of you together, eh? I have observed that a certain frostiness still exists between you. I wonder if this is a good idea."

"I can assure the Colonel that no personal difference that I may have with Captain FitzHugh would be allowed to interfere with my duty."

"And you?"

"I feel the same way as the Rittmeister, Colonel. Our difference of, er, opinion must wait until after the war."

"You might both get killed."

"Then, Colonel, the problem will be solved."

The Colonel grunted and remained deep in thought for a time:

"Very well—I will consult Major Lubin. If he will take you, then you can go. Dismiss!"

The two men saluted, about-turned and marched out of the office. Outside, they paused and stood side by side, still not looking at each other; it was Charles who spoke first:

"Look Czerny, it ain't no good us setting off like this. We've got two thousand miles to travel and God knows what in between. If I say that I was wrong about the girl, will you take a handshake?"

For a moment, Mischa stood stiffly, staring into the distance:

"It was not correct of me to have thrown that drink in your face."

They turned solemnly to face each other and, after a moment's hesitation, clasped hands.

"After all," said Charles, "the girl's managed to steal my horse and your dog without speaking a bloody word. That makes us something of comrades in adversity, I suppose."

"Bloody dog," said Mischa gloomily.

"Bloody horse," said Charles.

Sirius came bounding to meet Mischa as he approached the Ryshkov's house.

"Turncoat!" said Mischa ruffling the shaggy head.

Sirius did a little pirouette of pleasure in front of him.

"Judas!"

Sirius grinned.

Sarah Ryshkova had been watching the performance from her chair under the oak tree, where she was smoking one of her small cheroots in the mellow autumn sunshine.

"Good afternoon, Herr Rittmeister—so you are off to the war with Our Lady. You must take great care of her. She is of the greatest importance to us Cossacks."

"I assure you, Madame, that I will guard the Lady with my life."

"Well and stiffly said, Sir! And you leave in the morning?"

"Yes Madame."

"And you have spared the time to come and say good bye to an old woman?" Sarah Ryshkova's eyes twinkled.

"And to thank you for all your kindness.'"

"La, Sir—you have caused great entertainment in a dull life."

Mischa stood silent for a moment, seemingly with a sudden interest in the toe caps of his boots. Sarah watched him with wry amusement through a cloud of blue smoke.

"Was there anything else the Rittmeister wanted?" she asked mischievously.

Mischa shuffled his feet and then blurted out that he would like to say goodbye to Anna.

"It would be extremely ill-mannered of you not to do so. Come into the house and we will drink a glass to your success and safety. Sirius! Warn the household!"

Sirius bounded up the path and, standing on his hind legs, pushed the door open and disappeared inside.

Anna was sitting in her usual chair by the window; Waif was standing behind her humming softly and brushing Anna's long golden hair. This had become something of an obsession with Waif, but Anna found it immensely soothing and laid her head back and closed her eyes.

There had been a time in the recent past when she hardly

dared to close her eyes, and so she would try to keep herself awake at night, because sleep brought dreams. Her dreams were a writhing horror of blood, smoke, pain and always that distorted leering face that for her personified evil. The face would come spinning out of the blackness, coming nearer and nearer until she could smell the stink of the man and feel the pawing of his hot hard hands on her body. She would wake screaming and sweating.

Waif, who insisted on sleeping in a cot at the foot of her bed, would come to her, wiping the sweat from her, and cradle Anna's head in her arms, murmuring softly to her as a mother would soothe a frightened baby, until Anna's whimpering and crying would ease and she would sink back into a more kindly oblivion. The dreams came less often now, and when they started Anna's unconscious would call on other faces to help her. There was the sweet dark face of the Lady, which would come floating in front of her and before which the terrors would flee.

Every day now, Anna would make her way to the church of St Lazar and kneel quietly in front of the icon. There she stared up at the gentle face of the Black Madonna and at the crude little cross of charred wood that lay at the foot of the icon. Sometimes the old priest would come and kneel beside her in silence. His presence would be a comfort to her—a man with no threat. Anna would never know the great peace of the soul that her praying and her little cross had restored to the old man—his Faith had returned.

Sometimes another face would float into her dreams: the face of a great bear of a man, but there was no threat there either. She would imagine the gentleness of the huge hands as they caressed her; the strength of the massive arms as they held her; the warmth and the strong male smell of him. Then her body would stir as she imagined... as she imagined... something that would drive the horrors away for ever.

She was thinking of this even now as Waif brushed her hair. Then she woke from her day-dream with a start as the door crashed open and Sirius came bounding in. Putting his hugefore paws on her, he began to lick her face vigorously.

He was obviously excited. Waif, who seemed to understand Sirius instinctively by now, hurriedly pushed Anna upright and, pulling her hair back, tied it up becomingly with a piece of black silk.

A cloud of rank cheroot smoke wafted in front of Sarah Ryshkova.

"Anna, my dear, we have a caller. Herr Rittmeister Czerny is off to the wars with the Black Madonna. He has come to say good bye."

Anna felt her heart turn to ice—the man and the Black Madonna were leaving—who would comfort her dreams now?

Mischa's great bulk filled the doorway as he entered the room and made a stiff little bow. He hoped that he was not intruding. He hoped that Fräulein Anna was greatly improved in her health. He could see that her riding had greatly ameliorated her condition. He hoped that his wretched ingrate of a dog was not being a nuisance and causing too much disruption to the Fräulein. He hoped... he wished...

At this point Mischa dried up and stood rather miserably, twisting the cap in his hands and shuffling his feet. He thought crossly that bloody Charles would have had all the right things to say. There was so much that he wanted to say, but in front of this girl's silent beauty he felt like some ill-conditioned hobbledehoy. What a fright he must be, standing there shuffling and mumbling.

Poor Mischa was struck dumb.

Then there was a sudden clear voice in his head. With it came the flash of a vision of the one-eyed man in a battered hat, who took his pipe out of his mouth and said in a clear and exasperated voice:

"Give her the book, man; for the sake of all the gods, give her the book."

Mischa pulled himself together, coughed and fumbled in the pocket of his coat. He coughed again and stammered out the little speech that he had prepared about how he hoped that Fräulein Anna would accept a small present as a token of his deep respect and esteem for her, and...

"Oh get on with it, man," said the Hunter.

Mischa took from his pocket the battered little German prayer book that had travelled with him all the way from Lippitz and, with another stiff little bow, offered it to Anna. Never taking her eyes from his face, Anna took the book. As she did so, something fell from it into her lap; it was the dried and pressed remains of the yellow rose. Anna gave a little gasp and, for a long moment, sat there looking at it.

Then a little miracle happened. Anna's face—for so long set in sorrow—moved. The mask cracked, her eyes flashed and her mouth widened in a brilliant and dazzling smile.

"By all the saints!" said Sarah Ryshkova to herself.

Anna got slowly to her feet, the little book and the rose clutched to her bosom. For a long moment she stood and stared at Mischa, who was still basking in the warmth of that wonderful smile.

Never taking her eyes from Mischa's face, Anna reached behind her head and pulled the black silk band free, so that the golden hair tumbled around her shoulders. She raised the ribbon to her lips and held it there for a moment; then, still smiling, she handed the ribbon to Mischa, who took it like a man in a dream.

Anna turned and darted from the room—with Sirius at her heels.

"By all the saints!" Sarah exclaimed out loud this time.

Mischa was still standing like a statue, the ribbon lying across his hands.

"I think," said Sarah gently, "that after that, we all need a glass of vodka."

* * *

The Khan slid from the saddle and handed the reins of his horse to one of the escorting brigands. He stopped for a moment to admire the new horse, a fine, bay, Kabardine stallion that he had recently 'liberated'. It was a fine horse, he thought, but he still allowed himself a grind of the teeth as he thought of the beautiful black stallion that the filthy Cossacks had so basely stolen from him:

"Wait here," he growled.

The escort also dismounted and settled themselves comfortably on the grassy patch at the foot of a waterfall. The Khan looked at the steep narrow goat track beside the waterfall and scowled—he hated walking. However, a summons from the Shaman was not to be ignored. He twisted his sword-belt round so that the scabbard hung behind him not to hinder his progress, and set off up the rock ladder.

The Khan was in high good humour. His stock, which had fallen so low with the clans after the débacle of Tearnause, had been somewhat restored by raids on several 'soft' villages; there was nothing like a bit of rape and pillage to restore morale, he thought. The nice plump little Kabardine girl that he had acquired along with the horse, had whimpered and screamed in a most satisfactory manner as a result of his 'ministrations'. This word made him think of the wives and the fact that they had been pleasantly quiet lately, with no more unsettling demands.

And had not his virility been amply demonstrated by the safe and satisfactory delivery of a fine male baby to the youngest wife? The Khan had inspected it closely—without actually touching it—and everything that should be there seemed to be in the right place. So, all in all, he felt satisfied with himself.

As he puffed and swore his way up the rocky ladder, he felt the satisfaction ebbing away. The Shaman had this effect on him. In fact the shrivelled little old man terrified him, although he would hardly admit that to himself let alone anyone else. He paused at the doorway of the mean hovel. As usual, the inside was thick with smoke, very little of which ever seemed to escape from the smoke-hole in the roof.

"Come in, my son."

The dry leathery voice rasped his nerves, and he shivered as he bent through the doorway and entered the acrid blue cloud. After a few moments, he could make out the wizened figure, hunched over the miserable fire, with the stiff leg stuck out as always.

"Sit."

The Khan settled himself cross-legged on the opposite side of the fire. Almost immediately the dank cold of the rough stone-flagged floor started to creep into his bones— why did that blasted fire never seem to give out any heat? The silence seemed to stretch interminably, but the Khan did not dare break it. He was there to listen. At last the old man spoke, the voice dry and creaking like weathered hide.

"My son, our time is coming—our moment of glory."

He stopped and let the words swirl round with the smoke. The Khan tried to ease himself from a sharp corner of flagstone that was sticking into him. He had a feeling that he was not going to like what was coming.

"The cursed icon the Black Madonna, has left the protection of the fort and is being taken to the Cossack army to help them fight in the west. Now is your chance to seize it and so will the Cossacks be destroyed. To lose the Black Madonna would be like losing their balls."

The Shaman made a sound that might have been a cough or a laugh:

"You must gather your men together at once; tell them what is afoot. Tell them that this is a holy war for all the spirits of the mountains. Tell them that when the Black Madonna is taken the Cossacks will be smashed and we will be able to come out of the mountains and rape the plump land below at will."

The Khan scratched his beard, thoughtfully:

"And how will I find the Black Madonna?"

"The escort is heading north-west from Pyatigorsk. You will be guided by the spirits."

The Khan chewed his lower lip.

"That's a long way from the mountains."

The Khan did not like to be too far from the sanctuary of the mountains.

"Exactly, my son, they will not be expecting any trouble."

"Even so, on the open steppe, surprise will be necessary."

"You have doubts?" The voice was like a snake's hiss.

"No! No!" the Khan threw back his shoulders. "I am the

Wolf of Elbrus, I fear no man!"

The dry cough came again:

"Quite. Listen, when you are out on the steppe, a storm will come in the night and you will come with the storm and cut the Cossacks to pieces."

The old man's voice had risen to a screech that descended into a fit of coughing. The Khan had often wondered how the Shaman knew these things, and had as often decided that he did not want to know. He just felt a chill in his bones—and that was not entirely due to the cold stones of the floor.

"One thing more."

The Khan waited.

"If you fail to get the Black Madonna, it would be unwise for you to return to the mountains."

The Khan shivered again.

"And one thing more; where you find the Black Madonna, there you will also find your German Gold."

* * *

"Back on the bloody steppe, Vlad me lad," said Trooper Bone, "and a bloody draughty spot it is too."

Bone was huddled into his cloak with his hands held out to the camp fire as the cold night-wind howled over the camp.

Vlad shrugged; to him weather was an act of God.

"Just an autumn storm, Bone. We shall have more of them before winter really sets in."

Lubin, Charles and Mischa were huddled around their own fire.

They had set off from Pyatigorsk in fine autumn sunshine and high spirits, which had been maintained for the three days of the westward march. The cold blast of wind and rain out of the east had come as an unwelcome surprise.

"Bloody weather," said Charles, fumbling in his pocket for his big silver hip flask.

"Just an autumn storm, Charles," said Lubin. "Mother Russia likes to remind you that winter is coming... and with it a war," he added.

"Let's drink to both." Charles unscrewed his flask.

"Permission to speak, Excellency!"

The huge bulk of the Sergeant Major loomed out of the howling night.

"Sarn't Major?"

"Excellency, I think that we are being followed."

"What makes you think that?" asked Lubin.

The Sergeant Major tapped his huge eagle's beak of a nose.

"I feel it—smell it, Excellency."

"How many and how far?"

"Maybe only one man and close"

Lubin thought for a moment:

"It could be a scout for a raiding party. One would hardly expect such a thing, this far into Russia, but..." he became silent again, then swung smoothly to his feet.

"Sarn't Major—my compliments to Captain Zorokin. He is to stand the men to and take command until I return. Then bring a section here and we will investigate this mystery man. And Sarn't Major..."

"Excellency!"

"Bring your nose with you."

The little party set off on foot into the howling night, the wind lashing their faces, and occasional dashes of hail making them curse quietly and hug their cloaks around their faces. They were roughly back-tracking on that day's path, moving in file, with the Sergeant Major leading in deference to his nose.

Mischa and Charles who were following behind Lubin could just make out his figure, now that their eyes had become used to the darkness. There was a darker mass in front of them, and Mischa decided it must be a small grove of scrubby trees in a hollow that the squadron had passed through earlier in the afternoon—maybe a mile or more from their camp.

All of a sudden the Sergeant Major stopped. They could

see his hand held up in the murk. His nose tested the wind like a dog. He turned to Lubin, bringing his bearded lips close to the officer's ear:

"Woodsmoke! Just over the rise, in the hollow!"

Lubin slid his sabre gently from its scabbard. Without orders, the section followed his action and, at a silent wave of Lubin's blade, the Cossacks spread out in skirmishing order.

They crept forward.

As they did so, the cloud wrack broke, and the moon—two days from full—illuminated the scene. Below the rise on which they were standing lay a small hollow, and in the trees of the far side, they could make out the dark shape of a hobbled horse. In the hollow were the smouldering remains of a miserable fire with a smell of rain-soaked ash. By the fire was a shape huddled under a blanket. Mischa thought that whoever it might be was having a miserable night, that was just about to get much worse.

Creeping carefully, the Cossacks surrounded the hollow.

Charles whispered urgently to Lubin:

"Let me take the blighter!"

Lubin shrugged: "We'll be right behind you."

Foot by foot, Charles edged forward until his moon-shadow touched the huddled form. Then, with a yell, he leaped upon it—wrenching at the blanket.

Several things happened at once.

Charles leaped back, cursing and clutching a hand from which, even in the moonlight, it was possible to see that blood was flowing.

The moon gleamed on a knife blade that appeared from under the blanket.

With a roar something huge and hairy launched itself also from under the blanket.

There was a flash of teeth and Charles was down, yelling and cursing as the monster worried him.

The Cossacks surged forward, sabres raised, with a great 'Hurrah!'

"Stop!"—it was Mischa's roar—"Halt!" He leaped forward to the centre of the circle, his hands spread.

The Cossacks, surprised, halted, their blades at the ready.

"*Sirius!* Leave it! Leave it, Sir!"

The monstrous shape that had Charles pinned to the ground, its teeth flashing at his throat, backed away growling. Then it turned and trotting up to Mischa gave him an ecstatic welcome. Seizing him by the skin under the chin, Mischa held the dog's face up until Sirius was forced to look into his master's eyes. The man held him there until the dog's tail drooped and he began to whine.

"But," said Mischa wearily, loosing the now cringing animal, "I suppose you are not really to blame. Come out, Fräulein."

Very slowly the blanket was pushed aside and Anna's head, hair shining in the moonlight, emerged. Mischa spoke in the same weary voice:

"Give me the knife, Fräulein, before someone gets hurt."

"What do you fucking mean, before someone gets hurt?" Charles was on his feet nursing his arm.

"Well, I don't want her knifing anybody else."

"The bloody bitch didn't knife me, she bit me—just like your bloody dog."

Anna was standing now, her face stubborn, the knife in her hand.

"Give me the knife, Fräulein."

Mischa held out his hand. The girl stared at him, her mouth set.

"No!"

"Give me the knife!"

"I won't!"

Something snapped inside Mischa:

"*Give me the damned knife or I'll put you across my knee and give you a damned good hiding!*"

"*You wouldn't dare!*" screamed the girl, spitting with fury.

The two of them stood glaring at each other.

Sirius, who had been watching with his head on one side, trotted across to Anna and, very gently taking her hand, clenched on the knife hilt in his huge jaws, shook it until the girl gave a little cry and the knife fell to the ground.

At this Anna fell to her knees, buried her face in Sirius's mane and began to cry.

Mischa's anger fell away from him to be replaced by a thought that hit him like a fist:

"She spoke!" he said to Charles.

"She bit me."

"You spoke!"

There was a small sniffle from the depths of Sirius's mane.

"Yes,"—the voice was equally small.

"But... What?"

"He jumped on me! I don't like being jumped on— especially by *him*."

"Why you ungrateful little bitch!"

"Charles! I really must ask you..."

"Mischa! I have been bitten by your woman..."

"I'm not his woman!" Anna was on her feet again.

"...by your woman and your dog, I think I might get a little courtesy, but I suppose that at least I shall get my horse back."

"No!"

At this point the hardly suppressed mirth of the Cossacks broke out, and the three protagonists were engulfed by waves of laughter.

"I think," said Lubin smoothly, "that we had best get back to the camp and sort it all out there. Charles, do you still have your flask about you?"

"Yes—that's a damned good idea." Charles unscrewed the top.

"Ladies first," said Lubin.

"The question is what are we going to do with the lady."

Lubin stretched back at ease in front of a fire when they were back at the camp.

They all turned to look at the lady.

Anna was wolfing down a large bowl of horse-meat stew, watched with a close and keen interest by Sirius. The fact that he had already consumed a large portion of gravy soaked bread did not seem to lessen his interest. His eyes followed each spoonful as it went to Anna's mouth. Occasionally, she would not be able to resist the accusation in his eyes and would throw him a gobbet of meat, which the dog would catch with languid grace.

"Send the b..." A warning growl from Mischa stopped Charles and he bowed towards Mischa. "Begging my comrade's pardon," he said sarcastically, "send the lady"—he stressed the word—"back. Surely she has caused enough trouble already."

He waved the hand, roughly bandaged by Bone, as a convincing argument.

"I'm not going back," Anna licked the last traces of stew from the spoon, wiped the bowl round with a piece of black bread, ate it and daintily wiped her mouth on the corner of the cloak that had been wrapped round her, "...and you can't make me."

"It would not be safe to send her back on her own."

Mischa was staring gloomily into the fire.

"She bloody well came here on her own!"

Charles was hardly in a good mood after the happenings of the night; both his hand and his pride were damaged—he knew that the story of the events in the hollow was even then circulating amongst the Cossacks of the escort and losing nothing in the telling.

"Which begs the question that none of us has been so indelicate as to pose, yet," said Lubin in his lazy drawl, "as to why the lady decided to follow us in the first place and how?"

Mischa raised his eyes and looked across the fire. Anna seemed to have shrunk into the folds of the too-large cloak. Her eyes met his:

"Don't let them send me back," she spoke in German.

Mischa replied gently, in the same language:

"Then you must tell us why you came, Fräulein."

"And stop jabbering away in Kraut." Charles was roused again. "I suppose that this is all some damned German plot, eh, what?"

"Certainly not!" Mischa's anger was rising.

"All this damned 'holier than thou' nonsense of yours, Mischa, but when it comes down to it, you just can't wait to get those damned breeches off her and... Shit! You bloody dangerous bitch!"

The bowl flung with unerring accuracy by Anna, hit Charles full on the bridge of his nose. It began to bleed.

"You see, Mischa? You see what your precious doxy has done?"

"I am not his doxy!" Anna spat out. "I am no one's doxy!"

"Stop this nonsense!" Lubin's voice had an unaccustomed edge to it. "May I remind you all that this is an active service mission, which I command. There will be no brawling!" Then his voice reverted to his usual amiable drawl: "Now perhaps the lady will explain just why she did follow us?"

Anna seemed to withdraw into the folds of the cloak again. She was silent for a moment, then spoke in a small voice, so quiet that the men had difficulty hearing:

"He told me to follow."

"Which he?" Lubin persisted.

"Sirius."

There was a pause of astonishment, then Charles threw his arms in the air with a bark of laughter:

"Well if that don't take the batter pudding! She came because a bloody dog told her to come! I tell you, Lubin, the woman's not only dangerous but mad as well! And, my God, I've been bitten by her! Any moment now I shall start frothing at the mouth and howling at the moon! So now Herr Rittmeister, what answer have you got to that, eh?"

Mischa had been staring across the fire at Sirius. The dog's eyes seemed to meet his and hold them. At last, he shook his head and said quietly:

"No, I don't think that she's mad, although, God knows, she has every right to be after what she's been through. No, she's not mad."

"I suppose that she's bitten you as well."—Charles was standing now and working himself into a fine old rage—"Well, I tell you what, Lubin. Either that girl goes or I do!"

"Beg pardon, Excellency," the great bulk of the Sergeant Major loomed out of the darkness.

"Yes, Sarn't Major?"

"I don't think that the lady should leave, not on her own, not now."

"Problems, Sarn't Major?"

"Could be something brewing up, Excellency."

"Your nose?"

"Yes, Excellency."

"Hmm." Lubin thought for a moment, then said crisply, "Right that's it. The lady stays. And, Sarn't Major…"

"Excellency?"

"Double the picquets."

"Christ Almighty!" Charles was in a splendid rage now. "That is it! That is definitely it! If she stays I go. I'm not staying with a rag tag that's run by a dog and the sergeant major's nose."

"You are here as a guest, Charles, and so is the lady. You may come or go as you please."

Without another word, Charles turned on his heel and strode off into the camp shouting for Bone. Mischa half got to his feet.

"Sit down, Mischa," Lubin drawled. "You will do no good with him in that frame of mind. Let him go and cool himself on the steppe for a couple of days. I feel it in my water that there is another storm coming. So… welcome to our little band, Fräulein. It looks as though we now have two ladies to escort."

The steppe rolled away to the horizon: a seemingly endless

land sea of rough grassy downland, with scrubby woodland and reed-thick marshes in the bottoms of the combes. Across this featureless plain the escort of the Black Madonna moved. To the eye of a soaring eagle they would have looked like a line of beetles crawling across the grey green expanse. Occasionally the track to the west would run through a village of wretched timber and turf hovels, scattered along a dirt road that the recent storms were already turning into glutinous mud.

The Cossacks moved at the easy, distance-covering jog that the tough little Cossack horses could keep up for miles, day in and day out. The wind stayed in the east, keeping the escort huddled in their cloaks.

Charles and Bone had disappeared in the previous night. Mischa worried about their safety. Lubin shrugged. He did not foresee much in the way of trouble out here on the steppe—"as long as Charles keeps his cock in his breeches, and does not try anything with the women in the villages."

He thought that hunger and boredom were much more likely to affect Charles:

"There is nowhere for them to go, except back to Pyatigorsk, and I don't think that Charles's pride will allow that."

Anna rode alongside Mischa. The hood of her cloak almost entirely hid her face and she had not spoken since the events of the previous night.

Mischa felt uncomfortable. He could not help wondering whether the business with Charles had driven her back into the prison of silent trauma from which she had emerged. He kept glancing at the slim, muffled figure riding beside him. He felt an almost overwhelming urge to touch her—just to lay a hand on her arm, perhaps—simply a gesture of comfort, he told himself. Once or twice he tried to steel himself to speak to her, but each time the silence baffled him. At last he could stand the situation no longer:

"I d-d-do h-h-hope,"—damn that blasted stammer—"I do hope, Fräulein, that the unfortunate events of last night have not upset you too much."

He knew that the words sounded stiff and formal. Formality was a refuge where he did not have to admit to himself how much the girl's presence stirred him. For what seemed an age, there was no response. Suddenly, the girl pushed back her hood. Her fine boned face looked set and serious, and the yellow hair cascaded over her shoulders. She turned her head and studied Mischa for a long moment, her face expressionless.

"Herr Rittmeister, do you still have that ribbon I gave you?"

Mischa was taken aback.

"May I have it back please?"

A slim hand appeared from the fold of the cloak.

"Y-yes, of course."

Thoroughly puzzled, Mischa, fumbled in the breast of his tunic, where the ribbon was carefully tucked away and, pulling it out, put it in the outstretched hand.

"Thank you."

The girl took the ribbon and, pushing the hood further back and dropping the reins on Bahram's neck, she deftly gathered her hair behind her head, tying it back with the ribbon. Then she turned to Mischa and flashed that amazing, dazzling smile at him.

"Thank you. My hair is a mess. Poor Waif would be horrified if she saw it."

Mischa seized the opportunity to continue the conversation:

"I hope that Waif is all right. She did not accompany you?"

"Certainly not. She wanted to, but she has suffered enough. She will be safe with Madame Ryshkova."

"And Madame Ryshkova—does she know that you followed us?"

"Certainly!"

"Did she not try to stop you?"

"No. She just looked at me for a long time then said that I must follow my star"

"Just that?"

Anna's face was solemn again:

"She said that I would be safe with you."

"Holy God!"

The green eyes were boring into his face.

"Am I safe with you?"

Mischa spluttered—utterly confused:

"F-Fräulein, I assure you that I... that I..."

The green eyes seemed to sparkle at his confusion.

"She also gave me this."

The 'this' was a large flask of vodka.

"Perhaps the Rittmeister would like a drink?"

The Rittmeister thought that he bloody well would, and tried to cover his confusion with a piece of hearty joviality:

"Come in jolly useful now that we have lost Charles and his flask."

"The Englishman is a pig!"

Anna disappeared into her hood and silence.

It was a miserable day's ride for the escort. The wind was set in the east and bringing with it a thin cold rain, that seeped through all clothing and seemed to penetrate to the very bone, chilling and numbing both mind and body. The men rode in sodden misery—too miserable even to grumble, that traditional military safety valve.

Since the morning, Anna and Mischa had ridden in silence, both huddled in their cloaks. Even Sirius seemed downhearted, trotting along with his ears back and his stern down, his rough coat sleeked with rain.

Mischa sought once or twice to break the silence with some cheering remark. Anna had remained silent, hidden in her hood. At last, Mischa gave up and retreated into himself. He tried to think of pleasant things. He tried to think of Lippitz and his friends in the regiment, but then he thought of

the thousands of miles of trackless howling steppe that lay between, and at last lapsed into dull, animal misery. Even the
Hunter seemed to have deserted him.

As the afternoon wore on, the weather got colder still, and
the rain turned to sleet. The wind took on a wolf's howl and a
black pall spread along the eastern horizon. There was a
storm brewing. Lubin watched the deteriorating conditions
and gave orders to make camp early.

The escort was on the open steppe with no shelter in sight
and no wood to make a fire. The men settled down to a night
of cold, with only some black bread to ease the pangs of hunger. The black pall in the east soon turned into a black,
howling darkness that made men shiver with much more
than cold.

Lubin was more tense than Mischa had ever seen him. He
had ordered that the horses were not to be off-saddled—they
stood tethered in their lines, heads hanging and their backs
turned to the blast.

Mischa sat on his sodden blanket, with the moisture dripping from the peak of his cap. He wondered, briefly, how
Charles and Bone were faring, and decided that they could
not be more miserable than he was at that moment as he
stared into the blackness.

In the darkness, he felt a figure move up beside him.

"I'm so cold," said a small voice.

Mischa said nothing. He just opened his cloak and pulled
the figure to him, putting his arm around the slim shoulders.
He could feel the girl shuddering with cold and pulled her
closer to him till she rested her head on his chest. A cold nose
prodded his face and a large expanse of wet dog wriggled
underneath the cover of the two cloaks. Mischa thought dryly
that Sirius had an advanced sense of propriety.

A larger shadow loomed out of the night:

"Excellency?"

"Sarn't Major."

"I have posted double picquets, Excellency."

"You expect trouble—on a night like this?"

"A bad night for bad work, Excellency."

"Your nose, eh?"

The Sergeant Major never answered, for at that moment a musket ball removed not only the famous nose, but the side of his face as well.

They came screaming out of the darkness as though they were devils from the pit of hell, riding on the storm.

In the darkness men ran cursing and stumbling trying to find their horses, but the devils were amongst them slashing and stabbing, cutting down the running men. A few shots flashed in the darkness, but many powder charges were wet and there was no second chance. It was a slaughter.

A ring of Cossacks surrounded the box containing the icon of the Black Madonna. They put up a stubborn and fierce resistance, but were cut down one by one by the encircling horsemen.

Mischa had been on his feet in an instant, sabre in hand. Instinctively he had pushed Anna behind him. As if by magic, Vlad appeared at his side. Lubin made up the rest of the little group, that was swiftly surrounded by yelling riders.

Steel clashed on steel.

A horse came down, screaming, hamstrung by Vlad, who swiftly dispatched its cursing rider.

There was a roar from Lubin, whose monocle fell from his eye and he staggered forward with the point of a lance sticking out of his back. A slash from a sabre took half his face away as he fell.

It was cut, thrust and slash, then there was a sudden burning pain in Mischa's arm as a lance thrust cut open his shoulder; the sabre fell from his hand. Anna seized it and as she did so her hood fell back, revealing the flash of her golden hair.

A voice roared in the darkness and the riders suddenly

drew back, leaving Anna and Mischa standing alone.

'Where was Vlad?' Mischa wondered to himself, but had no time to wonder further.

A horseman spurred out from the others.

Even in the darkness, Anna could recognise the shape—it had filled her nightmares for long enough.

She screamed. Her grip tightened on the hilt of the sabre.

The Khan roared with laughter.

"So you have not forgotten me?"—the wind carried his words like a whip—"You scream all you like, girl, I will soon give you good cause. But first I will cut your friend so that he dies—but not too quickly."

The Khan spurred his horse forward, his sabre raised.

Then something shot out of the darkness and rocketed through the air. The Khan gave a yell of pain and fear as Sirius's teeth fastened in his shoulder, and the force of the dog's weight sent him tumbling backwards out of the saddle.

"Now Excellency! *Now!* I have the horses!"

Vlad's voice was desperate.

10 Sirius Triumphant

$\mathcal{T}$HE cold morning air bit into Mischa's naked torso. He shivered.

"Keep still!"

Anna's voice was severe, but indistinct because of the knife that she held in her mouth. The little party had stumbled into a stretch of scrubby woodland in their headlong flight through the howling storm and darkness. There they had taken what shelter they could and spent a night of discomfort and misery, with Mischa and Vlad taking it in turns to stand guard. Not that any of them slept, what with cold, hunger and the reaction to the appalling violence of the night.

At first Anna had called for Sirius, until Mischa told her sternly to desist, lest her calling attract unwanted attention:

"Sirius will find us," he said. But Sirius did not come.

Anna wept silently as she huddled in her sodden cloak. She felt sure that the great dog was dead, hacked to pieces by the infuriated brigands. He had died protecting them and through that night, Anna wished that she might die too. Life just seemed to consist of violence, misery and the loss of all that she loved.

The awful storm passed in the night. The morning dawned bright and clear, with a rind of hoar frost that made them shudder with cold. Mischa was not in good order and was shivering with more than the cold. He could hardly move his wounded arm and he felt feverish.

There was a small stream at the bottom of the wood and, seeing Mischa's condition, Anna forgot her own misery and became brisk and business-like. Here was something practical that she did understand. She made Mischa kneel by the stream and, with Vlad's help, removed his torn tunic. The shirt was more of a problem. The blood-soaked material had dried and clotted in the deep gash on the shoulder. Mischa was obviously in deep pain. Anna snapped a twig from a bush:

"Bite on this," she said to Mischa. "It is going to hurt."

Vlad brought a water canteen from one of the saddles and, using the fresh water from the spring, Anna soaked and softened the clotted blood on the shoulder. Then, with her knife, she cut the sleeve away from the rest of the shirt.

"Hold him still, Vlad—this will not be good."

Biting her lip with concentration she began to ease the sleeve away from the wound. Mischa threw his head back, the sinews taut in his neck, his teeth biting deeply into the twig. With a triumphant "Ha!" Anna finally pulled the sleeve clear. Fresh blood flowed from the wound and Mischa would have collapsed had not Vlad got a tight hold of him.

Anna washed the wound, then went to Bahram's saddle bags. For a second she paused and looked at the neatly folded and wrapped dress which Sarah had given to her as a parting gift—"Look forward to the day that you can wear this with happiness, child," she had said.

Anna ripped it into strips. She poured some of the Vodka into the wound, causing Mischa to arch his neck again as the raw spirit burned him. Then the girl bandaged his arm.

"There, that's the best I can do. How are you feeling?"

Mischa spat out the deeply bitten twig:

"Like shit!"

Without a word, she handed him the flask of Vodka. Mischa drank deep, grunted and shook his head as it coursed and burned its way down his gullet.

"To kill the fever," said Anna handing the flask to Vlad.

Finally she took the flask herself and stood looking at it for a moment. Then she raised it:

"To the memory of Sirius."

"He may still be alive," said Mischa, as Vlad helped him to his feet.

"Sirius is dead," said Anna miserably; and to Mischa, "So what do we do now?"

"We go back."

Anna felt cold inside:

"But what about the bandits?"

Mischa moodily kicked a tuft of grass:

"They won't hang about. They've got what they wanted. They've got the Black Madonna. They'll be making back for the safety of the mountains as fast as they can."

Mischa kicked the tussock again. For a moment Anna wondered whether the fever was gaining on him, then she realised that Mischa was full of a rage—a cold dangerous rage:

"We ran like rabbits last night. We deserted our comrades. We cannot skulk here in this wood, like... like..."

He kicked again. Anna said nothing. She knew that if they had not run last night, the two men would be dead and she would be wishing that she was too. But she also knew that it would be useless to argue with Mischa in his present mood: Mischa was ashamed.

Vlad was leading. Anna stayed beside Mischa, who was swaying a bit in the saddle, weak with exhaustion and loss of blood.

Suddenly Vlad held up his hand and pointed. A *verst* away on the crest of the next roll of the plain was a group of horsemen. There was nowhere to hide on the open steppe. They had obviously been spotted, as the distant figures swung their horses towards them and began to gallop.

"Go!" said Mischa to Anna. "Go! Vlad and I will hold them for as long as we can."

"You couldn't even hold a spoon." Anna became cool and practical and checked the knife in its sheath. "I'm tired of running away and there's nowhere to run to."

She touched her fingers to her mouth and leaning over gently touched them to Mischa's lips:

"Go with God, Herr Rittmeister!"

Mischa seized her hand, but at that moment there was a shout of triumph from Vlad:

"Excellency! Excellency! It's all right! They're Cossacks!"

Ten men and a Sergeant—all that remained of the escort—

some of them wounded, but none too seriously; somehow
they had individually managed to fight their way out of the
slaughter of the night and had come together, one by one, in
the light of day. The Sergeant, whose cheek was open to the
bone, explained all this in a voice heavy with defeat and exhaustion.

"So what do we do now, Excellency?"—the Sergeant
paused—"You are the only officer left."

The men waited; they were sunk in a dull and sullen
mood, too tired and sick of heart to think of anything.

Mischa roused himself from his own pain. He realised that
he had to grip the situation.

"We go back," he said.

The bodies were strewn across the trampled and bloodied site
of the ambush. The crows were already at work and rose tor-
pidly as the men approached—some of the bodies had only
bloodied sockets where their eyes had been. A few horses
were wandering aimlessly about. The bandits had driven
most of the horses away with them.

"Check the bodies," Mischa ordered grimly. "Take whatever weapons you have need of and gather up all the rations
you can find and catch up the horses. Where are *you* going?"

This to Anna who was turning her horse away.

"To find Sirius," she said simply.

Mischa nodded. With Vlad's help he dismounted and
wandered amongst the bloody shambles, recognising the
faces of men that he had come to know well.

"Excellency!" It was the Sergeant's shout.

There was a piled ring of corpses around where the box
housing the Black Madonna had lain. The box was gone.
From the pile came a pitiful moaning. The Cossacks pulled
some bodies aside. A young trooper lay, his face ashen with
pain. He had been covered by his fallen comrades. He was
clutching his belly.

Mischa knelt beside him.

"It's all right, my son—we are here now to help you."

"You cannot help me, Excellency."

The Sergeant gently opened the man's tunic. The sabre slash ran from groin to chest. In spite of himself, Mischa took a sharp breath. He realised that it was only the man's hands that held the belly together; his face was haggard with pain.

"I am dead meat. Do not leave me here for the crows and the wolves to find. In God's name, Excellency, make an end."

The little troop had gathered round as Mischa got stiffly to his feet. They were all watching Mischa. Without a word, the Sergeant pulled the pistol from his belt, checking the priming. The double click as he cocked the hammer, echoed in the stillness. He handed the pistol to Mischa.

Mischa felt cold.

"Do you want to pray, my son?"

"I have prayed enough—for God's sake and mine, Excellency, end it."

Mischa raised the pistol.

"May God forgive me and receive you."

The sound of the shot echoed across the steppe.

The watching men crossed themselves, their faces hard.

Anna came galloping at the sound.

"What...?"

Then she saw Mischa with the smoking pistol and the man without a face, whose guts were now spilling through the gaping slit in his stomach.

"Oh my God!" Leaning from her saddle, she vomited.

"What shall we do with the bodies?"

The men all looked at Mischa again. Mischa thought for a moment. With so few men and no spades, burial was out of the question.

"We will lay them out in ranks. They died like soldiers, let them lie like soldiers. Their souls are now with God, but let us leave their bodies with what respect we can."

In silence the little band set about its grisly task.

Anna was pale and composed now.

"Anything of Sirius?"

She shook her head.

"Perhaps he escaped?"

Anna bowed her head over Bahram's neck:

"He is dead," she said and her tears came fast and silent.

"Horsemen!"

The Cossacks immediately left their awful task, seized their weapons and gathered around Mischa. Vlad handed Mischa his spy-glass. By resting the glass on his saddle, he was able to focus on the distant moving black dots.

"Bandits?" asked the Sergeant.

Mischa let out his breath in a deep sigh of relief.

"Two horsemen and they are Captain FitzHugh and Trooper Bone. Thank God for that."

"Amen!" growled the Sergeant.

The two riders came spurring up to the group.

Charles's face was slack with surprise and horror as he took in the scene:

"Jesus Christ! What the hell has happened here?"

The little troop had formed a rough rank.

Mischa ran his eye over them, coughed and spoke:

"I have no authority over you men, except what you give me. What has happened touches my honour and yours. I intend to follow and recapture the Black Madonna, and I must go now whilst the trail is still warm. Any man who wishes to ride with me is welcome with all my heart, but there can be no shame for any man who wishes to return to the fort."

There was silence. Then a great burly Cossack spoke:

"Go skulking back to the fort, with our men lying here like carrion! We should be dead too! We will come and die with you, Excellency. There is no honour to be had anywhere else." He turned his head and spat onto the ground.

"Are you all with me?"

There was a rumble of assent.

"What about you, Charles?"

"Oh, I'm coming old dear—just look at the fucking awful trouble you get into without me."

Bone raised his eyes to heaven:

"Trouble?" he said to himself. "When have we ever been in anything but trouble?"

Sirius heard the footsteps approaching his hiding place. His lips curled back in a silent snarl. He had dragged his broken leg and his bleeding flank into this patch of scrub. Instinct had told him that he could go no further for the weakness and the pain. He had curled up and lay waiting for the blackness that was hovering over him. Now a man was approaching his hiding place. No man was going to touch him again.

"Sirius! Sirius!"—the man's voice was deep, but gentle—"Come on old dog. I know you're hurt."

Sirius's snarl disappeared. Inch by inch he crawled out of his hiding place.

"There's a good lad!"

The Hunter was squatting outside the bushes. Sirius crawled to him on his belly and began to whine like a puppy.

"Poor old dog!"

Sirius closed his eyes and felt the great rough hand stroking his head. The dog lolled over on his side. He felt the hand exploring the torn flank and, where the hand went, so the pain eased.

Sirius felt the fingers gently manipulating the broken leg. A wonderful feeling of warmth and comfort came over him and he stretched out luxuriously as the fingers carefully probed the break. The Hunter began to chant a verse that came from time before consciousness: from the time of fire and ice, when the great forests of the north were young.

" *Bone to bone! Blood to blood! Limb to limb! So that all will be whole again...*"

Sirius drifted into a deep, healing, sleep.

"No," said Mischa, "it is better if I go alone."

Anna pouted:

"You should not be allowed anywhere on your own."

"Quite right, old boy—you're bound to make a pig's breakfast of it. I'll come with you."

"No, you must stay here and take charge. I will take Vlad with me. The rest of you will stay here until I report."

It had not been difficult to follow the trail of the bandits, especially as the pursuers knew where the band was headed. Also, the Khan's men had made little effort to conceal their passing; they were returning in triumph and had no thought of being followed.

Even so they made best haste across the steppe, until they were in the loom of the foothills, with the safety of the deep mountain valleys before them. Here they slowed their pace as the story of their victory ran before them over the mountain passes, and the mountain people came out to welcome the returning victors. Outside the still partially ruined town of Tearnause, the band halted and prepared for a more serious celebration of their triumph.

It was this camp that Mischa intended to reconnoitre. His plan was to ride to within some distance of the camp, leave the horses with Vlad in the trees and creep forward on foot and under the cover of darkness. He would then spend the day, hidden, watching the camp with his spy-glass. On the basis of his observations, he and his followers would try to make a plan.

"I don't like it,"—Anna's face was set—"it is too dangerous. What if you get caught?"

"I won't," said Mischa confidently.

* * *

The Khan was in exceedingly good spirits. His credibility had been restored in heroic portion. Already songs were being composed in his honour.

There remained one more thing to do. He must deliver the Black Madonna to the Shaman and receive that weird man's blessing. Then he could return to a feast of slaughtered sheep and looted vodka. Mightily would he feast—after all, was he not the Great Khan, killer of Cossacks and destroyer of their spirit. With the Black Madonna safe in the mountains, all the fat lands below would be his to rape and pillage as he thought fit.

All of this he thought as he pulled up his breeches. He cast a satisfied eye on the Kabardine girl crouched naked and

whimpering in the corner of the hut. He had given her something to cry about and there would be many more weeping
women before he was done. He strode through the broken
door of the hut and stood, arms akimbo, letting the warmth
of the autumn sunshine meet that of his self approval. He
looked around him and, as he did, he caught a flash of reflected light high on the hill above.

Mischa swum in and out of consciousness. The pain was
frightful. He reckoned that at least two of his ribs were broken and his wounded shoulder had opened up again.

He had been tied face down across a saddle with his hands
and feet tied underneath the horse. The jolting motion of the
trotting horse caused him physical agony, but the feeling of
stupid failure was almost worse. He had been stalked and
clubbed down like some half-witted rabbit. He had fully expected to be killed and, as the jovial bandit who tied him with
excruciating tightness to the horse explained, he would be,
but he would pray for death many times before it came to
him.

"You will be the star guest at our feast," the bandit said.

His companions guffawed with laughter.

"A welcome guest indeed!"

The Khan was in high good humour. Was it not his own
quick eye that had been responsible for the capture of this
prize? And what a prize—a foreign officer. This would be
really most entertaining:

"Help our friend dismount."

The jovial bandit cut the thongs round Mischa's wrists,
then pushed him back over the saddle. As his feet were still
tied he landed on his back with a terrible crash. The pain
made him gasp with agony.

"Ah Ha! Listen my children—our friend is tuning up. He
will sing most tunefully for our celebrations."

Through the red mists of pain, Mischa looked at the
bearded face full of laughing cruelty. He knew that there was
worse to come.

They hung Mischa up by his thumbs. He prayed for relief,

for unconsciousness, because in unconsciousness the faces of the two women, one fair, one dark, floated in his head and whispered to him words of comfort that he could not understand, but which gave him strength.

A bucket of water thrown into his face brought him spluttering and coughing back to the reality of pain. The Khan was standing in front of him and behind him in a row were the four hideous women, whom Mischa vaguely remembered from when the Cossacks had sacked Tearnause. One of them was carrying a baby in the crook of her arm. The Khan turned and indicated the women with an expansive sweep of his arm:

"These fair flowers are my beloved wives—the stars of my firmament—and behold, my first born son! I am sorry to keep you hanging about,"—at this the Khan was overcome by his own wit and laughed himself into a coughing fit—"but I have a mission to carry out. This evening, when I return, we will feast and, whilst we are feasting, my wives will remove every scrap of skin from your body. Then shall you sing indeed."

There was a manic giggle from one of the women:

"Can I do his ministration bits?"

"His Excellency is taken." The tears streamed down Vlad's face. "From where I was hiding with the horses, I could see the bandits creep up on him. I should have gone and died with him. I am as a cur."

"Worse than a cur!" the Sergeant spat savagely.

"No!" Charles was decisive. "You did the right thing, otherwise we would not know what had happened. Now, are you sure that the Rittmeister was killed?"

"I saw them club him, Excellency."

"Hmm! Well in that case they probably meant to capture him. If that is the case he might be wishing that he was dead," Charles added grimly.

"Sweet Christ! What can we do? We must save him."

Anna's face was a mask of horror: "The Khan is a monster."

Charles twitched his face wryly:

"The trouble is, there ain't many of us. How many bandits do you think, Vlad?"

Vlad pulled himself together and stood stiffly to attention:

"Many have left, Excellency. But I would reckon there are still at least fifty camped in the ruins of the village and the women were arriving to join them."

"Ha! Party time eh! Well, that might work to our advantage. You didn't see any sign of the Rittmeister after they took him to the village?"

"No, Excellency, but there was a lot of shouting and cheering."

"Well," said Charles grimly, "it is very probable that the Rittmeister is being kept alive, not very comfortably, to provide the high point of the celebrations tonight."

"Oh God! No!" Anna buried her face in her hands.

"Now steady on, old thing—that ain't going to help Mischa. We have got to make a plan."

It came flying through the air and knocked Anna into a heap on the ground. She gave a scream of surprise. Then it began to lick her face.

"Sirius! Oh, Sirius!"

Anna sat up and buried her face in the dog's rough neck:

"Oh Sirius! Is it really you?"

"Trooper Sirius reporting for duty: present and correct in every detail," said a deep voice.

"Heavens above! Mr Hunter!"

Charles's mouth was open with astonishment.

Anna looked up at the Hunter. This was the man whom she had last seen as an itinerant blacksmith. Now he had appeared from nowhere, bringing with him the beloved dog that she had been mourning. Who was this extraordinary man? She was bewildered and dumbfounded, but at last she managed to stammer out:

"Was Sirius much hurt?"

"Let us say that he was a little tattered and torn when I found him, but I effected some emergency repairs."

Anna took a deep breath and hugged Sirius to her more closely. Then she looked at the Hunter again and said:

"Mischa…"

"I know about Mischa." The Hunter sounded grim.

"Is he alive?"

"He is alive, but not in a good state. They will keep him alive until tonight. We must act then," he paused, "if we are to get him back alive and in one piece."

"They will flay him," said the Sergeant soberly. "They let the women do it. It is the custom of the bandit scum."

Anna felt her whole mind screaming.

Hunter picked her up from the ground and she buried her head in his chest. He gently stroked her hair:

"Don't worry! I have a plan and I have brought some friends to help,"—he gestured down the valley where a large herd of horses was being driven up the valley by Kabardine herdsmen in their distinctive wide brimmed felt hats—"the Kabardines have suffered much from the Khan."

The Khan paused. He was feeling monstrous pleased with himself. He had the Black Madonna. It only remained for him to take the icon to the Shaman so that that strange being could burn it slowly on his smoky fire. Then, the Shaman had said, the power of the Cossacks would perish in the flames along with the icon.

It would be a good moment and the Khan relished the prospect. It was the Shaman's order that the icon should be brought to him without delay. But, the Khan argued to himself, what with the excitement of capturing the foreign officer, the day was now far gone. It was too late to get to the Shaman's hut and back in time for the festivities—the festivities to celebrate the victory over the hated Cossacks, to display his man-child to the tribesmen and last, but not least—here the Khan licked his lips—the flaying of that foreign bastard. How he would scream, they all did! The thought gave him an erection. The Shaman could wait until tomorrow.

The waves of agony wracked Mischa, interspersed with mer-

ciful periods of unconsciousness. He was bruised and battered now, with casual blows and stones thrown by passers by.
His testicles came in for particular attention. They felt enor-
mously swollen, but, as one wit pointed out to him, that
would make them easier to skin. He knew that his situation
was hopeless.

As darkness fell and the fires lit up the scene, he knew
that his slow and painful demise could not be far off. The
bandits were roasting sheep on the fires and drinking themselves into a fine mood of celebration and anticipation. The
shouting and the jeering had become just a background
sound of hell, but the sound that did penetrate his consciousness was the 'snick, snick, snick' of the four silent women
sharpening their little skinning knives.

"Now," said the Hunter, "you are all clear on the plan? Remember our biggest weapons are surprise and aggression."

"Sirius!" said Anna. "You will stay with me."

"No," the Hunter rammed his battered hat firmly on his
head, "Sirius is coming with me. I have a special purpose for
him."

It was now pitch dark outside the light of the circle of fires.
Mischa knew that it only needed the arrival of the Khan for
his torment to begin. Closing his eyes, he prayed yet again to
the Holy Mother to help him through the pain, and to look
after Anna. He kept his eyes closed most of the time—one
was closed by a flying stone anyway—but some instinct made
him open his good eye and look down. There, as always, were
the four dreadful women. The youngest had her baby in a
basket beside her: what a monster that would be.

He closed his eye to shut out the horrid scene and then
opened it again. Holy Mother of God! There it was! A huge
shaggy dog had slipped through the crowd and was standing
on the edge of the firelight, grinning at him. Then, swiftly
and smoothly, it slipped forward, picked up the sleeping infant in its huge jaws and was gone into the darkness with only
the thin wail of the frightened child to mark its passing.

The mother came screaming to her feet. There was instant turmoil. Everybody was shouting. Then out of the
darkness came the sound of thundering hooves, hundreds of
hooves and the Russian "Hoorah!"

"Attack! Attack!" screamed the milling crowd.

The Khan really thought that he would have to get rid of the
Kabardine girl; she kept snivelling all the time. He liked a bit
of whimpering, but this slut never stopped—except when her
mouth was fully occupied as it was at that moment.

His thought strayed to the Golden Girl; she had not sniv-
elled, but by all the spirits he had enjoyed hearing her
scream under the whip.

The thought aroused him even more than the Kabardine's mouth and tongue. He became fully erect once again.
With a grunt, he came up into the kneeling position and
pushed the girl's head down so that she crouched in front of
him. The sight of the deep purple welts on her buttocks excited him even further. He was still slippery with the girl's
saliva. This would give her something to snivel about.

The girl cried out as the Khan thrust into her roughly.
She cried so loud that for a moment the Khan failed to hear
the shouting and the fists pounding on the door of the hut:

"Attack! Attack!"

With an oath the Khan withdrew from the woman and
leaped to his feet buckling up his breeches. He seized the box
in which lay the icon of the Black Madonna and leaped to the
door. He could hear the screams, the shots, the thunder of
hooves and the "Hoorah" of the Russians. The Khan made a
split-second decision. It was quite clear where his duty lay.
He tucked the box under his arm and, sprinting to his horse,
swung into the saddle. He paused for a moment to look and
listen to the mayhem behind him.

Then with the box tucked under his arm, he spurred his
horse towards the mountains.

To the bandits, fuddled as they were with drink and gorged
with meat, the night seemed to be full of demons. There were

hundreds of horses charging amongst them and by definition each horse had to carry a sabre-swinging Cossack—a whole regiment must have fallen upon them. They were being cut to pieces—massacred—slaughtered. They must flee—retreat—live to fight another day.

The screams of their women added to the fear and confusion. The loudest of the screams came from the Khan's youngest wife. Had she not seen her baby, her first born, snatched from its cradle by a devil dog? All those who had witnessed this dreadful act compounded the fear of the crowd: the very fiends of hell were riding with the Cossacks. The panic fear spread like fire through a straw stack as the horses thundered amongst them and pistol flashes flamed in the darkness.

All of this Mischa witnessed through his pain, and for the first time he allowed himself a flicker of hope as the crowd surged and trampled past his gibbet. In all the panic there was one small group who did not run: the four black-clad figures who had sat below him sharpening their knives. The woman whose baby had been snatched was in a frenzy. She had thrown herself to the ground in hysterical grief, rubbing dust and ashes from the fires into her hair. Suddenly she rose to her feet, her teeth bared in an animal snarl:

"It's him," she screamed, pointing at Mischa. "He is Satan and he has called up his devils from the pit of hell to steal my baby, my precious, my jewel. Kill the devil, sisters! Kill him and revenge my baby!"

With this she fled into the heaving darkness, wailing the name of the child.

"We should go," said Number Three Wife rather tremulously. "We should go and find the lord and keep our own babies safe."

"We will go," the Senior Wife spoke grimly, "but the girl was right. We must deal with this scum."

She gestured at the hanging Mischa with her knife.

"Can you kill the devil with a knife?" Number Two Wife sounded doubtful.

"He is not the devil, he is just a man—but not for much

longer!"

She moved purposefully to Mischa and seized his genitals roughly. Mischa closed his eyes. The blast of the pistol shot roused him. The hand fell from him and he saw the hideous crone fold in two as though she were hinged, the knife falling to the ground from her senseless hand. Next moment the ground in front of him was full of galloping, maddened horses. He heard the screams of the other two women as they disappeared under the thundering hooves.

"Not a bad shot for the distance and a galloping horse, if I say so myself, Sir."

"Bone!"

"At your service, Sir, and just in time to save your wedding tackle, by the look of things. Now don't you worry, Sir. I'll have you down from there in two shakes of a duck's arse. Them bloody old women are dog meat," he added with evident satisfaction.

Mischa fainted.

"There's a good lad, then!"

The Hunter was leaning on his staff, watching the bedlam in the village below him. Sirius came trotting out of the darkness, head and tail held high, and the still wailing baby hanging from his jaws. He came up to the Hunter and laying the baby at his feet, stood back grinning, his tongue lolling and his ears pricked.

The Hunter bent down and examined the baby:

"Good lad, Sirius—not a mark on him."

The Hunter and the dog stood looking at each other, their minds linked.

Sirius put his head on one side.

"What!" The Hunter was shocked.

Sirius fixed his stare on the baby, swallowed convulsively and licked his lips.

"No you damned well can't! The very idea!"

Sirius cocked his head the other way.

"That's as may be but you're a dog not a wolf! Now come along and leave the baby here. I can feel the mother coming this way. She'll hear her brat wailing."

Hunter and dog faded into the shadows of the night.

"Really, Sirius! I am surprised at you!"

Sirius grinned.

The sharp frosty sunlit dawn showed a scene of devastation, of scattered, smouldering fires and crumpled bodies. The dawn also brought reinforcements; a band of Kabardine tribesmen came to recover their horses and loot whatever they could. They prowled the ruins of Tearnause, hunting out hiding or wounded bandits. The sound of the occasional shot marked their progress.

There were no casualties amongst the little band of Cossacks and they were in high good humour, grouped round the ruined hut where Mischa lay on a makeshift bed, being alternately scolded, fussed over—and occasionally wept over —by Anna.

"Well, well, well,"—Charles came in rubbing his hands— "absolutely splendid job, what? And Bone tells me you're all in one piece, what? Not that it's going to be much use to you for some time, he says. What do you reckon, Anna? Don't tell me you haven't inspected the armoury." Charles was undoubtedly slightly drunk.

"I think that you are disgusting!" Anna flushed scarlet. "Mischa is badly hurt."

"Well I've liberated some bandit vodka. Here, give the patient a swig of this—put a crack on him like a coachman's whip, what? Can he ride?"

"No, he..." Anna blushed again.

"Only side-saddle, Sir," said Bone bluntly. "His scrote's swollen the size of a cabbage—and as for his poor old John Thomas..."

Charles took another swig from the flask:

"Spare me the gory details, Bone. I haven't had my breakfast. And yes, Bone, why haven't I had my fucking breakfast? Bloody well stir yourself!"

"Sir!" Bone was unperturbed. "And he's got three broken ribs," he added as a parting shot.

"Grüss Gott!" said a deep voice from the door of the hut. "I wonder if I can be of assistance?"

"Bone to bone! Blood to blood! Limb to limb! So that all will be whole again!..."

Through his good eye Mischa watched as the Hunter towered over the bed. When he first felt the touch of the huge rough hands, he had flinched instinctively at the prospect of yet more pain. Then as the hands ran over his naked body, he felt an amazing sensation of heat running through him. Starting at the feet the Hunter smoothed, probed and worked with his fingers. As his hands worked their way up his body, and as the Hunter intoned the incantation, Mischa felt a great feeling of peace and healing. Where the hands went, so the pain went, and by the time the hands worked on his face, Mischa felt only a great drowsiness and desire for sleep. He drifted off into deep, blessed darkness.

At last the Hunter stood back, rubbing his hands together in a satisfied manner. Sirius came up and inspected his recumbent master, sniffing the path of the Hunter's hands with an air of informed interest; he had been there himself. His inspection complete, the great dog lay down beside the bed and rested his head on his paws, a pleased expression on his face. The Hunter pulled the rough blanket over Mischa's body.

"How is he?" Anna's face was full of anxiety.

"Let him sleep. In half an hour he will wake whole and hale."

Anna reached up and kissed the Hunter on his bearded cheek.

"Thank you," she said simply.

"Now," said the Hunter briskly, "we must decide what to do next."

* * *

The exhausted horse was down to a walk. It was too far gone for the Khan's whipping and cursing to have any effect. With an awful suddenness it collapsed, throwing the Khan head first onto the side of the track, where he lay, momentarily stunned. When he came to, he sat up and did a mental inventory of his body: nothing seemed to be broken, but he had a nasty cut on his forehead that streamed blood down his face. Wiping the blood away, he looked round hurriedly.

He was alone in the narrow rock-strewn pass, with the river roaring in its straitened, bouldery bed. In front of him at the head of the pass, loomed the vast bulk of Elbrus, its cap white with everlasting snow. To his left, the dirty ancient ice of a small glacier spilled out of a narrow defile. It was through the stunted pines to the side of the glacier that the track to the Shaman's hut lay. It would be a long walk and the Khan hated walking. A snort from the foundered horse disturbed his self-pity. He kicked it viciously in the belly.

Then a panic gripped him. The icon, where by all the angels of Shaitan was the icon? He was not looking forward to explaining to the Shaman that he had let himself be surprised and routed by the Cossacks yet again. He must have the Black Madonna to assuage the anger of the old man. Where was it? He searched frantically in the road, then—praise to all the spirits of the place!—there it was, lying on its end just below the rim of the river bank, where it must have been flung by the force of the fall.

One corner of the box was split and splintered, but it was intact. With a great feeling of relief the Khan seized the box and tucked it under his arm. Then, pausing only to kick the horse once more—son of a whore to collapse like that—the Khan turned to the steep path by the glacier.

The Kabardine girl was on the verge of hysteria. The relief of her rescue from a life of hell had opened the flood gates of her emotions, and all the pent-up fear and suffering came pouring out in screams and great gulping tears. She sat on a stool, wrapped in a blanket.

The Hunter knelt beside her questioning her gently. The Khan had fled? For a moment the horror of the memory of that awful experience threatened to overwhelm the girl, but she pulled herself together.

The Khan had fled—she was certain of that. The tears

overcame her. The Hunter spoke soothingly to her, gentling
her with his voice as he would a hurt animal. The girl responded and between sniffs and sobs said haltingly that, yes,
there had been a small wooden box and that, yes, the Khan
had tucked it under his arm as he ran from the building.

The Hunter sat back on his heels with a sigh. Then, very
gently, he leaned forward and, picking up the girl's hand,
raised it to his lips.

"Now," he said briskly, rising to his feet, "we will leave this
poor child to the care of her own people and to her God. We
have work to do. We must find the Khan and retrieve the
Black Madonna."

"Damn good idea! The feller's a complete shit! I mean
look what he's done to this poor girl! I mean…" Charles's
tone of rather smug righteous indignation stuttered to a halt
as both Anna and Mischa turned their gaze upon him,
"…well, I mean dammit, what, we'd never have the bugger in
White's, what?"

A noise from the Hunter, that might have been a cough or
a laugh, brought their attention back to him.

"The trouble is"—Mischa was wriggling his shoulder as
though still amazed that the pain was gone—"we haven't got
a clue as to where he might be. He knows his way around
these mountains like a rat round its run. He could be anywhere by now."

"I know where he will be heading," said the Hunter
grimly.

No one even considered asking him how he knew.

"What we have got to do is to get to him before they have
time to destroy the Black Madonna."

"Who are 'they'," Mischa asked.

"You'll see. Now what I suggest is that Anna goes back
with the Kabardines. They will look after her and get her
safely back to Pyatigorsk and…"

"No!" Anna was pink with fury. "No! Do you think that I
have gone through all this just to turn tail now?"

"It is dangerous up in the mountains," said the Hunter.

"We are only thinking of your safety." Mischa sounded
rather smug.

"Dangerous! Safety!" Anna flew at the amazed Mischa and started pounding his chest with her small fists. "And who thought about your safety back on the steppe? Who bandaged you when you were hurt, eh? Answer me that! I want to see this snake, this vermin, this devil, crushed and finished! *He killed my family!*" she screamed at Mischa, who had been retreating step by step in the face of her wild-cat fury.

Now he took her by her shoulders with his huge hands and held her. Her fury suddenly subsided:

"Besides, you silly great bear, you are not safe to be allowed out on your own. From now on, where you go, I go!"

"It were better for him that a millstone were hanged about his neck..." Charles intoned in mock piety.

"One day," Mischa was in quiet fury, "I just might break yours, Charles."

Anna gave Charles one of her sweetest smiles:

"Not until I have finished with him," she said to Mischa in a voice of poisoned honey.

They followed the Hunter. As the road climbed up the valley, the mountain walls became steeper, the vegetation sparser. Sometimes they would pass mean clusters of houses that seemed to cling precariously to slopes amongst tumbles of boulders and slides of scree. There was no sign of life in the houses, as though the inhabitants had fled before their coming and disappeared into the steep and rocky quarries that occasionally split the bare, barren mountain faces. A few ribby cows and ponies grazed in the wretched fields beside the tumbling river. Wretchedness was written across everything in this wasteland, and laid its burden on the travellers, as the valley walls narrowed until they almost blocked the pale autumn light. Always before them was Elbrus, its great bulk filling the view ahead. The little party was grim in its resolution and silent as the mountains closed in on them.

Anna nudged Bahram closer to Mischa's horse, to feel his knee against hers. Mischa, whose eyes constantly swept the slopes around them, reached across and gently squeezed her arm; it was a dreadful place.

The horse was still alive, lying on its side and giving the occasional feeble struggle.

It rolled its eyes as they approached.

"Poor bugger!" said Bone. "Well and truly stuffed he is."

The Sergeant said something to the Hunter. The Hunter nodded:

"But no shot, mind."

The Sergeant slipped from his horse and with practised ease slid his long dagger into the wretched animal's heart. It kicked twice and lay still.

"So," said Mischa, "now he's afoot. But where in this hellish wilderness might he be?"

The Hunter was silent. He and Sirius were looking at each other, their eyes locked.

As the others watched, Sirius's tail and ears shot up. He put his nose to the ground and worked carefully around the stiffening corpse of the Khan's horse. He stood facing the side of the valley and the narrow defile from which the glacier tumbled into the valley. For a moment, Sirius stood: ears, mane and tail erect, nose working the air. Without a backward look he set off for the trees at a steady trot.

The Shaman sat staring into the smoke of his fire. His stiff leg was paining him badly. It was always particularly acute when there was trouble in the wind. He knew that things had not gone well. He sat staring into the smoke, wrinkled, unblinking and expressionless as an ancient reptile, but his mind floated up with the blue smoke wreaths.

He let it leave his motionless, shrivelled body and fly above like the eagle that hovered the thermals far overhead on outstretched wings, its eyes attuned to the slightest movement on the ground below.

The eagle watched the tiny figure of the Khan as he struggled up the steep path towards the waterfall, the box clutched firmly to his chest.

The thought of the box and its contents caused a tremor to run through the Shaman's body, the only indication of the extreme excitement that coursed through his mind. The box and its contents—a fine crackling blaze he would have with them and make an end of his enemy.

A rise of warm air lifted the eagle still higher. It could see the tiny figure of the man as it approached the steep climb beside the waterfall, up through the rocky gully where the warming sun had not yet penetrated.

'Ice!' thought the Shaman. 'The clumsy oaf is going to slip on the ice and hurt his leg! The cursed fool!'

The eagle soared higher still and saw new movement. Ant-like figures crawling out of the dark smear of woodland at the top of the glacier. It looked like a hunt. There might be a kill.

The Khan was gasping for breath as he arrived at the jumbled rock ladder beside the roaring fall. The water was rimed round with ice. Ice glistened on the rocks in the dark chasm. He would need both hands free. Undoing his cloak, he formed it into a rough sack to carry the box. He knotted it and hung it over his back. Very carefully he began to climb.

Sirius was still moving at a steady trot as the pursuers broke out into daylight from the gloomy darkness of the pines. The faint path that they had been following continued, twisting and turning through the boulders on the steep side of the rushing torrent that fed into the glacier. The path climbed ever upwards. Every time the riders thought that they had reached a crest, another climb and another crest appeared in front of them. The sun was warm on their backs now, and shone with blinding whiteness on the saw-teeth of the snow-covered mountain peaks. Far above in the pale frosty blue of the sky, an eagle wheeled and soared on motionless wings.

The horses picked their way cautiously along the narrow track, still slippery in places with the night's frost. There was a dusting of fresh snow on the slopes.

"A bugger of a climb!" Charles took off his cap and wiped a sleeve across his forehead. "Oh do hold up you clumsy bastard!" as his horse stumbled. "You sure we're going right, Mr Hunter?"

"Sirius thinks so."

"Christ! I sometimes reckon you think that dog's cleverer than we are."

"Perhaps," said the Hunter without looking round, "that's because he didn't go to Eton."

Now a hand-hold there, a step-up onto that large boulder, and he would be nearly at the top. The Khan had climbed the rock ladder many times before. It was nothing to worry about. Another ten yards. Step up... His foot flew out from under him on the sheet of ice. He fell back fifteen feet and crashed into a huge rock. The rock saved him from going down the waterfall, but it also cut his knee to the bone. The Khan's curses rose to a sky that was empty save for a speck that was a gliding eagle.

"Get up you sow's git," the Shaman shouted suddenly into the smoke. "Bring me that icon! Bring me the Black Madonna! Then burn in the flames along with Her, for all I care! But get up!"

Dazed and cursing with pain, the Khan somehow scrambled and pulled himself the last few feet to lie gasping on the level plateau at the head of the falls. It was as he was lying there that he glanced back and saw the little band of riders coming over a crest in the track about a *verst* below him. A wave of cold fear washed over him, and climbing to his feet he began to hobble as fast as he could across the rough grass to where there was a distant smudge of smoke hanging on the still air.

Sirius stood with his forefeet on the first boulder of the rock ladder. His ears were pricked. He began to whine.

The Hunter studied the jumble of boulders:

"Up there, by the looks of it, and we'll have to leave the horses here."

"Hell's teeth!" said Charles, looking up. "I joined the cavalry so that I wouldn't have to climb bloody places like that."

"Perhaps the Captain has no head for heights?"

Anna flashed him her sweetest smile. Charles looked at her gravely:

"Madame, I can assure you that I have never fallen off a whore yet."

Anna's smile vanished.

Mischa had a small fit of coughing.

But there was no time for more talking. Sirius and the Hunter were already feeling their way up the slippery climb.

As the party reached the top, they could see Sirius standing on his hind legs, his ears pricked. He was obviously watching something. The Hunter joined him. Far across the meadow they could see the small figure of a man, hirpling along as fast as a lame leg would allow.

"Go!" said the Hunter softly, and Sirius was covering the ground in great arching bounds.

The Khan was wallowing, his leg agony, his breathing laboured; only his fear kept him staggering on. The Shaman's hut was in plain sight now. He must keep going and seek the safety of the Shaman's powers. He cast a quick glance behind him and in spite of his lack of breath, gave a yell of fear. The huge dog was almost on him. He turned and ran even faster.

Sirius took a great leap and hit the Khan right between the shoulder blades, sending him sprawling on his face on the frosty grass. He could feel the dog's hot breath on his neck. He waited for the crunch of the teeth. Instead the dog tugged at the cloak-made sack that was hanging over his back. With fumbling hands the Khan dragged the knot over his head and felt the cloak with the box being dragged away.

He dared to turn his head.

The dog was standing over the bundle, grinning at him, its head cocked on one side.

Very carefully the Khan dragged himself forward.

The dog did not move.

Whimpering with fear and pain, the Khan got slowly and carefully to his feet and began to back away.

The dog just stood. The Khan felt sure that it was laughing at him.

The man backed away still further, then turned and bolted for the Shaman's hut and through the open door. Panting with tension and exhaustion he pushed the heavy door shut and rammed the bolt home.

"Well done, Sirius!"

The feathery tail wagged.

"Now," said the Hunter, "let us see what we have got."

Kneeling down, he undid the knotted cloak to display the battered and splintered box. The little group, still breathless from their run across the meadow, gathered round. Very carefully, the Hunter opened the box.

The Black Madonna lay serene and undamaged in the thick velvet lining.

The Hunter doffed his hat.

Mischa crossed himself.

The Cossacks had fallen to their knees at the sight of the icon. The Hunter picked up the box and took it to each Cossack in turn. In turn, each man kissed the box and crossed himself.

Charles was not quite sure what to do, so he followed the military maxim of 'if in doubt, salute it'.

Anna knelt and looked at the little darkened picture of mother and child as she had done so many times in the recent past; as always she thought that the Madonna was smiling faintly. She felt a tear run down her cheek.

"Now," said the Hunter briskly, "there is some business to finish."

"Sit!" the voice croaked from the smoke.

The Khan felt his way round the wall and eased himself to the floor.

"I'm injured."

There was a dry cackle from the other side of the fire:

"That's as nothing compared to what's coming to you."

"You must save me."

"*Must!*"—it was a screech—"*Must!* Who are you to say 'must' to me? Did you bring me the Black Madonna?"

"Well, I..."

"Spare me—I know what happened. I also know that, but for your bungling, the Black Madonna would be crackling merrily on the fire at this moment—just like you will be soon."

"What do you mean?"

"They will fire the hut, of course, to burn us out, or burn

us in. I don't think they are in the mood to be fussy."

"You'll burn too!"

Again the dry leathery laugh:

"I shall rise above it, but you, you will sizzle and crackle like the pig you are."

The Cossacks collected brushwood and piled it around the walls of the hut.

"Should we not give them a chance to surrender?" Mischa sounded a little doubtful.

"Like the vermin gave my family?" Anna spoke with quiet venom.

"It is time to make an end of this business."

No one questioned the Hunter's right to command; he nodded to the Sergeant who fell to work with his tinderbox.

"What's happening?" The Khan stirred uneasily.

"They've piled brushwood round the hut and the flames are just beginning to take hold. You'll hear them crackling in a minute."

The Khan felt the panic rise in his throat.

"Aren't you going to do something?"

"Oh yes, I know exactly what I'm going to do."

The shrivelled form sat unmoving in the smoky darkness.

"Damn you! You scrawny old snake!"

The Khan was screaming now:

"I'm not staying here to roast!"

He scrambled to his feet.

"I'll take my chance outside."

"You might wish you'd burned."

But the Khan was already scrabbling at the door. As he burst out of it, the last thing he heard was the Shaman's mocking laugh.

"Stand back! He's coming out!"

The flames were licking up the walls of the hut as the door opened. The men stood back, their weapons ready. Anna had her knife in her hand. She looked at Mischa.

"I want to kill him," she said simply, "for my family."

The Khan burst into the open and stood for a moment looking at the ring of men. Then with a yell of defiance he raised his sabre over his head.

No one saw the eagle until it was on the Khan. The force of its swoop knocked him over. The watchers were dumbfounded, rooted to the spot by the awful suddenness of what happened.

The eagle sunk its talons deep into the Khan's eyes.

It seemed to sit there for an age calmly looking around it, before rising into the sky with huge lazy wing-beats, until it became a hovering speck once more.

Blood poured from the Khan's empty eye sockets.

He began to scream and crawl frantically away, back into the burning hut.

The roof collapsed in a roar of fire and sparks.

"Definitely only one body in the hut, Excellency."

"But the Shaman could not have got out. There was only the one door and no windows."

"Perhaps the old devil went up in smoke, quite literally," said Charles cheerfully. "Anyway who cares—that's the end of both of them, eh, Mr Hunter?"

The Hunter did not reply. He was watching the distant eagle as it soared over the crags.

11 Intermezzo at Telez

"**S**o what do we do now?" said Mischa.

Ever since the events at the Shaman's hut, the little party had ridden in virtual silence, eyes scanning the mountainsides, always alert for signs of attack. None came.

The mountain villages they passed on their way down the valley seemed totally deserted. Tearnause, still smoking from the attentions of the Kabardines was like a town of the dead, indeed it stank of death.

All the way down the valley the Hunter had walked ahead of the riders, his long stride easily keeping pace with them. He had walked in silence and no one had dared to break his mood. Now, at last, they had left the dreadful valley behind them.

They had made camp in a grove of trees amongst the rolling hills. The picquets had been posted and a sheep, liberated by Bone and Vlad, was roasting over a generous fire. The smell of the cooking meat reminded everyone that for several days they had existed on stale bread. Sirius watched the operations with keen interest, in spite of the fact that he had feasted noisily and messily on the discarded entrails.

The Hunter sat cross-legged, his hat tipped over his face, brooding and staring into the fire, as though watching pictures in the flickering flames. At Mischa's question, he reached out a booted foot and kicked a smouldering log back into the fire, then he spoke:

"You must go west, as fast as you can travel. You must find the Russian army and get the Black Madonna to the Cossacks."

He paused and threw another branch on the fire causing it to flare up. The Hunter seemed to be watching the flames intently for a moment then he shook his head and to those watching him, his eyes became hooded.

"There will be a great battle and the Cossacks must have the Lady riding with them, otherwise there will be disaster."

"But, how will we know where to go?"

"Head towards Austria. That is all I know at the moment. Events are moving fast and so must you."

"Will you come with us?" Anna sounded anxious.

"No. I must be about my business, but I will be with you and I will see you in the west."

"Well," said Charles, "this is all jolly fine, but if we don't eat this damned sheep soon, I ain't going to be strong enough to get up in the morning, let alone travel a thousand fucking miles or whatever it is. I say we eat. What do you reckon Sirius? You seem to control most of what happens round here." Sirius's ears shot up. "I'll take that as a 'yes'. Bone! Come hither and carve this damned thing or whatever it is you are supposed to do."

"Is your stomach the only thing that you think about?" said Anna acidly.

"Absolutely not, my dear lady, but I like to have a full stomach before I start to think of other things."

"You're an animal!"

"So's Sirius," said Charles imperturbably, "and he seems to have a damned sight better life than most people round here. What do you think Mr Hunter?"

But the Hunter was nowhere to be seen.

"Damned odd chap," Charles grumbled. "Here one moment, gone the next. Popping up here, popping up there."

"I wonder…" Mischa began.

"Don't wonder, old dear, it doesn't suit you," said Charles firmly. "The Hunter is the Hunter and that is the end of the matter. Bone! Stir yourself for fuck's sake—my belly thinks my throat's been cut."

"Horses?" The Moldavian gypsy dealer in Tschenowzy scratched his head. "Horses are bad to come by, Excellency. All this talk of war to the west, the soldiers are looking for all the horses they can lay their hands on, and for what they pay they might as well rob me. I am a poor man, Excellency, with many mouths to feed. It is hard to find horses and they would be expensive—especially if you want horses to get you through the high passes of the Carpathians; the snows have come early this year."

"Who said I wanted to cross the Carpathians?" Mischa was suspicious.

The dealer shrugged.

"The Excellency has come from the east: where else would he be going but west. To go west, he must cross the mountains, but I am a simple man, what do I know?"

"Too much for your own good," growled the Sergeant.

The gypsy's bearded face broke into a broad smile:

"There speaks a true Cossack, renowned for their charm and honesty."

Mischa checked the Sergeant.

"Look," he said wearily, "we have come far and have far to go. We need fresh horses and good ones, and we will pay."

The gypsy smiled happily:

"Yes, I have good horses and, yes, you must pay, but"— and here he studied the tattered and travel-stained band with many hundreds of miles of dreary storm-blasted steppe behind them—"first, I would like to see the colour of the Excellency's money."

The Sergeant growled again:

"Better I pay the pig with my knout!"

"Then," said the gypsy cheerfully, "I would assuredly have a sore back, but you would assuredly get no horses."

At this point his eye fell on Anna, who sat sagging wearily on Bahram—Bahram, who alone amongst the horses appeared to have worn not at all upon the journey and who stood now, fit and muscled, with his ears cocked.

"Now that is something special."

Stroking his roughly bearded chin, the gypsy walked round Bahram, but as he did so his eyes licked Anna as well. At last he reached up and smoothed Bahram's mane.

"I tell you what, Excellency, you throw this horse and the girl in and I do you a really good deal. What do you say?"

As he spoke he laid an exploratory hand on Anna's thigh. Before Mischa could reply, Charles's whip struck like a snake and the gypsy was lying on the ground clutching his face, which carried a livid red weal from mouth to ear. Bahram looked down at him and snorted. Charles's drawl was icy:

"Neither the horse nor the girl are for sale and even if they were, you would not be man enough to ride either of them."

The gypsy's eyes blazed and his hand moved instinctively for the knife in his belt, but a lance point at the throat is a convincing argument. He got to his feet slowly, rubbing his smarting face:

"A lesser man would be upset by that," he said thoughtfully, "but I am a businessman. There will be some small adjustment to the price of the horses and a small outstanding debt to pay, if ever any of you come this way again. It might be better if you did not."

The gypsy spat on the ground and, very deliberately, ground the spit into the mud with his boot. Then he looked Charles full in the face:

"And you, my fine gentleman, certainly will not. Remember what I say—there will be two bridges and you will never cross the second."

"Here it comes again." Bone wrapped his cloak more firmly over his head, as the first flakes of yet another fall of snow settled on him. "I tell you what Vlad, my son, I am pig sick of this fucking snow, these fucking mountains and this fucking journey. What I wouldn't give for a good warm by the fire, a square meal and a dry bed, eh?"

"And perhaps something to warm the bed, Bone?"

Bone's great crumpled nose poked out of the folds of the cloak for a moment.

"You 'orrible, dirty little, Cossack, you! That's all you think of is getting your bloody end away. Well I tell you this, mate, I'm that fucking cold that I don't think I've got an end no more. I reckon it fell off the last time I had a piss. It's lying back in that bloody godforsaken pass somewhere."

"It will be gobbled up by the wolves," said Vlad whose humour no hardships seemed to quench.

"Well there ain't been much else volunteering for the job lately," came the gloomy response from the depths of the cloak. "Roll on fucking death, I say. It got to be better than these bastard mountains."

The crossing of the Carpathians was hard going. Winter was hitting early. The high passes had already been deep in snow. It had been weary work for men and horses, and they were constantly chilled to the bone. The men retreated into themselves and had become too cold, miserable and hungry even to grumble.

Charles, as an experienced regimental officer, recognised the signs of decaying morale. He rode up alongside Mischa as the snow began to fall with more serious intent:

"Look, old dear, we've got to get out of this bloody weather for a day or so. Have a bit of rest. The whole bloody thing is coming apart at the seams. The men are in a bad way."

Mischa had been riding with his chin sunk on his chest and his mind sunk in sullen endurance:

"We must keep going. You know—the men know—the importance of our mission."

"You keep on regardless and you won't have a bloody mission. And what about Anna?"

"What about Anna?"

Mischa raised his chin from the depths of his coat collar and looked at Anna as she sat her horse beside him. She was huddled deep in her cloak and sat slumped in the saddle. She did not look at him.

"What about Anna?" he said again.

"Dammit, man, she's unwell. Are you blind?"

"Are you ill?" Mischa turned to Anna.

She still did not look at him:

"I'm all right," she mumbled. "I'm really all right. It's just..."

"Just what?" said Mischa sharply. "Tell me girl!"

"Don't shout at me, you bloody man!"—Anna's furious face appeared from the folds of her hood—"It's my time, all right? It's my bloody time!"

She disappeared into her hood and sobs. Charles looked at the total mystification on his friend's face and shook his head:

"Sweet suffering Jesus, Mischa! You really know bugger all about women, don't you? No sisters?"

Mischa shook his head.

"Well you just carry on thinking that babbies are brought by the stork, and in the meantime take it from your Uncle Charles that what that girl needs is a couple of day's rest and warmth. It wouldn't do us any harm either."

Mischa shook his head as though trying to clear it. He knew that Charles was right and cursed himself for not noticing Anna's discomfiture.

"There are some cousins of my father's who live in this area somewhere. They are very old. He was ambassador to the court of Louis Seize. I have never met them, but perhaps they might give us some shelter for a day or two until this damned storm passes."

"Well," said Bone to Vlad, "that's about the most sensible fucking thing I ever heard an officer say."

Breakfast at Castle Telez was a silent meal. This was partly because the Count and Countess seldom spoke—after more than sixty years of marriage they had little left to say to each other. Also the length of the table in the great hall, which they sat at either end of, would have necessitated shouting as they were both deaf.

In spite of the fire in the huge fireplace, the cold in the hall was considerable. The Count was dressed in an ancient quilted dressing gown, whilst his spouse fought the chill in a once magnificent, but now rather dilapidated sable coat. Everything in the castle was like the sable coat. The castle had once been a scene of light, luxury and laughter. Now the fine tapestries decayed on the walls, the damp ate away at the magnificent portraits and the once fine liveries of the many servants were threadbare and dirty. The Count had long since given up buying them shoes and stockings, so they went barefoot and blue legged in the cold.

The Count was dipping a roll in his tea to soften it—he had few teeth left—when the ancient major-domo approached him and whispered in his ear.

"What?" cried the Count, dropping his soggy roll in surprise. "Here? After all these years? Are you sure? Well, bring him in, you fool, bring him in!"

The Countess raised her lorgnette to study all this unseemly movement at the other end of the table. She thought of asking what it was all about, but found the effort too much.

The major-domo had left the hall and now returned. Sitting on his wrist was a huge raven with a lively wicked eye and a dagger of a beak. The major-domo approached the table and bowed. The Raven popped onto the table.

The Countess raised her lorgnette again, the better to study this phenomenon. The Raven put its head on one side and returned her scrutiny.

"Xavier," remarked the Countess, "the Raven is here," and she returned to her porridge.

The Raven turned its attention to the Count and hopped down the table to stand in front of the old man. It then picked up the remainder of his roll, swallowed it and stood there watching the Count.

"Well," said the old man, "do you bring news from your master? It has been many years since we heard of him. Still wearing that bloody awful hat, is he?"

The Raven bobbed up and down.

The Count stretched out his arm:

"Come and tell me."

The Raven walked sideways up the outstretched arm until it perched on the man's shoulder. With its great beak, it delicately plucked a tuft of hair out of the Count's ear, then stood still. The Count was also still. He appeared to be listening to something. At last he spoke:

"We must prepare for guests."

The mountain village was a wretched place of tumble-down hovels. The people looked starved. They stared at the party of horsemen, listless and sullen: nothing good came from soldiers. When Mischa asked for directions to Castle Telez the men just shook their heads.

"Christ's blood, Excellency!" The Sergeant was enraged. "Let me open a back with my knout—that might refresh their memories."

The harsh croak made them all look to the roof top where sat the largest raven that Mischa had ever seen. It croaked again. One of the peasants removed his hat and turned to Mischa:

"Excellency, if you follow me I will put you on the road to Castle Telez."

"Damn me, Mischa! Your relatives live in some style!"

Charles was looking up at the soaring turreted ramparts perched on top of the crag above them. The troop climbed the twisting track that had been carved out of the hillside and rode through the arch into the central courtyard of the castle.

Closer examination suggested that the castle might not live up to its distant promise. Tiles from the steep roofs lay scattered and shattered in the yard. An empty window frame showed like a black tooth in a wall from which huge chunks of plaster had fallen.

"Some things don't pay for close scrutiny, as the whore said to the parson," muttered Charles to himself.

"At least we might get a roof over our heads," said Vlad to Bone.

"From the look of that roof, we'll be bloody lucky not get most of it *on* our heads, lad. What a bloody dump!"

"You're sure that your cousins still live here?" Charles stared around. "Look! There's a bloody tree growing out of that wall."

Mischa rubbed his unshaven chin:

"I really don't know. I just remember Father talking about them. He used to come here when he was young. They used to have the most fantastic hunting parties. You wouldn't think it now."

They surveyed the dirty rubbish-strewn courtyard with its heaps of discoloured snow. As though to emphasise the desolation, another slate slid from the roof and shattered in the yard.

"Even if they are still here, they won't have a clue who I am. So don't be surprised if they turn us away or set the dogs on us."

"If I saw us in my yard, I'd set the dogs on us," said Charles gloomily.

At the far end of the courtyard was a broad flight of steps that lead up to an imposing double door. As they sat their horses looking about them, the huge doors creaked open. The old man who hobbled through the opening was wrapped in a sumptuous fur-collared cloak, with a stain of grease down the front of it. His head was bare, but as he stood on the top step a pair of hands appeared through the opening and jammed something that closely resembled a tea cosy onto his hairless pate. The old man ignored this interruption and raised the ebony cane that he carried:

"Welcome Cousin Mischa!" he cried. "Welcome to the son of my cousin! And how is your father? Well I trust. But come now. All is ready for your arrival. We have put ourselves 'en fête'. What a treat for us! We see so few people now. Come in! Come in! My man will show your people where the stables are."

"How in God's name does he know who I am?" the amazed Mischa asked Charles. "And how did he know that we were coming?"

"Quite frankly, Cousin Mischa," said Charles, sliding stiffly from his saddle, "I don't give a damn. Perhaps a little bird told him. All I know is that I smell food, bed and brandy, and I ain't looking no gift cousin in the mouth."

A ragged barefoot footman was appointed to show the Sergeant and the troop to the stables. Mischa, Charles and Anna—with Sirius in close attendance—followed the Count into the great hall where the Countess sat with one foot swollen with gout propped up on a footstool.

Anna was still wrapped in her cloak and silent misery. Her golden hair was piled up under a woollen cap. To the Count's rheumy eyes she looked like a boy. Like many deaf people the old pair were accustomed to conversing with each other in bellows.

"Three fine young men the gods have brought us, my dear," shouted the Count.

The Countess raised her lorgnette and studied the ragged trio in silence for a moment:

"That one is the cousin,"—she pointed her stick at Mischa—"the Czerny features are unmistakable. The tall one is an English officer,"—the lorgnette took in every detail of Charles's now tattered uniform—"he is of the Royal Cavalry. I remember them when we visited London all those years ago."

The lorgnette swung to Anna.

"Who is the young man, Xavier, he is very pretty. Is he the English officer's catamite? The Czernys were not much of that persuasion."

"There was Uncle Hugo." The Count fingered his badly shaven chin and peered closely at Anna.

The old lady nodded:

"There was your Uncle Hugo, but he was a Cardinal."

This was too much for Charles who began to shake with silent laughter. Poor Anna went bright pink and clutched Mischa's arm. Mischa began to stammer with embarrassment. Then, without a word, Anna pulled her cap from her head and her golden hair fell around her shoulders.

"A woman!" cried the old couple simultaneously.

"Bless my soul, cousin, but you have chosen well!" said the Count, studying Anna myopically and closely.

"Come here, child." The old lady was imperious and Anna, in desperate confusion, obeyed silently. A bony, bird-like hand gripped her wrist and held it for a moment. "This poor child is exhausted and sick,"—she fixed her eyes on Mischa—"shame on you Cousin for seeking to impose yourself on her. She must be looked after. Fetch Greta and that other slut, what's-her-name."

The major-domo bowed and turned away. Mischa stood rigid and silent as though he had been struck like Lot's wife. Charles could contain himself now longer and, turning away, he clutched one of the great stone pillars and began to howl with mirth.

"That's all right, Sir," said the Count cheerfully, "you may piss behind there if you want to."

"Well, well," the Count looked at the contents of the battered wooden case with interest, "so that's the famous Black Madonna. I've heard about Her, of course, but I never thought that I would actually see her." He crossed himself. "Well, we must make Her comfortable. Let us put her in the chapel with our own Lady, the Madonna of Telez. They can chat together."

Anna was pink and glowing from her bath. She felt clean for the first time in what seemed an age.

The two peasant women chattering happily in their impenetrable dialect, had removed her stinking clothes and had scrubbed and sponged her from top to toe without any embarrassment. The older woman was now towelling her vigorously. Anna found the sense of warmth and well-being was wonderful.

The door opened without warning and the Countess came stumping in, leaning on her cane to ease her swollen bandaged foot. The two maids curtseyed, which meant that Anna was left standing stark naked in the light of the large fire that roared in the fireplace of the bedroom. Up went the lorgnette. Anna wanted to cover herself, but the towel had been take away.

"You have great beauty, child. I hope that you use it well and I hope that that great bear of a cousin of my husband's uses you well, too."

"But he's not..." Anna began.

"I used to like big men too,"—the old lady ignored the

attempted interruption—"I remember when we were at the French court at Versailles, there was the Duke of Anjou. He was a great big fat man. Oh, but what a lover! I still burn when I think of it. Does the cousin make you burn too? He doesn't say much, but 'still waters run deep' they say. Now those clothes of yours are filthy. I have sent them for washing and mending. Come in Gretchen! Come on you idle slut! Where are you?"

An elderly maid, panting with fat and exertion waddled through the door, a pile of dresses spread out across her outstretched arms. The old lady extended her hand and stroked the flowing silk.

"These dresses were made for me when I was your age. You may not think it to look at me now," she gave a cackle of laughter, "but I was counted a great beauty at the court of Louis Seize." Here the old lined face took on an expression that might have once been coyness. "Indeed I was privy to His Majesty's most intimate councils at one time." She was silent for a moment. "He wasn't very big though," she added thoughtfully. "Now," she continued briskly, "these dresses were made for me by the finest dressmakers in Paris. Let us see what we can find to fit you. Lay them on the bed, Gretchen. You really are so slow and clumsy."

"Right Bone—a bit more scrub-a-dub-dub on the back. That's it. A drop more of that brandy, I think. Better than mother's milk, that is. How are things below stairs? Looking after you all right, are they?"

"Bloody rum old place, Sir, all falling to bits, like, and rats as big as cats. Got a regiment of servants all tripping over each other and not a pair of shoes between the lot of them. Never get paid, neither, so far as I can make out, but the food's good and they seem to reckon it's better to stay here for nothing than to go and starve in the villages for nothing. 'Nothing' seems to be the only thing there's plenty of in these mountains."

"Any wenches?"

"Lifting with them. That little bugger Vlad reckons he's

had two already."

"What about you, Bone, eh?"

"You know me, Sir. Wouldn't want The Household Cavalry letting the side down, would we?" said Bone enigmatically.

"Reckon I can get me bed warmed, Bone?"

"No trouble at all, Sir. One each side, Sir?"

"Where on earth have we got ourselves now, Sirius?"

Mischa was towelling himself vigorously in front of a roaring fire. Sirius who was actively engaged with an enormous bone was too busy to answer.

"...and where did you get that bone? It looks like half a peasant."

Sirius looked up for a moment and grinned.

The dress had been in fashion fifty years before, with its huge billowing skirts and a bodice that showed Anna's neck and shoulders to perfection, accentuating the swell of her bosom.

The Countess had been sitting on a stool with her gouty foot extended, watching as the maids fussed round Anna and occasionally prodding one of them with her stick for good measure. Three dresses had been tried and rejected until Anna stepped into a gown of pale cream silk.

In fact she had liked all of them. Never in her life had she seen such sumptuous clothing or felt the soft smoothness of such beautiful silk. However she was much too overawed by the dilapidated grandeur of her surroundings, which to her was something out of a picture in some of the old German books of fairy tales that she had read as a child. She was also overawed by the imperious old lady. When she had hesitatingly suggested that one particular dress appealed to her, the Countess tapped her stick on the floor:

"Stuff and nonsense, child; that one makes you look like a dairymaid."

Which, thought Anna rather sadly to herself is exactly what I was, and the notion of what now seemed another world increased her sadness, which was compounded by her

tiredness and malaise. This must have showed in her face, because the old lady said sharply:

"Why the long face, child?"

Anna said simply:

"I was thinking of my family."

For a moment her lip trembled, a fact not missed by the
lorgnette:

"Where are they, child?"

"Dead."

The old lady was silent for a moment, studying the girl's
face. Her tone was gentle now and she reached out a bony
hand and gripped Anna's wrist:

"We all die and we do no honour to our dead by being
miserable about them. Do you think that they would want
that of you?" Anna shook her head silently. "Well then we
must cheer you up and make you knock out the eye of that
man of yours."

"But he's not my man!"

"If you really think that, then you are as stupid as you are
beautiful, which I do not think to be the case," said the
Countess crisply. "Now in that dress you will have him rolling
over in front of you, and you can scratch his belly with your
foot. Look at yourself in the glass."

Anna looked amazed at a vision of herself such as she had
never seen before.

"Now sit there and let the maids put your hair up.
Gretchen! Fetch my case—there is still something lacking. A
neck like that should not go unadorned. Do you like the bed,
child?"

Anna had regarded the huge four-poster bed with
amazement; it looked as big as her house back in the German
village. She nodded. The Countess produced a dry cackle of
laughter:

"The Margrave of Krönstadt deflowered his bride in that
very bed. I hope that my cousin is merry in bed. You should
romp well there."

The truth suddenly dawned on Anna that she and Mischa
were to be put in the same bed. She opened her mouth to say

something, but she was suffused by a creeping warmth, as though her whole body was blushing. At that moment Gretchen came waddling back with a large leather case in her hands, and somehow the moment seemed to pass.

"By Jove, Bone, not exactly the height of fashion these clothes. I shall look like my father in that portrait in the library at home."

The Count had had some clothes laid out for his male guests: clothes that had been the *bon ton* at Versailles, but fashion flies with the times—and quite a bit of the clothes had flown with the moths—but they were dry and reasonably clean. Charles took another deep draught of brandy. He was really starting to feel much better.

"You'll not be wanting this, Sir?"

Bone held up the great full wig.

"Why ever not Bone? Let's have the full fig, what?"

Bone placed the huge wig on Charles's head and Charles pirouetted in front of the looking glass as a couple of startled moths flew out.

"Tol-lol! Ain't that something? I wonder what they'd say if I walked into White's or Boodles dressed like this, eh?"

"They'd say you looked a complete cunt, Sir," said Bone stolidly.

Mischa was not having such success. Only with the greatest difficulty was he able to get into any of the Count's clothing. His nether regions were already turning numb in breeches that were tighter than his skin.

Vlad had to lever him into the velvet coat, the sleeves of which came little below his elbows and the front of which had no hope of meeting across his massive chest. Vlad, whose humour was always dangerously close to the surface, was containing it with difficulty. Breaking-point came when he put the old-fashioned wig on Mischa's head. Vlad took one look and hysteria took over. With a howl of laughter, he threw himself onto the bed in the room and rolled about in a paroxysm of mirth. This was too much for the tired and wormy timbers of the bed which gave way, and the whole thing closed like a book on Vlad.

Mischa could take no more of this. He too was overcome by the ridiculous. All the tensions of the past weeks came roaring out in great bellows of release and happiness. This was too much for the coat that split down the back. With tears running down his face, Mischa sank onto a stool.

Sirius who had been watching all this with bright-eyed interest and his head on one side, got to his feet, walked across to his master and, very gently, took the wig in his teeth and took it off into a far shadowy corner, where he tried to bury it.

The great hall, for the first time in many years, was a blaze of light. The grand chandeliers—in one of which pigeons had nested undisturbed in recent times—had been lowered and filled with candles. The table and sideboards were spread with magnificent gold plate and priceless crystal which had been immured deep in the castle vaults for half a generation. Fresh pine branches had been spread on the weeping stone flags to soak up the damp, and their sharp fragrance helped to combat the dank, musty atmosphere.

The Count in his old-fashioned finery had been fussing about the hall like a bantam cock—his sagging jowls held up by his too tight stock tie—getting in everyone's way. He had even made a foray into the cavernous kitchen, until the cook, who had been with the family all her life and feared no one, drove him forth with blows from a soup ladle.

He was usefully distracted by the descent of his two male guests, which gave him the excuse of ordering and fussing over the opening of cobwebbed bottles of Champagne.

"Dammit Count!" said Charles, who had already sunk a considerable amount of the excellent brandy, "I must say you keep a damned good cellar."

The Count bobbed and grinned with pleasure:

"It is seldom that I have the honour of sharing it with proper gentlemen. We see so little company here now. Madame and I often talk about travelling to Vienna, but we are old and the roads are hard and in these uncertain times..."

—he spread his hands—"but, my dear Sir, your glass is empty!"

Charles, whose amazing wig was already slightly awry was nothing loath. Mischa who was drinking sparingly watched his friend's gradual dissolution with a certain detached amusement. But he kept one eye on the staircase. Anna had hardly been absent for so long from his presence since the demise of the Khan.

At this moment the door into the hall opened and the major-domo entered in a stately fashion with the Raven sitting on his wrist.

"Ah-ha! Splendid," cried the Count, "you have returned to join us. Come my friend and welcome!"

As the two young men gawped, the Raven walked crabbedly up the Count's outstretched arm, settled on his shoulder and added to the stains on the back of his once sumptuous velvet coat. Sirius, who had been chewing his bone contentedly by the fire, rose to his feet and cocked his ears. The Raven turned and regarded the dog with his wicked black eye.

"There child, now look at yourself in the glass."

The Countess cleared the maids back with a sweep of her cane. Rather timidly, Anna turned to the looking-glass and gave a small involuntary gasp. Her hair had been swept back in two waves over her ears and coiled at the back. The cream-coloured silk dress displayed her perfect shoulders and accentuated the swell of her breasts, but it was her long slim neck that made her gasp, set off as it was by the many-rowed pearl choker that the old lady had herself clasped round her neck, chuckling gently the while.

Anna had never been vain, although she had always realised at the back of her mind that men considered her to be attractive. She had often—when she had thought that nobody else was looking—studied her features in the small stained glass that used to hang on the wall at home, and where Papa sometimes used to brush up his moustache. But this tall, slim girl who looked calmly back at her from the full length glass, was someone she hardly recognised. This was a beauty. This was a princess from the pictures in the old books; if only Mutti was there to see her...

"There now," came the Countess's dry little voice, "what a sensation you would have made at Versailles, and not a touch of paint nor powder. Come, child, it is time for your entrance. Gretchen! Come here, you fool, and help me down the stairs."

There was a crash as Mischa's glass fell from his suddenly nerveless fingers. He stood transfixed at the vision that was descending the stairs, her skirts lifted in each hand, her head held high, her face serene.

This was Anna. But an Anna such as he had never seen. He was besieged by desire. This was a girl that he wanted more than anything else in the world: more than... more than..... Suddenly—horrid and unbidden —the bloated face with the reeds tangled in its hair floated across his mind. Was he cursed?

The other two men were also entranced:

"Jesus, Mary and Joseph!"

"I say! I mean, what, I say!"

It was as though Anna's stately descent had cast a spell over the room.

The spell was broken.

Sirius and the Raven had been staring at each other and had entered into telepathic conversation:

"Who the hell are you?"

Sirius bitterly resented the intrusion of a mere bird into a situation in which he was a recognised hero—one whose exploits had been much praised to an admiring audience since arriving at the castle. The Raven preened a feather in a deliberately offensive manner:

"Who are you to question me?"

Sirius felt a frisson around the hackles.

"I am Sirius! Killer of deer! Slayer of wolves! Stealer of babies! I am a great hero," he added modestly.

"Oh is that all? I am the servant of a god."

"I have served the Hunter."

"A mere spear carrier! I am his trusted herald."

The Raven spread a great black wing and began to feel under it with his beak, as though he no longer considered the dialogue worthy of his attention.

Sirius uttered a low growl:

"You are verminous!"

The Raven continued his under-wing explorations before eventually shaking himself and deigning to return his gaze to Sirius:

"As a near divine," he said superciliously, *"even my vermin are divine. You—you just have fleas like any other common mutt."*

"MUTT!"

This was much too much for Sirius. With a bellow of rage he took a sudden leap at the Raven, still sitting on the Count's shoulder. The Count was knocked flying. With a few lazy flaps the Raven took himself to the nearest chandelier.

In hot pursuit, Sirius used Charles, who was in the act of rising from his chair, as a scaling ladder to storm the table, which he took in a shower of shattering crystal and crashing plate. He then proceeded to bay the Raven, who watched with sardonic and insulting amusement from its swaying perch.

Mischa rushed to help the old man to his feet.

Anna had stopped her descent, and put her hand to her mouth in dismay at this horrid scene. At that moment Charles's head emerged from behind the table—the magnificent wig knocked all askew and sitting drunkenly over one eye.

The sight was too much for Anna.

All serene dignity forgotten, she sat on the stair, put her head in her hands and began to cry with laughter.

"Bless my soul!" The old Count wiped his eyes again. "I haven't laughed so much in years."

Order had been restored. The Raven had returned in triumph to the old man's shoulder, where it contested every forkful of food with its host. Sirius had been severely reprimanded by Mischa and was simmering with resentment.

He had sought refuge, lying beside Anna as she sat at the table and using as a rug the wig that a furious Charles had hurled at him.

Anna was restored to serenity—almost. Every time she looked at the bareheaded Charles, she could feel the laughter bubbling up inside her. She countered this by looking down at Sirius and telling him that he was a 'bad dog'. Sirius was not amused.

"Caviar!" cried the Count, rubbing his hands. "I love caviar!" He noticed that Anna was looking at the little black pearls on her plate with some perplexity. He leaned across to her and whispered, "You are not familiar with caviar, my dear?"

Anna shook her head slightly and lowered her eyes. She did not wish to look foolish in front of Mischa.

"Come," said the Count, who might be eccentric but was no·fool, "we will do this *à la Française*, as was the fashion at Versailles."

And, taking a larger spoonful he held it to Anna's lips. It was delicious.

The caviar was followed by a consommé of quails.

"Jolly little birds," said Charles, "I bet that they are damned difficult to hit."

The Count launched into a long tale about the excellent quail shooting that he had enjoyed whilst once on a diplomatic mission to the Sultan of Morocco; this lasted through the stuffed carp.

Anna surreptitiously slipped a titbit of fish to Sirius.

Sirius ignored it. He was still huffed.

Mischa could not stop his eyes wandering towards Anna, whilst he listened politely to the Countess's tales of the wonders of the French court. The sharp eyes of the old lady did not miss this:

"She is very beautiful. Are you a strong lover? The Czemys have always been strong lovers."—this was said in the bellow of the very deaf.

Anna blushed scarlet.

Mischa had a choking fit.

The moment was saved by the arrival of the roast wild boar complete with an apple stuffed in its mouth, which enabled Charles to slip smoothly into the tale of Mischa's exploits at the boar hunt at St Petersburg.

"Splendid! Splendid!" cried the Count, stamping his feet and drumming his knife handle on the table. "You are obviously a great hunter, Cousin. I remember hunting with Prince Radziwill in Poland in... oh I forget the year..."

At that moment his sharp eye caught Anna slipping a bit of meat to Sirius. He paused in his story and with a forkful of meat poised in front of his mouth—the Count saw nothing wrong in talking with his mouth full—"No, no! You mustn't do that, my dear... Damn *your* impudence, Sir!"—this to the Raven who had calmly expropriated the poised forkful. "No, no, you mustn't feed the dog like that. It won't do."

Poor Anna—covered in confusion—felt that once again she had committed some dreadful social sin. The Count shouted for the major-domo who brought a large gold salver, on which he carefully arranged the scraps that Sirius had studiously ignored.

"That's better." The Count reached across and lifted Anna's hand to his lips. "A dog belonging to such a beauty as you should not be expected to eat off the floor: the very idea!"

Sirius rose to his feet, looked at Anna, looked at the food on the golden plate and, very delicately, began to eat.

The Raven expressed its feelings down the back of the Count's coat.

As the final litter of plates was cleared away, the Countess rose stiffly to her feet:

"Come, my dear," she said to Anna, "you must be exhausted. We will leave the gentlemen to their wine, although,"—here she shot a sharp glance at Charles, who was swaying slightly and clutching the table as he stood up—"not, I hope, to the total dissolution of their senses. Or," and her bright old eyes fixed on Mischa, "their sensitivities."

With this she took Anna's arm and limped away towards

the stairs. Anna took a swift backwards glance at Mischa in whom nervousness, hope and longing were mixed.

"Sit down, gentlemen, sit down." The Count waved a hand round the table, "I must admit that the stirring events of the evening have left me somewhat fatigued, but we will have another glass before we retire. I expect that you young men will be ready for bed."

His rheumy eyes twinkled.

"Ready, aye, ready," said Charles, " and may I say, Count, that this is really excellent brandy. Just the thing to take a chap to his lonely couch, eh Mischa?"

The look that he gave Mischa combined a wink and a leer, which Mischa affected not to notice. He was feeling slightly fuddled by the evening, but the flow of wine had served only to increase an overwhelming desire. God! Anna was incredibly beautiful!

Anna had never been accustomed to undressing in front of people, but she had no choice as the maids fussed around, removing her dress and helping her into her night gown—a gown of silk, trimmed with delicate lace.

The Countess, with her foot up on the stool, superintended the operation, scolding the maids for clumsiness and remarking matter-of-factly on the beauty of Anna's body:

"Your breasts are nicely pert, child, and you have long slender thighs."

Anna felt as though she was being assessed like a prize heifer. From the smirks of the maids as they helped her into the great bed and arranged the down-filled cover over her, she realised that they were in no doubt as to what her fate would be that night. Neither, it seemed, was the Countess in any doubt as she hobbled round the bed and bent to kiss Anna on her forehead:

"Goodnight, child, and may it be a night of wonder and pleasure for you."

Anna lay watching the flickering shadows that candle and fire light threw on walls and ceilings. She felt both frightened and full of desire. Her eyes kept wandering to the large expanse of empty bed beside her. She knew that Mischa would come to her that night. She knew that she wanted him to. She knew that she wanted to feel the warmth of his naked body against hers.

At this point she sat up and, pulling the night dress over her head, dropped it on the floor. Now she was naked and ready for his embrace.

She wished he would come. She could feel the warmth spreading over her body. She wanted him so badly, why didn't he come and soothe her fears? She must think of something.

The face of the Black Madonna floated into her mind. Putting her hands together above the quilt, she began to pray:

"Dear Lady..."

The three men tackled the stairs. The Count led the way, his candle held high. Charles stumbled twice, until Mischa took away his candle stick and holding it together with his own in his huge right hand, gave Charles some well-needed support with the other, in spite of the fact that Charles kept assuring him that he was "absholutely fine, old boy."

They reached the door of Charles's room and the Count, with a dry little cackle of a laugh, hoped that everything had been arranged for Charles's comfort. He opened the door and Charles grasped the door post. The room was candlelit. The light revealed two heads already on the pillow with long dark hair spread out. At the sight of Charles, both the heads began to giggle:

"I say!" Charles seemed suddenly to straighten up. He took a step away from the door and stood ogling the bed. "I say! Tally-ho! Bloody well, Tally-ho, what!"

With that he began to lurch his way towards the bed. Still cackling the old man, closed the door and set off down the passage until he paused by another door:

"Here you are, Cousin. I am certain that I need not enquire about your comfort."

Chuckling to himself, the Count and his flickering candle

disappeared into the shadows of the great cavernous corridor.

Mischa stood looking at the door. Twice he raised his hand to the door knob. Twice it fell back to his side. Then he took a deep breath, knocked and turned the knob.

Fire and candle light flickered round the walls of the room. The candle on the table beside Anna lit up her face and gave it a luminous quality. She lay very still, her naked arms above the covers, her hair spread like a golden cloud on the pillow. Her face was set and serious. Only her eyes moved, watching Mischa as he stood silent and uncertain in the doorway.

Suddenly she smiled, a smile of such warmth and welcome that it lit up her whole face. Mischa felt a sudden surge of warmth, happiness and desire. Very carefully he shut the door behind him and, still moving slowly and never taking his eyes from Anna's face, he advanced and set his candlestick down on the table at the empty side of the bed.

Again he stood irresolutely.

Anna's smile deepened.

Then she held out her arms to him:

"Come!"

Mischa walked round the bed and knelt beside her. Very gently he put out a hand and began to trace his fingers over her face. He traced the line of her eyebrows, smoothed his fingers across her cheeks.

Anna lay still, her eyes fixed on his.

Tentatively, Mischa drew his fingers to the corner of Anna's mouth.

Her hand clasped his and drew the fingers to her lips. She kissed each finger up and down. Then, lifting the hand slightly, she ran her tongue catlike across the open palm, tasting the salt of the sweat there. She took a finger to her mouth and, with great delicacy, closed her teeth on it.

Mischa gave a deep moan and, taking her face between his hands, lowered his mouth towards the girl.

Anna's arms twined round his neck pulling him down and at the same time pulling herself up, so that the covers fell away to show her perfect, pink-nippled breasts.

They kissed—slowly and gently at first, then with increasing passion.

Mischa pulled back, slightly. He was frightened by the intensity of the physical passion that was surging in him. He was frightened by the knowledge of his own physical strength as against Anna's seemingly fragile beauty. He was terrified of hurting her. He was also frightened by the battle inside him: the battle between what he wanted to do, and the sense of sin to add to the other sin that had weighed so heavily on his soul for so long.

Anna felt no sense of sin: only an intense desire: a desire that had simmered and grown inside her over the past months: a desire to be as one body and mind with this man— a desire for him to do the things that sometimes came hot and splendid in her dreams. She knew that he might—would —hurt her, but she did not care. Beyond the pain lay ecstasy:

"Come, my darling."

Reaching across she pinched out her candle.

Mischa was like a man in a fever. He staggered round the bed and snuffed his own candle. Only the firelight lit the room now. His nerveless fingers fumbled with awkward buttons. In his impatience, he ripped his shirt as he pulled it off and slipped underneath the thick down-filled covers.

Anna slid into his arms, and their burning naked bodies entwined.

Mischa took one of her breasts in his hand, caressed it with his fingers and felt the nipple hardening. Then he raised himself on his arms and stared down at her.

Anna's eyes were sleepy with desire. Her lips parted. She ached for what she knew was about to happen.

Mischa also felt desire: desire such as he had only felt once before—once before. Oh Sweet Jesus! Suppose it were all to happen again. Suppose that he were to do to this girl what he had done to the girl at Lippitz?

He looked down at Anna. She looked so beautiful and yet so fragile. She had suffered so much. Suppose that all he did was to add to her suffering? Suppose that by an act of love he were to betray this girl also? An awful agony of the spirit wracked Mischa. What he was about to do was a mortal sin. In his anguish, he moaned. Anna's eyes opened wide—full of concern:

"What is it, darling?"

Mischa could not answer. His eyes were screwed shut and beads of sweat formed on his brow. For a moment longer, he stayed poised above Anna's body, then he rolled away from her and, burying his face in the pillow, he began to cry with great aching sobs.

Anna sat up in the bed and stared at the shaking, prostrate figure beside her. This sudden change shocked and frightened her; something had gone horribly wrong. But as she sensed Mischa's obvious agony, she was overwhelmed by a great wave of compassion and love. She loved this man and that was all that mattered. She stroked his naked, shuddering shoulders. Then she began to kiss them, very slowly and gently, until the sobbing abated and Mischa turned to face her on the pillow. His cheeks were wet with tears.

She took his face in her hands and continued her gentle kissing.

Mischa gave a gulp:

"I'm s-so s-s-sorry," he stammered. "So very s-sorry. I'm..." But Anna stopped his mouth with her hand:

"It doesn't matter, darling."

"But I've disappointed you! It's just that..."

"Nothing matters except love," she said simply. "Everything else can be sorted out."

"I..."

Once again the hand stopped him:

"You silly great bear! I've told you, it doesn't matter. Now my darling you must sleep. It is my turn to look after you. Put your arm round me."

She moved into the angle of his shoulder so that their bodies lay gently and easily together. Then she began to sing. She sang the old lullabies that Mutti had sung to her and to Matthias in their cradles.

She felt the tension flowing out of Mischa's body, and she could feel him sinking into exhausted slumber. Anna smiled to herself as she watched peace come to the man's face. She looked up to the ceiling, said a little prayer to the Black Madonna, then, warm in the arm of her lover, she too drifted off to sleep.

Very carefully, Anna laid out the dress on the bed. The sharp frosty morning sunlight shone through the window and a stray shaft lit up the old silk. Anna stroked the dress and gave a sigh. She thought that she would never again see such a beautiful dress, or look as she had last night.

She wondered about the future. When she had woken that morning and stretched out a hand for Mischa, she had felt only a cold empty bed. Mischa had gone. Would the rest of her life be as cold and empty?

With a rather heavy heart she pulled on her patched and weathered breeches and boots. She felt that life had become a seemingly endless journey, plagued with snow and ice. She sighed again and picked up the pearl necklace, running it through her hands and watching how the pearls glowed in the sunlight.

She was so wrapped in her thoughts that she did not hear the door open. The tap of the cane on the floor made her start. She turned. The old Countess was standing there, regarding her quizzically:

"Well, child, and did you pass a good night?"

Anna, with the pearls in her hands, stammered out a confused reply. The old lady smiled gently and, taking Anna's hands in hers, she closed them over the pearls:

"Don't worry, child, you must just be patient. Men are such funny creatures with all their 'honour' and 'duty'. They can be very stuffy and stubborn at times, but remember: *Omnia vincit amor*."

Anna looked perplexed. The Countess squeezed her hands:

"Love conquers all. Keep that in your heart. You will also keep the pearls and the dress."

Anna gasped:

"No! I couldn't. I…"

The Countess gave one of her dry little laughs:

"Don't be silly. I shall never wear that dress again and you may well find a use for it; in fact I am sure of it. As for the pearls..."—she opened Anna's hands—"they never looked so well as they did on you last night. They are yours."

She turned her head and called, "Gretchen! Here's some packing for you."

The Count was wiping a rheumy eye:

"My boy! My boy!" he said, clasping Mischa's hand and once again laughing until he coughed. "Such lovely fun! It's years since I have laughed so much as last night. The Englishman in that awful wig—used to be the height of *ton* at Versailles, ye know—and your splendid dog and the Raven, what d'yer call him?"

"Raven, I suppose."

"No, no, the dog you fool, what d'yer call the dog?"

"Sirius."

And Sirius who had been lying by the fire pretending to be asleep rolled a watchful eye.

"Sirius, of course, Sirius. Now, Sir, d'ye know your name? Come here, Sir."

"Sirius!" Mischa spoke crisply. "Come!"

Sirius, who suspected that he was being laughed about, got reluctantly to his feet.

"Sir Sirius! That's the ticket. We shall dub you, 'Sir', damned if we don't."

The old man hobbled across the hall and began to rummage through a large oaken chest.

"Ah-ha! Here it is. Knew it was there somewhere."

The dog collar was wide, made of fine red leather and covered in plates of yellow metal which, by the way they glowed deeply in the firelight, could only have been gold.

"Now, Sir Sirius, what do you say to that, eh?"

Sirius pricked his ears, and sniffed the collar with obvious interest and approval.

* * *

The blizzard hit them on the open plain between Budapest and Vienna.

"Sod this for a lark." Bone and Vlad were riding together as usual. "Wish we'd stayed at that bloody castle."

"No good, my old Bone. You would be pricked out by now."

"Well at least I rediscovered my John Thomas for a bit. Bloody thing's disappeared again now—shrivelled. The Captain made a pig of hisself as usual. How did your bloke come on?"

Vlad shrugged:

"I don't think he is very happy."

"What, didn't get his wicked way, you reckon?"

"There are other things, Bone."

"I dunno," said Bone gloomily. "It all comes down to that in the end."

"There must be a village somewhere on this blasted plain," said Charles, "somewhere we could lie up during this storm."

Mischa grunted. He had been in poor fettle since Telez. In the whiteout they nearly rode into the back of the oxcart, piled with firewood, that filled the middle of the road.

"He must be going to a village."

Charles turned to the snow-covered figure of the driver huddled up on the front of the cart.

"Village? Houses? Bloody Magyars—can't speak any known language"

Charles held up two hands in the shape of a roof. The ox cart driver pointed in front of him in the murk.

Mischa halted the column when the dim shape of the houses appeared through the snow and sent the sergeant to reconnoitre. The man was quickly back in some excitement.

"There's an inn, Excellency. I did not enter, but I had a look in the barn and there are some horses there—Cossack horses."

The men were in the inn. They were Tersk Cossacks, tired, dirty and dispirited. One man was wounded. Their story was not easy to piece together, but it seemed that there had been a skirmish at a place called Amstetten, some 150 miles to the west. The Austrian and Russian forces had had a mauling and were retreating: that was all they knew.

Their regiment had had a bad time and they had been lucky to escape. Mischa wanted to know where the Allied army might be. The men shrugged: east, north, gone to the devil for all they knew. They were heading home.

Mischa gave orders to march at first light. They must get on.

12 Mariazell

*D*ECEMBER was well and truly setting in with fog,
frost and snow. The little party was heading west
along the old Roman road that ran past Budapest
and Vienna and had always been one of the main
arteries from east to west. Mischa, ever more dogged, silent
and determined, would brook no delay to their mission
which instinct told him was becoming ever more urgent. This
urgency was renewed when, during a brief stop for victu-
alling at the hamlet of Mayerling in the wooded hills south of
Vienna, they heard rumours of a great battle somewhere to
the north, between the French and the allied armies of Russia
and Austria.

The rumours were conflicting, as is the way with rumours
—the French had received a bloody nose and were retreating
westwards—the battle had been a hard-fought draw—the allied armies had been roughly served. All these conflicting
stories were related as actual facts. This uncertainty served
only to fuel Mischa's impatience. This impatience was
matched by that of the Cossacks, who believed deeply in the
importance of the presence of the Black Madonna for the
success of their comrades.

Anna was confused and uncertain. After the night at Castle Telez, Mischa had withdrawn totally into himself. All his
energy and thought was concentrated on the Black Madonna.
With Anna he had reverted to a formal courtesy and he
seemed to avoid contact with her. There had been no signs of
love or tenderness from him and certainly no question of
them sharing a bed again.

Anna had been deeply grieved by Mischa's withdrawn attitude, although she knew that it was a carapace for his own
misery. In her direct way she thought it ridiculous that they
should both be unhappy. She had no way of knowing the

root cause of Mischa's guilt and unhappiness, but she just
wanted to comfort him and soothe him as she had done that
night. She felt that with time she could gentle him out of the
dark corner of his soul where he now seemed to be chained,
but he would give her no opportunity. She covered her unhappiness with a bright and cheerful manner. This certainly
did not fool the sharp and cynical eye of Charles, who
broached the matter with his customary brutal cheerfulness:

"What's the matter with you two, my sweet?" he said to
Anna. "Couldn't the old boy get it up? Well any time you feel
the need for a cuddle and a canter, come to old Charles. I'll
bring the roses back to your cheeks—all of them."

Anna's stinging slap rocked him back on his heels:

"If Mischa heard that he would kill you!"

"Well he might and then again, I might kill him. Then
where would you be, my pretty? Anyway he won't hear, because you ain't going to tell the po-faced old misery, are
you?"

"I thought he was your friend."

Anna's fury was rising, especially as she knew that what
Charles had said was true; she would not tell Mischa.

"Of course he is, but that's got nothing to do with tupping
wenches. I've helped quite a few of my friends out in that
line."

"Have you no conscience?"

"I have, but my cock ain't."

"You disgust me!" Anna stormed away.

Charles laughed.

They pressed on westwards and, as the snow thickened and
worsened, so did the rumours; the only thing that the rumours agreed upon was that there had been a great battle.

"I pray to God that we are not too late," said Mischa to
Charles.

"Don't worry, old thing," said Charles breezily. "Battles
are like women—there's always another one just over the horizon."

"Have you no sense of honour and duty?"

"Oh yes, but at the moment it's so shrivelled up with the cold that I can't feel a thing"

"Horsemen, Excellency!" The Sergeant appeared at Mischa's side.

"Where?"

The Sergeant pointed. Out of the freezing fog that blanketed the road appeared the dim shapes of a straggling column of horsemen. The Sergeant barked an order. Lances were unslung from shoulders, sabres eased in scabbards and pistols checked.

Then, as the horsemen came into clearer sight, the tension eased. This was no threatening force. Both men and horses were exhausted. Some horses carried two men. There were men afoot as well, men who clung to the stirrup leathers of their mounted comrades. Uniforms were torn and bloodstained. Some men had dirty bandages tied about them. Some had open wounds, clotted with dried blood.

Even as they watched, one man who was bent over his horse's neck, collapsed and slid silently to the ground. Ignoring the fallen man, one of his comrades grabbed the animal and, with some difficulty, managed to pull himself into the empty saddle. The others shambled past him without a backward glance.

Anna slid from her horse and ran to him.

At the head of the column rode a man with a battered shako over one eye; his uniform proclaimed him to be an officer. Mischa reined his horse beside him. The man, with his head bowed and his eyes on the ground, did not even glance at him.

"For God's sake man, what's happened?"

"Home," the officer's voice was dull. "We're going home."

"But what's happened?"

"What's it to you?"—sullenly.

"I have to find the Russian Army."

There was a short bark that might have been a laugh:

"You'll be lucky. You might find bits of them," again the bark, "cut to bloody pieces—and I mean bloody pieces—and heading east with their tails between their legs. It's a toss up who's running faster—us, or the bloody Russians."

"But what happened?"

"What happened? The fucking French happened, that's what, and they whipped our arses."

"Where did this happen?"

The man waved his hand vaguely towards the north:

"Up there, a shit hole of a little village called Austerlitz. Got any brandy?"

Anna got up from the fallen man:

"He's dead," she said simply.

Mischa and his party sat beside the road, watching as the ragged column dragged its way past them until only a few limping stragglers were left and, finally, even they were swallowed up in the dank pall of freezing fog. The men were silent as though the additional dank pall of failure had settled on them—all those weary miles and months—all the fear and desperate fighting—all those dead comrades—all the struggle to get the Black Madonna to her rightful place with the Cossack army, and all for nothing. They were too late.

The Cossacks knew nothing of politics or strategy, or the manoeuvrings of emperors and generals. They were simple men of simple faith. They *knew* that if the Black Madonna had been with the Cossack army, then no earthly power could have defeated it. They *knew* this and believed it. It was as though the glazed eyes of those dead soldiers were staring at them and their failure. They felt that they had betrayed a sacred trust. The men were dumb in their misery.

This misery seeped through to Mischa. He sat huddled in the hood of his cloak, staring blankly into the mist and, as though to add to the bleakness of his mood, it began to snow again.

Anna, remounted, pushed Bahram alongside him. She looked at the bleak misery of his face and put a hand on his arm:

"You did your best."

Mischa continued to stare straight ahead. At last he spoke, but still without looking at her:

"It was not good enough. We failed. The Cossacks had to fight without the Black Madonna and have been defeated—destroyed. If only we had moved faster, harder…"

"You did your best. No man could have done more."

Mischa did not reply, but sat slumped in his saddle.

"Well," said Charles, "it looks as though we are stuffed. We must take immediate military action. Bone!"

"Sir!"

"Immediate Military Action Number One!"

"Sir!"

Bone reached down into his saddle bags and pulled out a bottle of brandy.

"You do have some brandy?" Anna was surprised.

"Never travel without it, but I was not going to waste it on that miserable bunch." He nodded his head in the direction of the departed soldiers. "Now, ladies first."

Anna took the bottle and the fiery liquid brought on a coughing fit.

"That bad is it?" said Charles cheerfully. He handed the bottle to Mischa, who ignored it. "For God's sake, man, snap out of it! We don't know where we're going and you sulking like some bloody girl who's lost her favourite ribbon ain't going to help!"

Charles took a healthy swig himself and made a sour face:

"Damn me! But that is awful stuff. Here you are Bone, pass it down the line. Everybody will welcome death after a mouthful of that rot gut. Talking about which, Herr Rittmeister, if we sit here much longer, we are all going to freeze to death. What are we going to do?"

The Raven appeared suddenly out of the murk and settled on a fallen tree beside the road. Sirius who had been sitting shivering, in the snow beside Bahram, got to his feet, hackles raised and teeth bared. The Raven cocked a wicked black eye at him:

"*Greetings, Mutt,*" it said.

"Sirius, no!" Anna's voice was sharp. "Stay, Sir!"

Sirius who had been poised to spring, subsided, grumbling deep in his chest. The look that the Raven gave him said all too clearly:

"Who's Mummy's good boy then?"

Sirius quivered with indignation. One day, he thought—one day.

The Raven gave a harsh croak, flew a few yards along the road to the west, landed and stood looking back at them.

"Is that the same bloody bird we saw at Telez," said Charles. "Is it trying to tell us something?"

Mischa shook himself rather as a dog does when it comes out of water:

"We follow it. Walk march!"

The Raven continued to flutter in front of the little column as it headed west, never going far enough for them to lose sight of it in the fog.

The Hunter was sitting on a milestone. He was so completely covered in snow, that he might have been a snowman had it not been for the curl of pipe smoke. As the party approached he rose to his feet and dusted the snow off his clothing.

Mischa grasped the huge calloused hand of the big man and felt a profound sense of relief, as though he was able to slip the heavy pack of command and responsibility from his shoulders for a short time.

The troop all gathered round the Hunter who was leaning on his stick. The Raven flew up and perched on the crown of his battered hat. Its eyes locked with those of Sirius who was now sitting behind Mischa's saddle:

"See how important I am, Mutt," said the Raven.

Then it gave a slight squawk and shifted uncomfortably. A thought had come up through the hat that said clearly and distinctly: "If you don't behave, I'll pull your tail feathers out."

Sirius also heard the thought. His tail thumped approvingly.

"Now," said the Hunter out loud, "you have heard the news. What were you planning to do?"

"We must go on. We must find the Cossack army and hand over the icon. It may not be too late to help them.

Surely there must be something we can do to help the Cossacks"—Mischa paused to choose his words—"even with a little divine intervention."

The Hunter stroked his chin and shook his head:

"Unfortunately, Napoleon does not believe in gods, only fate, of which he considers himself master. He will learn his lesson, but not yet. No, there is nothing you can do for the Cossacks. You have done all, and more, that any men could."

"But we failed."

"A failure in one thing can lead to success in another," said the Hunter cryptically. "Now, what was your immediate plan?"

"We were going to head for Amstetten and find out more about the situation there."

"What you will find at Amstetten will be a whole boiling pot of French troops, who will solve all your problems by killing you and looting the Black Madonna. No, what you must do now is to save yourselves,"—he paused for a moment as though listening to something far away—"well most of you, anyway," he added rather sombrely, "and to save the Black Madonna. You must turn south and head into the mountains."

"At this time of year?" Mischa was doubtful.

"I will help you," said the Hunter, "and, as I cannot be with you all the time, I will send the Raven with you."

The Raven looked up from preening its feathers and turned its beady eye on Sirius:

"You hear that, Mutt? I am to be in charge."

Sirius scratched an ear and pretended not to hear.

Past St Pölten, the party turned south, following the fertile valley of the river Erlauf with its broad pastures and prosperous looking farmsteads. The road they were on was one of the main routes through the mountains. The weather improved and a cold wintry sun sparkled on the white forested slopes of the foothills.

In spite of the knowledge of the failure of their mission, the clear, crisp, windless weather raised the spirits of the party. The Cossacks even began to sing, the Sergeant's fine deep voice providing the base for the harmony

The Raven had taken a particular liking for Charles, with whom he seemed to be able to communicate. Sometimes, as the bird sat on his shoulder, Charles would give a loud guffaw.

"What is it?" asked Mischa, as Charles was spluttering with laughter:

"This bird has an enormous fund of remarkably revolting stories," he said, wiping an eye on the back of his glove.

"Then he has certainly chosen the right ear to whisper in," said Anna in her most honeyed tones.

At every village they passed, in the broad peaceful valley, Mischa would ask for any news of other soldiers. The villagers shook their heads.

"You can see that the French have not passed this way, Excellency," said the Sergeant. "The houses have not been burned and the women are not hiding."

His words were prophetic. Later that day, one of the Cossacks who had been scouting the road ahead, came galloping back:

"Horse tracks, Excellency! They have come out of a side road and must be ahead of us on this road."

"You're sure that it is not just some peasant carts?"

"No, Excellency, many, many, horses and wagons."

Leaving the rest of the troop halted, Mischa, Charles and the Sergeant galloped forward with the scout. The signs were plain to see in the hoof-trampled snow, the droppings and the tracks of heavy wagons. The Sergeant dismounted and inspected the signs.

"Well?" asked Mischa.

"I would say at least two squadrons of cavalry, with baggage wagons and infantry."

"How far ahead do you reckon?"

The Sergeant shrugged:

"Perhaps two days, no more. It looks to me that wherever they are going, they mean to settle in."

"What would the next place of any size be?" Charles scratched his chin.

Mischa thought. It was some years since he had travelled this route:

"Gaming. As we go further up the valley it narrows. Gaming is like a cork in a bottle. Who controls the town, controls this road."

"Could be Austrians retreating."

The Sergeant spotted something dark in the snow beside the road. It was an empty brandy bottle. He picked it up:

"French!"

"I have known Austrians to be partial to a little Cognac."

Mischa rubbed his face:

"I think that we must assume the worst and move very carefully from now on."

The worst was soon confirmed. The next village on the road was a smoking ruin and bodies lay scattered in the streets where they had been casually slaughtered. The body of a woman lay in a shattered doorway. She was naked in the blood stained snow.

Anna stared at the scene of carnage, her face white and pinched:

"Sweet Christ! Is there to be no end to this bloody business?"

Mischa put his hand on her arm.

With a harsh croak the Raven took off from Charles's shoulder to land in the bloody snow, where it began hopping about the bodies with obvious interest and intent.

"Oh God, no!" Anna buried her face in her cloak. "Stop him!"

"Sirius!" snapped Mischa, and the dog was gone like an arrow.

The Raven rose with a startled squawk and settled on a roof beam. Sirius, with a tail feather in his mouth, grinned up at him.

"How dare you attack a servant of a god?"

"They didn't want you pecking out any eyes."

"Stuff and nonsense—that's what ravens do!"

"Not today, oh divine one, unless you want to lose more of your divine feathers."

"Bah!" The Raven ruffled his plumage.

"Bone!"

"Sir!"

"Any cigars left?"

"Precious few, Sir."

"Well break one out. I need to think about this bloody Gaming. They can't even pronounce it properly in this be-nighted country. God! What I wouldn't give for a good game of whist. Is there any way round this town, Mischa?"

Mischa shook his head:

"I don't think so. The valley is narrow and steep and the only bridge across the river is in the town. If the French intend to garrison the place they will have it heavily guarded."

Charles nicked the end of his cigar and lit it, his brow furrowed in thought:

"Well, if we can't go round it, then we must go through it."

Mischa shook his head:

"If we attack the bridge, we'll have the whole wasp's nest buzzing about us. We'd never fight our way through."

Charles was wreathed in smoke and deep in thought:

"What we need is an act of God to impress the Johnny Crapauds on the bridge."

"The French have abolished God," said Mischa gloomily.

"Officially, yes, but I'll wager you a fat purse that they have not managed to change what people believe deep in their superstitious little Republican heads. Also remember that it's nearly Christmas. The Frogs may have abolished that as well, but the old beliefs run deep. Now think of our Frogs on the bridge—far from home in a foreign country—the festive season approaching and them far from their families: a little bit of eau de vie to ease the gloom and the loneliness. Now how do you think that a sentry in that state would react to a vision of the Blessed Virgin, eh?"

Pierre Lebrun, Private in the 112th Regiment of Foot in the

Army of France was not a happy man. Like many of the men in the regiment he had been conscripted in Provence. He was not enjoying the army. Here he was, far from home, far from the more kindly climate of the Mediterranean, far from his parents' little farm, far from his mother's wonderful fish stews. He did not like the army. He did not like the harsh discipline. He did not like the fear, the marching and the lack of food. Most of all he did not like standing up to his knees in snow, with more of it blowing into his face, on this godforsaken bridge, in this godforsaken country, amongst these godforsaken mountains, staring out into a frozen darkness that contained God knew what.

From the town behind him he could hear occasional distant snatches of revelry; the bloody cavalry were having a high old time in the captured town. The bloody cavalry always did. It was always the poor bloody infantry who froze their balls off doing guards, whilst those other snooty bastards enjoyed themselves. It was not fair and it was not right and he would like to tell Sergeant Fèvre so, but he knew what would happen to him if he did.

Sergeant Fèvre was the biggest bastard of all. So Private Lebrun huddled in his cloak and stamped his feet against the cold. It was then that he saw the vision.

Pierre had been brought up a good Catholic. Although religion had been officially frowned upon after the Revolution, the beliefs that had been driven into him as a child remained with him. The Rosary that his mother had given him when he joined the army was still buried deep in his pocket. In moments of stress and fear he still prayed to the Blessed Virgin. Therefore he had no doubt when he saw the vision:

"Holy Mother of God!" he said, for it was She.

The Vision was of a beautiful women dressed in flowing white robes. Behind her golden hair was a golden halo. He could see this because the vision was floating above the ground and was lit by four flaming torches, very likely carried by the Four Apostles for all Lebrun knew.

He managed a strangled shout and his comrades of the

guard who had been warming themselves around a meagre
fire, ran to his shout. They saw. They also knew. As one they
fell to their knees in the snow, dropped their muskets and
raised their hands in supplication to the vision. This made it
very easy for the Cossacks, who had been creeping in the
shadows alongside the vision, to slit the throats of the entire
guard with silent enthusiasm. The bridge was taken without a
sound.

"Quick!" said Mischa.

The rough stretcher on which Anna had been standing
was lowered to the ground and the four torches quickly ex-
tinguished. The gold plate that had formed the halo was
handed back to Bone.—"Where the fuck did you get that,
Bone?" "Made it, Sir."

Mischa wrapped a cloak round the bare shoulders of the
shivering girl: shivering not just with the cold, but with
nerves.

"Are you all right?"

Anna nodded, silent except for her chattering teeth.

"Well done, my dear. Worked like a charm, eh?" Charles
rubbed his hands "Mind you, if they had been Church of
England we'd never have got away with it."

"No talking! Where's Bahram? Quick, Anna, mount! We
must be on!"

"My dress…"

"No time, no time."

Anna swung into Bahram's saddle. She thought sadly to
herself that when the Countess had pressed her to keep the
dress she had suggested, coyly, that 'it might come in for another occasion, child'. Anna felt that this was not quite the
occasion that either she or the Countess might have had in
mind.

The bodies of the bridge guard were dragged into the
shadows beside the bridge. The column fell in and moved
into the town at a steady trot, the men tense and silent.

Gaming was a long town with the main road running
through the middle of it. It was this road that they had to
pass. As they got further into the town, they began to meet

more soldiers, most of them reeling with drink.

"Pissed as bloody mattresses, the lot of them," Bone muttered to Vlad. "Lucky. bastards!"

The column, all muffled in heavy cloaks, looked suitably anonymous as they trotted through the dim street, lit only by the occasional lantern and the lights from various windows. No one took much notice of them, except for the occasional shout of drunken greeting, to which Mischa would answer:

"Vive la France!"

The night was heavy with coarse laughter and shouts from houses and inns. It was obvious that Gaming was getting its induction into the meanings of 'Liberty, Fraternity and Equality'. Men staggered out of houses with bags of loot on their backs. Behind a brightly-lit upstairs window a woman was screaming again and again. Mischa reached out to grip Anna's arm and rode grimly on. It could not be much further to the end of the town.

The platoon of infantry that came marching out of a side turning was not drunk. It was marching in good order with an officer at its head. This was obviously the new guard on its way out. The officer saw the column and halted his men. The French filled the road ahead.

"Qui va là?"

"I have to report to the Commanding Officer," said Mischa in French.

"Then you are going the wrong way, my friend," said the officer. "What is the password?"

Mischa hesitated.

"We have not been told yet."

"Then how did you pass the bridge?"

The officer made a sign and there was a hiss of steel as the bayonets slid out of their scabbards. As one, the hilts were rammed home into the muzzles of the muskets.

"The password?" the officer asked again.

"Raven!" cried Mischa.

The great black bird appeared out of the darkness and hit the officer full in the face. With a cry of shock and horror, he clutched his face and fell to his knees.

Sirius seized him by the throat.

"The devil! The devil!" cried Charles in French. "Demons from Hell!"

The disciplined line of steel wavered and, as the officer screamed in pain and terror, broke.

"Now!" roared Mischa, drawing his sabre.

With a yell the Cossacks charged, cutting and slashing to the sides of them.

The dawn was cold and crisp and clear.

They had galloped out of the south of the town, leaving Gaming in a total confusion of shouts, shots and bugle calls.

"Very excitable, your Frog-eater," said Charles cheerfully. "Shouldn't wonder if they don't shoot a good few of their own before they're done."

"They'll be after us like hornets soon enough," said Mischa grimly. "We must be over the Grübberg pass, by dawn."

But they were not. The twisting pass was deep with snow. The tired horses had to take turns in breaking through the drifts:

"Making a bloody good track for the Frogs," grumbled Bone.

They had no choice but to pause at the head of the pass; men and horses were exhausted.

Mischa moved amongst the men, talking quietly and encouraging them. The little party seemed to have escaped very lightly from the skirmish at Gaming. One Cossack had received a bayonet wound in his thigh, but it was only a flesh wound. Mischa and the Sergeant inspected it. Mischa ordered a treatment of vodka—internal and external. In fact, he thought, vodka all round would be good. There was no time for anything else. As he turned away from the wounded man, Anna screamed.

"Fucking hell, Sir, quick!" It was Bone shouting.

Charles had slumped to the ground and was lying on the snow.

Bone ran to him and putting an arm round his shoulders raised him up.

There was a red stain in the snow.

Anna was beside Charles now, her face serious and determined. She began to unbutton his tunic. As she did so, Charles opened his eyes:

"Never thought I'd ever get you to do that," he said and laughed. The laugh became a cough. There were flecks of blood on his lips.

They opened the tunic. The shirt on Charles's left side was stained and black with dried blood.

"Sweet Jesus!" said Anna horrified.

"Just a scratch." Charles sounded his usual jaunty self. "Here, let Bone have a look, he's been patching me up for years, eh Bone? Any of you Christians got a drink?"

A Cossack brought a flask of vodka and held it to Charles's lips. Charles took a deep draught and had another coughing fit. There were more flecks.

Bone said nothing, but went to his pack and came back with a pair of scissors. Very carefully he began to cut away the shirt and ease the blood-stiffened material away from the wound. As he did so, fresh blood poured out of the gaping hole on the side.

Charles fainted.

They bandaged the wound as best they could. Charles, who had come round again, was assuring everybody that it was only a scratch and where was that bloody vodka?

"Have a word, Sir?" Bone motioned his head to one side and Mischa followed him:

"What do you think?"

"Not good, Sir. You see how some of that blood was sort of pinky? Well, I reckon it's nicked a lung."

"Can he ride?"

"He ain't got no fucking choice, begging your pardon, Sir. We best tie his legs to the leathers. Stop him falling off like."

Mischa scratched his chin:

"I wonder..." he began.

"Excellency! Excellency! Look!"

The Cossack was pointing back the way they had come.

The road twisted and looped its way up the contours of the mountain to reach the pass. Some of the loops were visible from their vantage point. Way below them, a line of mounted figures, made tiny by distance, was picking its way up the road past the high walls and steep shingled gables of the ancient Carthusian monastery.

Mischa took his spy glass from its case and focused on the figures: French dragoons.

The snow was less deep on the far side of the pass and, with the slope in their favour, the party was able to make better time, ever-mindful of the fact that the pursuing dragoons with their fresher horses would also have the same advantage.

It was obvious that Charles was not in a good way. In his lucid moments he was his old cynical, cheerful, blasphemous self, but sometimes the pain was too much for him and he would slump in the saddle, semi-conscious. Anna and Bone rode either side of him, quick to support him if he looked like falling.

"I don't like the look of him, Madam," said Bone. "Reckon he could have a fever coming on him."

With an effort Charles, jerked himself upright:

"Don't be such a bloody old woman, Bone. For Christ's sake give me a drink. No, no, you fool, not water—you know what it does to gun barrels—give me some vodka."

Through all of this, the Raven remained perched on the sick man's shoulder.

Any attempt to dislodge it resulted in a stab from the savage dagger of a beak.

"Leave him alone," said Charles, "he wants to get my eyes nice and fresh when I croak."

"You are not going to die, Charles." Anna sounded determined

"Yes, I bloody am. Raven has told me and he's welcome to my eyes. He cheers me up with his stories. Come on Raven, tell me the one about the two priests and the milkmaid again." Bone just shook his head.

They came to a fork in the road. To the right the main road zig-zagged down into the next valley. The road to the left climbed into a steep-sided, thickly-forested ravine, which ran high into the mountains. There the infant river Ybbs roared and tumbled down over its boulder-studded bed.

The little column halted. Mischa who had been in the lead, turned his horse back to the others. He took off his cap and scratched his head. Anna noticed again how haggard and care-worn he had become—so many dangerous and difficult decisions, and now another one:

"That is the pass to Mariazell," he said. "I have not been over it since I was a boy, but it is very narrow and steep. That is the way we ought to go, but if it is blocked with snow we would be trapped like rats. If we go down the main road then the French will surely catch us, and then..." he shrugged hopelessly.

At this moment the Raven gave a harsh croak and, with a few flaps of its huge wings, landed at the foot of a gnarled and twisted ash tree by the fork. The Hunter was leaning against the tree, although any one of them would have taken an oath that he had not been there a moment ago.

"Well strap me vitals," cried Charles, within whom vodka, pain and sepsis were struggling violently, "if it ain't old Hunter. Waidmannsheil, old cock!"

"Waidmannsdank!" The Hunter was smiling.

"Oh Hunter! Can you help him?" Anna pleaded.

"Yes! What about a bit of that 'bone on bone' stuff, eh, what? No, not you Bone! One of you is quite enough."

Charles was beginning to babble.

The Hunter walked across and put a hand on Charles's knee:

"Look at me."

Charles tried hard to focus on the Hunter.

"Look at me. You will soon be out of all pain and sickness —after you have done what you must do."

As he spoke his grip tightened on the sick man's thigh. Charles gradually straightened in his saddle and his face cleared as though some current of strength was running through him:

"Yes, I understand," he said in his normal voice. "Bone! Where's that fucking vodka?"

The Raven landed back on his shoulder.

The Hunter turned to Mischa:

"You must take the road to Mariazell. You will get through. At the head of the pass, there is an inn. Wait there for me."

"But the French...?"

"The French will not follow you."

"The French are following us, Excellency."

"How far, Sergeant?"

"Less than a couple of *versts* behind."

They could go no faster. The track was steep and covered in snow and ice. It continuously twisted to suit the course of the icy torrent, which it often crossed on sturdy wooden bridges. On either side the rocky slopes, with their stunted trees, rose almost sheer, cutting back the daylight. It was a sombre place and they were going to die there.

Mischa felt despair seeping into him. To have travelled so many weary miles only to have failed in his mission, and now to lose everything—everything that he had fought for, hoped for and dreamed of—it was... it was, almost too much. He felt his throat thickening.

Then he felt a hand on his. Anna had brought her horse alongside him. She was looking intently into his face:

"Don't worry, my love, you have done everything you could, and if we die then we will truly be together."

"But you...."

"Don't worry about me. The bloody French won't get me alive, and I'll take some of the bastards with me."

Mischa bent his face to hers and their lips met.

"That's the stuff, Herr Rittmeister! Nothing like putting on a bit of a show for the troops, what!" Charles's cynical drawl made Mischa and Anna turn angrily. "This is the place," said Charles before either of them could speak. "This will do nicely."

They had just rounded a sharp bend in the road where it twisted round a hillock of jumbled, snow-covered boulders. The river curved round the other side of the hillock, where the waters scoured against the sheer side of the mountains. There were two bridges, one on either side of the hillock.

"What the hell are you talking about?"

"My dear old consumer of sauerkraut, have you lost all tactical sense? All you need is a chap up on those rocks with a musket or two. The Frogs have got to come over that first bridge single file. Pick a few off and they'll soon lose their enthusiasm. Meanwhile you and your merry men can chop the shit out of the second bridge. And hey presto! You're safe! They ain't going to cross that torrent."

"But what about the man?"

"Crow bait, old boy."

The Raven gave a little squawk and jumped on Charles's shoulder:

"Sorry. Slip of the tongue. Of course you get first go. I promised you."

The Raven snapped its beak in a satisfied manner.

"Oh God!" said Anna and put her face in her hands.

"I can't let you do this."

"Mischa, you can't stop me. And anyway, I've never liked taking orders from you."

"Charles, you can't!"

"Oh yes I can, sweet Anna. I'm dying anyway, and think of that Roman chappie, what they call him? Horatius, that's it. I'll be like Horatius. And what's more you will never have to worry about me lusting after your smooth body again."

Anna gave one of her sudden dazzling smiles:

"I shall miss you," she said simply.

For a moment they sat smiling at each other, then Charles bent as far as his wound allowed him and, taking Anna's hand, raised it to his lips:

"It wasn't all lust," he said quietly; "not quite anyway. Now take care of that old bear."

He held out his hand to Mischa. They clasped hands and looked into each other's faces for a long moment.

"Good bye, Charles."

"Good bye, old boy."

Charles wheeled his horse round.

"Now I want all the muskets and pistols you can spare—all loaded and primed. I ain't going to be able to load very well on my own with my side as it is."

"I'll be loading for you, Sir."

Ex-Trooper Bone was standing stiffly to attention.

"What are you fucking on about, Bone?"

"Coming with you, Sir."

"No you're not and that's an order."

"Stuff your order, Sir. I've had all the bloody orders I'm going to take and, anyway, what would the Corporal Major say if he heard I'd let you loose on your own?"

The two man stared at each other. Then they both began laughing.

"Let's go then, Bone."

They watched them go back and disappear round the corner. For one last time, Charles turned back and raised a hand. Then they were gone.

As the Cossacks fell to furious work on the bridge with their axes, they heard the first shot from the other side of the hillock.

The snow storm hit as the party climbed towards the head of the pass. It had been a silent journey except for the occasional curse as a tired horse stumbled on the snow-covered ice. The driving snow made them huddle even deeper into their cloaks and their muffled thoughts. They were passing a series of dreary reed-fringed lakes, and still the pass climbed in front of them.

The Raven came gliding out of the murk and with a few flaps of its great black wings, settled on a snow-covered fallen tree and gave a harsh croak. Sirius gave a half-hearted rush at his adversary, but was too cold and tired even to bark at him. The Raven ignored him, flapped off its perch and landed on Mischa's shoulder.

Mischa was too dispirited to complain. He was amazed

when his brain heard the words, spoken in a harsh, guttural, voice. He knew that Charles had claimed that the bird spoke to him, but Charles was a joker, Charles was... Charles was dead.

"*He died well,*" said the Raven, as though reading Mischa's thoughts. "*Bone also.*"

A sudden awful thought passed through Mischa's mind. The Raven gave a ghastly chuckle:

"*No I didn't. There were plenty of Frenchmen dead. I had a feast off them.*"

There was a sound of the smacking of lips. Mischa shuddered.

"Are we ever going to get to the top of this bloody pass?" he said out loud.

Anna's head appeared from her hood:

"What did you say?"

"I was talking to the Raven," said Mischa rather testily.

Anna retreated into her cloak: 'Dear God!' she thought, 'now he's going mad.'

Out of the murk and the swirling snow, the shape of some houses began to emerge.

"Thanks be to the Blessed Virgin!" thought Mischa. "Maybe we can shelter here."

"*No you can't,*" said the Raven. "*It's only a collection of tumble-down hovels and a decaying church. Newhouse they call it, which is a joke in very bad taste. You must keep going to the inn at the top of the pass. My master is there.*"

The blizzard howled about them as they climbed still further past the miserable village, which was as the Raven had said it was. Then through the wrack that swirled about them there appeared a flickering glimmer of light.

"*That's it,*" said the Raven. "*I'll tell them that you're coming.*"

With a flap of his wings he disappeared into the snow.

The inn sat right on the summit of the pass. It was a small place, but with extensive outbuildings. The windows of the inn blazed with light. The innkeeper was standing at the door with a raised lantern:

"Welcome! Welcome!"

With curses of relief and fatigue the party dismounted.

"Have you somewhere for the horses?"

"Stables a-plenty, Sir. Franz! Franz! Where is that idle boy? Now shift yourself and show the soldiers the way to the stables. Come in, Sir! Come in! And the lady too."

Amazed by this welcome, Mischa turned to Anna. She still sat on Bahram, slumped with cold and weariness. Mischa reached up and very gently pulled her out of the saddle. She fell against him and for a long moment they stood there, her face buried in the frozen snow on his chest.

"Come," said Mischa gently, "let me get you inside. You are exhausted."

The innkeeper was still standing with his raised lantern:

"That's it gnädige Frau, come on inside. There's a good fire and a welcome to warm you."

Sirius, who was not waiting to be asked, had already shot through the lighted doorway. They heard him barking inside.

"Oh God ! Now what?"

Mischa put his arm around Anna and hurried through the door.

The Hunter was sitting on a bench by the roaring fire, his pipe billowing clouds of blue smoke and a glass in his hand.

Sirius was bouncing up and down in front of him, wriggling and baying with joy. The Hunter rose to his feet:

"Peace, Sirius, peace!" He ruffled the big dog's head. "And welcome to you, my children. A long hard journey you've had of it."

"And a failed one," said Mischa miserably.

The big man looked at him shrewdly with his one eye:

"Why? Have you lost the Black Madonna?"

"No, She is here."

Mischa put the battered wooden box on the table.

"Then you have not failed. The Lady is safe and in your care. But what about the other lady?"

Anna had thrown off her sodden cloak and was crouched in front of the fire with one arm round Sirius's neck. She still wore the creamy white dress, although now it was torn and stained. Her head was bowed so that her hair hid her face. She was weeping silently, her shoulders shaking.

Mischa went to her quickly. He lifted her to her feet. Again she buried her face in his chest. He stroked her hair, until the sobs gradually subsided. Then she raised her tear-stained face:

"I'm sorry, so sorry."

"What on earth for?"

"My dress, my beautiful dress; it's the most beautiful thing I ever owned and I wanted to keep it for... keep it for... keep it for you," she finished with a gulp.

Mischa stroked her face:

"The dress doesn't matter. It's you that matters."

Anna sniffed:

"It mattered to me," she said in a small voice.

"Hrrrmph! I hate to strike a practical note, but what you need now is some dry clothing. Here is Frau Hofner"—the Hunter held out his hand towards a plump beaming lady who dropped a curtsey to Anna—"go with her and she will look after you."

"We've only got the one spare room, I'm afraid, gnädige Frau." Frau Hofner held up the lantern to light up the tiny room that was nearly filled by an enormous bed. "But it's a good bed. I do hope that you and your husband will be comfortable. It's not often that we get gentry staying here, you understand..."

"But he's not..." Anna began.

"...except for Mr Hunter, of course, but he's different isn't he? I must say we were very excited when he told us you were coming. A gentleman and his wife, he said, and I said to Hofner..."

"But I'm not..."

"...Hofner, I said, there's quality coming to stay and you just make sure there aren't too many fleas in that bed..."

"Frau Hofner, the Rittmeister and I..."

"Such a fine looking gentleman, and you such a lovely lady and that lovely dress nigh ruined. I can't think what you was thinking of. Never mind, I've put out some clothes of my daughter's. She's in service down in Mariazell; she's about your size, but nothing like as pretty if I say it myself. Of course, they'll not be the sort of clothes that a grand lady like yourself is accustomed to, but they're clean and dry, and I'll see what 1 can do with this poor dress of yours. Now you don't often see workmanship like that these days. Pure silk I'd say..."

Anna, wrapped in a blanket, gave up the struggle and sat silently on the bed until Frau Hofner, still chattering, had faded away down the short ladder that led to the little room. Anna sat staring into the flickering shadows thrown by the lantern and fire. She thought of the Black Madonna, to whom she had prayed so often during the last months:

"Oh Lady! What is going to become of me? I am not a wife or a fine lady. I wonder what will become of me?"

But the flickering shadows had no answer.

There were great sides of pork with pickled cabbage, there was soup with dumplings, there were piles of sausages, sweet apfelstrudel and cream; there were great mugs of beer and bottles of obstler.

As soon as a plate was empty, it was filled again. The men ate like wolves—gorged themselves until they could eat no more. They were alive, their bellies were full, their horses were comfortable and there was plenty of dry warm straw in the stable for them to sleep on. For Cossacks there was little more to ask of life.

Mischa also ate well and drank rather more deeply than usual. The strain of the journey was behind him. Lippitz and home was only a few days in front of him. He had already decided that was where he would head. The Cossacks would come with him and they would decide what to do then.

And Anna? What of Anna? He watched her as she sat across the table from him; they were either side of the Hunter who sat at the head. She was picking at her food with down-cast eyes, although she must have been hungry. Most of her food seemed to be going to Sirius, who sat gazing at her soulfully, swallowing occasionally in expectation of the next morsel. She raised her eyes and found Mischa staring at her. He smiled at her, a deep warm smile. Her eyes fell back to her plate. Anna got suddenly to her feet. She did not look at Mischa, but addressed herself to the Hunter:

"If you will excuse me, I think that I will go to bed."

The Hunter rose:

"Of course, child, you must be exhausted."

"You must get some rest," said Mischa solicitously.

Anna did not look at him.

The Sergeant extricated himself from his chair with some difficulty and stood swaying slightly.

"Well what I say is—what I say is—we've all come a long way and I don't know where we are, but it's bloody good food and bloody good drink. So what I say is—what I say is—three bloody good cheers for Gospoza Anna!"

The men rose to their feet and raised their glasses:

"HURRAH!—HURRAH!—HURRAH!"

Anna felt herself blushing and felt a lump in her throat:

"Thank you!" It was almost a whisper.

Then she turned and fled.

Anna lay in bed staring at the ceiling. She tried to keep her mind blank and hoped that sleep would come. Downstairs the roar of voices gradually subsided and she heard the noisy stamping, and the occasional shout and burst of song as the Cossacks made for the stables. Then there was silence. Silence until she heard the footsteps approaching the bottom of the ladder.

The footsteps stopped and Anna held her breath.

Then came the sound of someone slowly and hesitantly climbing the ladder. The square of dim light from the doorless hatch was suddenly blocked out.

"Anna," came Mischa's whisper. "Anna? are you awake?"

Anna turned on her side so that her back was towards the hatch and lay silent staring into the fire. She heard his steps crossing the floor and felt the bed give as he sat on it.

"Anna," he said again.

Anna remained silent and still, except that she turned her head into the pillow and bit on it.

"I must talk to you."

She felt like screaming, but she stayed silent.

She felt his hand on her shoulder and she began to shiver in spite of the warmth of the bed.

"Anna, I love you, I love you more than anything in this world, but..."

She turned violently so that she could look up at his face. Even in the dim light, she could see that it was drawn and haggard—the face of a man in pain.

"If you truly love me, there are no buts." Her voice was almost savage.

Mischa shook his head silently. He was in torment. Very gently she reached out her arms to him:

"Come!" she said quietly.

But he did not move except to shake his head again. When he spoke it was the voice of a man in the pit:

"I can't. I can't. I am a shameful creature. If only you knew... you would not want me then."

"Only I could judge that and I can't if you will not tell me. All I know is that I love you." As she talked she began to stroke his haggard face.

The dam burst suddenly. The words came not in a rush, but in a flat, hesitant monotone. He told her of the fair-haired girl at Lippitz. He told her of their love, of getting her with child, of her suicide, of his shame and the burden of guilt that he had carried.

All the time he was speaking she continued to stroke his face and, when the hot tears began to run down his cheeks, she very gently wiped them away. At the end, Mischa said simply:

"There, that is the sin I carry."

Anna reached up and put her arms round his neck.

"Come, my darling," she said quietly.

"You mean...?"

"I mean, come here to me."

Mischa obeyed.

Anna leaned on an elbow. She kissed his forehead, his eyes and brushed her lips against the corners of his mouth.

Gently she pulled his head down onto her breast, stroking his hair all the time.

"The past is past. You think that you killed that girl and your child. I know that I shot my own brother and strangled that woman. That is all behind us. We must bury the dead bodies in our past. Unless we bury the past, how can we find peace in our future?"

"Our future? Do you mean that you would m-marry me?"

Anna's fingers began to play with the hair on Mischa's chest. Then, hesitatingly, she stroked her hand down his body. Mischa caught her hand and pulled her towards him.

"Anna, please..."

Anna lay back on the rough white linen sheet.

A pine log burst on the fire, sending out a shower of glowing red sparks...

"You'll have to marry me now."

Mischa leaned up on one elbow looking down at Anna, her hair still spread wildly on the pillow. With his other hand, he gently stroked her damp forehead.

Anna pouted:

"I might."

Mischa tensed:

"Might? What do you mean?"

"Well," said Anna demurely, "you haven't asked me yet."

It was a morning of bright sunshine and ice-glittering beauty. The air went to the head like wine. Not that Mischa and Anna needed wine; they were intoxicated with each other. They ate a huge breakfast waited on by the smiling Hofners.

"Isn't it romantic?" said Frau Hofner in the kitchen. "Just look at the way they stare at each other."

Herr Hofner's reply was to pinch his wife's ample bottom.

"Oo! You just wait, Hofner!"

"Not for long, I won't!"

"Where is the Hunter?" Mischa asked Frau Hofner. "Is he up yet?"

"Bless you, Sir, up and gone these many hours. He said that he had someone to see in Mariazell."

"Mariazell?" Anna looked up inquiringly from the roll she was smearing with honey.

"It is a little town in the next valley, where there is a wonderful church. It is a very holy place, even from the old times. Would you like to see the basilica?"

"Oh, yes."

The Sergeant appeared at the door and saluted:

"Beg leave to report, Excellency, that the men are present, correct and ready to mount,"—there might have been the slightest pause, but the man's craggy face was devoid of expression—"if you are, Excellency."

As the Sergeant said this, Mischa felt a soft, naked foot caressing his leg under the table. Anna was apparently totally absorbed in watching her plate. Mischa felt himself colouring:

"Very good, Sergeant," he said hurriedly, "we'll be out in a minute."

The foot was still at work as the man left. Anna looked up smiling, and reached for his hand.

Sirius dropped his head onto his paws and gave a deep sigh.

The Raven was sitting on top of the inn sign as they came out:

"*Not before time,*" said the voice in Mischa's head. "*I can't think why you humans take so long over it.*"

Sirius leaped snarling at the post:

"*How dare you speak to my master like that.*"

"*Stupid Mutt, you just wait. They'll have you shut away in a kennel next.*"

"Silence the pair of you!" said Mischa, and to the Raven, "Where is your Master?"

"*You are to meet him at the basilica in Mariazell.*"

"The basilica?"

The Raven flew down and landed neatly on Mischa's

shoulder:

"Certainly—you want to get married, don't you?"

"Here? You mean we can get married here?"

Anna stood awe-struck inside the basilica of Mariazell looking at the great marble pillars that swept up to the intricate carvings of the vaulted roof, inset with paintings. The pillars marched away on either side of the wide nave to the baroque, gold-leafed splendour of the high altar, shining in the winter light that came down from the great dome of the cupola.

"Here?" she whispered.

In front of her stood the shrine of the Madonna. The elaborately crafted pillars, gates and arches of the shrine were all of solid silver. At the back of the shrine above the silver and marble altar, was the tiny figure of the Madonna in her silver dress.

Anna remembered the little shrine where she had prayed so hard in the church at Pyatigorsk. She had thought that magnificent, but this, this was beyond words:

"They will let us get married here? Today?"

She looked up at Mischa who was standing beside her, the battered wooden case of the Black Madonna tucked under his arm. He looked nervous:

"I don't know, but the Hunter thinks so. He has gone to see the priest. He says that he is a 'good enemy' of his."

"An enemy?"

Mischa shrugged:

"Who understands the Hunter?"

Footsteps echoed through the nave. The Hunter appeared. Beside him hobbled an ancient Benedictine in a soutane. Mischa was surprised to notice that the Hunter was still wearing his hat. He and the priest appeared to be squabbling amiably as they approached. Anna slipped her hand into Mischa's. He gave it a reassuring squeeze. The old priest fumbled in his soutane and eventually produced a pair of eye glasses with which he studied the young couple in silence.

"Getting a bit short-sighted are we, Father?"

The Hunter, who was standing behind the priest, winked with his one eye at Mischa.

"I may be getting a little short-sighted, Hunter," said the priest testily in a voice as dry as crackling parchment, "but I am still able to see things more clearly than you ever have."

"Even with my one eye, I can see that your thinking is like your vestry—in a complete muddle."

"It is a matter of perspective."

It was obvious that the two of them were continuing what must have been a long-running argument.

"Ah, but my perspective has the advantage of historical depth."

"Historical twaddle, more like," said the priest tartly. "I..."

"This," said the Hunter, cutting him short, "is Father Jakob. He wishes to have a look at you."

"What, what?"—the old man was fumbling with his eye glasses again—"Yes, yes, you distracted me. You are always distracting me. Now let's have a look at them." He gave Anna and Mischa a close scrutiny. "Well, they look a handsome couple, I'll say that. What's your name child?"

"Anna."

"Anna what?"

"I wish it to be Anna Czerny," said Mischa firmly.

"Ah-ha Herr Rittmeister! So you are a Czerny, eh? Fine family, good Catholics. There was a Cardinal Czerny I seem to remember. Now there was something about him, now what was it? Ah well, I can't remember, can't remember—old age you know."

The Hunter had a coughing fit.

"But the young lady is not of the one true faith?"

"No, but she intends to take instruction."

"Quite so, quite so, but still a bit of a problem."

"It is better to marry than to burn with lust," said the Hunter blandly.

The Priest rounded on him:

"You dare to quote scripture to me! Anyway the Blessed Paul never mentioned lust."

"That's what he meant though."

"How dare you! You..." In his agitation the old man dropped his eye glasses. Mischa picked them up for him and carefully wiped them off with his kerchief. "Thank you, my boy. Now where were we? Yes, marriage, hmm! Well we live in troubled times and I gather that the two of you have had your share of them. I suppose that you are already married in the eyes of God, hmm?"

Mischa went scarlet and Anna dropped her eyes to the floor.

"Yes well, we had better tidy it up a bit, then. But no choir, no flummery."

"Could you not marry us here in front of the shrine of the Madonna?" Anna asked quietly. The priest considered:

"Why not?"

"And what about Sirius and the Cossacks?"

"Sirius?"

"Our dog."

The old man raised his eyes to the shrine:

"Blessed Mother forgive me: dogs, Cossacks!" Then he suddenly rounded on the Hunter. "But not you, or that spawn-of-Satan Raven of yours. God's mercy is infinite, but not that infinite."

The Hunter was shaking with laughter:

"You can teach me nothing about infinity, Father."

"Oh Hunter!" Anna was obviously distressed.

"Don't worry, child. When it is over, you will find me in my place. The good Father knows where that is."

"Well, Herr Rittmeister Czerny?"

"Well indeed, Gräfin Czerny."

They stood looking at each other in front of the shrine of the Madonna of Mariazell, their hands clasped. The old priest looked at them happily: a handsome couple.

"No!" he shouted suddenly. "No!"

Anna and Mischa looked up in horror.

"No! I knew this would happen! Out! Out! Out!"

Sirius, who had been marking the importance of the occasion on one of the marble pillars, watched in mild surprise as an inaccurately thrown missal shot past his head. Heroes can be most obliging. Sirius, whose gold-embossed collar matched the splendour of the basilica, picked up the fallen book and, trotting across, laid it at the priest's feet.

"Father, I'm so sorry." Mischa was mortified.

The old man was frowning. Then he saw Anna who was struggling to keep a straight face. The priest's face also began to twitch:

"I am sure that he was only trying to pass his own form of blessing on the occasion."

Then suddenly they were all laughing. The priest linked his arms between them and they came, still laughing, to the door of the basilica.

Mischa smote his head:

"God what a fool I am!"

He turned and bolted back into the church, leaving the priest and Anna open-mouthed. He returned with the battered wooden box in his hands:

"What a fool I am! To have forgotten Her after all we've been through."

He handed the box to the priest who reverently opened the lid. The old man crossed himself:

"So! That is the famous Black Madonna."

The three of them stood and looked at the little icon in silence.

"So small, so small—and yet so great."

"Father," said Mischa suddenly, "do you think that She should stay here, in your church?"

The priest rubbed his chin in thought:

"No," he said at last. "She is in your care—both of your care. You have brought her all this way, or She has brought you. You must take care of Her until God and Our Lady decide otherwise."

He closed the lid of the box and stood back.

"Take Her with you and keep Her safe, as She will keep both of you. Now go and God bless you both."

As they walked out of the door, the ragged little band of Cossacks was drawn up at attention.

"Beg leave to report, Excellency, the troop is present, correct and ready for inspection." Mischa returned his salute:

"No inspection is necessary, Sergeant. I know that this is the most excellent troop in His Imperial Majesty's army. However there is one thing I want to do."

Mischa walked down the line and, as he came to each man, he shook his hand and then embraced him in the Russian fashion. His eyes were wet. Then he turned to face the troop.

"There is only one more thing I want to say: thank you!"

"Three cheers for their Excellencies!"

"HURRAH!—HURRAH!—HURRAH!"

Anna bowed her head.

"What will you do now?" Mischa asked the Sergeant.

"We will follow you, Excellency," said the man simply. "Then, when the Black Madonna is safe, God will tell us what to do."

"Then I will tell you what to do now. Take the men to an inn. Here is money. But have them ready to march in one hour."

"It is an honour to obey your order, Excellency."

The priest told them where to find the Hunter. Behind the basilica, there was an open slope. On the slope there was the massive stump of what must once have been a mighty oak tree. The stump was so old that it had become almost petrified. The Hunter was sitting on the stump, puffing his pipe with the Raven perched on his shoulder.

"You defiled the church then, Mutt."

Sirius sat down and began to scratch an ear reflectively, his golden collar glinting in the sunlight.

"They wouldn't even let you in."

"I wouldn't want to. They should have sprinkled some holy water on those fleas of yours, Mutt."

"Verminous bird!"

"Stop it, the pair of you!" The Hunter's thought stopped them both. "So my children," he said out loud, "Mother Church has blessed you?"—he patted the stump—"Come sit with me for a moment."

"Oh Hunter!" said Anna. "We so wished you had been there."

The Hunter chuckled:

"As I told you, I know my place and you know that you have my blessing."

"What is this place?" asked Mischa looking around.

"Do you not know? This is the remains of the mighty Wotan's Oak. I told you that this had always been a holy place. Long before the coming of Christianity there was a stone of sacrifice here."

"Where is it now?"

The Hunter laughed again and pointed with his pipe stem:

"Under the high altar of the basilica. The missionaries chopped down the oak tree, but they realised that there are some things that are best changed by keeping them the same."

The three sat silent for a time. It was a comfortable silence. Then Mischa said:

"We must march soon."

"I know. Your father will be pleased to see you. He is much looking forward to welcoming Anna."

"But he does not know about me."

"He has been told," said the Hunter simply.

"Shall you come with us?" asked Mischa.

The Hunter shook his head:

"I shall stay here for a bit, in my place. But I will see you. Go now and my blessing and the Black Madonna go with you."

Hand in hand, Mischa and Anna walked down the slope. At the bottom they turned back to wave to the Hunter.

The old stump was empty.

PUBLISHER'S NOTE

The Battle of Austerlitz, a small village in Moravia north-east of Vienna, was fought on 2nd December 1805 between the French 'Grande Armée' of 68,000 troops, and the combined allied armies of Russia and Austria with nearly 90,000 men, whose supreme command was assumed by Czar Alexander I.

It was also known as 'The Battle of the Three Emperors' because Napoleon, Francis I of Austria and Alexander I of Russia were all present on the field.

The outcome was a resounding rout of the allies which historians have attributed to Bonaparte's inspired generalship. However, had the icon of The Black Madonna been present to lead the Cossack cavalry into battle, virtually nothing could have stood in their way and the result may have been different; there would have been no contemplation of the disastrous Peace of Pressburg and the entire course of European history might well have been rewritten.

My great-great-grandfather, a Hanovarian Rittmeister, had become attached to the Grande Armée and fought under General Prince Murat at Austerlitz. My father has told me the story of The Black Madonna.

Lieselotte Loyd, Eynsham, 1997